PAUL SLAVONIK

Legacy Drive

First published by DMG United, LLC 2019

First edition

ISBN: 978-1-7330253-1-7

Editing by Sam O'Neal
Cover art by Bespoke Book Covers

This book was professionally typeset on Reedsy.
Find out more at reedsy.com

To my amazing wife, Christina. Thank you for your love, support and inspiration during the entire six-year process of writing this book. I thank God for you every day.

To my high school English teacher, Angela Scopel, who saw something in me which no one else saw at the time—a writer. Thank you for believing in me.

"To do something well is so worthwhile that to die trying to do it better cannot be foolhardy. It would be a waste of life to do nothing with one's ability, for I feel that life is measured in achievement, not in years alone."

—Bruce McLaren

Contents

Prologue iii
Chapter 1 1
Chapter 2 15
Chapter 3 28
Chapter 4 40
Chapter 5 63
Chapter 6 78
Chapter 7 91
Chapter 8 109
Chapter 9 122
Chapter 10 151
Chapter 11 160
Chapter 12 170
Chapter 13 189
Chapter 14 197
Chapter 15 205
Chapter 16 220
Chapter 17 234
Chapter 18 246
Chapter 19 259
Chapter 20 270
Chapter 21 282
Chapter 22 295
Chapter 23 311
Chapter 24 322
Chapter 25 337

Chapter 26 348
Chapter 27 365
Chapter 28 378
Chapter 29 385
Chapter 30 397
Epilogue 412
About the Author 417
Also by Paul Slavonik 418

Prologue

For such a beautiful day, the atmosphere was somber and reminiscent of days long gone. The clear blue skies above were void of clouds as the warm sun pierced the morning air. The stillness that surrounded the area made every sound an intrusion.

The long walk from the car with his son by his side was slow but that was to be expected considering the older man's need of a walking cane. As his son walked along beside him, the old man stopped every now and again to find his footing on the gravel path.

It was a few minutes before they finally arrived at their destination. Upon arrival, both the older man and his son immediately became aware of just how quiet the surrounding area was. Without the sound of the gravel crunching under their feet as they walked, the only audible sounds were the slight breeze blowing in the air and the occasional bird chirping as it flew by. There were no crowds or cars to be heard, just the sound of silent memories as they stood before the markers.

The old man watched as his son knelt down, unsure of what to say or do. Finally, after several seconds, his teenage son lifted his head and softly asked his father, "Are you finally gonna tell me the story? You said you would."

The old man looked down at his son and could already feel the tears beginning to well up in his eyes. He tightened the grip on his cane slightly as he suddenly felt the weight of more than 50 years of memories—many of which he had kept to himself—rest upon his shoulders once again. He had been waiting until this very moment to tell the story to his son. He had waited so long, in fact, that he had never asked himself how to begin.

Where does one begin a story of such magnitude?

He started to speak but choked up. More than anything, he was afraid that he would somehow tell the story incorrectly.

Then he remembered who this story was about. He remembered what that person meant to him. The vivid memory alone gave him the strength he needed, and he knew that was a good place to start.

A stray tear fell down his cheek as he took a deep breath and gathered himself. After what seemed like an eternity, he slowly knelt down and sat on the ground beside his son.

"This is the story of someone who refused to give up," he began. "Someone who stood strong in the face of adversity, looked their own fate in the eyes and kept on going ..."

Chapter 1

Bill Watson gripped the steering wheel tighter and tighter with each passing lap. Checking his mirrors again, he saw what he had been seeing for the past 20 laps: a bright yellow Chevrolet Camaro which never seemed to go away no matter how hard he pushed.

Bill's engine screamed as he raced down the front stretch of Road Atlanta, starting another lap with the 35-car field behind him. The vibrations from the nearly 500 horsepower engine coupled with the bumps on the road and the crushing G-forces ripped through Bill's body. These forces were enough to wear out even the strongest of drivers over a period of time. Bill, however, was focused on the prize which now seemingly lay before him. Everything else happening in this moment was nothing more than a minor inconvenience.

Casting a quick glance at the lap board as he drove by, Bill saw that there were only two laps remaining. If he could hold off the field for a little while longer, he would have his first victory in motorsports.

Bill had never been in the lead before during a race. Surprisingly, that made it very easy to spot his wife, Lena, and son, Chad, in the bleachers on the front straight. They were the only ones jumping up and down as they cheered him on. This was Bill's third time racing with the Sports Car Club of America's Trans Am series. The first time ended with mechanical failure at Sebring International Raceway, and the second resulted in an 8th place finish at Mid-Ohio Sports Car Course.

Today, however, Bill knew that the third time was indeed a charm.

Today was the day he was going to win.

He threw his black SCCA Trans Am Series TA2 class Ford Mustang down into second gear as he approached the quick right-handed Turn One. Turning it in and the easing onto the accelerator, he felt a smile slip onto his face as he perfectly executed the uphill turn—but he was somewhat disappointed to see the yellow car still on his back bumper. His nerves were high and his grip on the steering wheel was so tight that he could feel his hands starting to go a little numb.

A slight bump from the yellow car behind him didn't help. This caused him to make a brief mistake as he jerked the wheel during the next turn-in and missed the apex of the corner by two feet. Regardless, the yellow car didn't move to overtake him. Bill wasn't sure if the other driver was toying with him or if he simply had to brake suddenly due to Bill's mistake and lost momentum in the process. Bill noted it as a mistake he would not make again as he wound his car around the tricky circuit.

As he entered the last corner—a downhill right-hander where car control and throttle management are critical—Bill passed the start/finish line to begin the final lap.

One more time around.

He knew all of his gear changes had to be perfect and his braking points had to be spot on.

Speeding down the front stretch, he made a quick glance down at the gauges and then was back in the race. Braking for Turn One, Bill wasn't fazed this time when another tap from behind came upon the exit of the turn. In fact, he was ready for it. Looking up at his rearview mirror, it was almost as if the pursuing driver was sitting directly behind him because of how close he was.

As he drove through *the esses* on the final lap, Bill could feel a fresh burst of adrenaline surging through his body. He knew the finish line—a line which would give him a major racing victory—was only a few corners away.

As they raced down the backstretch and approached the signature

10a and 10b corners—a sharp left-then-right combination where your momentum carries you up the hill which leads to the finish line—Bill saw with his peripheral vision that the yellow car behind him was swinging towards the inside for a very late pass while heading towards the braking zone. Instinctively, the distraction caused Bill to look up at his mirror, which led to him taking his eyes off the road for only a brief second.

It was enough, however, for him to make a costly mistake.

With his adrenaline rushing hard, the momentary distraction caused Bill to miss his braking point. A slight wheel lockup followed as Bill was forced to brake harder to slow the heavy car down. Unfortunately, it wasn't enough to make the corner.

Electing to abort the Turn 10 sequence instead of risking a spin or, even worse, an incident with the other car, Bill drove straight through the grass in front of him, which ultimately spilled him back out onto the track. With his car's momentum lost, however, Bill cursed aloud but could barely hear the sound of his voice as he slammed the throttle down after straightening the car out. Instead of seeing open track in front of him, he now had the view from *behind* a yellow Camaro as it passed him on the outside of the final turn and crossed the finish line to win the race.

He had just been outmaneuvered and made to look like a fool in the process. Even as he crossed the finish line to take second, Bill punched the steering wheel and cursed in frustration for falling for such a maneuver.

The long cooldown lap around the circuit again to get to the pit lane entrance was a quiet one as Bill was finally able to take a deep breath and calm himself down. He wanted to kick himself for falling for a trick he'd seen on TV countless times before. He knew he'd probably be ridiculed by the other drivers but he didn't care. Other than taking it as a learning experience, it wouldn't do much good to get even more worked up about things like that.

As Bill continued his cooldown lap back to the pits, the winning driver pulled up alongside of him to give him a thumbs up as a sign of respect for a hard fought battle. Bill returned the gesture in kind. As the driver accelerated away, however, Bill flipped him a hand gesture which was not so kind.

He entered the pits to find his wife and son waiting for him. Shutting the engine off after bringing the car to a stop at his pit stall, Bill climbed out and removed his helmet, HANS device and balaclava as he climbed over the pit wall. His young son, Chad, ran over to congratulate him.

"Alright, Dad! Second! You're getting better every race!" said Chad as he hugged his father's leg.

"He's right," his wife, Lena, said with a smile on her face as she leaned in to give him a kiss. "Great race, babe!"

"Thanks guys," said Bill as he scooped Chad up into his arms. "I almost had it, though."

"It's okay, Dad. You'll get 'em next time."

"Next time! That's the great thing about racing: There's usually always a next time," said Bill as he faked a smile.

Chad may have been too young to know that his dad was in fact very upset at himself. Lena, on the other hand, knew all of his tricks. She gave him a look which seemed to say everything he needed to hear.

It's okay. Your son is in the arms of his greatest hero and your wife loves you regardless if you win or lose. You gave it your all and that's what matters the most.

Bill felt his anger subside as he smiled and looked into the eyes of his wife. He leaned in to give her another kiss and said, "I love you, too."

"You'd better," Lena said as she wrapped her arms around him. "You sure aren't going home with any of these racing broads," gesturing toward a few scantily clad women.

Bill laughed as he put his son down.

"Plus," Lena added, "you smell like wet dog. I don't think too many women would find that appealing but I'm kind of stuck with you."

"Well lucky you!" said Bill as he pulled Lena in close to him and rubbed his sweaty face all over hers. The three of them screamed with laughter together as many people began to look on.

Let 'em watch, Bill thought to himself.

After a few minutes, a small group of people came down and approached Bill.

"Great race, Bill!" one person shouted. "You'll get 'em next time!" said another.

Bill knew that one of the great things about having a very social wife and son was that they were always telling friends and coworkers about his racing schedule. They sold a few t-shirts and stickers here and there but mostly they brought folks from all over down to the track on race day to support Bill when he raced.

As Bill shook hands and took a few pictures, a voice came on the loudspeaker and said, "Drivers Elliot Hughes, Bill Watson and Roger Jennings please report to the podium."

"I guess that's me," Bill said. He turned to walk away but stopped all of a sudden. He stood still for a moment and then smiled as he turned toward the crowd which had come to see him.

"Which way to the podium?" he asked.

Laughing at the sight of the now lost racing driver, Bill's entourage began leading him towards the location which he had been summoned to.

As they walked, Lena came up beside Bill and held his hand. Any indication or sense of false emotion or anger was now replaced with pure happiness.

He had loved Lena since the first time he laid eyes on her back when they were both freshman in high school. Bill liked to think that the feeling was immediately mutual but if you were to ask Lena, she would tell you otherwise.

At the time, Bill was the guy that the 'good girls' avoided and the one who the good girl's parents told them to avoid even more. In those days, he had long shaggy hair and couldn't care less about popularity.

Lena, on the other hand, was a ballet dancer and classical musician who lived a very prim and proper life. When the two first crossed paths at their local church's youth group, the first words came from Bill and were, "Howdy there!" as he oftentimes tried to imitate the southern accent which had an obvious presence in their hometown of Austin, TX.

At first, Lena was repulsed by him. Over time, however, she began to notice small but significant changes in him. He had cut his hair, for one. He would also go out of his way to oftentimes just be able to say a few words to her. Over time, she couldn't help but be drawn to him as she began to see Bill for who he really was.

Soon the two began dating, much to the dismay of Lena's parents—her mother in particular—who never liked Bill. Lena soon discovered how passionate Bill was in his work ethics and took notice of how he poured himself into whatever project he had in front of him at the time.

The high school years passed quickly and, before they knew it, they had graduated and were engaged. Bill could still remember the feeling of taking Lena's hand for the first time after they were officially husband and wife. Now as he held her hand walking to the winner's circle, he felt just as in love as the day he said "I do".

Since Bill had gotten out of the car, Chad had not left his side. Bill put his hand on Chad's head and asked, "What's on your mind, little man?"

With an almost embarrassed look on his face, Chad looked up and quietly asked, "Are you gonna do it, Dad? You said you would if you ever came in second."

Bill knew exactly what he was talking about. Unfortunately, so did Lena.

"Bill Watson, what are you teaching your son to do? Don't even think about it."

His pace slowed briefly and a perplexed look came on Bill's face. As they approached the podium, however, he saw the race winner, Elliot Hughes, who would be taking the top step of the podium. Just then, a massive smile broke out onto Bill's face. He looked down at his son who instantly knew what that meant.

"Go for it, Dad!" said Chad excitedly.

"Bill!" said Lena who tried to stop him but it was too late. Bill turned toward her, gave her a quick kiss and ran off.

"Lord, help him," she said to herself but even she couldn't help but smile.

When he got to the podium, Bill took his place on the second level. As the crowds gathered around, the announcer began:

"Ladies and gentlemen, thank you for attending today's event. On behalf of the Sports Car Club of America's Trans Am series, it's my pleasure to introduce to you the winners of today's TA2 race!"

Just then, the respective trophies were handed to each of the drivers along with a bottle of champagne. A few pictures were taken—and then came the moment that Bill was waiting for.

As the other drivers uncorked their champagne bottles and began spraying each other and the crowd, Bill uncorked his, put the bottle to his lips and started to drink.

As the other drivers finished spraying theirs, they noticed that Bill was still drinking, with the bottom of the bottle getting higher into the air. The seconds passed on and before long the crowd had hushed and stopped their applause as murmurs of support for Bill's cause began brewing.

Bill kept drinking as the crowd began to cheer him on. So did the third place driver, Roger Jennings. The winner, Elliot Hughes, didn't find this to be humorous at all, but there was nothing he could do to stop it without looking like a jerk in front of the crowd.

The bottle rose higher and higher as the cheers rose in volume.

"Chug! Chug! Chug!" the crowd chanted.

Then, when he thought it couldn't get any louder, Bill finished off the bottle and held it upside down over his head. The crowd erupted in cheers as Bill then raised both of his arms over his head as if he had won the series championship. He looked out to see his son cheering and jumping up and down as his wife was shaking her head with her characteristic *I love you anyways* smile on her face.

He also saw out of the corner of his eye that Elliot, the man who'd out-maneuvered him on the track, was now smiling as well.

As the crowd dispersed, Bill approached Elliot and shook his hand to congratulate him.

"You just have to get the last word in, don't you?" commented Elliot.

"You know me too well," Bill said with a smile. "See you next time?"

"You can count on it," replied Elliot as he turned back towards his team's garage.

Bill turned towards his family to see his son smiling ear to ear and his wife still shaking her head. "What am I going to do with you?" she asked sarcastically.

Stumbling his way back to her, Bill gave his wife the best smile he could and said, "Whatever you want."

She returned his comment with a sly smile of her own as she said, "I guess this means I'm driving home. You glutton, you."

They began to walk back to the car as Lena put her arm around Bill and pulled him tightly to her side. This succeeded in squeezing out a very loud belch from Bill which echoed throughout the stands.

* * *

After Bill's crew got his TA2 Mustang loaded up onto the hauler, they were on their way back home. With Road Atlanta being a bit of a trip back to their hometown of Austin, TX, having family members traveling to races with you had its advantages, especially when the person in the passenger seat had just downed an entire bottle of champagne.

As Lena drove, she saw how all of the day's excitement had taken its toll on their son, passed out in the back seat.

Looking over at Bill, however, Lena noticed that her husband was staring off into the distance with a blank look on his face. Unable to tell if he was in deep thought or just drunk, she poked him softly on his arm with her index finger.

"Hey, you awake?" she asked, more so just to get him to snap out of it.

"Yeah," replied Bill partially startled. "Just thinking, that's all."

"About second place?" It was a loaded question, but Lena was a very direct person.

Bill sighed. She took that as a yes.

"There's nothing wrong with second place. You haven't even been racing in this series for a year yet. Some people race all of their lives and never get second place," she said.

"It's not just the second place. It's the fact that I keep making mistakes. If I had run a solid race, then I would be okay with second. But it was just a foolish mistake to fall for a trap like that—and on one of the last turns of the last lap," said Bill.

"Give yourself time. With every race you're getting better and more confident. Plus, if you were in second place right behind Elliot Hughes, wouldn't you have tried the same move on him?" asked Lena.

Bill chuckled. He knew she was right. He knew she was trying to tell him to stop beating himself up. He was indeed very new to this type of racing. Although he had grown up around cars, had been watching races on TV for as long as he can remember, did some karting when he was younger and eventually worked his way up to the SCCA Pro Series, racing a car as fast as a TA2 car still took a lot to get used to.

"Oh, and you should've seen Chad's face while you were going around that track. He's so proud of you," said Lena.

Bill smiled.

"I'm just glad we have something we can do together and that we both enjoy. That and with what he's been learning about racing just from being around the track, it'll probably be him out there one day lapping his old man," said Bill.

"Just like with your dad?" said Lena with a smile on her face.

Bill gave an exaggerated laugh. "Not quite. I may be a little too old to ever accomplish what he did."

"You never know. You've definitely got the talent for it. You just need to start believing in yourself…like your son does." Lena cast him a quick glance.

"Yeah I suppose you're right. Just don't tell my dad what happened," said Bill jokingly.

"Bill, your dad wouldn't care if you came in first place or if you just cruised around on the track with the windows down and your feet hanging out. He's just happy to see you following in his footsteps in a race car."

"It would've been nice to see him today. He still doesn't leave the house much anymore."

"You should go visit him after work sometime this week. Or better yet, why don't you invite him over for dinner? I know Chad would love to see him again too," said Lena as she glanced into the rearview mirror to see Chad still fast asleep.

"I'll talk to him. No promises, though. He can be a tough nut to crack."

"As tough to crack as my family?" Lena asked with a smile.

"Don't even get me started on your family," said Bill as he suppressed his laughter. "I've already got a pounding headache. The last thing I need is to start imagining the sound of your mom's voice in my head."

"What's the matter?" replied Lena. "You don't like the sound of a chainsaw right after guzzling an entire bottle of champagne?"

"The Texas Chainsaw Massacre..." said Bill.

It was well known within Bill and Lena's families that once Lena's mother, Helen, got onto a rant of any sorts, her voice had the distinct qualities of a chainsaw. Thus, whenever she began a conversation with you—which most of the time was against your will—it was nicknamed the Texas Chainsaw Massacre.

"Hey, I'm the only one who's allowed to call her that," said Lena as she was trying not to laugh.

"Well at least she wasn't at the race today. I probably would've heard her voice over all of the cars."

Lena shot him a numb look and said, "Bill, I don't think you'll ever have to worry about my mother showing up to a race."

* * *

After the long trip home, life returned to normal for Bill and his family. Arriving on time at his workplace the following Monday, Bill pulled into his assigned parking spot at the business he had helped build from the ground up.

Named *Dynamis Engineering,* the company began as a partnership between Bill and his longtime friend, Pat Henderson.

Upon graduating from college together, the two shared mutual ideas for an engineering firm and started laying the groundwork for what would become their own business. After moving into a new office building, the early months rolled on and the startup company quickly gained traction. Thanks in part to Pat and his business-savvy marketing skills and Bill's mechanical expertise, *Dynamis Engineering* now enjoyed a fruitful market with clients from all over the world. Bill was the CEO and Pat was the President.

As Bill put his vehicle in park, he noticed that Pat was just climbing out of his own car. Immediately, Bill took notice that Pat was wearing his typical short-sleeved dress shirt and tie. Although Pat was slightly older than Bill, one could easily be fooled into believing that he was ten years his senior by the way he often dressed.

"Well you're still in one piece, so I guess that means you survived again," said Pat in his typical monotone voice as he greeted Bill in the parking lot. "How did your race go?"

"Meh," answered Bill, which was his way of saying he'd rather not talk about it.

"That bad, huh? Well, look at it this way: at least you don't have a case of the Mondays," said Pat quoting a line from his favorite movie, *Office Space*.

It was a line Bill had heard countless times from his counterpart ever since they were roommates in college. Even so, he still chuckled every time he heard it.

"How could you have a case of the Mondays when the day hasn't even started yet?" asked Bill.

"Where do I start?" replied Pat as he adjusted his tie which, due to the red complexion of his face, always appeared to be choking him. "Cindy pooped on the carpet again, I ran out of coffee and I had to get a jump from my neighbor because my car wouldn't start."

"Well that's what you get for driving that old clunker," said Bill with a chuckle.

"That doesn't explain the poop, though."

"Maybe it does," chuckled Bill. "Either that or maybe you need to keep Cindy in another room at night. It'd probably keep your bedroom from smelling like cat, too."

"I can't kick Cindy out," said Pat. "She'd never forgive me."

"Depending on what you ate the night before, she may actually end up thanking you," said Bill as the two walked through the door of the office suite.

Wanting to get a jump on the day, Bill sat down at his desk to check his emails, which typically built up considerably on race weekends. After a few minutes, Pat strolled in with a large coffee cup in-hand.

"So did you crash or did Lena finally talk you out of doing it anymore?" asked Pat in his typical dry-humored tone.

Bill looked up from over his computer monitor.

"No."

Pat chuckled at his friend's well played response. "Wow. You must really not want to talk about it. Did you at least finish the race?"

A master of probing questions, Pat rarely gave up on something once his interest was piqued. Despite the fact that *Dynamis Engineering* was the primary sponsor for Bill's racing endeavors, Bill knew that Pat had no interest in racing but was more or less just trying to make conversation.

He obliged. "Yeah, I finished…in second," replied Bill.

"Second? That's great! No disrespect but you're doing a lot better than I think we both thought you'd do," said Pat. "That and it really looks good to have our business name on a car that's toward the front." It was no secret that Bill was a nervous wreck during his first few races and felt it was luck if he simply finished on the lead lap. The fact that he was now challenging for race wins was a boost of confidence for him, despite his previous mistake in the race.

"No disrespect taken," replied Bill. "Plus, how come you didn't come out to watch me race? Atlanta isn't too far for a traveling man like yourself."

"That's what I came in here to tell you!" said Pat as he suddenly got excited. "I was working a deal with that new *possible* client from Greece! We should be hearing something from him in the next few weeks."

Although Bill was excited to hear the news of new business for the company, he couldn't help but shake his head as he smiled.

"Do you ever *not* work?" asked Bill. "I mean, it's great for the business but all work and no play makes for an exhausted man. You've gotta take some time for yourself and relax."

"This *is* how I relax, old friend," said Pat as he lifted his arms into the air as if he were a gladiator who just achieved victory in an arena of battle. "I do business for business because business is good!"

Bill couldn't help but notice that Pat's shirt had now become untucked from his pants and, with his arms still lifted, out popped a rather large belly button.

This wasn't the first time the sighting had happened but Bill still had to fight to maintain composure.

"Well I can't complain but you're gonna make me look bad," said Bill as he tried to subdue a chuckle. "You're out there breakin' necks and cashin' checks and I'm out driving a race car."

"Either way, you should be out there enjoying the fruits of our labor. Business is what I do for fun and racing is what you do for fun," said Pat.

"Now that I'm actually somewhat competitive, you'll have to come out and watch me race some time," said Bill.

"Tell you what. If this deal goes through with our Greek friend, I'll come out to one of your next races. How about that?"

"I'll take what I can get," said Bill. "I guess you'd better get crackin' with Greece, then. I'm sure you won't mind that. Is he flying into town?"

"He'll be here all next week," replied Pat. "He even requested that we go to a Greek restaurant while he's here. For the life of me, I'll never understand why people go to different countries and eat food from their home country."

"Well at least bring me some baklava," said Bill as he went back to work.

Pat laughed as he walked out of Bill's office. "I'll order some for you and the family. No promises that it'll survive the trip home, though."

Chapter 2

He sat motionless in his old recliner, just as he had been doing for the past several hours. With no lights on, the house was slowly becoming dark as the day pushed towards the evening hours. He sat still with his head turned slightly to the left so that he could see the last rays of light being given off by the setting sun through his window. He didn't mind the approaching night. He could live with the dark but what he could never get used to was the silence.

It was so quiet now.

There used to always be something going on in the house as it was full of its own comings and goings. People were always swinging by to say hello and ending up staying for dinner. The house always had a fresh fragrance to it as well which felt like a warm embrace when you walked through the front door. Now, that embrace was gone.

The various friends and acquaintances he had made ever since he moved to the United States from Australia nearly 40 years ago were nowhere to be found. Many had simply moved on but the lot of them had either grown old or passed away. Now as he sat in complete silence, he wondered when his turn would come. Time had already claimed more than he was ever willing to give.

He thought of his wife.

He wanted to see her again. He couldn't bear the silence any longer.

All he wanted was to hear her call his name one more time.

As he sat, he remembered all of the times he would get so bothered at how she would yell at him for leaving a mess in the kitchen or how he sat in front of the TV all day. But he also remembered how she was with him through every victory and every defeat.

What he would do just to hear that voice one more time…

For 35 years he had had his best friend by his side. As he turned his head to see the now empty chair where she normally sat, he felt alone.

Lost.

Without purpose.

He closed his eyes and tried hard to think of what it was like before he was married. He tried to remember the things he accomplished before his great voyage overseas but his clouded mind betrayed him. He glanced up at the wall in front of him to see his various racing trophies, pictures and newspaper clippings from his time as an Australian Touring Car driver, but they meant nothing to him. They felt as empty as the house he lived in.

He tried to think of the victories he'd had in life: Winning the Bathurst 1000 and the series Championship in his debut year, moving to America and meeting his wife, having a son who grew up well, buying his son and daughter-in-law their first house, becoming a grandfather…

An outsider would look at this and see a long and prosperous life.

But an outsider doesn't see the full picture.

William reopened his eyes with the faint hope that perhaps this was all just a bad dream but it was in fact his reality. He was still sitting in his old recliner in an old empty house with the memory of his now deceased wife haunting his mind.

A knock on the door startled him at first but he paid it no mind.

If it's important, they'll come back, he thought to himself. *Probably someone selling something or wanting to tell me that I need their version of Jesus. Hmm. Maybe they won't come back.*

After the second knock, however, he began to get curious.

A neighbor, perhaps? Maybe that yappity little dog got out again.

The jingling of keys coming from outside confirmed his next guess.

The door opened and his son, Bill, walked in. Closing the door behind him, Bill initially had trouble seeing as all of the lights were off.

"Dad? You in here?" Bill called out.

"In here, son," said William.

Bill made his way into the living room, turning lights on as he walked. As he entered, he found his dad in his usual spot: sitting in his old recliner with his feet up. Bill knew exactly what was going on.

He sat down in the chair beside his dad and asked, "How ya been holding up?"

William thought about lying and saying that everything was okay. But he was better than that and he could never lie to his son. Plus, he knew he wouldn't fool Bill.

He softly said, "I miss her."

Bill dropped his head somberly. "I miss her too, Dad. She was a great mom who managed to be married to you and raise this mess of me at the same time."

William chuckled as the memories of Bill's youth made him smile for the first time all day. Raised in private school through the end of middle school and then transferring to public school for high school, Bill was never the social butterfly that his mom, Charlotte, was. She was always trying to get him involved in sports or after school activities but Bill never seemed very interested. He'd rather be at home working on the family car with his dad.

With a smile William said, "Yeah. You were a good son."

"Were? I like to think that I still am."

"Well, you're here now visiting an old fart like me, aren't you?" William held out his arm to Bill. This was the universal sign that William was getting up and he wanted you to help him up.

Bill obliged.

As both men stood, Bill gave his dad a hug.

"It's good to see you, Dad," said Bill.

The words caused William to have to fight to keep his eyes from watering up. "Good to see you too, son." He slapped Bill on the back.

"So what have you been up to? How's work going?"

"Oh staying busy. Work always keeps my hands full but I manage to find time to do other things," said Bill as he tried not to sound too obvious that he was hinting at something.

"Everything going well at the shop, I assume?" asked William.

Bill knew he'd have to try harder. "Yeah, it's all going well. Pat says 'Hi', by the way. We're both always just racing around over there trying to stay ahead of the game."

"That's good," said William. "I'm glad that all of that big college money we spent on you is still paying off!" William said with a laugh as he headed towards the kitchen.

Bill tried again. "Well you know when you push hard in life and work your way to the front, it's a good feeling to stand on the podium in victory circle."

William opened the refrigerator and stooped down to look inside. "Well, working hard is something I've tried to press onto you from a young age. I'm glad to see you're walking the straight and narrow. Not many people do that nowadays."

Bill sighed and gave up. He knew that his dad was getting up there in years, so to say, but he hoped he hadn't forgotten about Bill's racing.

William emerged from the fridge with two beers in hand and a giant smile on his face. Bill instantly recognized it as the *Haha! Fooled you!* look which he had come to know over the years. He was glad to see his dad back in true form.

"So, you going to tell me how your race went yesterday, or not?" asked William.

"How did you know I raced yesterday?" Bill asked as he joined his father in the kitchen.

"C'mon, I may have been born at night but I wasn't born last night. Go on, how'd you fare?" asked William in his thick Australian accent.

Bill knew that his dad only talked that way nowadays when he got excited.

"Second place. Gave up the lead on one of the final corners of the last lap," Bill said as he sat down in one of the chairs by the kitchen table. William was quick to join him.

"Second place, huh? Not bad at all! Standing on the podium after any race worth racing is no easy feat and you've managed to do it. You're really getting the hang of this racing stuff, aren't you?"

"I'd like to think so. All of that karting when I was younger looks like it paid off. I feel like I can handle the car okay but I just seem to make so many mistakes towards the end of the race. Now I can officially say that it's cost me a race win," said Bill.

"To be nervous while driving a race car at speed is to be human, Bill. If you weren't nervous, it probably means you're in last place. Driving a full-sized race car is a lot different than the go-kart you drove when you were a kid. Plus, all great drivers have been guilty at least once of choking up at the end of a race, myself included. However, it's not *that* race that counts. It's what they do with this knowledge and experience in the *next* race which matters the most."

Bill nodded in acknowledgment. It was the advice he needed to hear.

"So how's the Mustang driving? You still taking care of her?" asked William of Bill's race car.

"Yep, I've still got the reins on her. She's a good car. Easy on the eyes, too," said Bill.

"Well nothing beats a good Ford," boasted William.

"Except a better Ford," they both said simultaneously.

The two laughed at the old saying as William suddenly realized that in all of the excitement of talking about racing, he was, in fact, still holding the two beers he had retrieved from the refrigerator. He handed one to Bill who held his hand up to decline the offer.

"Not before dinner," said Bill.

William, with a somewhat puzzled look on his face, asked, "What's for dinner?"

"Steak."

"Hmm. Charcoal or gas barbie?"

"Charcoal."

"Filet Mignon or T-Bone?"

"New York Strip"

"Is this my invitation?"

"Yes."

"Can I bring the beers?"

"You sure aren't drinking all of mine."

They both chuckled as William stood up and put his shoes on which were on the floor by the front door. As he slipped them on, he suddenly felt something which he wanted to feel all day: happiness.

He turned to Bill who was still sitting at the table. "I'm glad you stopped by here, Bill."

Bill smiled as he could tell his dad genuinely missed social interaction. He felt bad that he wasn't able to come by more regularly but he made up for it as often as he could. "C'mon, let's get going. I've got two hungry humans at home waiting for us. They'll turn to cannibalism if we wait too long."

William laughed as they both headed for the door. He turned and asked, "How are the wife and kid doing? Is little Chad keeping his grades up?"

"Straight A's again. I don't know where he gets the brains from," said Bill.

"Well it's gotta be from his mother's side. He sure didn't get it from us!" William said along with a mighty laugh. "But I'll be honest with ya, Billy. I hope he doesn't take *too* much from his mother's side of the family if you know what I mean."

"You and me both, Dad. You and me both."

* * *

The ride to Bill's house from his father's normally took about 15 minutes depending on who was driving. William opted to drive himself as he refused to "be driven 'round." Although he was in his mid-60's, he certainly didn't act like it. Nor did he drive like it.

As soon as he was in his car, William launched it down the road like it was the start of a championship race. Bill hadn't even gotten in his car yet as he saw the 1968 Mustang become a red blur as it bolted down the road. As Bill got into his car and took off, he tried to keep up but was a little more conscientious of the speed limit in the area. However, he couldn't let it be said that he was beaten by his old man. He slammed the gas down and went after him.

Although his SUV was no Mustang, it was surprisingly quick. He knew his dad had a good head start so if he wanted to beat him, he had to think outside of the box. Or in this case, outside of the road.

As he approached the neighborhood park, he turned in and cut through the open fields, the running track and the picnic area, narrowly missing two teenagers making out in the grass. He exited back onto the road on the other side of the park just behind his dad. He had caught up with him just in time to see his dad power slide his car to make a left turn. The tires screeched loudly but not nearly loud enough to overpower the almighty roar coming from the big V8 engine inside the mustang. The sound alone got Bill's heart racing even more.

Bill doubled down and used every bit of available road while making the left turn his dad had just made. SUV's are known for many things and tipping over during a hard turn was one such feature. Pushing his vehicle to the limit, it was now a straight shot down the road to Bill's house. He punched the gas but the SUV was no match for the power behind his father's old Mustang. He reached the house a few seconds behind his dad.

Second place again.

William parked his car along the curb in front of Bill's house as Bill pulled in and parked behind him. William couldn't help himself as he exited his car with both arms extended into the air while laughing aloud as if he had won the Great Race again.

As he lowered his arms, he walked toward Bill's vehicle with an ear to ear smile on his face. As he gave Bill's SUV a few pathetic pats on its hood, William said, "Never worse for wear, I'm afraid."

Bill acknowledged his father's victory by giving him a slow round of applause as he exited his vehicle. "I've never seen pond water move so fast," Bill said.

"Ay, don't be a freckle. I gave you a fair go!" said William as he smiled.

"A fair go?! Have you seen what I'm driving?" asked Bill.

"Hey, I've had this beauty since I moved here and..."

"It still runs as good as the day you bought it. I know, I know," said Bill as he finished his father's sentence.

They were both laughing as they walked towards the front porch when they both stopped suddenly. There standing in the doorway was Lena. Even from the distance they were apart from her and it being in the evening hours, Bill and William could see the look she had on her face with the accompanying hand on her hip.

"Well that'll burn a hole in your head," said William softly.

"You have no idea," Bill said in return.

After a moment, Lena said, "I think I could hear you both coming from the moment you left." She paused for a minute and held her nose up to smell the obvious scents which still surrounded the area.

"I smell burnt rubber," she said as she looked at William, "and fresh cut grass," as she turned to Bill. "Are you guys trying to get yourselves killed or arrested?"

Bill knew better than to speak right now since he was already in the dog house. His dad took the cue and said, "Darlin', I was just keeping his skills sharp. You look lovely, by the way," as he let out a playful laugh.

It didn't work.

Lena let her head dip down a bit and let out a sigh. She looked up and said, "Boys, save the racing for the track. Please."

"Sorry, love. It won't happen again," said William with as much suave as he could muster up.

Lena always loved hearing William's accent. She was trying so hard to keep a serious face but she couldn't help but smile as she heard his charming voice. She finally cracked and said, "Get in the house, you two."

As they entered the house, they were greeted by Chad.

"Grandpa!"

"Hey! There's the little ankle biter!" He scooped Chad up into his arms which strained his back slightly. "Oh, you're getting so big!"

Bill, who was walking into the house behind his dad, said, "Easy there, Chad. He's not getting any younger."

As Bill walked past Lena, he kissed her on the cheek as she slapped him hard on his rear.

"You're not out of the woods yet," she whispered in his ear.

* * *

After they finished eating, the three adults sat around the table enjoying a cup of coffee and good conversation. Lena still hadn't forgotten the men's grand arrival and because of it, wasn't her usual talkative self. The occasional gaps in conversation were quickly filled by Chad, however, who was very eager to tell his grandfather all of the details of his dad's previous race. Bill had to admit that everything about the race sounded much more interesting coming from the mind of his enthusiastic child.

After many of the details had been shared, Lena finally spoke up. "Chad, why don't you take your Grandpa and show him your report card from school?

Chad didn't need any motivation. He quickly got up and took

William's hand as he led him away. "C'mon, Grandpa!"

William laughed as Chad pulled him along. "Don't pull too hard, now! I'd like to go to bed tonight with all of my limbs still attached!"

As they exited the room, Bill and Lena sat quietly at the table. Bill knew that it was best if he waited for her to speak first. It didn't take long for her to begin.

"Bill," she said softly, "when we first bought your race car, we did it under the condition that you would keep the racing on the track. You promised me. But the more and more you race, the more and more I see it taking control of you."

Bill wanted to speak up but he knew she had more to say. He bit his tongue.

"I know you're excited to see your dad and you're glad he's still able to do things with you, but you need to control yourself and not let your emotions control you. I don't mean to sound like the nagging wife, but we've had this conversation before. Too many times, actually. Either you get a grip on this racing business, or it's gone. I'm not going to have our son raised thinking that he can race down public roads with no consequence and I'm certainly not going to raise him as a widow. Please, Bill. I love you and I'm glad that you enjoy racing, but we're not having this conversation again. You promised me and I'm holding you to it."

Bill wanted to be upset at his wife for putting her foot down so harshly but he couldn't. He was a man of his word.

At first, he found himself actually driving slower on the public roads after a race. But in the recent months, he noticed that as he got closer and closer to victory, his driving on the public roads was getting more and more out of control. He wanted to win so bad that everything he did in a car turned into a race. Whether it was closing a gap in front of him to stop a car from merging into his lane or racing a car to be first onto an exit ramp, Bill saw how it was beginning to affect him. She was right. He needed to cool it.

"You're right. I'm sorry. When I saw my dad take off in his car, it just took me back to when I was a kid and how he would do the same thing. But I'm not a kid anymore. I'm a husband and a father and I have a responsibility to you two. It won't happen again."

"One more chance, Bill. I hate that I have to put ultimatums down, but this is your safety we're talking about. One more chance. Please don't make me regret it."

"You won't. I promise," said Bill.

They sat in silence for the next few seconds unsure of how to proceed. After Lena took a sip of her coffee, she asked, "Were you still planning to ask him tonight?"

"I was. Just waiting for the right moment."

"You still think he'll say no?" asked Lena.

"He *will* say no. He loves company but he doesn't like intruding and that's exactly what he would feel like he's doing," Bill said softly as he heard footsteps going down the hallway. He heard the door leading to the garage open and then close a few seconds later. He knew that Chad was showing his grandpa his dad's race car.

"Well, no time like the present," said Lena.

She stood up from the table, grabbed as many of the dishes as she could and headed toward the kitchen. She stopped along the way and kissed Bill. He sat for a few more seconds as he got his words together. Finally, he stood up and headed for the garage.

With the success of Bill's business, he'd been able to furnish the third bay in his three-car garage with the equipment he needed to repair and maintain his race car. From a hydraulic lift to multiple tool boxes to a small paint booth, the third bay in Bill's garage had been transformed into a bonafide race shop. Like he had done when he was a kid, he enjoyed working on his car during his time off.

Walking into the garage, he found Chad in the driver's seat of the race car and William kneeling down by the driver's side window showing Chad how to properly hold the steering wheel.

"Keep your hands at *nine* and *three* but don't hook your thumbs on the wheel," said William. "That way you can still have a good grip and not have a serious injury should you ever have an incident on the track. A steering wheel snapping left or right all of the sudden can do some heavy damage to your wrists should you not be able to release your hands in time."

Bill remembered when his dad had told him the very same thing. He looked in the car to see Chad following his exact instructions and turning the wheel as he pretended he was racing.

"Alright, Andretti. It's time for bed," said Bill.

"Oh c'mon, Dad. Can I stay up just a little longer?"

"Not on a school night. Come on. Say goodnight to grandpa," said Bill.

Chad exited the car and gave William a big hug and told him goodnight. He stomped towards the door with his head hung low.

As he left the garage, William said, "He's a good kid. You used to kick and scream when it was time for bed."

"I still do," said Bill.

As his dad stuck his head inside the car, no doubt looking to make sure that Bill was taking care of everything, Bill said, "Dad, I need to ask you something."

William pulled himself out of the car and leaned up against it.

"Shoot."

"Lena and I have been wanting to know if you would be interested in moving in with us."

Before even a full second had passed, William replied firmly by saying, "Absolutely not."

Bill sighed. He knew he had an uphill battle in front of him. "Dad, you're lonely. You said it yourself at your house. You sit home all day by yourself and we're worried about you."

"Son, I don't need someone to wipe my ass for me. I may be getting older, but I can take care of myself," William snapped back.

Bill looked him straight in the eyes and asked, "Are you happy, Dad?"

"Am I happy? What kind of question is that?" William said.

"A yes or no question."

"What does that have to do with anything?"

He knew why his dad wasn't answering the question. "This isn't an interrogation, Dad. Just answer the question. Are you happy?"

William dropped his head and sighed deeply. "No, son. No. I'm not happy," he said.

"Then why won't you move in with us? You'll always have us to talk to and your grandson would love to see you more often. We have the extra bedroom downstairs and you'll have your own space."

"Because I have my house. I've had it since I moved to the states. It's the house your mother and I raised you in," said William as he lowered his head. "I feel like giving it up would be like losing her all over again."

"I can certainly understand where you're coming from," replied Bill. "There isn't a day that goes by that I don't think of her. But you know that Mom was never one to sit on her hands and if anyone knew how to make a bad situation turn to good, it was her."

William smiled.

"What would mom do if your roles were switched?" asked Bill. "Would she sit still or would she try to enjoy the time she had left while being surrounded by those who loved her?

William stood motionless. With his head still dropped, he simply stared off into space.

Standing across from him, Bill wondered what was going through his father's mind. A thousand beautiful memories from all the years his parents spent together? Or perhaps one unbearable memory which he was both running from and clinging to?

Feeling like he had nothing more to say, William slowly turned and walked past his son as he headed toward the door. Just before he was there, however, he stopped. With his back to Bill, he turned his head slightly over his shoulder and said one word.

"Alright."

Chapter 3

The weeks passed quickly as both Bill and Lena prepared for William's move. In the meantime, Bill began making more frequent trips after work to his father's house to help him pack and assist with selling the house.

One Friday evening, Bill was making one such trip to William's house and was accompanied by Chad.

William had insisted on packing everything himself—with the help of Bill and Chad of course—but had forgotten just how much stuff he had gathered since first moving there after marrying his wife, Charlotte, nearly 35 years ago.

Bill and Chad walked in just as William was setting a newly sealed box aside with the other sealed boxes.

"You know," said William, "I moved to the states all of those years ago with only enough stuff to fill a small apartment. Mostly just racing memorabilia and the likes, but you never know how much stuff you can accrue over the years until you pull it all out and have to pack it!"

Seeing that many of the boxes in the room had yet to be sealed, Chad immediately gravitated toward the open boxes of racing trophies which were sitting in the corner of the living room. Except for his favorite, the Bathurst 1000 trophy, William kept most of his racing awards boxed up.

Upon moving to the United States, he initially had many of them out on display in elaborate setups for all who visited to see. As he took a step back from racing, however, he desired some degree of normality with his family and peers. That and he simply didn't have the room for them anymore after getting married.

This was the first time Chad had seen most of the trophies. "Wow, grandpa! Did you win all of these?"

"I did, indeed. I imagine your father will be earning his share as well," said William as he shot a wink toward Bill. "But it's not about the trophies, it's about the racing. Every driver takes a trophy away from a race in their own way." Putting his hand on the open box of trophies, he added, "These trophies are simply rewards for the ones who happen to come out on top on race day. Speaking of race day, I hear someone has a race coming up soon."

"Nothing seems to get past you," said Bill.

"I thought you would've learned that by now," replied William with a smile.

"Are you gonna come and watch, grandpa?"

"You'd better believe I'll be there! It's been awhile since I've been to a proper race."

"I'll try not to disappoint," added Bill.

"Oh don't worry about disappointing me. I'm proud of you for just being out there," said William.

As William was talking, Chad had pulled out a smaller but fancy looking trophy from the box and brought it over to his grandfather.

"What's this one from, grandpa?" asked Chad.

With a smile on his face, William examined the trophy and said, "Oh, you won't believe what I went through to win this one."

As William began sharing the story behind that particular trophy, Bill started walking through the house to see the progress his dad had made in packing. He entered the guest bedroom where many of the sealed boxes were being stored for the time being. As he walked further into the room toward where the closet was located, he noticed a single open box sitting on the floor by the closet doorway. Inside this box, sitting on the very top, was an old picture which Bill hadn't seen in some time. He picked it up and carried it over toward the window where the golden evening sunlight allowed him to see the picture with more clarity. Wiping his hand across the top to remove some of the dust, he smiled as he looked at the wedding photo of his parents. It reminded him of Lena and himself: so young, happy and full of life.

It felt as if it had been such a long time since he had seen a picture of his mother. Although his dad would be the first to tell anyone, Bill could personally attest to his mother's fiery personality. He remembered the countless times that his father would tell friends and family members that he married Charlotte because "they don't make 'em like that in Australia."

Bill smiled at the memory. It had only been about a year since his mother passed away but it still felt like it had happened just yesterday. Thinking back, Bill remembered the severe headaches which never seemed to subside. Then she began forgetting simple mundane things like their home address or how to get to the grocery store. Upon visiting the doctor, she was diagnosed with a rare form of brain cancer which was causing her to deteriorate very quickly at her age.

Due to the cancer not being found until it was in an aggressive state, there was little to nothing which could be done. Three weeks later, she had passed away.

The hole that her death left on the family was difficult to bear. It was so all-of-the-sudden with how she was gone, the person who took the brunt of the loss was, of course, William. Bill often wondered how his dad kept himself together. He knew that if something like that were to happen to him, he'd more than likely fall apart.

"She was a looker, wasn't she?"

Bill looked up to see his dad standing in the doorway.

"I know I've never asked you this but how did you do it?" asked Bill as he held the picture up toward William. "With how mom passed, how did you move on?"

William let a slight smile surface as he said, "Honestly, it's you and the family. Seeing you become the man you are and watching my grandson grow gives me the inspiration I need to get up every morning. You guys are what keep me going. These legs still have some life in them and I know that your mom would want me to keep going. Like you said, she would've done the same thing."

Bill smiled as he looked down at the picture again.

"Alright, alright. Don't get all sentimental on me," said William sarcastically as he took the picture from Bill and handed him a roll of packing tape. "Don't quit your day job yet, either. One day he'll be able to do it but right now I don't think we could kick back and let Chad pack the rest of the house just yet."

"He's got to earn his keep somehow," said Bill with a smile.

"And so do you. Remember, this was all your idea!" exclaimed William as he let out a mischievous laugh. "C'mon. This house won't pack itself! Off you go!"

* * *

Staring out the window as his father drove them both home, Chad often daydreamed of what adulthood would be like. He'd met teachers, firefighters, police officers, professional athletes and even an astronaut while visiting Houston. Although he found them all to be interesting, he found something else to be much more fascinating.

As his father continued the drive home, Chad sat still for several seconds with what looked like a face overcome with deep thought. Finally, he turned to his dad and asked, "Why did you get into racing, Dad?"

Bill, more than slightly shocked at the sudden question, didn't exactly know how to answer it at first. He knew what it was about racing that he loved—the speed, the thrill, the danger—but it had been some time since he'd stopped and asked himself *why* he had gotten into racing.

"Honestly, I think it has more to do with being able to communicate with grandpa. It's what excites him and I guess it's also in our blood, too. That and growing up around someone like grandpa gave me the knowledge I needed to be competitive on the track. But knowledge is nothing out there without the skill to back it up," said Bill.

Turning toward his dad again, Chad asked, "Could I be a race car driver, too?"

Bill, mirroring the words he had just asked himself, asked, "Why do you want to be a race car driver? You're a smart kid. You could be whatever you wanted to be in life."

"Grandpa's a race car driver and so are you. I just thought it's something that our family does," replied Chad. "I mean, I really like going to the track when you race and I like working on cars with you, too."

Bill couldn't help but feel touched by his son's comment. He was fortunate enough to have a great relationship with his dad, and he wanted to have that very same thing with his son. Racing was indeed in his blood and Bill knew that it was only a matter of time before it would one day manifest in its own way with his son.

"It takes a lot to be a driver," said Bill. "It's one thing to have the money to buy a good car and maintain it but it takes years to develop the skills needed to drive at high speeds with other cars on a track. It's a big commitment."

Chad began thinking about the word 'commitment'. At his age, he'd been able to commit to his studies at school and the results were obvious. He was the smartest kid in all of his classes.

"I can do it, Dad. It'll be a family thing or something," said Chad.

"Chad, you're my son. I'll support you in anything you chose to do. But don't feel that you need to follow any particular path in life just because your dad and grandpa did it. The whole world is at your fingertips. You can do whatever you want to do," said Bill.

Chad's mind wandered upon hearing the statement.

Does he know how long I've been thinking about this? Maybe he thinks I'm just trying to make him happy—like a good son.

He's just a boy, thought Bill. *I shouldn't discourage him from trying his hand at something. It was only a matter of time anyways.*

Turning to Chad, Bill said, "Tell you what. After my race this weekend, how about we swing by the go-kart track here in town and I'll show you the basics? Then we can see what you're made of."

"Really?! Can grandpa come, too?" asked Chad.

"I'm sure he'd love to tag along. He knows more about this racing stuff than I do," replied Bill.

"Thanks, Dad! I can't wait!" said Chad. He became so overcome with excitement that he could hardly sit still. Extending his arms as if grabbing an imaginary steering wheel and was driving the SUV home, Chad mirrored the movements of his father while adding a bit of racing flair.

"I wouldn't exactly call driving 25 mph in a neighborhood a thrill ride," replied Bill as he smiled at his son.

"I've gotta start early. I need to work on my racing line and late braking skills," said Chad with complete seriousness.

Bill, totally amazed to hear his son using racing lingo, glanced over at Chad and noticed how he was locked in the moment. He laughed as he said, "You've been hanging around the track too much if you're already talking like that."

Chad laughed as he continued steering the car with his imaginary wheel. It wasn't until Bill's cell phone rang that he froze in place. Looking at the caller ID, Bill saw that it was Lena.

"Go ahead and answer it," he said as he handed the phone to Chad. Picking up the phone, Chad tried to mimic his father's voice by deeply lowering his own.

"Hello?"

A brief second passed and Chad handed the phone back to his dad. "She wants to talk to you," he said.

Oh no, thought Bill. *Did I leave the garage door open again? Maybe it's just a grocery store run.*

He put the phone on speaker and answered, "Yes, my loving wife?" A very soft and overly polite voice from Lena came on the other end, "You might want to take the long way home tonight."

Even worse, thought Bill. *Helen.*

"10-4. I love you." said Bill as the other end hung up.

Bringing his vehicle to a stop at a stoplight, Bill sat quietly for a few seconds as Chad, totally oblivious to what was going on, looked at his father curiously. Finally, Bill made a decision. He turned to Chad and asked, "How does ice cream sound to you?"

* * *

"I'm not leaving until I see my grandson! You can move that foreigner into your house but you won't even let me see my own grandson?" barked Helen. "I raised you better than that, Lena!"

It had been over an hour since Lena had called Bill and given him the coded message that her mother had invited herself over. At almost 9 pm, however, Lena knew that Bill and Chad would be home soon. She also knew that her mother was showing no signs of giving up. If anything, her aggravation had reached a boiling point.

"Mom, you really need to be nicer to William. He's been through a lot," said Lena as she tried to diffuse her irate mother.

Lena's mother, Helen Godbey, was a large woman who often allowed her size to work in parallel with her mouth. Making a habit of cornering the person who was unfortunate enough to be caught in her crosshairs, she would oftentimes use her mass to seal off any escape routes while she berated her victim with whatever it was which she felt was ultimately necessary for that particular person to hear.

Helen was a Texas native who had the accent and the hairstyle to show for it. And if she wasn't raising her voice at you, she was killing you with her poisonous kindness, which involved speaking softly and often with a smile as she hurled demeaning and insulting words your way.

Lena recalled back to when she was dating Bill in high school and, while he was at her house on one occasion, Helen approached the two of them, looked Lena in the eyes and said, "You can do better than this," as she indicated towards Bill.

"Don't you tell me what I should do! You let that husband of yours keep my grandson out this late at night and now you want to boss *me* around? Who do you think you're talking to? And how do you even know Chad is okay? With the way that man drives, he's probably crashed into something. I can't believe you let him drive like that. And it's all because of that old man that you're now bringing into this house," said Helen.

"*This house*," replied Lena sharply, "belongs to Bill and me, and it was paid for by William. I think that Bill and I will be the judge of what goes on in here."

The expression on Helen's face was evidence enough that she didn't take too kindly to those words.

Here it comes, thought Lena.

"So I guess I can fully expect to be moved in here when I get older, too? It would only be fair. Plus, what kind of a person has enough money to buy a house but not to hire a moving company? The kind of person that's using you! That's who! I knew from the first time I met him that he was always up to no good. I still can't believe that you didn't listen to me when I told you not to marry his son. Now you're caught in this mess and you're stuck with it. I can't believe..."

Helen's speech was cut short as the sound of the garage door opening caught her attention. At this, Helen rose from her seat and made her way toward the door which led to the garage. She stopped about three-feet shy of the door, folded her arms and made ready for the scolding she was prepared to unleash upon an unsuspecting Bill. She knew that there was no way around her.

Stiffening her upper lip and lowering her brow, she waited.

And waited.

After what seemed like several minutes when in reality it had only been about 15 seconds, Helen made an audible *Hmph!* as she gave in and swung open the door to the garage. At the same time, the front door of the house opened slowly as Bill and Chad snuck in. Having discussed this plan ahead of time, Chad went directly upstairs as Bill snuck past Helen from behind.

"What kind of a game is this? Is he trying to give me a heart attack? Where did they go?" rambled Helen.

Turning around to enter the house, she said, "I bet he ran off since he knows I'm here. He's always been afraid of me. Wait until I…" As she turned to face Lena who was still seated at the kitchen table, she was surprised to see Bill sitting in what was up until this point Helen's seat.

The awkward pause as Helen stared with a look of disbelief was ended when Bill broke the silence. "Helen, so wonderful to see you! Wow, you really warmed this seat up well. Have you lost weight?"

"You snake!" replied Helen. "What did you do to my grandson?"

"I fed him this horrid substance known as ice cream. On a Friday night, nonetheless. I would've gotten you some but I think you've had too much already," said Bill as he made no attempt to hide his disdain.

"Bill, please," said Lena under her breath.

"You worthless, arrogant prick! How dare you!" was all that Helen could say.

"Okay, mom. Time for you to leave," said Lena as she saw where this conversation was going.

"No! I told you that I'm not leaving until I see Chad! Now where is he?!" said Helen.

"He doesn't want to talk to you. As a matter of fact, I don't want to talk to you either. Now get out of my house," said Bill as he pointed towards the front door.

Helen rose up to her full height of 5'3" and slowly closed the distance between her and Bill, stopping just inches away from him.

"You think I'm scared of you, little boy?" said Helen in a low and sinister voice. "That's all that you were then and all that you'll ever be: That little insecure boy from high school that nobody liked and nobody wanted to be friends with. So why don't you just keep driving around in your little car until you crash and get yourself killed so you can do us all a favor and rid the world of yourself."

Bill had enough. Letting a defiant smile creep across his face, he slowly stood up from his seat and, with his fists clenched, advanced on Helen.

"You wanna know what happens to people who come into my house and disrespect me in front of my wife?"

Lena, seeing where this was going, stepped in.

"Enough!" shouted Lena. "Mom, you need to leave. Now." Completely ignoring her daughter's comments, Helen fixed her gaze upon Bill and met his advance with that of her own.

"You think I'm scared of you?" asked Helen as she balled up her own fists. "You won't be the first man I've destroyed."

"Get the hell out of my house!" shouted Bill. At this, Lena stepped in between the two of them and faced her mother.

"I said enough!"

The sudden outburst caused a brief respite from the action. Lena took a deep breath as she turned towards her husband.

"Bill, please sit down," she said calmly.

Bill, hearing the wisdom in her words, let his anger subside for the moment and sat back down at the kitchen table.

Turning towards her mother, Lena continued. "You've crossed the line, mom. You can't come into this house and talk to my husband like that. To be honest, I don't think you should come over anymore. You're a bad influence on Chad, and I don't want you around him."

Helen's face became a twisted mess of rage. Looking past her daughter and directly at Bill, Helen pointed her finger at his face.

"Look at me, little boy. I hope you die and go to hell!"

At this, Helen grabbed her purse and began walking toward the front door. With every footstep being a heavy but intentional *stomp* along the way, Helen opened the front door and, upon exiting, swung the door shut. The door, however, was caught just before impact. Chad, who appeared from behind the corner, closed the door softly as he walked into the kitchen where his mom and dad were.

"Well that got ugly really quick. Why is she always like that?" asked Chad.

Lena, still in a state of shock at what had just unfolded in their kitchen, walked over and knelt down in front of Chad. "Because she is a very controlling person. She doesn't like people telling her what to do and she doesn't want anyone to be happy unless she *allows* them to be happy. It's hard to say that about my own mom but she's always been that way."

Lena gave Chad a hug as Chad asked, "Why doesn't she want *us* to be happy?"

"Because of me," said Bill as he remained seated exactly where he had been when Helen said those horrible words to him. Feeling his anger slowly dissipating, he stared with disbelief up at the ceiling as he sighed. "She's never forgiven me for marrying your mother against her wishes."

As he sat, Bill recalled back to when he was once speaking with Lena at her house weeks before their wedding. He remembered telling Lena that he thought her mother—who'd previously stated she wouldn't be attending their wedding—was crazy and that she needed to get away from her. Unbeknownst to the two of them, Helen had been eavesdropping on their conversation and immediately began accusing Bill of trying to drive a wedge between her and her daughter. Lena would later tell Bill that ever since that moment, her mother had hated him.

"You'd think that we'd be safe from idiocy while inside the walls of our own house."

"She won't be coming over anymore, Bill. I promise," replied Lena. At this, Lena also sighed as she stood up and patted Chad on the back while she said to him, "Time for bed, mister. You need to get some sleep."

"After what just happened, I'm not even gonna argue with you this time," said Chad as both he and Lena went upstairs.

Bill remained seated at the kitchen table as several thoughts whirled through his mind. He knew he had tried to live a good life by supporting and providing for his family. He had a successful career, a beautiful house and he truly lacked for nothing. As he sat and pondered about the previous incident, however, none of that was on his mind. He could still feel the burning sensation of anger running through his body and the only thing he could hear was that sinister voice which now seemed to be ingrained in his mind.

I hope you die and go to hell!

Chapter 4

An early bird by nature, Bill remained in bed for some time as his wife lay by his side. Unlike Bill, Lena was always the deep sleeper. She could lie absolutely still all night long and not awaken even if Bill was tossing and turning. Unfortunately for Bill, he'd been doing just that all night.

It had been several days since the incident with Helen, but Bill had yet to be able to put it fully behind him. He was eventually able to get some sleep and let the day along with all of its happenings pass away. Waking up this morning with his mind renewed, he knew that neither a restless night of sleep nor an angry mother-in-law would be able to quell the excitement which began to brew up in him as he lay there.

Today was race day.

He had been looking forward to this day since the conclusion of the previous race, and as he lay there in bed, he began making a mental checklist for himself concerning things which needed to be done before they set off for the track. Although a slight headache had been harassing him since he woke, which made his thought process a bit difficult, he simply assumed that he was needing his daily dose of coffee. Feeling confident that everything would be in order, he glanced over at the clock to check the time.

6:30 am.

He turned to look out the window which answered his question as to why it was still dark as he noticed heavy rain clouds moving in.

It's never stopped us from racing before.

He rose from bed and stood up tall as he stretched his arms up high and let out a quiet groan. Turning around to check if he had woken up Lena—which part of him had hoped that he had—he noticed she was in the same position as when he had gotten out of bed. She hadn't moved a muscle.

As she slept like a baby, Bill thought, *If only we could all be that lucky. Oh well. Time to get moving.* Beginning with the first item on his mental checklist, he knew that on the floor of his closet was his racing bag, which normally contained his helmet, fire suit, shoes, gloves, HANS device and balaclava.

He realized, however, that after spending the last several evenings helping out at his father's house, he had been so weary that he had gone to bed without packing it. Leaning down and unzipping the bag, he searched through it and saw that it was missing his fire suit, balaclava and helmet. He knew his helmet was in Chad's room as Chad liked to keep it there and had a special place for it amongst his various racing toys. But where were the other two items?

As if on cue, Lena said, "They're hanging up in the laundry room."

Turning around to see his wife lying there with her eyes partially open, Bill said, "I'm sorry. I didn't mean to wake you."

"It's okay. I need to get up and get everything ready too."

Even though Bill and Lena were still relatively new to the life of auto racing, Bill was genuinely surprised at how quickly Lena had adapted to it. Although there were certainly days where Lena would've preferred to stay home, she always woke up early on race day to help Bill get ready.

Walking over to Bill, she gave him a quick kiss on the lips as she said, "I'll go make the coffee if you go and wake the mom-magnet." She smiled as she headed into the closet to fetch her robe.

Letting his eyes follow her into the closet, Bill said, "I didn't apologize to you the other night and I feel like I need to. I didn't mean to let things get out of hand like that with your mom." Bill had been thinking about this for the past several nights.

"You don't need to apologize to me, Bill. I would've done the same thing if I were in your shoes," said Lena from inside the closet. Sticking her head out, she smiled and added, "I'm just glad you didn't punch her."

"I can't say the thought didn't cross my mind," said Bill under his breath.

She emerged from the closet wearing her robe and walked up to Bill. Wrapping her arms around him, she looked into his eyes as she softly spoke and said, "Look, I know she said some terrible things to you. You know how she gets when she gets angry."

"And hungry..." added Bill.

Lena slapped his arm. "I'm being serious," she said, but she couldn't help but smile at the comment. "I need you to tell me that you don't believe anything she said."

Smiling, he let out a sigh as he looked into his wife's eyes as he said, "I don't believe anything she said."

"Are you being honest with me?" asked Lena.

Bill kissed her on the forehead and smiled. "Ask me again after I've had coffee."

Lena dropped her arms from his side as he walked toward their bedroom door to go wake Chad up. He was stopped short as Lena said, "I love you."

He had heard her say those words countless times since they've known each other but this time it felt different. It was almost as if she had poured every bit of her love for Bill into those three simple words and made a point to make sure he recognized it. He knew Lena had a unique way of communicating with him and this was one such way. She wanted to tell him that she believed in him, trusted him, loved him and cherished him all at the same time.

She had done just that.

He turned around to face her as she stood in the center of the room. Smiling with his youthful and charming face, Bill looked into her eyes and replied, "I love you too, babe."

He turned and exited the master bedroom and proceeded down the hall toward Chad's bedroom. Bill approached the door and noticed that it was still cracked open after Lena had tucked him in last night. As he peered inside, Bill heard and saw something that made his heart melt.

There was Chad sitting on his bed with his father's helmet on his lap. Rubbing the fingerprints off of it with an edge of his bed sheet, Chad was also saying a simple prayer: "God, I ask that you watch over my dad today on the race track. Keep him safe and help him to do the best he can. Help him kick everyone's butt today, too. Amen."

Bill knocked softly on the door and pushed it open slightly. Nodding his head toward the helmet, Bill said, "I appreciate it. Both the helmet cleaning and the prayer."

"It's the least I can do," replied Chad. Handing the helmet to his dad, he said, "I just wish there was more I could do to help out."

Taking the helmet into his hands, Bill sat down next to Chad on his bed. "You do a lot, son. More than you know," said Bill.

"Like what?" asked Chad.

"Well you take care of mom when I'm out on the track, for one. She'd be a nervous wreck without you. But there's something else you do that's very important. The most important, if you ask me," said Bill.

Chad looked up at his dad and asked, "What's that?"

"You inspire me. You know that? When I'm out on that track and it's scalding hot in the car and I'm tired and I just want the race to end, I know that you and your mom are out there watching me. You guys are what keep me going and I honestly couldn't do this without you," said Bill.

Chad smiled and let his head drop in shyness as he said, "Thanks, Dad. I don't know how I do it but I'm glad that I do."

"You know," said Bill, "your grandpa told me the same thing when I was about your age. That I inspired him. I never really understood what he meant by it until I had a family of my own. Now I know what it feels like. One day you will, too."

"But I thought that grandpa was done with racing by the time you were born?" asked Chad.

Bill smiled as he stood up and said, "Racing isn't the only thing in life that requires inspiration, son. Plus, despite his age your grandpa has never been officially *done* with racing. He's got a lot of friends overseas in Australia who are still involved in racing that he keeps up with."

"Are we still going to visit there one day?" asked Chad.

"One day, yes. But not today."

"Because today we've got a race to win!" said Chad.

Giving Chad a high-five, Bill exclaimed, "That's right! But we're not going to win any races sitting here on our butts, are we? We'd better get going before they start without us!"

* * *

The early start paid off for Bill, Lena and Chad as the three of them arrived promptly at the location of the next race—The Circuit of the Americas in their hometown of Austin, TX—to find William's red mustang already there. William had gotten there so early, in fact, that he was waiting at the gates when the first track workers arrived.

This was his first visit to a race track in quite some time so he was anxious to hear the sounds of the first motors starting up and to see the sights of teams and individual drivers getting their cars ready.

Currently the only Formula One track in the United States, William soaked in the majesty of the Circuit of The Americas as a pack of cars drove by. The sounds of their engines reverberated through the front grand stands which caused William's skin to get goosebumps.

There were a number of smaller races going on throughout the day and William was keen on watching all of them. Being in the racing atmosphere made him feel young again. As he watched the various practice sessions throughout the morning, a coy smile slipped onto his face. *I may have stepped away from racing, but I could probably still go out there and show those young drivers a thing or two.*

Looking at his watch, he knew that Bill and the family would be arriving shortly. Leaving his seat, he headed down to the pit area just as they were arriving. Bill was driving the SUV which was hauling his race car on a large enclosed trailer up to the loading area as William made sure the area was clear.

Emerging from the vehicle, Bill greeted his father with a smile. "You made it!"

"So did you! I was thinking you were going to leave me here all day!" William said jokingly as he extended his hand.

Bill met his handshake and asked, "How's the track looking so far?"

"Good enough but don't you be worrying about that right now. You just focus on what you need to do out there today," barked William. Bill raised his eyebrows at the comment which had just caught him off guard.

Lena emerged from the passenger side of the SUV and, after hearing William's previous remark, said, "You need to come to these races more often. He needs someone to kick his butt into gear." She smiled and gave William a hug. "Good to see you, Dad."

"Good to see you too, darling. And where's the youngster at?" asked William.

"Grandpa!" shouted Chad as he emerged from behind Lena.

Kneeling down, William said, "There he is!" as he gave Chad a hug.

"Grandpa, Dad almost punched Grandma Helen in the face the other night."

"Chad!" shouted Lena.

William laughed aloud and smiled as he said, "Almost? You didn't miss, did you?"

"Not quite," said Bill as he laughed.

"So that means she's still out there somewhere. Should I be hiding?

I always thought I was on her hit list, too," said William who then began looking around as if Helen were hiding behind the nearest fuel drum.

Lena, not thinking it was funny, said, "Hey, I know she can be a pain but she's still my mom."

William chuckled as he patted her on the shoulder.

"I didn't mean any harm, Love. C'mon. Let's get our boy ready for this race."

Lena and Chad began unloading Bill's gear from their vehicle as the crew Bill had hired arrived on the scene and began unloading the car from the trailer. With a vehicle as complex as a TA2 car, running it was one thing but preparing it and servicing it on race day required the attention of a full complement of experienced personnel. Although their services came with a hefty price tag, the return on investment was worth the cost if it meant having a competitive car.

Looking up into the sky, Bill saw that it was still an overcast day but at least the rain had stopped. With the practice sessions and races which were going on throughout the day, he knew the track would probably be dry enough by the time his race began.

Once the car was off-loaded, the crew went to work with getting the car ready for the upcoming race. As always, Chad was right there watching and learning the skills of the trade. Initially, Bill thought the rough and tough crew members would be mildly annoyed by the small figure lurking behind them. To his surprise, however, the crew were always very polite with Chad and, when things weren't going at a hectic pace, often showed Chad what they were doing and why.

Putting the car in neutral, the crew began pushing it towards the pit stall as Bill and Chad walked alongside the car. William and Lena walked behind them and smiled at the two as they worked together.

Knowing that this was a rare moment where she found herself alone with William, Lena said, "I need to talk to you about the other night."

William let his head drop as he shook it and said, "Look, I'm sorry.

I didn't mean any harm. I was just joking arou..."

"It's not about that," interrupted Lena. Knowing that her time with William was short, she continued by saying, "My mother said some pretty horrible things to Bill. He said that they're not bugging him but I know him better than that. He's always struggled with my mom and she knows it. She tears him down whenever she can and it takes its toll on him after a while. He may never admit it but I know it affects him."

"You want me to talk to him?" ask William.

"Discretely, if you wouldn't mind. He's been looking forward to today since the last time he raced and I just want him to enjoy himself and not worry about this stuff when he's out there," said Lena as they arrived at the pit stall and handed Bill's race bag to William.

Taking the bag, William said, "I'll say a few words to him, Love. Don't you worry about a thing."

Lena smiled a *Thank you*.

They both looked over as Bill, Chad and the crew began the work of preparing the car. As time passed and the car was about ready to hit the track, Bill, who had been wearing the bottom half of the full-body fire suit with the sleeves tied around his waist, pulled the top half over him and zipped it up. He then began looking around as if he had lost or dropped something. He checked in the car, under the car and in his pockets but couldn't find them anywhere.

"Looking for these?" a voice said from behind Bill.

Turning around, Bill saw his dad standing there holding his racing gloves.

"Thank you," said Bill. "I don't want to lose these. They've been through a lot."

"And there's a lot more for them to go through!" said William as he handed the gloves to Bill. "They have a way of taking care of you but only if you know how to take care of yourself out there. I'm not just talking about gloves, mind you, but up here too," he said as he put his finger up to the side of Bill's head. "Make sure your head is in the game and try to stay focused. A calm mind will allow your body to do the rest."

As Bill put the gloves on top of the car, he looked back at his father and asked, "Lena's been talking to you, hasn't she? About what happened with her mom the other night."

"Don't you worry about it. The only time that crazy woman can exist in your mind is when you allow her to. Don't give her the control that she wants," said William as he reached into the bag and pulled out Bill's helmet. As Bill reached out to take it, William held onto it. He looked Bill directly in the eyes and said, "When you put this on, block everything else out, son. Everything. You only take out on that track what you bring with you so don't bring any unnecessary weight—physical or emotional."

As William released his grip on the helmet, Bill had trouble remembering the last time he'd heard his father speak this directly.

William added, "I don't need to say it so I won't."

"I'll be careful," said Bill as he placed his helmet on top of the car alongside of his gloves. He gave his dad a hug and said, "I'm glad you're here, Dad. I really appreciate it."

"I'm glad I can be here. Now get out there and show these jokers what you've got," said William with a smile.

Chad and Lena approached as William took a few steps back to give Bill's family some space.

"Good luck, Dad. I know you can do it." said Chad as he hugged his dad's leg.

Lena gave Bill a hug, looked directly in his eyes and said, "Be safe out there."

"Fast and safe; that's my motto," said Bill jokingly.

Lena shook her head while smiling and said, "You're a crazy man, Bill Watson. That's why I love you."

"I know," said Bill with a smile.

Lena put her hand on Chad's shoulder and said, "C'mon, Chad. Let's go find a seat with grandpa."

The family waved one last time as they exited the pit stall.

Alone now, Bill took a brief moment to collect himself as he squatted down and leaned his back up against the driver's side door of his Mustang. He closed his eyes and took several deep breaths, already beginning to feel the butterflies in his stomach.

Despite all of the action and racing that awaited, this moment of solitude was enough to draw him back to reality as he noticed that his headache from this morning was still there. Only a minor nuisance, Bill shook it off and allowed his mind to focus on what was about to happen.

The air was cool at that moment as the sun had yet to expose itself through the heavy cloud cover. He enjoyed these simple and quiet moments before the madness of the race. Then, like a rolling thunder moving through pit lane, he heard the sounds of several engines starting up. He opened his eyes slowly and took one more deep breath.

As Bill stood up and turned around to enter his car and get himself strapped him, he looked down pit lane and saw Elliot Hughes, the driver who beat him on the final lap at their last race at Road Atlanta, hugging his own family. Elliot turned and noticed Bill staring in his direction and gave him a slight nod as he entered his own car.

Bill returned the nod and said to himself, "Time to get busy."

* * *

With races in the SCCA Trans Am Series being 100-miles in length with no mandatory pit-stops for fuel or driver changes, they are a flat-out dash from start to finish. Before the race begins, however, there are typically two practice sessions which last between 30 to 45 minutes. This gives the driver ample time to not only get a feel for the track but also to give their respective crew feedback on what the car is doing so that appropriate changes can be made.

After the practice sessions are complete, they are followed by qualifying, which is also between 30 to 45 minutes. In this session, drivers attempt to set the fastest possible lap time as this determines the starting order of the race from fastest to slowest.

Coming back into the pits at the end of qualifying, Bill was very happy with how the car felt. With the cooler weather due to the overcast skies, the conditions were favorable for fast lap times.

Setting a decent lap time, Bill qualified in third just behind Elliot. Although he missed out on a front row start by a tenth of a second, Bill couldn't beat himself up too much. Third place was the best he had ever qualified and this was also the first time he'd ever raced on this particular track.

Although there was a buzz in the air because of how close Bill's time was in relation to Elliot's, the main focus seemed to be on the new driver who qualified on pole position.

A young driver who made his start in go-karts, did a brief stint on oval short-tracks racing Legends cars but later moved to the Mazda MX-5 Spec Miata series, Sam Wells was new to the Trans-Am Series but no stranger to racing. Despite the fact that Wells wasn't even 20-years old yet, he had signed a handsome deal which made him a factory driver for Dodge which, in turn, put him behind the wheel of the TA2 Dodge Challenger.

After the qualifying session, Bill had a chance to meet Sam and congratulate him on sticking it on the pole in his debut race.

Extending his hand in greeting, Bill, along with several other drivers, introduced himself. Much to Bill's surprise, however, Sam knew who he was.

"You're William Watson's son, right?" asked Sam. "I've heard a lot about him over the years but I've never actually met him."

"Well, maybe I can arrange a meeting," said Bill. "He's here today in the stands."

"That'd be great! You know, my dad used to watch him race when he was growing up and now here *we* are. Fate's a funny thing, isn't it?"

"It is, indeed."

This wasn't the first time that Bill had to play secretary for his father. Although the Australian Supercars series wasn't very popular in the United States, word got around of William's accomplishments once Bill formally entered the Trans-Am Series. Having mentioned that his dad had grown up racing in Australia, many other drivers were quick to search the internet for his name and were very surprised at what they found.

"Good luck in the race today, Sam. And watch out for this guy," said Bill as he nudged Elliot Hughes in the ribs with his elbow. "He can sure put the heat on you."

Elliot, an older man in his early 50's, had worked his way up to where he was on his own and with his own money. Unlike Sam or even Bill for that matter, Elliot had no fancy sponsors other than for a few local businesses from his hometown in Topeka, KS. It had taken decades for him to get to where he was today, and he never looked too kindly on the young kids who came into motorsports "with a silver gas pedal under their foot" as he often said.

The snarling look on Elliot's face said everything he'd wanted to say.

Sam, with a boyish smile on his face, took a long look at Elliot and calmly said, "I'll be careful." Bill could sense the tension developing between the two.

"Well, we'd all better get back to our crews," said Bill. "Good luck, guys."

Elliot and Sam said nothing as they turned in opposite directions and walked away.

"Geez, Elliot. It's his first day on the job. Give the kid a break," said Bill.

Elliot just shook his head. "Kids like that can't appreciate what it takes to get here on their own. I have no respect for them," said

Elliot.

"Well, he wouldn't be here if he couldn't drive. Plus, he just beat the both of us and stuck it on pole."

"By less than a tenth of a second and with a factory team."

"Still ahead of both of us though."

Elliot couldn't help but chuckle at the comment.

Bill slapped Elliot on the shoulder and said, "Have a good race, buddy," as he turned and headed towards his pit stall.

Turning and shouting towards Bill, Elliot replied as loudly as he could, "I probably would've had a lot more good races if I had just chosen the right parents like he did."

* * *

The field began to form on the starting grid as Bill and his crew did a final check of the car. The twenty-eight cars which were in this thirty-lap race were gridded side by side, two cars per row, with the pace car in the front which would lead the pack to a rolling start. This put Bill directly behind the leader and on the inside lane for the first left hand turn. It was going to be a sprint race, so Bill knew he had to push himself but not do anything crazy too early in the race. With the field as condensed as it is at the start, any incident or misjudgment would be catastrophic to not only Bill, but potentially other cars in the field.

With all of the cars lined up and the race about to begin, Bill closed his eyes for a moment and took a deep breath. His mind focused on what he needed to do, he envisioned the apexes of certain turns, the tricky driving line through the first half of the track and how he would start the race. As he reopened his eyes, his attention was pulled to the slightest drop of rain which fell on his front windshield.

Oh great, he thought.

Bill had only a few brief experiences of racing in the rain, so he crossed his fingers and hoped that the floodgates would stay closed until after the finish line.

The pace car rolled off and led the field on a brief warmup lap. Using this time to warm their cars up, many of the drivers began swerving left and right to put some heat into their tires before the green flag dropped. Additionally, it was common to see drivers accelerate and brake repeatedly in an attempt to warm up their engines and brakes. This accelerating and braking action, while heating the brake rotors, also causes the wheels to heat up which in turn causes them to slightly expand into the tires. This helps to heat the tires up more quickly.

Following suit, Bill used the available time to warm his tires up as well. As the pace car led the field toward the final turn, however, Bill straightened out and got ready.

The pace car peeled off the track and into pit lane and the cars formed up tightly into their two columns. It was a long run down the front stretch at the Circuit of the Americas so they had to maintain their speed until the green flag was waived.

After the field snaked its way through the final corner, every car was now on the front stretch when the lights finally turned green.

Easing his foot onto the throttle to avoid wheel-spin, Bill accelerated up to race speed in what was a good enough start to maintain his position. The same could not be said for newcomer Sam Wells, however. Whether by inexperience or sheer nerves, Sam hit the gas too hard and too soon as he was victim of early wheel-spin which cost him both time and speed.

Heading towards the uphill Turn 1, Bill saw a brief window of opportunity to go down the left side of Sam for a possible overtake but it would've put him three-wide with Elliot on the outside and Sam in the middle. Not wanting to cause a first-turn incident, Bill backed off and filed behind Sam even as he was hoping he wouldn't regret his decision later in the race to err on the side of caution.

However, Bill knew that it's better to be safe and live to fight on rather than let his ego get the better of him and finish the race on the back of a tow truck.

Despite his early wheel-spin mishap, Sam was able to hold onto the lead after the first turn with Elliot Hughes directly beside him. Bill decided to stay behind them both and hope that one or both of them would make a mistake which would open the door up for him to lead the race.

As both lead drivers entered the tight S-turns, Elliot attempted to stay side-by-side with the younger driver but soon yielded and gave Sam the undisputed lead for the time being. Even though it was a safe move to keep the race going smoothly, Elliot was more than likely having the same argument in his head as Bill and hoping he would have another chance.

The pack of cars wound their way through the turns as Bill began putting the pressure on Elliot. He wanted to pass him early in the race if only to give himself the psychological edge he needed over his competitor. That and he knew he could take full advantage of Sam's nerves which were sure to be high after his mistake at the start.

As the first few laps chipped away, Bill was still in third when he began to set Elliot up for the pass. The majority of the field were single file at this point, but Bill was going to shake it up a bit.

At the start of the fifth lap, Bill continued behind Elliot as normal and waited until after they had gotten through the first few turns. He knew that the best shot would be at turns 11 and 12 because of the long straightaway between the two turns and a hard braking zone at the end of the straight.

As the cars approached the left handed turn 11, Bill brought his car to the right side of Elliot. This limited the amount of space which Elliot would have to turn with and caused him to have to slow down much more to make sure his car didn't go off the track. Elliot ran his car wide and towards the right side of the track. Bill, on the other hand, was able to capitalize on this with a cross-over.

Slowing down, Bill made a slightly sharper turn-in, which allowed him to get on the power earlier and effectively change to the opposite side of Elliot.

As Elliot straightened up, he found himself again going side-by-side with Bill down the long back stretch. Only this time, he was on the outside for the upcoming left turn with Bill on the inside. In perfect position, Bill braked hard and was able to pass Elliot on the inside of Turn 12.

With his adrenaline kicking into high gear, Bill couldn't help but feel a bit of satisfaction in passing the seasoned veteran. "Yeah baby!"

Looking in his rearview mirror quickly, Bill had a flashback of the last race where he remembered that yellow Camaro following closely behind him. This time, however, his resolve was stronger. He ignored the urge to constantly look in the mirror and instead put his head down focused on the younger driver who was in front of him.

As the laps ticked by, he knew he had plenty of time to chip away at Sam, who had used the fight going on behind him for second place to extend his lead. With each passing lap, Bill was getting closer to Sam and further away from Elliot.

About halfway through lap 9, Bill had about a two car-length distance between himself and Sam. At first, he thought that he could simply pass the rookie and be done with it. Unfortunately for Bill, Sam was putting up quite the fight.

Although Sam didn't quite have the race pace that Bill had, he wasn't leaving any openings for Bill to take advantage of. Bill knew he was quicker out of the corners, but Sam always aligned himself so that he would have the ideal position for the next turn. The battle for the lead might have been what every race fan at the track today wanted to see but in the car, Bill was getting frustrated.

At the start of lap 21, however, things changed drastically as a light rain began to fall.

Bill had hoped to beat the rain but with several laps still remaining, he knew he had his work cut out for him. Given the fact that they were also driving on slick racing tires with no tread, conditions were changing quickly on the track and it was up to the drivers to modify their technique to adapt to the increasingly slippery racing surface.

Despite the light rain, Bill continued to put the pressure on Sam. Bill thought that maybe he could intimidate him enough and cause him to make a mistake, but Sam wasn't having it. Bill was trying everything he knew to get around Sam but every chance he got, he had to either pull back because of Sam closing the open gap or because he was being extra careful due to the slick track conditions from the light rain.

As they continued to race through the corners, the laps continued to tick away. To make matters worse, Bill looked in his rearview mirror and noticed that Elliot had caught back up. All of the fighting between Bill and Sam had indeed cost them both a considerable amount of time. As the three drivers headed down the front stretch and crossed the start/finish line, Bill saw on the illuminated sign that there were only two laps remaining.

He tried to calm himself down, but his mind and heart were racing just as hard as he was. Bill was getting desperate.

While approaching the left handed Turn 1, Bill decided to go for a dive down the left side of the track and hopefully get on the inside of Sam who was moving to the right side of the track. Sam, however, saw this coming and suddenly decided to keep just enough of his car on the left side of the track to effectively block Bill from making the move. Caught off guard, Bill had to slow down greatly to complete the turn and in doing so, allowed Elliot to slip past him on the outside. Now frantic, Bill could feel his heart beating heavily.

Looking in his rearview mirror, he saw that because of the antics caused by the top three drivers, many of the other cars on the lead lap had now caught up with them.

Bill stayed close behind Elliot and Sam through the S-turns. As they came to the left handed turn 11, where Bill had previously passed Elliot, he tried to replicate the maneuver—but this time Elliot was ready.

As Bill went to take the left turn by going wide right and then turning hard left to get on the left side of the coming straightaway, Elliot went with him and duplicated his move which caused Elliot to wind up on the left side and Bill on the right side of the straightaway. With Sam only a few car lengths ahead of them, both Elliot and Bill were on a side-by-side drag race down the long back straight. Bill knew his only hope of winning was to out-brake Elliot going into the turn or at least stay side-by-side with him until the next corner. That would put him on the inside of Turn 13. He knew that Elliot was thinking the exact same thing.

Sam, however, was not.

At full speed and flat-out throttle, the three drivers approached the braking zone of Turn 12. As it was a left turn, Bill was effectively boxed in with Sam in front of him and Elliot on his left.

Upon approach of the turn, Sam braked earlier than his normal braking marker due to the now steadily falling rain and began to turn his car into the left turn. Elliot, seeing that Sam was now directly in front of him and going slower than normal, braked hard to avoid crashing into the back of him due to the wet track surface.

That's when Bill saw the opening he'd had been looking for. Seeing that both cars were now on the left side of the track and driving slower, Bill made a split second decision to try to pass both cars on the outside of the turn and beat them both to the next right turn. He knew it was a brave move, but it would probably be his only chance to pass them both before the end of the race.

Despite the risks from the wet track, Bill decided to send it.

Braking very close to his normal braking zone, Bill turned his car into the left-handed turn and was already halfway past Elliot and poised to pass Sam when the laws of physics decided to pass judgement on him. Going into the turn too fast for the wet conditions, the rear tires on Bill's car lost traction as the rear end of the car spun to the right. Unable to catch the spin due to his entry speed and the slick track, Bill was nothing more than a passenger as his car spun far off the track and into the sand trap.

The sand trap—which was there to slow cars down and prevent them from crashing into the wall which was further away—was very deep and provided no traction whatsoever. As it was put there to stop cars, it was difficult to get out of once you came to a stop, especially in the wet conditions.

As Bill's spinning car came to a stop in the sand, his first instinct was to get the car back out onto the track and salvage whatever he could from the race. He put the car back into first gear and hit the gas. He watched as the car's tachometer gauge rose and heard the sound of the engine roaring—but the car didn't even move an inch.

"You've gotta be kidding me! C'mon!" shouted Bill.

Putting it in reverse, he tried to rock the car loose but only succeeded in digging himself deeper into the sand. He watched as several of the other competitors began to pass his trapped car as the local yellow caution flags waved to warn the other drivers of the incident.

Feeling all of the blood in his body rush to his face, he panicked and tried putting it in first gear and slamming the throttle again but to no avail. As the last pack of cars passed him, Bill froze as he stared out onto the now empty track with utter disbelief.

As he sat there for a moment and listened as the roaring sounds of the engines got further and further away, he knew that even if he could magically get his car back out onto the track, he would never be able to catch up with the cars in front of him.

Angry, shocked and beyond disappointed in himself, Bill knew his race was over.

* * *

The ride home was filled with an awkward silence. With nobody really sure how to act, Lena and Chad chose not to say anything just yet, as Bill was obviously not in the mood to talk. Not even bothering to stay for the awards ceremony after the race, Bill sat quietly in the passenger seat of the SUV as Lena drove home.

As he sat, he thought about what he did wrong and how he had done it. Above all, he thought about how he had just finished in last place. He thought about how he was forced to wait for the tow truck to come and pull him out of the sand. He also thought about the embarrassment he felt as the other drivers passed by him and how he could feel their stares as they drove by.

Sitting still now as he stared off into space with an array of endless *what if* questions circling around in his mind, Bill thought about that foul dark voice which kept repeating itself, saying, *I hope you die and go to hell!*

William had stayed for the duration of the race and helped Bill and his crew get the car along with the rest of the equipment loaded onto the trailer. He tried to cheer Bill up but it was obvious that Bill wasn't having it. Saying goodbye to the family, William left the track to try to beat the approaching storm.

The rain, which was only a light drizzle during the race, was now coming down in droves. Normally, Bill would be the one driving in these conditions. Lena, however, insisted on driving as Bill was clearly lost in deep thought from the earlier incident.

Lena knew that the quiet was only adding to the aftershock. Hoping that talking about it would help Bill, Lena said, "You know, you were doing really well today. I know that you're doing it right now but there's no need to beat yourself up over this. You're okay and so is the car. That's all that matters."

"No, that's not all that matters," said Bill plainly. "I pulled yet another amateur move and paid the price for it. What little credibility I thought I had before is probably gone now. That tends to happen when you repeatedly make foolish mistakes on the track."

Unfazed, Lena continued. "Bill, it's just like your dad said: You saw an opportunity and you went for it. There's no shame in that and you certainly didn't lose any credibility."

Bill could sense the well of anger opening within him: The same anger he'd felt when he last confronted Helen. He could feel heat rising in his face as his mind raced through the thought process of what happened earlier. He wasn't in the mood to be cheered up. If anything, he *wanted* to feel the weight of his actions. Nonetheless, he was now feeling the need to justify this feeling.

"I came in last place after I started in third. I was the ONLY ONE TO SPIN OUT! I think it's safe to say I've lost some credibility!" shouted Bill.

"It's not the end of the world, Bill," said Lena who was clearly trying to keep things calm. "There's always the next race and then the race after that! It's no big deal!"

"No big deal?! Do you realize what everyone's going to be talking about now? The guy who spun out when nobody else did. The guy who thought he could out-brake himself in the rain. The amateur who can't keep his car on the damn road! Oh, and it also happens to be William Watson's son!"

Chad, who was sitting in the back seat, tried to intervene. "Can you guys just calm down?" Ignoring their son, they continued.

"It's just like you and your dad always say, Bill. It's just racing," argued Lena as she tried to pull a play from Bill's playbook. "If you stick with it long enough, these things happen."

Bill could only laugh.

"You don't even know what you're saying," said Bill. "It's one thing to be caught up in someone else's mess but when it's you getting *yourself* into the mess over and over again, nobody takes you seriously!"

"So whatever happened to 'racing is for fun'?" asked Lena. "Is that gone now? I thought you told me that this was just a fix and that you only wanted to do this as a hobby? Now you're suddenly worried about what other people are thinking about you? I think you've got your priorities mixed up a little."

The heat he'd felt building within him earlier had now begun to burn. He may have lost the race, but he wasn't about to lose this argument.

"It's not just about me! It's my company's name on the side of that car, too! It's everything I stand for and everything I believe in! It's my reputation and it's my family's reputation! What part of that are you not understanding?"

"I knew it, Bill. I told you that this racing business was going to start getting the best of you and you didn't believe me," replied Lena. "I mean, do you care more about what people from the track say about you than what your own wife and kid think? And now you're wanting to live up to your family name after you've told me before that none of that mattered?" Lena shouted back. "You've let your priorities get twisted. Your family should come first. There's nothing I'm saying right now that we haven't talked about before."

"Oh, so this is my fault now, right? I spin out while chasing some kid driver and embarrassed myself in front of everyone and now everything is my fault? How great is that," said Bill as he threw his hands in the air in frustration.

"Everything isn't your fault, Bill. You're really overreacting here. You just have your priorities backwards. You care so much about these things which don't matter at all but it's all you talk about and it's all you think about. This isn't just a hobby anymore, Bill. You're obsessed and addicted to it."

Bill threw his hands into the air once again.

"So that's it then. I guess I should just quit because I'll never be good at it, right? I have one thing I enjoy doing. One thing! And now that's not good enough?"

Lena turned to look at Bill and asked, "Is your family good enough?"

A shout came from Chad in the back seat.

"Watch out!"

The rain was coming down so heavily that Lena, who had only briefly turned to look at Bill, didn't see the 18-wheeled tractor-trailer at a complete stop in front of them. At the sound of Chad's voice, she turned and slammed on the brakes—but it was too late. The weight of the SUV combined with the car and trailer attached behind them sent them hydroplaning towards the back of the large truck.

The last thing that Bill remembered before blacking out was the impact of being pushed into the air bag.

Chapter 5

Why don't you just keep driving around in your little car until you crash and get yourself killed so you can do us all a favor and rid the world of yourself!

Is your family good enough, Bill?

Can you guys just calm down?

I hope you die and go to hell!

Watch out!

Bill opened his eyes suddenly, as if startled awake. The dark dream which he had awakened from was something that he hoped to God he never would have to revisit. He had dreamed that all of his family members had morphed into one single dreadful looking being which seemed to be floating above him. This being was shouting at him using the voices of his family. Upon awakening, however, he found his current reality to be just as frightening.

His vision was very blurry, as if he had been asleep for some time, but it felt like his entire body was in a vice clamp. His muscles were sore and stiff and all that he could see was a white blur which he guessed was a ceiling light. He tried to move but his achy muscles caused him to groan in protest. As he tried to move again, he heard a sound which seemed to be coming from the foot of the bed. The sound of rustling fabric stopped suddenly as he heard a familiar voice.

"Bill? Are you awake?" asked the voice.

"I think so. Where I am?" answered Bill.

There were more sudden sounds as if the person was standing up quickly. "I'll get the nurse," said the familiar voice.

Bill knew that voice. He knew that dialect as if it were his own. "Dad?"

The voice only repeated its last statement but louder this time saying, "I'll get the nurse!" as he heard a door open and then close.

As Bill lay there in bed, he tried putting some of the pieces together in his mind. He remembered a race and he remembered an embarrassed feeling from something. He remembered the ride home and an argument as they drove in the rain…

The rain…

Bill felt fear surge through his body as he vaguely remembered an accident. He heard sirens in his head and could remember the sensation of being on his back as rain poured on top of him as he was put into a vehicle of some sort. Frantically, he tried to get up but could only get as far as lifting his head. His body protested in pain throughout and he started feeling dizzy as Bill gave up and laid his head back down in anguish. Finally, he did what he thought was the only thing he could do.

"Dad!" cried out Bill.

A few seconds later, William came into the room accompanied by someone who appeared to be a nurse.

William rushed to Bill's side. "It's okay, Bill. Try to stay calm," he told Bill.

"Where's Lena, Dad? Where's Lena and Chad? What's going on?" Bill asked frantically.

"Bill, please calm down," said William as the young female nurse stood over Bill and looked into his eyes.

"How are you feeling, Mr. Watson? You have a concussion, so try not to move too much. Are you seeing double or is it just blurry right now?"

Bill had had enough. "I don't care about my damn vision! Tell me where my wife and son are!"

William and the nurse paused and looked at each other.

"Give us a minute, Miss," said William as the nurse nodded and exited the room.

Turning to look at Bill, William felt his eyes begin to water up.

"Dad," said Bill. "What happened? Where are they?"

William sat down on the side of the bed and took a deep breath as he said, "You were involved in a bad accident, son. You were lucky. Only a few broken ribs, some bruises and a knock to your head."

"But where's Lena?! Where's Chad?!" asked Bill.

Looking down at his feet, William said, "When they brought Lena in the hospital, she was in bad shape, Bill. They tried everything and did all that they could. Lena...she, uh, she didn't make it."

Bill felt his stomach tie into a knot. "What?! What do you mean *she didn't make it?!*"

With tears starting to fall heavily down the side of his face, William answered, "Bill, Lena's dead."

They both sat in complete shock looking into each other's eyes. William began to sob aloud as Bill, who was now ignoring the pain and sitting up on his elbows, was frozen in place with his eyes wide open and his jaw dropped in a horrified expression. His mind, bewildered by what seemed to be the very life inside of him being extinguished, subconsciously returned to the dream he had awakened from moments ago. He shook his head quickly as if he was trying to come back to reality as he knew it.

"How? I... I didn't..." said Bill aimlessly. Tears began to fall down his face as William took his hand. Bill, who knew what he had to ask next but was too horrified to do so, couldn't manage to get a word out of his mouth. He tried to hold back the river of emotion which seemed to be dammed up inside of him but the sight of his father crying sent him over. He fell back onto the pillow. Putting his hands over his face, he felt the swollen area around his eyes as well as a bandage over his head.

"No...Dad. No," cried Bill.

William moved closer to his son and slid his hand under his back to sit him up. Bill felt lifeless as his father pulled him up into his arms. Holding him as if he were a child again, William couldn't think of anything to say that would bring comfort to his son as he wept in his arms.

Bill remembered the question he didn't want to ask but he knew that he it had to be done.

He withdrew from William's arms and took a moment to collect himself. Slowly he asked, "Dad...what about Chad? Is he okay?"

William took a deep breath and said, "Chad's in ICU right now. He was banged up pretty badly but I'm still waiting to hear from the doctor on how he's doing."

Struggling to get up, Bill said, "I need to go see him. He needs me!" William put his hands on Bill's shoulders to keep him in bed. "He needs you to take care of yourself. There's nothing you can do for him right now. You need your rest."

Wiping the tears away from his eyes, Bill asked, "How, Dad? How did this happen?" Throwing his arms up into the air, he added, "I don't even remember what happened."

"The police said that with the amount of rain that was falling, Lena must not have seen the tractor trailer in front of you until it was too late," said William as he wiped the tears from his eyes.

Bill, still shocked, couldn't comprehend any of it. "I don't remember her going that fast. How could that impact..." Bill couldn't finish the sentence. He lay there and gave William a hopeless look. He almost thought that he could convince himself that the accident wasn't bad enough to have killed Lena and that he could somehow bring her back because of it.

"It wasn't the impact that did it," said William as he stood up and walked towards the window. "When she hit the brakes, the car hydroplaned and the trailer behind you fish-tailed. The initial impact caused the trailer to jerk your vehicle hard enough that it flipped and rolled into the ditch on the side of the road. That's where they found you."

Bill stared off into space hoping that he would be able to remember some part of what happened but he couldn't. His mind was still in shock from the news as everything seemed to be spinning around uncontrollably. He looked at the chair at the foot of the bed and noticed the bed sheets on them. He knew that his dad had been sleeping there.

"How long was I out?" asked Bill.

William took another deep breathe to prepare himself. "You've been in a coma for five days, son. I've...uh...I've made sure everything's taken care of." More tears began to fall down his face.

Confused, Bill asked, "What are you talking about? What's been taken care of? Tell me!"

William was crying even harder than he was before when he gave his son even worse news. "Lena...she's already been buried. We had the funeral yesterday."

Bill couldn't take any more as he began to feel sick and light-headed. With an empty sinking feeling in his stomach, he fell back onto his pillow and became completely numb.

* * *

Bill was awakened by the sound of his hospital room door opening. As he opened his eyes ever so slightly, he noticed that it was the nurse bringing food in for him. Quietly walking over to his bed, the nurse set the food dish on the tray attached to the top of Bill's bed and started to leave the room.

Though it was the sound of the door that woke Bill up, it was the sight and smell of the food that awakened his appetite. He couldn't remember the last time he had eaten anything. His stomach, suddenly growling loudly, caused the nurse to stop just shy of the door. Knowing that Bill was awake, she turned around with a smile on her face and said, "Let us know if there's anything we can get for you, Mr. Watson."

"Thank you," murmured Bill with his face still half buried in the pillow.

As the nurse left the room, he turned his head around to see that his dad was not in the room. Lying on his side, he slowly turned over onto his back and adjusted the bed so that it sat him up closer to the tray of food.

He noticed that it was morning and the sun was shining brightly through his room's windows. Unsure as to how much time had passed since he was last awake, Bill tried to gather his thoughts and piece together some sort of timeline but the plate of food in front of him was too distracting.

As he grabbed the fork, he was just about to shovel a chunk of scrambled egg into his mouth but stopped just shy. He was missing something. It actually took him a few seconds to realize that ever since he was a child, he had always prayed before he ate. His parents has raised him as such and he had passed to his son this way of giving thanks in the same manner.

He set the fork down on the tray, closed his eyes and said, "God..." His mind betrayed him at that very second. An image of the tears coming down his father's face burned its way into the forefront of his mind as he told him "Lena's dead."

Lena's dead.

LENA'S DEAD!

He imagined his son lying in a hospital bed. But worst of all, he imagined his life without Lena. He would never see his wife ever again.

As he sat there with his eyes still closed, he could feel himself begin to shake as he fought off the tears. He had no idea of what to say as a prayer to God. What did he have to be thankful for?

Foolish ambition? Pride?

These things had become his downfall at the expense of his wife's life and possibly that of his son, as well. He could feel himself continuing to shake as all of the blood in his body rushed to his face. He realized, however, that it wasn't tears he was fighting back this time.

It was rage—rage towards the weather, rage towards racing and ultimately, rage towards himself.

Himself.

"It's my fault, isn't it?" he said aloud.

His eyes were closed tightly as he felt his face getting hot.

If I hadn't have spun out and convinced Lena that I was too shaken up to drive, she'd still be here. We'd be back home right now. None of this would have ever happened if I had only...

"Hey!" a voice yelled.

Startled, Bill opened his eyes to see William standing in the doorway along with a crowd of nurses gathering behind him to see what the commotion was about. William stepped in and closed the door behind him.

"I know what you're doing to yourself and I won't let it happen," said William sternly. "I won't sit by and watch my son tear himself apart by blaming himself for something that he had no control over."

"I did have control over it, Dad. All of this is because I lost that control in the race," argued Bill.

"You spun out because the laws of physics made you spin out. You spun out because you saw an opening and went for it in less than ideal conditions! That's it! Nothing more! If I were in that car, I would've spun out too because I would've done the exact same thing you did. Any driver worth his salt would have gone for that gap!" said William. "I realize you're not in your right mind right now because of everything that's happened. But you're never going to be able to move on if you keep thinking that it was your fault!"

"Move on?! My wife's dead, Dad!"

"So is mine!" yelled William as a tear fell down his face.

Bill replied, "At least you got to say goodbye! I didn't even..."

Stopping mid-sentence, Bill saw the stern look on his father's face and realized he'd crossed the line.

"You think this is hard for you?" asked William. "Imagine watching your wife die a little bit every day right in front of your eyes and being powerless to stop it. Imagine waking up one morning and having your wife forget who you are! Thirty-five years of marriage erased overnight. There were no goodbyes! My wife withered away and I was forced to stand by and watch so I'll be damned if I'm going to let that happen again with you. I'm not going to sit here and coddle your ass until you're done feeling sorry for yourself over something that you had no control over and wasn't your fault!

"I know it's tough and it's only going to get worse before it gets better," William continued. "But you have a son that needs you to be strong for him so, by God, if you can't find it in your heart to be strong for yourself, at least be strong for Chad. You lost your wife, but that little boy lost his mother. Don't you ever forget that."

Bill could only sit there feeling like he had just been punched in the gut. His dad was right. If anybody knew what he was going through, it was him. With that thought in mind, Bill had only one thing he could ask.

"So what do I do now?"

William gave a slight smile and said, "You finish eating whatever that crap is on that tray and then you go see Chad. He finally woke up not too long ago and the doctor wants to speak with you."

Bill, smiling for the first time in days, said, "Chad's awake? Let's go see him now!"

Trying to get up, William once again restrained him and said, "Not so fast." Pointing to the food in front of Bill, he said, "Eat something. You'll need your strength and a sound mind for what's to come."

Confused, Bill asked, "What do you mean by that?"

Turning around and heading for the door, William said, "You'll see. I'll be waiting outside his room. Just have one of the nurses take you over."

As William left the room, an older man whom Bill assumed was a doctor stepped in.

"Mr...Watson," said the man as he looked for Bill's name on his clipboard. "I'm Dr. Owens. How are you feeling?"

"Still a little dizzy but I'm just wanting to go see my son," said Bill as he was hoping to keep the visit—which he assumed was simply a routine check-up—as short as possible.

"I understand," said Dr. Owens. "I won't keep you any longer than I have to, but there are a few things I'm needing to talk to you about."

Suddenly alert and sitting up as straight as he could, Bill asked, "Is this about my son?"

Taking a seat on a chair across from the bed, Dr. Owens exhaled softly. "No, Mr. Watson. This is about you."

* * *

Slowly but surely, along with the help of a few of the nearby nurses, Bill was able to finally get out of bed and stand up on his own after finishing his meal. By his own power, he was able to walk himself over to the shower in his hospital room to freshen up as well. Other than the sponge baths the nurses gave him while he was in a coma, it had been days since his last shower so it was an obvious need. It required such an effort to simply get into the shower that Bill had completely bypassed the clear plastic bag which lay on the counter. It wasn't until he had finished and stepped out of the shower that he noticed several of his personal belongings inside the bag. Making his way over to it, he noticed his wallet, cell phone and car keys were inside.

As he opened the bag, however, he removed his wallet to find his wedding band sitting underneath it. It immediately sent chills down his spine. Memories flashed in his mind of the day the ring was first put on his finger by Lena. Leaning on the counter and letting his head drop, he knew that Lena's death would never fully sink in. He thought of his bed at home and how he would never share an intimate moment with his wife ever again.

He imagined a cold grave where his wife now lay.

Lifting his head, he stared into the steam covered mirror on the bathroom wall and looked himself in the eyes. It was almost as if he could visibly see the stress, the anguish and the abandonment in his eyes and on his face. He didn't shed any tears this time. He had cried enough for a lifetime already and he knew that more tears and a time to mourn were a guarantee in the near future. This time, as he gazed into his own eyes, it was a conversation of sorts—one without words or body language. He simply stared and wondered what the person staring back at him was thinking. He stood for several moments before a lone thought entered his mind.

I hope you die and go to hell!

He felt anger rising up in him. In the span of only a few seconds, he suddenly remembered every word ever spoken to him by his mother-in-law, Helen. None of those words had ever showed any degree of kindness. He dreaded their next confrontation but he knew that it was inevitable. His mind became suddenly overwhelmed but he didn't break his stare into the mirror. He felt his grip tightening on the counter top when suddenly he felt very light-headed. He closed his eyes briefly and stood up straight.

You still have a concussion, numb nuts.

After gathering himself, he reopened his eyes and met his stare again in the mirror. This time, however, it was almost as if the sudden lightheadedness had allowed his mind to go free from the torment of the former thoughts.

For a brief moment, his mind went blank. He closed his eyes and used this moment to his advantage.

Chad needs me. I can sit here and cry about something I can't change or I can be there for my son who needs me now more than ever.

With new resolve, he let his gaze fall down to the ring which still lay inside the plastic bag. He didn't think twice about it as he slipped it onto his finger.

* * *

William had been waiting and reading the newspaper outside of Chad's hospital room when Bill finally arrived. Being pushed along in a wheelchair as a precautionary measure, Bill didn't object as he was still feeling light-headed at times. As Bill was wheeled around the corner to see his dad sitting outside the room, he gave a slight wave to William as the nurse who was pushing the wheelchair stopped a few feet short of where he was sitting.

Turning around, William looked at the nurse and said, "I'll take care of him from here, miss. Thank you." The nurse blushed as she smiled and walked away.

Turning his attention towards Bill, William said, "The doctor just stepped into the room to check on Chad. Now would be a good time to go in if I were you."

For a moment, Bill just stared at the door. Unsure of what he would find on the other side, he felt frightened. He had been through so much since regaining consciousness that he didn't know if he could take anymore. But giving up wasn't an option. He was a parent—a dad. His responsibility was to his family or to at least what was left of it. He knew that he had to see this through to the end no matter what the outcome was.

Making his first move into the unknown, he wheeled his wheelchair towards the door. Stopping just shy, he turned and noticed that William wasn't following him.

"You're not coming?" asked Bill.

"No, son. I've done all I can do for now. The rest is up to you," William said softly.

Bill could see the fatigue in his father's eyes and heard it in his voice. He had no idea how long it had been since his dad had slept.

"Go get some rest, Dad. I'll take care of things from here," Bill said. William grinned and said, "I won't argue with you. But you call me if you need anything."

"Will do," said Bill.

As William turned to walk away, he stopped as Bill added, "Dad, thanks for everything."

William gave Bill a slight nod as he turned and continued his weary walk.

Bill turned and faced the door that led to his son. Taking a deep breath, he turned the handle and slowly pushed the door open.

Nothing in this life could have prepared him for what he saw next. There was Chad lying asleep in a bed which was propped up. His face was visibly swollen from bruises which caused his skin to be various shades of blue and purple. His right arm was in a cast, and both of his bare feet were sticking out from under the covers. Bill noticed that they looked morbidly pale compared to his normal skin color.

The doctor in the room smiled and introduced himself as Bill wheeled himself in. "You must be Bill," he said quietly as he extended his hand. "I'm Dr. Morris. I've been treating Chad ever since he first arrived."

Shaking the doctor's hand without making eye contact, Bill

couldn't take his eyes off his son. He felt his stomach churn at the sight of what appeared to be a giant bruise lying in the bed. He had never seen anyone, much less his son, in a state such as this.

Noticing where Bill's eyes were, Dr. Morris said, "I'm sure you have a million questions so I'll tell you everything that we know so far. Because of the accident, we believe he has what we call an incomplete spinal cord injury. Right now, there's a lot of inflammation around his spinal cord which is causing him to lose the feeling as well as the ability to use his legs."

Bill could feel the blood draining from his face as the doctor continued.

"I say we *believe* because we're going to have to wait until the inflammation subsides before we can give him a full neurological examination. Until then, however, we don't know the full extent of the damage. For now, though, it's safe to say that he has temporarily lost the use of his legs," said Dr. Morris.

Bill sat speechless. He didn't know what to say or what to ask. As he felt tears begin to well up in his eyes again, he just sat there looking at his son as he rested. Bill couldn't help but realize how at peace he looked.

Seeing that Bill was unsure of how to handle the news he had just shared with him, Dr. Morris pulled up a chair and sat down next to Bill.

"I have a son, too, you know. About the same age as Chad," said Dr. Morris. "I would be feeling the same way you're feeling right now if this had happened to him. I know that it may look bad, but the important part is that he's still here with you. I see hundreds of kids involved in car accidents each year. Some of them aren't this lucky."

"Lucky?" Bill snapped back. "You just told me that my son can't walk and you call that lucky?"

"I said temporarily," Dr. Morris replied. "We don't know the full extent of it, yet. And yes, he's lucky. Call it a blessing, an act of God or just old fashioned luck, but he sustained a spinal injury in a way that many don't ever walk away from."

Bill let his head drop into his hands.

"I'm sorry," said Bill. "I didn't mean to snap at you like that. It's a lot to take in combined with what's already happened."

"I'm sorry for your loss, Mr. Watson. I've heard what happened."

Bill lifted his head and looked Dr. Morris in the eyes.

"Does Chad know?"

"No, we haven't told him. That's not our place to say to him."

Bill turned his attention back to Chad, he asked, "Has he said anything yet?"

"He's on pain medication right now which is causing him to sleep quite a bit, but he was asking for you earlier," said Dr. Morris.

Bill rolled his wheelchair up to the bed and asked, "Doctor, could I have a few minutes alone with him?"

"Of course," said Dr. Morris as he stood up from his seat. "Take as much time as you need. I'll be back to check on him again in a little bit."

As the doctor left the room, Bill reached onto the bed and grabbed Chad's hand. He didn't want to wake him up but, at the same time, he wanted to do just that. He wanted to hear his voice and know that he was okay. He had lost so much in the past few days that he knew he had to cling to what he could. His mind became so overwhelmed with things to say that he had no idea of how he was to go about saying what he needed to tell Chad. It was on that line of thought that he felt a slight twitch coming from Chad's hand.

Chad squirmed slightly in bed as he always did when he was just waking up. His eyes hadn't opened yet but he groaned as he stretched his left arm over his head. When Chad finally opened his eyes, Bill felt like his heart had jumped with joy. He smiled ear to ear at the sight of his son awake. It wasn't until Chad put his hand on top of Bill's hand that Bill felt his eyes water up again.

After a moment, Chad asked, "Dad? Is that you?" Noticing that Chad's eyes were still adjusting from being asleep for so long, Bill was still smiling as he said, "I'm here, son. It's me."

Still squinting his eyes, Chad asked, "Are you okay?"

Bill felt a tear fall down his cheek as he fought back his emotions. "I'm a little banged up but I'm okay. How are you feeling?"

"Sore," said Chad. "I don't think I can feel my legs, Dad."

Bill was on the verge of going off another emotional cliff as his son spoke. He softly put his hand on Chad's head as he said, "Don't worry. We're going to get that taken care of. You just try to relax, okay? I'm here now. Grandpa's been keeping an eye on you, too."

With a confused look coming to the surface of the young boy's face, Chad asked the hardest question: "Where's Mom?"

Chapter 6

Several weeks passed before Chad was finally discharged from the hospital. The doctors, who had ran a series of tests, confirmed Bill's worst fears: Chad had lost the use of his legs and would be required to go through extensive physical therapy if he ever hoped to walk again.

But that wasn't the worst of it.

Upon hearing the news that his mother had passed away, Chad had not spoken a single word since. Despite both Bill's and the doctor's best efforts, Chad simply wasn't speaking. Later to be diagnosed with Post Traumatic Stress Disorder from the accident, the harsh reality had taken a toll on him in a way which was different than anyone thought possible.

Bill, who himself was gradually recovering from a concussion and a few broken ribs, now had the enormous task of not only raising a disabled child by himself, but also coming up with the money it would take to pay for both his medical bills and also a physiatrist for Chad's physical therapy. He had a well-paying job as well as health insurance, but he was by no means making enough to where any of this could sanely be called affordable. Regardless of his mounting medical debt, he had a responsibility to his family which he fully expected to meet.

It was a clear evening when the transportation the hospital had provided for Chad, who was now in a wheelchair, arrived at Bill's home. Although his right arm was still in a cast, the bruises on his face had all but disappeared. As he was helped out of the medical van by the driver, Bill and William came out of the house and into the cool evening weather to greet him. Both of them were all smiles as they walked down the driveway towards Chad.

"Welcome home, Chad!" said Bill as he knelt down in front of his son. Bill grabbed his hand and said, "We're glad to finally have you back!"

Chad's face showed no emotion whatsoever. He simply stared past his dad and grandfather and looked at the house behind them.

Bill glanced over at William as they were both wondering what was going through Chad's mind. His face gave no expression as to what he was thinking.

Thanking the hospital staff as they departed, Bill got behind Chad's wheelchair and started to push it up the driveway as William walked beside them.

"I've got some good news, Chad," said William. "I'm all moved in! Now you can spend all the time you want with your Grandpa!"

Nothing.

No expression came upon Chad's face as they continued their walk towards the house. It was William this time who glanced over at Bill as he gave a slight sigh and a look of disbelief. Both of the adults were so used to the energetic and talkative Chad. The boy who now sat in the wheelchair, however, seemed as if the life which was once in him had been extinguished.

As they arrived in the house using the wooden ramp which Bill and William had built to get the wheelchair up the stairs and in through the front door, Chad stared up the staircase towards his room.

William had prepared dinner for both Bill and Chad but it was done in an awkward silence. William and Bill had both tried to elicit some sort of response from Chad but had failed each time.

Knowing that it was getting pretty late after dinner and Chad was needing to get some rest, Bill knelt down beside Chad and said, "Let's get you ready for bed. You've had a busy day."

Picking Chad up from the wheelchair, Bill carried him upstairs towards his room as William slipped away while waiting downstairs. As they climbed the stairs, Bill said, "Don't worry. We're going to have one of those electric chairs installed in the stairway soon to take you up and down".

Getting to the top of the staircase, Bill was huffing for air.

"You never seem to get smaller. That's for sure," said Bill as they neared Chad's room.

A second wheelchair awaited Chad upstairs and Bill gently placed his son in the seat. Helping Chad through his bedtime preparations, Bill couldn't help but have brief glimpses of Lena flash in his mind, since she was the one who typically helped Chad get ready for bed when he was younger. He noted to himself that this would be the routine every night for a very long time.

Once his teeth were brushed and his face washed, Bill pushed the wheelchair toward his son's bedroom. Walking through the bedroom doorway, Bill picked Chad up and laid him down in his bed as he knelt down beside him.

"I know you must be thinking about the negative," said Bill. "It would be easy to. But we have to be thankful for what we still have. I have you and you have me and grandpa. We'll always be close by if you need anything."

Still no response. Chad simply stared up towards the ceiling with a blank look in his eyes.

Taking his son's hand, Bill said a short prayer, kissed Chad on his forehead and closed the door behind him. As he walked down the hallway towards the stairs, Bill couldn't help but feel a sinking feeling in his stomach.

Heading back downstairs, Bill saw that William was on the phone. This struck him as odd because not only did William not have many friends, but it was also late at night.

Seeing Bill coming down the stairs, William retreated to his room and closed the door behind him. This action further raised Bill's suspicion. A few moments later, William reemerged with a big smile on his face.

"Who was that?" asked Bill.

"Oh just an old friend," replied William as he walked past Bill and sat down on the sofa in the living room.

"What kind of old friends are you talking to at this hour?" Bill asked curiously.

"The kind that live across the big pond," said William with a smile. Knowing that the reference was to someone he knew in Australia, Bill said, "You don't talk to anyone over there too often anymore. What made you decide to start now?"

Having enough of the questions, William replied, "You just mind your own business. If it pertains to you, I'll let you know."

Bill raised his eyes at the scoff. He noticed, however, that his dad was still smiling. He knew he was up to something.

Quickly changing the subject, William asked, "So when are you planning to visit Lena?"

Ever since finding out Lena had passed away and had already been buried before he had regained consciousness, Bill had refused to visit her grave without Chad. With Chad back at home, however, he still felt reluctant to take him to his mother's grave so soon.

"I'm not sure yet. I just don't know how Chad will react," said Bill.

"You need to make up your mind, son," said William. "This will bring closure for both you and for Chad."

"He's just been through so much already. I'm afraid that this may send him over the edge," said Bill.

"Or it could pull him away from the edge. The only way to find out is to do it. But if you don't think he's ready, I'll stay and look after him while you go by yourself," said William.

"I'm not going to go without Chad," replied Bill. "We're a family and we stick together."

William started shaking his head ever so slightly.

"What," asked Bill.

Taking a moment to gather his thoughts, William replied, "When are you going to grow up and become a man?"

Normally, Bill would've shot back with an argument, but he knew he couldn't hide his thoughts from his dad. William knew him too well.

"Stop hiding behind your family. Step in front of them and lead by example. It may not seem like it, but Chad is looking to you to make all of this right. He's depending on you to do the right thing. In order to make the decisions which you'll need to make, you need to get your own head on straight. To do that, you need closure for yourself."

Nodding, Bill said, "I know. I'm trying to be strong but it's still unreal to me, too." Pointing toward Chad's room upstairs, Bill said, "I can't even imagine what he's feeling right now."

Bill lowered his head. As much as he still couldn't fathom that his beloved wife was gone, he had tried to appear strong in front of his father. He knew full well, however, that William could see through this masquerade in less than a second.

"Look," replied William, "you just need to stay strong. When Chad looks at you, he needs to see strength and resolve. I'm not saying to hide what you're going through from yourself, but hide it from Chad."

"But he won't even talk to me," said Bill. "How can I know what he's going through if he doesn't talk to me about it?"

William shrugged his shoulders and said, "Welcome to another stage of fatherhood, son. Remember back when you were in middle school and you were dating that fat buck-toothed girl from a few roads down?"

Bill chuckled. "She wasn't fat," he said.

"She was," snapped back William. "I swear that I also saw a sign on one of her front teeth which read 'One Mile to Next Tooth' but you never believed me."

Bill erupted in laughter. "You're exaggerating," said Bill.

William lowered his head, raised his eyebrows and said, "Really?"

"Okay you're exaggerating a little," replied Bill as he kept laughing.

"I remember when she broke up with you because I wouldn't let you borrow money to take her out to eat," William said as he tried to contain his laughter. "Like she needed anything else to eat."

"Okay, Dad," said Bill in an attempt to stop his dad's tantrum, but William was already on a roll.

"You didn't talk to your mother and I for nearly two weeks. The only time we'd see you is when you'd come to the dinner table. I learned right then and there how to tell exactly how your day went by your body language," said William. "From the way you squirmed in your seat when I asked you a question you didn't want to answer or the way your eyes would open wide when I'd talk about racing, it eventually came to the point where your mother and I could read you like an open book."

William looked over at Bill who was staring off into space, lost in deep thought.

"You still here?" asked William half-jokingly.

Shaking his head slightly, Bill replied, "Yeah. You just reminded me of something I haven't thought of in weeks."

Without even needing to probe his son for answers, William replied, "Racing."

Nodding his head up and down, Bill said, "I think this is the longest I've ever gone without even thinking about racing in some way." Bill took a deep breath as he said, "And you know what? It feels good. I feel almost relieved in some ways."

"Seasons come and go in our lives, son," replied William as he rose from the couch and walked toward the garage. "I gave up racing because I wanted to start a family and devote all of my time to them."

Following William into the garage, Bill stopped and stared at the colossal mess which used to be the TA2 Ford Mustang he raced. During the accident, the enclosed trailer which contained Bill's race car had flipped several times as the inertia from the impact sent it catapulting into the air along with the SUV carrying Bill, Lena, and

Chad. For all intents and purposes, it was the second casualty of the accident.

"Your decision was by choice," said Bill. "With the Mustang totaled and all of the money I have going into medical bills now, I'm gonna have to sell it for parts…or scrap."

Bill let his fingers run down what used to be the smooth surface of the hood. He briefly remembered the life he felt as he raced it on the track. Now, all he saw when he looked at it was a reminder of loss.

"I hate to say that I was forced out but that's the way it looks," said Bill. "What's strange is that I'm not complaining about it."

"Nor should you," replied William. "Your family needs you. All of you." Leaning against the wall which faced the destroyed car, William shrugged his shoulder. "But you never know. Maybe one day you'll be able to get back into racing."

Bill gave a slight chuckle as he turned to leave the garage. "I'm in no rush."

* * *

The following morning, Bill awoke with a sense of dread. He didn't want to get up. He almost felt like a kid again as he buried his head back under the covers and tried not to think about what the day ahead would hold. Bill lay half-awake in his bed as the new day's sunlight began peering through a nearby window. The warm feeling of the sun on his skin combined with the comfort of his soft bedding caused him to close his eyes again and drift off into a type of twilight zone. The sounds of the birds singing their morning songs as the wind swept softly through the trees only seemed to ease his passage into the unknown.

With his eyes now closed, he thought back to when he has was once *encouraged* by Lena to go see her mother on her birthday. As they both lay in bed, the dread was unbearable as the thought of visiting the bane of his existence came into his mind. Lena, not wanting to go either, tried to pretend that she was serious.

"Alright, we'll get up of on the count of three. One...two..." A long pause arose as neither person moved. "Three," said Lena. At that point, Bill began to make a snoring sound to show that he was in fact not interested in moving as Lena playfully slapped him on his chest. The two laughed as he swung the covers back over the both of them...

"Dammit!" Bill shouted as he swung the covers away and sat up on the edge of the bed. Burying his face in his hands with his elbows resting on his knees, he squeezed his head as if that would somehow force the memory out of his mind.

He didn't want to think of the good times. He didn't even want to think of the bad times. He glanced over his shoulder at the empty bed as a cold chill ran up his spine. He couldn't help but think about how he would never see his wife lying there ever again.

"Get up, Bill," he said out loud to himself. "Get moving."

Finally, he stood up slowly. As he took a deep breath, the dread which he felt as he laid in bed returned to him once again. Today was going to be a tough day. Today was the day that he had been dreading for a long time.

Today, he was going to visit Lena, and he was taking Chad with him. Grabbing his robe, he went down the hall and peered into Chad's room to find him still asleep.

Some things never change. The kid can still sleep in all day if he wanted to.

Bill went downstairs as the fresh aroma of coffee tickled his nose. Knowing it meant his dad was already awake, Bill looked out the back door to see William doing what he had always done almost every morning for as far back as Bill can remember: sitting on the back patio with his coffee and his newspaper.

This sight, along with the sight of his young son sleeping, brought some measure of comfort to Bill. He knew that he needed to take the very advice that he had given to Chad only the night before.

"I know you must be thinking about the negative. It would be easy to. But we have to be thankful for what we still have."

Indeed, Bill was thankful. He was thankful for his family, his home and for the fresh coffee which he now poured into his favorite Peter Brock coffee mug which his dad had bought for him several years ago. Opening the backdoor, Bill stepped outside into the cool morning air and sat down across from his dad.

"Morning," said William without even looking up. "You're up earlier than usual."

"Yeah. Woke up and had trouble going back to bed," replied Bill as he took his first sip of coffee. After a few seconds, Bill said, "Today's the day, you know."

William lowered the paper enough so that his eyes were just looking over the edge as he made eye contact with Bill. "Lena?" he asked.

"Yeah."

"Chad too?"

Bill lowered his head a bit and took a deep breath. "Yeah. Chad, too."

"Good," was all William said. He raised the paper back up and resumed his reading. "I'll hold down the fort whilst you're away."

Bill couldn't help but smirk at his dad's *matter of fact* mentality sometimes.

William again lowered the paper and sat up in his chair. "Look at this," he said pointing to an advertisement in the paper, "A chartered fishing trip. Sounds like fun. They practically do everything but catch the fish for you."

Bill chuckled. "Sounds expensive and full of rich people who are too afraid to get their hands dirty."

"Or people who are too old to do that themselves," countered William with a smile as he made no attempt to hide that he was talking about himself. "Plus," he added, "it includes an open bar."

Laughing again while holding his coffee mug, Bill lifted the pinky finger of the hand holding the coffee and said with an overly dramatic British accent, "Would you like us to wash your ass for you before you go fishing this morning, Mr. Watson."

Both men laughed at the idea of William sipping wine with a bunch of people on a fishing boat who made way more money than the both of them. The laughter was cut off all of the sudden by the sound of a heavy *thud* coming from inside the house. For a brief second, both men paused and looked each other in the eyes before dropping everything and racing inside.

Hurrying up the stairs, Bill and William immediately went straight to Chad's bedroom where they found him face down on the floor.

* * *

Lying in the same position as he was in when his father laid him down to sleep last night, Chad couldn't help but feel relieved as he opened his eyes to find himself in his own bed on a bright and sunny day. The diffused sounds of birds chirping on the other side of his windows caused him to smile slightly as he closed his eyes again to soak in this peaceful moment.

It reminded him of the numerous occasions where he'd wake up on a Sunday morning to the smell of the coffee that his parents drank and the sounds of laughter. His parents would usually find a humorous story in the morning paper or a rare comic strip which they actually found funny.

He remembered jumping out of bed and running downstairs to the corresponding sight of a delicious breakfast waiting for him as his parents wondered how it's possible for someone to sleep in for so long.

As if living the memory again, Chad couldn't help but take a deep breath as the all too familiar scent of fresh coffee crept into his room and took him back to those wonderful mornings just as he had remembered.

He felt free. As if he had just completed a prison sentence which was served in an internal cage, Chad could sense that the prison door was finally opening. Now, the only thing he needed to do was walk through it.

Still feeling groggy, he squirmed ever so slightly and couldn't help but squint his eyes as he realized how stiff his body felt.

How long have I been sleeping?

Still only partially awake, the sound of laughter coming from the back patio seemed to complete the memory. At once, he flung the covers off of him and rolled out of bed in an effort to run downstairs towards the familiar sound.

Hitting the ground face first, however, he returned to his harsh reality as the prison doors slammed shut once again.

* * *

"Chad!" said Bill as he ran and knelt by his son's side.

At first appearance, Bill judged that he had tried to get up out of the bed by himself and fallen, but he couldn't figure out why he had done so.

Bill rolled Chad onto his back and could now see that Chad had tears coming from his eyes.

"Hey, you're okay," said Bill frantically as he lifted Chad into his arms and hugged him. "I know it's going to take some getting used to, but we're going to get through this."

With tears in his eyes, Chad began striking Bill on his arms and back.

Bill could feel the tension in his son's body as he tightened his embrace. "I know you're mad, son. Mad at me and mad at the world," said Bill.

Chad, burying his face in his dad's shoulder, lowered his arms as they now hung loosely as if lifeless as Bill continued to embrace him.

The tears continued to flow down Chad's face as William knelt down behind Bill which allowed him to look Chad in the eyes as his head hung on Bill's shoulder.

"Chad," said William softly, "who was it that studied harder than anyone in his class and got straight A's in school?"

Chad, refusing to look his grandpa in the eyes, didn't answer and continued to hang his head low.

"Who was it that helped encourage this old man to pick himself up and live his life to the fullest?" asked William as he pointed towards himself.

The tears began to fall heavily down Chad's face as Bill had to work extra hard to keep himself from breaking down in front of both of them.

Noticing that Chad was still looking down and not making eye contact with him, William said, "Chad, look at me."

At once, Chad's teary eyes looked into William's. Letting the moment sink in for both of them for several seconds, William asked, "Who is it that's going to walk again?"

Chad continued to stare into his grandpa's eyes as William said, "Do you want that? Do you want to walk again, Chad?"

In what was the first type of social response they'd seen ever since Chad had stopped talking, Chad nodded his head up and down.

"Good," said William softly. "If you believe it here and here," tapping on his own head and heart, "it'll be so. But you can never give up."

Now with a firm grip on his emotions, Bill asked, "Remember the first time I raced the Mustang and I got a flat tire? Do you remember what I did after that?"

The memory seemed to bring a slight smile to Chad's face along with a single quick chuckle.

"I pulled into the pits, got out of the car, changed the tire myself and went back out. There were people who were laughing and nobody came to help me either but that didn't matter. The point is that I never gave up and I finished what I started. We're a team, and you're a Watson. Together, we're going to finish this race. Do you understand?"

At this, Chad's limp arms wrapped around Bill's neck as he buried his head in his father's shoulder once again.

Still holding Chad in his arms, Bill stood up and said, "You're okay, little man. Now let's get you some breakfast. We've got a big day today." As the three left Chad's bedroom, William exited first and stepped to the side to allow Bill, who was carrying Chad, to go in front of him. As Bill passed his father, however, William leaned into Bill's ear and whispered, "Come talk to me later."

Chapter 7

The forty-five-minute drive was long and quiet. Travelling down one of the many Texas Farm-to-Market roads, Bill held onto the steering wheel of his father's 1968 Mustang as Chad stared aimlessly out the window, as he often did when they drove together. Bill couldn't help but smirk at the short order his father had given him just before they left the house.

Tossing the keys of his Mustang to Bill, William had said, "Take it. Don't argue. Drive it like you stole it."

The feeling of being behind the wheel of his father's car again took him back to his childhood when he first learned how to drive. Recalling what it was like learning how to drive a car from a former Australian Touring Car champion, Bill chuckled out loud at the memory of his dad repeatedly telling him and grinding into his head to, "brake later, turn in, hit the apex and power down."

The chuckle from Bill caused Chad to break his daze and look over at his dad. Glancing over at his son, Bill said, "You know, this is the car I learned to drive in. Your granddad is quite the teacher. You've never really learned how to drive until you have a champion race car driver show you how."

Bill smiled as he looked over at Chad again. He noticed, however, that Chad was no longer looking back at him but was, instead, looking down towards his feet as if in dismay.

Bill cursed internally as he realized what he had just done.

How could you tell your son about how exciting it is to learn how to drive when he may never be able to do just that? How can you tell that to a kid who just weeks ago told you he wanted to be a race car driver but may never be able to feel the pedals underneath his feet because he can't use his legs?

Suddenly Bill had an idea. *He can't use his legs...*

Still driving on the empty country road, Bill pulled the car off to the side of the road and stopped. Chad, now confused, looked over at his dad as if asking what was going on.

Bill turned and looked at his son. "So," said Bill, "you wanna drive?" At first, Chad's eyebrows furled and his chin tilted as if confused.

That's when Bill pulled Chad up onto his lap.

"We'll do this together, like a team," said Bill. "I'll push the pedals; you steer and shift, okay?"

At first, Chad just simply sat on his father's lap with his arms down at his sides. Bill knew he'd be a little nervous, but he also knew just how to get him going.

Only the slightest push of the throttle was all the engine needed to rev up and bring a smile on Bill's face. Looking at Chad through the rearview mirror, Bill could see that Chad was now smiling too. He leaned forward and put his small hands on the nine and three position just as William had shown him.

"Alright, we'll start out slow," said Bill.

Slowly revving the engine, Bill began to lift his foot off the clutch and the car began to move. "Just keep it between the lines," said Bill.

A little shaky at first, Chad seemed to be doing just fine. As they began to build up speed, Bill said, "Alright, get ready to shift into second."

Lifting his foot off the throttle, Bill pushed in the clutch pedal and, without even needing a cue, Chad grabbed the shifter and threw it down into second gear.

Surprised, Bill couldn't help but lift his eyebrows as he said, "Very good. Somebody's been watching me."

As they continued to build up speed, this sequence continued up to fourth gear until they saw an intersection up ahead.

"That's where we need to turn," said Bill. "We need to make a right." Bill brought the car to a complete stop at the stop sign as Chad put the blinker on. As they accelerated, Chad executed the turn perfectly. "Well, I must say, I'm very impressed, son," said Bill proudly. "We're almost to where we're going."

Not knowing how Chad was going to react, Bill hadn't told his son that they were going to the cemetery to see his mother. As it stood, Chad had no idea where they were heading. It wasn't until they approached a sign on the side of the road which read, "Cemetery" that Chad began to piece things together.

Choking up all of the sudden, Chad took his hands off the wheel and the car began to drift off to the side of the road. Fortunately for Bill, he had his hands ready and was able to catch the wheel before the car drove itself into the ditch. Nevertheless, the act still caught Bill off guard but he didn't need an explanation as to why.

"I'm guessing by now you've figured out where we're going," said Bill somberly. Chad began to slide himself off of his father's lap and back to the passenger seat. Once he got back, a tear slid down his left cheek as he let his head drop.

"We've got to be strong, Chad. We've got to be strong for mom. It's what she would've wanted for us," said Bill as he was fighting back his own tears. Bill remembered the words his father spoke to him just the night before: *Chad is looking to you to make all of this right. He's depending on you to do the right thing. In order to make the decisions which you'll need to make, you need to get your own head on straight.*

Bill knew he needed to be strong. He needed to take charge of the situation and lead by example. Vowing to press on, Bill took a deep breath as he made the right turn into the cemetery parking lot and brought the car to a stop.

* * *

A small cemetery in what some would describe as the middle of nowhere, this was the same location where Bill's mother was laid to rest not too long ago. Upon Lena's death, a heated argument arose between William and Lena's mother, Helen, as to where her final resting place should be. Being the controlling person that she was, Helen had demanded that Lena's body be buried in the same cemetery where her other relatives had been laid to rest. However, per William's advice, both Lena and Bill had previously written in their will their desire for their final resting place in the event of something catastrophic coming to pass. William remembered all too well how Lena loved the peace and quiet of the country cemetery when her and Bill accompanied William to visit the grave of his wife, Charlotte. As Bill was still in a coma at the time, William honored her decision and had Lena laid to rest out here—much to the dismay of Helen, of course.

It was a quiet and simple place. There were no noisy interstate roads anywhere around nor were there any airplanes flying overhead. It was simply quiet. The grounds were very well maintained by a small detail of landscapers and the most stringent effort was made to keep the area in tip-top condition. Like an oasis of sorts, the tall ironclad fence surrounding the well maintained grass, groomed bushes and tall trees seemed almost out of place as it rose out of the middle of the Texas countryside.

After Bill had parked the car, he removed Chad's wheelchair from the trunk as well as a bouquet of red roses from the backseat and, after assisting Chad into the wheelchair, they both set off.

Despite the fact that there were a handful of others who were visiting their own lost loved ones and relatives, it remained a very quiet and somber place. Listening to the wind blow, they could almost hear the tall grass shaking as the birds sat perched in a nearby oak tree and sang their afternoon melodies.

As they approached the sidewalk from the parking lot, they found a neatly maintained gravel walkway which led them underneath an ornate archway and into the cemetery itself. For Chad's sake, however, Bill opted not to take the walkway as the bumpy road of gravel under his wheelchair wouldn't be the most pleasant experience. Instead, Bill steered the wheelchair through the grass which was on either side of the gravel path.

As they walked, they were met with row upon row of perfectly lined up headstones of various shapes, sizes and types of stone on either side of them. Glancing at one occasionally as they walked by, Bill noticed some people who had been over 100 years old when they were laid to rest. Others he saw, however, were barely more than a few months old.

Previously receiving directions from William, Bill now knew exactly where to go. As they continued their journey, Bill felt his heart begin to race as he approached his wife for the first time in over a month. Counting the rows as he walked, he arrived at the eighth row and, per William's instructions, turned right and went two headstones down.

That's when he saw it:

LENA WATSON
Beloved Wife, Mother and Friend

Although he knew that this was the reason he had come all the way out here today, Bill's heart and mind still couldn't believe it. He could immediately feel his knees begin to weaken as he knelt down beside the newly placed headstone. His nose began to run as tears began to well up in his eyes. He didn't need to look back to know that Chad was crying as he could hear his son sniffling and trying to fight back his own tears. Placing his left hand on the top of the smooth granite stone, Bill had his eyes fixed on Lena's name as he still tried to come to the realization that she was gone. The sight of her name on the headstone caused him to feel as if his very soul was being torn in two.

He wanted to say something. He knew he should say something. His thought had always been that he would speak what was on his mind when the time was right. Now, however, there were only two words on his mind which he could think of.

Letting his head drop, tears fell from his eyes and landed on the green grass which separated him from his wife. "I'm sorry," said Bill over sobbing tears. "I'm so sorry, Lena."

He had tried to keep himself together but the sight of his wife's grave sent him over. As much as he had tried to prepare himself for this, he never imagined that he would be kneeling at the grave of his wife who was his high school sweetheart and best friend. It was almost as if he were hearing the horrible news from his father all over again that Lena had been killed.

Killed because he was too shaken up to drive home. Killed because he started arguing with her while SHE was driving during a torrential downpour of rain. Killed because he spun out while chasing some futile sense of glory. Killed because…

Bill…

The touch of a small hand on his shoulder snapped him back to the present moment. He quickly shook his head and turned to see that Chad had reached out to do what Lena often had to do: bring him back to reality. For a brief second, however, he almost felt as if he could hear the sound of his wife's voice in his head.

I think I'm finally losing my mind.

Looking at his son, he grabbed his hand from his shoulder and held it tight. "We need to be strong," he said, repeating what he had said earlier in the car. "This is hard on both of us but now more than ever, we need to be strong."

Turning his body to face Chad, Bill said, "I promise you that I'm going to do everything I can to make sure you're taken care of. I promise that I'll always have your back, no matter what."

Chad let his head drop as tears continued to fall from his eyes.

"Chad," said Bill, causing his son to lift his head. "Can I count on you to stay strong, too? For Mom?"

Wiping his nose with his sleeve, Chad looked his father directly in the eyes and gave a slight nod up and down.

"Good," said Bill. "I knew I could count on you."

At that point, Chad extended both of his arms toward his mother's gravestone. Bill recognized this as Chad wanting to be brought closer. Picking him up and setting him down on the ground, Chad leaned his body up against the headstone and wrapped his arms around it.

Still holding onto the bouquet of roses he had brought with him, Bill placed them down in front of the headstone and took a step back. What he saw next was something he knew would haunt him for the rest of his life.

There in front of him was the sight of an empty wheelchair belonging to his crippled son who was now lying on the ground while embracing the tombstone of his dead wife.

* * *

The ride home was even quieter than before. Both Bill and Chad seemed to be in deep thought of varying degrees as the red Mustang charged along the long country road. Glad to have that step behind him but already missing the presence of his wife...

I'll always be here with you, Bill.

There it was again.

Shaking his head again, Bill began to think that the lack of a full night's rest was indeed beginning to get to him. He did miss the sound of his wife's voice but what he was hearing now was nothing more than his own mind betraying him.

He remembered back to when his mother passed away and how his father would tell him similar things about how, when he was alone, he could still hear the voice of Bill's mother, Charlotte. Connecting the lines, Bill knew that the secret to insanity was being alone and having an idle mind with nothing to think about other than the past. He knew from now on and until further notice that he'd have to keep his mind engaged with something. Anything.

Now I know why some people drink.

Bill had never been a heavy drinker or a smoker simply because of the fact that he had seen so many great men in his life succumb to addictions and fall. What they often took with them when they fell, however, was not only the people whom they had built up along the way, but also the legacy they spent the majority of the lives constructing. Bill refused to have any part in that and, therefore, always knew his limits.

He began to think of what he could do to fill his time with. He had taken an extended leave of absence from his work since the accident so he knew that he'd be playing catch-up with his job when he got back.

That's a start.

He knew, however, that this would only last for so long and he would eventually catch up and need to find something else to further occupy his time. He already had plans to meet with several doctors over Chad's physical therapy treatments which he knew would be taking a large chunk of his time…and money.

What he needed, however, was something to help him take his mind off of everything: an escape of sorts. Inevitably, his mind took him back to racing.

Racing was his original and, for the longest time, his *only* hobby. He had invested so much time and money into it that he felt that Lena may had been right: it had turned into an addiction.

Similar to an addiction to alcohol, Bill looked back and asked himself what good had ever come from racing.

Nothing. If it hadn't been for racing, Lena would still be alive and Chad wouldn't be in a wheelchair.

For several minutes, his mind replayed the events which led up to his present circumstance in his mind: the race, the spin, the crash, Lena's death, Chad and this present trip. As he thought about it more, all of it had been a direct result of one thing: racing.

Gripping the wheel tight, he made a silent vow to himself that he would never sit in a race car again.

Would William be upset? No. Disappointed, maybe. But Bill knew that it wasn't the end of the world and his sole priority right now was to take care of his son.

Bill was so in the zone with his thoughts that he was surprised to see how quickly the trip had gone by. Passing a sign which told him he was closing in on his exit, he sat up in his seat and reaffirmed to himself once again: *No more racing. I'm done with it.*

* * *

Pulling up to the house, it was now midafternoon. He parked the car in the driveway, popped the trunk and got out. Chad, who had dozed off in the passenger seat, was just starting to wake up when Bill gently tapped his arm.

"We're home now, buddy," said Bill as he exited. He unfolded the wheelchair from the trunk and pulled up to the passenger side door and opened it for Chad. Positioning the wheelchair alongside the passenger seat, Bill was just about to pick Chad up and move him to the wheelchair when he heard a car pull up behind him. Looking over his left shoulder, he saw the unmistakable sight of the hybrid car driven by none other than the last person he wanted to see right now.

"Bill," said Helen with as much venom in her voice that she muster up as she exited the small car. "I thought you'd be out racing that toy car of yours," she said as she pressed her forefinger to her lips.

Sticking her heavy finger into the air as if surprised by her next sentence, she said, "Oh that's right. You wrecked it and killed my daughter while doing so. But I'm so glad to see that you're still alive and doing well."

She hates me. Always has and always will.

As far back as Bill could remember, Helen had always been vicious with her words, and right now was no different.

"Is there a reason that you're here, Helen?"

"I'm just here to collect a few things of mine that Lena was supposed to give back to me. Since she's no longer able to do so because, you know, you killed her, I figured I'd just do it myself."

She was baiting him. Bill had been around the block with her enough times to know that. He'd be lying, however, if he said that her words weren't shooting bolts of rage through his body.

Bill looked down at Chad who was staring blankly back up at him.

"You're not coming into my house, Helen. Get back in your shoebox and leave," said Bill dryly as he pointed out to the road.

"Well," she said while taking a few steps forward, "I called before I came over and your foreign father said he'd have it all ready for me."

"Oh," said Bill, "well in that case, please wait here. I'm sure the foreign minister will be out shortly to greet you."

Bill turned around to resume helping Chad when Helen's voice rang out again.

"How does it feel, Bill?" asked Helen.

Bill froze in place.

"How does it feel to know that you're alive and she's dead? How does it feel to know that your son will never see his mother again?"

Noticing the sadness in the eyes of his son, Bill had taken enough. He stood up and faced Helen.

"You would say something like that in front of my son? After all he's been through?" shouted Bill. "How does it feel to know that your husband died of treatable cancer?"

Helen stood up as straight as she could. "How dare you! He died because we couldn't afford the treatments!"

"You couldn't afford the treatments but you could afford satellite TV, clothes shopping every weekend and a brand new car?"

"I outta slap you upside your head, you worthless liar! You have no idea what you're talking about and if I were you, I'd mind my own business," said Helen.

"Just like you mind yours, right?" asked Bill as he threw his arms up in the air.

"You don't tell me what to do! You don't get to talk to me like that! I'm here because you killed my daughter! It should've been you! It should've been you and you know it!"

Bill could feel the anger burning in his face. He decided he'd had enough. Mother-in-law or not, he wasn't going to be talked to like this and he certainly wasn't going to subject his son to her words any longer. He was going to shut her up one way or another. Clenching his fists, he started to approach Helen when, all of the sudden, William emerged from the front door holding a small cardboard box.

"Helen!" he said with a smile on his face. "How nice it is to see you!"

"Well look what floated to the surface from down under," said Helen. "Get your twisted son away from me before he does something he regrets."

Moving to stand between the two, William handed the box to Helen and said, "There you go. It's everything you've been asking for."

Examining the box, Helen started to shake it softly. "I thought I told you it was my old jewelry. This doesn't feel like there's any jewelry in here," said Helen.

"Oh it's jewels alright. I wrapped 'em all up good and tight," said William. "It's very fragile so if I were you, I wouldn't open it until you got home. Speaking of home," he said as he turned to Bill, "I think it's about time we part ways for now," he said as he turned back to Helen.

Bill took this as a cue to go inside, but he wasn't budging until Helen was gone.

Helen took a deep breath and sighed. "Very well."

Turning to get into her car, she opened the door, put one leg in and said, "Until next time, Bill, try not to screw up any more lives."

Entering the car, she closed the door before Bill or William could say anything in response.

That was the way with Helen as Bill remembered. Years back, Lena had once told him how she would always get the last word in. Even if it meant she had to stay in an argument longer, she would continue to argue until she could manage to get the final word in before either she or the person she was arguing with would make their escape.

Putting his hand on his son's shoulder, William said, "C'mon, son. Let's get inside."

William and Bill helped get Chad, who was still in the passenger seat, into the wheelchair and inside the house. Knowing that Chad heard the entire argument as he always seemed to do, Bill said, "Chad, I'm glad you're smart enough to know that none of the things she said were true."

Chad's facial features were expressionless as they escorted him inside. Once up the outside front steps and through the front door, Bill looked down and could tell that Chad was very tired from today's events.

"I think it's nap time, bud. I know I could use one," said Bill. Heading into the house with his back turned to Bill, William turned and said, "Come talk to me when you're ready."

Carrying him upstairs, Bill helped Chad change his clothes and then laid him down in bed. Bill couldn't help but notice that Chad was already fast asleep before his head even hit the pillow.

"This will get easier," whispered Bill. "I promise."

Kissing Chad on his forehead, he stood up to walk out but stopped at the doorway. Turning around to look at his sleeping son, he could only imagine what he was going through right now.

"I wish I could hear your voice again," said Bill softly.

Taking a deep breath, he stepped back and closed the bedroom door.

***

Walking downstairs, Bill found his father sitting on the couch with his feet propped up on the ottoman while holding a beer. His head was leaning back on a pillow which was placed behind his neck and his eyes were closed as Bill stopped beside him.

"Is this how you shake it off?" asked Bill referring to the incident with Helen.

"Yes," said William calmly and without opening his eyes, "and you should learn to do it, too."

Walking over to the refrigerator and grabbing a beer for himself, he went back over and sat down across from his father.

For a moment, they sat in silence. It was Bill, however, who moved first. "I'm sorry I let her bait me like that. I shouldn't have said what I did in front of Chad," said Bill regretfully.

"You should be sorry," said William as he opened his eyes and lifted his head to look at Bill. "He may not be able to speak but Chad can hear everything you say. But, I know it's been an emotional day for you two so I can't hold that against you. Plus, I should've given you fair warning ahead of time."

"Yeah, you should've. What were you doing?" asked Bill. "Why didn't you let me know she was coming over?"

William, slowly sitting up in his seat and now smiling suspiciously, said, "I…uh…was preparing her package." Still smiling ear to ear at Bill, William let out a slight chuckle.

Bill couldn't help but be curious but he knew this was probably just one of his dad's many antics. Smiling and shaking his head, Bill asked, "What did you want to talk about?"

William put his beer on the coffee table and got serious as he folded his hands together and leaned forward. "Many years ago, back when I was young and handsome, I had a friend I grew up racing with. We raced go-karts all through our time in school but he got smart and decided to go to university instead of pursuing racing like I did," said William.

He paused briefly to see if Bill was paying attention. Continuing, he said, "While he was in school, he and his family lost everything in a house fire. At that particular time, I was doing well for myself in racing so I let them bunk in my place until they were able to get on their feet again. Although his parents still had their jobs, I helped out financially whenever I could. It took several months, but eventually they were able to get another home and start over."

Bill was looking more than slightly confused at this point. "I'm not sure I'm following."

"Well there's nothing to bloody follow yet! I haven't even gotten to the point!" said William with a smile.

Bill held up his beer to William and said, "Please proceed, sir."

"Thank you," said William. "As I was saying, they were all able to get back onto their feet again and my friend, Greg Foster, was able to go on to finish his school. He promised me a long time ago that if there's any favor he could do for me, to name it. Now, I know you American kids aren't very good at keeping your word anymore but to us Aussies, our word is who we are."

Rolling his eyes, Bill asked, "So is this the person you were talking to the other night?"

"Yes it was."

"So...what did you guys talk about that was so important that you needed to bring me into the mix?"

William looked directly into Bill's eyes and said one word: "Chad."

Sitting up in his seat all of the sudden, Bill said, "Chad? What about him?"

"I told him what was going on with everything and asked him if his offer for a favor still stood. He said 'yes.'"

"I still don't understand. What does your friend Greg have to do with any of this?" asked Bill who was getting tired of the subtleties.

"He's a doctor, Bill."

"What kind of a doctor?"

"The kind Chad needs: a Physiatrist. And he's offered to care for Chad...for free."

At first, Bill wasn't sure how to take this.

"Isn't this Greg guy in Australia?"

"Yes, he is."

"Dad, how is this guy going to care for Chad in Australia? What, do you want me to ship Chad over there by himself, or is he coming over to the U.S.?" asked Bill who was now clearly frustrated.

"No, you're going over there *with* Chad."

"To Australia," said Bill with an undertone of disbelief in his voice.

William nodded his head up and down.

Bill began to laugh as he sat up and grabbed the beer that his father had sat down on the coffee table. "I think you've had enough of these for tonight, Dad," said Bill.

"I'm serious, son. You don't think I know how much this is going to cost you? I would love to help and I could for a while, but I don't exactly have an infinite amount of money. Sooner or later, I won't be able to help anymore and then what? You're going to start working two or three jobs just to pay for medical bills and stay afloat?" said William.

"If that's what needs to be done, yes," said Bill. "I gave Chad my word that I would do everything I could to take care of him."

"And what happens when you give everything you can and it's still not enough? These are hospitals, not charities. They don't care about your sympathy stories; they just want your money."

"Dad, you're talking about me moving to Australia with Chad.

What am I going to do in Australia?"

"You're going to take care of your son, that's what you're going to do."

"What about me? What am I going to do in Australia? How am I going to be able to put food on a table—which I'll also have to buy—in Australia?"

"It's all part of the favor. Greg has agreed to let you and Chad stay at his place until you're both back on your feet, doubly so for Chad."

"What about my job here?"

"You talk with your buddy, Pat Henderson, and explain the situation. He's more than capable of taking care of things for the time being," answered William. "Plus, you youngsters know how to do all of that remote working nowadays.

"And the house?" asked Bill shrugging his shoulders.

"I'll stay back and take care of it. It's not like it'd be a permanent move, son. Trust me. A way has been offered for you and for Chad that you won't find anywhere no matter how hard you look. There's no reason whatsoever for you to turn it down," said William.

"You better believe there is!" shouted Bill. "I've spent my entire life building up what we have here and you're asking me to drop it all and run to Australia."

William stared at Bill for several seconds before asking softly, "Are you happy, son?"

"Are you serious?" asked Bill, knowing where this was headed.

"Are you happy knowing that you're going to have to pay more than you make from your job in medical bills, still have to pay your regular bills and at the same time, fend off that mother-in-law who will never leave you in peace? Are you happy?" asked William again.

He was using his own words against him but Bill knew the truth: his dad was right.

"No, Dad. No, I'm not happy."

"I'm offering you a way out, son. It's the best option and you know it. Just like you reminded me of how your mother was never one to sit still, I'm reminding you of how Lena was one who always did the right thing even if it meant being taken out of her comfort zone," said William. "Do this for Chad, son. I hope I'm not overstepping my boundaries but I think you can see that this is what's best for him."

Bill stood up from his seat and walked to the kitchen. He began slowly pacing back and forth as if in deep thought.

"You trust this guy?"

"Like a brother," said William firmly.

Finally, Bill looked up and around the house. He'd gotten so used to living here for so many years that he hardly ever just stopped to appreciate everything about it. He looked over at the family photos on the wall, the cabinet holding the China which Bill and Lena had received on their wedding day, the decorative pictures and artwork which they had picked out together and all the various furniture throughout the house.

It was home to him.

But then Bill realized something very important: home wasn't a mere building or simple items which fill a room. Home was wherever Bill's family was, and it was now up to Bill to protect that. Doing that, he knew, meant leaving certain things behind today so he could have a better life with his family tomorrow.

Turning to look towards his father who was now sitting on the edge of his seat, Bill simply said, "Alright," as he turned and walked away.

Suddenly, Bill stopped midstep. "Before I do anything, I need to know something." He turned to look at his father who had a very serious look on his face.

"What in the hell was in that box you gave to Helen?" asked Bill.

William laughed and said, "Let's just say I didn't need to flush this morning."

Both men erupted in laughter as Bill added, "Well, you did say that she'd been asking for it, right?"

Getting ahold of himself, William said, "If I were you, I'd be running to Australia as soon as I could."

Chapter 8

The plane landed with a *thud,* and the physical jolt caused Bill to wake suddenly from his sleep. Never a big fan of flying, the last time Bill was on an airplane was several years ago during his honeymoon with Lena. The two newlyweds travelled to the island of Kauai, Hawaii, which meant several tormenting hours of flying over water. Not helping Lena's efforts to get Bill to relax was the fact that they were playing the movie *Cast Away* during the flight.

This flight, however, despite the fact that it was several times longer than his previous honeymoon adventure, was more of an exodus of sorts for Bill and Chad.

It had been several weeks since Bill's decision to make the move. Much now rested on his shoulders and he could feel it. Considering the look of shock that his business partner, Pat Henderson, had given him when he informed him of his decision to leave, the good-byes to his friends, coworkers and neighbors—and when he had to explain why he needed a copy of Chad's medical records at the hospital—he more or less felt relieved to finally be sitting still in one spot despite the fact that the spot had just landed in a completely different country.

Leaning to his left to look out the window which he was sitting next to, all that he was able to see were the runway lights illuminating a somewhat foggy night sky of Sydney, Australia.

I can't believe I'm actually in Australia.

Beyond that, there was little else to see at the moment other than the additional lights from the approaching airport terminals. After several minutes of waiting followed by helping Chad get out of his seat and onto the provided wheelchair, the two were off to the baggage terminal where they had arranged to meet William's friend, Greg Foster.

In the days leading up to Bill and Chad's voyage overseas, Bill had done a considerable amount of research into Greg; or Dr. Foster as he would soon find out. The more he looked, the better he began to feel about this trip.

With a PhD from the University of New South Wales along with a Masters in Physiotherapy (MPhty) from the University of Sydney, Dr. Foster had elevated himself to become one of the most highly sought after Pediatric Neuromuscular Rehabilitation specialists in Australia. The author of numerous books and a regular contributor to several medical journals, Bill found it strange to think that someone as esteemed as Dr. Foster was once as crazy as William.

As they waited in the baggage claim, Chad was looking around curiously at the massive airport. Having never flown before, Bill initially thought Chad would be a mess throughout the entire flight. Much to his surprise, however, Chad lived up to his name as a heavy sleeper and was out cold almost as soon as he sat down. Only waking a few times for Bill's assistance to use the restroom, Chad would almost immediately fall back asleep once in his seat again.

Now fully awake because of the hustle and bustle of the busy airport noises, Chad couldn't keep his eyes fixed on something for more than a second before another object grasped for his attention. Whether it was a crazy product advertisement that wasn't seen in the United States or hearing someone say "G'day, mate," for the first time, he had plenty to cause his mind to go adrift.

They continued to wait for the baggage claim to come to life and release their luggage. As they waited, Bill couldn't help but notice the odd stares he caught from people's eyes as they glanced at him standing by a wheelchair which held a child. It had indeed been awhile since he had taken Chad out in public in his present condition. Not because he was ashamed of his son, but simply because so much has happened since Chad was first brought home after the accident.

And now here we are in Australia.

Looking to his right, he caught the eyes of an older woman who was looking down at Chad. The woman looked up to meet Bill's eyes and immediately looked away. Bill knew that it would be awhile before he would get used to this.

"You can never get used to it", said a thick Australian voice coming from behind him.

Turning around, he saw a very well dressed man who appeared to be around the same age as Bill's father. Wearing a black suit jacket with gray slacks, the man appeared to have just gotten off from work as his neck tie was loosened and the top button of his white dress shirt was undone. The silvery white haired man extended his hand to Bill and said, "You must be Bill."

"I am. And you must be Dr. Foster. It's good to finally meet you," said Bill as he shook Dr. Foster's hand.

"Likewise and please, call me Greg. I've heard a lot about you."

"Same here."

Looking down at Bill's son in the wheelchair, Greg knelt down in front of him. "And you must be Chad," he said as he extended his hand to Chad.

For a moment, Chad simply looked at the extended hand.

"Chad," said Bill. "It's okay. He's going to help you."

Very slowly, Chad extended his hand and met Greg's handshake.

"It's very nice to meet you," said Greg. "I promise you're going to enjoy yourself while you're here."

Standing up, Greg looked at Bill and couldn't help but smile.

"What is it?" asked Bill.

Giving a slight chuckle, Greg said, "Oh…it's just like looking back in time when I look at you. You have that same look in your eyes as your father did when he was your age."

"What, that same tired, bloodshot, sleep deprived look?" said Bill jokingly.

Greg laughed. "Well only when your father won a race and got off his face."

Looking at Greg with bewilderment, Bill asked, "Off his face?"

"Yeah, you know...drunk."

Both men stared blankly for a second before Greg erupted in laughter.

"Ah...Australian lingo," said Greg. "I reckon you've got a bit of a head start in learning it because of your old man but you'll be catching on in no time."

At that point, the baggage claim came alive as suitcases began to fall into the rotating carousel. At once, a mass of people flooded the carousel to find their bags. Bill did not want to fight through a crowd so he was content on waiting.

"So how is the old man? Still causing a bit of a ruckus?" asked Greg.

Thinking about the trick he pulled on Helen, Bill said, "You have no idea."

"I can only imagine. If he's still pulling half of the pranks he did when he was here, it's a wonder that he's not in prison yet," said Greg. "There was this one time back when we were young—he somehow got ahold of three goats and released them into our school. But before he did that, though, he painted numbers onto the side of them: One, two and four. I tell you, the school officials were looking for that third goat for weeks."

Both men erupted in laughter, which drew the attention of just about everyone in the vicinity. Looking down, Bill even noticed that Chad had a smile on his face.

After several minutes, Bill finally went forward and retrieved the four bags which contained all of what remained of their old life—clothes, files, books and various other items. Bill found packing for a new life in only four suitcases to be the hardest part of the preparation.

Greg grabbed a small baggage trolley, helped Bill load up his luggage and led the way to the parking lot where his car was waiting. After a few minutes of walking, they finally approached Greg's car and Bill immediately stopped.

"What the hell is that?" asked Bill as he pointed towards Greg's car.

Laughing slightly, Greg answered, "I forgot that you American's don't have the same cars we have over here. This fine specimen is a Vauxhall VXR8 GTS."

Bill immediately began walking around the car as if inspecting it. One of the first things he noticed, however, was that the driver's seat was on the right.

"Well that's different," said Bill.

"I imagine it'll take some getting used to," said Greg as he popped the trunk open. "But from what I hear, you're quite the driver like your father was."

Bill shrugged his shoulders and said, "I don't really do that sort of thing anymore."

"Fair enough. But if you ever want to take her out," Greg said as he pointed to the car, "you just let me know."

Greg helped Bill get the remaining suitcases loaded into the car and folded Chad's wheelchair up after getting him inside. Once everything and everyone was inside, they set off.

They had only been on the road for a few minutes when Bill turned around to see Chad staring up at the sights around Sydney. Despite it being night, the many buildings throughout the city were lit up and Chad was awestruck by the new scenery and sounds. Bill smiled at the nostalgic sight of his son being mesmerized by the country which his grandfather had been raised in.

"It'll probably take you both a few days to get used to the time change," said Greg as he noticed Chad wide awake at a late hour. "Other than that, I'll make sure you feel right at home."

"I can't tell you how much I appreciate you doing this for Chad," said Bill.

"It's not a problem at all, mate. Speaking of Chad, how long has it been since he…you know," asked Greg as he made a speaking motion with his hand.

"Almost two months now. Ever since I told him about…" Bill paused and hesitated to say her name.

"I gotcha, mate," whispered Greg as he gestured towards Chad. "We'll talk more about it later."

"Fair enough," replied Bill.

"Well," said Greg, trying to change the subject, "I can start with Chad in the next few days. That'll give you both some time to settle in and get situated. But for now, let's get you boys home. I'm sure you're both exhausted."

They were only a few minutes away from Greg's house when Bill began to doze off slightly. As the car was still moving, he could feel his head slowly start to spin. Still in a half sleep stupor, Bill could feel his head dipping from side to side as he tried to go to sleep…or tried to stay awake. He couldn't quite decide what he was doing. One thing was for certain, however. He felt like he was getting sick.

As they pulled up to Greg's house—which Bill wasn't even able to get a good look at—they came to a stop near what appeared to be a gate. As the car stopped moving while the gate opened, Bill snapped awake and immediately began to feel lightheaded.

"Did they give you a good feed on the plane, mate? I've got all sorts of food, and you're more than welcome to help yourself to whatever you'd like," said Greg as they passed through the gate but failed to realize what was going on next to him.

To Bill, the entire world seemed to be spinning. He was unable to see straight or clearly and he felt a ringing in his ears.

As Greg pulled the car into his driveway, he pushed the garage door opener button and looked over at Bill.

"Well, here we are. Home sweet…" Greg couldn't finish. "Are you alright, mate?"

"Yeah, I'm good. Just feeling a little dizzy, that's all," said Bill.

"When was the last time you ate or drank something?" asked Greg.

"You know, I don't quite remember. I'm sorry, would you mind if I get out now and get some fresh air?" asked Bill.

"Of course, mate. Go right ahead," said Greg.

Bill opened the car door and stepped his left foot out. The last thing he remembered was that he was face down in the grass before he blacked out.

* * *

"What did you feed him before he left? A rotten chicken?"

A long pause filled with undecipherable murmurs was all that could be heard. "No, mate. I haven't even given him an Aussie beer yet. The man just collapsed before I could give him a good feed."

It was hard to understand what the murmurs were saying but it sounded distinctively like laughter.

Laughter?

Bill slowly opened his eyes to find himself lying on a large leather couch with a cool damp towel on his head. The room he was in was massive. A large sectional furniture set of dark brown leather which he was currently lying on sat across from a fireplace which had a small fire going. Various types of plants were spread out over the room with modern art pieces all over the walls. As his eyes wandered more, he could see Greg pacing in the large kitchen while talking on the phone.

At that moment, Greg looked over to see that Bill was now awake. Bill didn't even need to guess who Greg was talking to.

"I think your stench woke him up all the way over here, Will," said Greg as he laughed out loud.

"Oh God," said Bill softly with a smile as he began to realize what had happened. He knew that he would never hear the end of it from his father…or from Greg.

"Alright, mate. I'll tell him…Yep. Cheers," said Greg as he hung up the phone.

Walking over to Bill, Greg retrieved a glass of water which was on the kitchen table and brought it to Bill as he pulled up a chair and sat down beside him.

"Here, mate. Drink this," said Greg.

Putting the glass to his lips, Bill slowly sipped the water until it was gone.

"You gave me quite a fright. I've never seen someone faceplant into the ground like that before. You're lucky you didn't break something."

Slowly trying to sit up, Bill asked, "Where's Chad?"

Pushing Bill back down, Greg said, "There's no need to get up, mate. Chad's in his bedroom upstairs, reading. I've taken care of everything. Sit tight and I'll get you some food."

Greg rose from his seat and went back to the kitchen where he retrieved something that Bill was not expecting.

"Here ya go, mate. Just how you yanks like 'em…I hope," said Greg as he handed Bill a large cheeseburger along with a plate of fries.

"You'd better eat all of it, too. You need the calories," said Greg.

"Spoken like a true doctor," said Bill as he dove into his American delicacy.

"Just don't make a habit of eating like this too often," said Greg. "I've never been to Texas before—or America for that matter—but I've heard everything is bigger over there…especially the inhabitants."

Bill, who was too busy chewing on his burger, could only give an annoyed look at Greg who was laughing away.

"Well you look like you take care of yourself so I won't give you a hard time," said Greg as he slapped Bill on the back.

Now already halfway through his burger, Bill could feel his strength return to him. He stretched his legs out in front of him as he remembered what Greg had just told his dad when they got off the phone.

"Just now when you were on the phone with my dad; he said something and you'd said you'd tell me. What was it?" asked Bill.

"Oh, it's nothing big. He just wanted me to tell..."

Greg's words stopped short as something caught the attention of his eyes. "There you are, you little bastard," said Greg with a low and sinister voice.

Bill, all of the sudden feeling afraid, turned to see what Greg had fixed his eyes on. Sticking out from underneath a chair across from him was the small, almost unnoticeable head of a snake. By the look of it, the snake appeared to be small in size. It was about ten feet away from them but Bill wasn't able to make out its features. For some reason, however, Greg was on high alert.

"What, that little guy?" said Bill.

"Don't let its size fool you, mate," said Greg softly as he slowly began to stand. "I've been looking for this one for a few days now and I haven't had a good night's sleep since I first saw him."

Not sure what all of Greg's worries were about, Bill said, "Why all of the fuss over a little snake like that? It's probably nothing more than a garden snake."

"Have you lost your head?" said Greg in a hushed but intense voice. "That's no garden snake, mate. That's a brown snake!"

Unfamiliar with brown snakes, Bill said, "I'm guessing brown snakes pack a bit of a bite, then?"

"They're one of the most poisonous snakes in the world. One this size probably has enough venom to kill a dozen humans," said Greg as he crept closer to the deadly snake.

Although Bill had been born and raised in Texas and had seen his fair share of snakes, he had no love for them. He was no expert on the various types of snakes but he also didn't want them anywhere near his yard, especially when Chad was younger and running around. Therefore, it was not a big deal for Bill to grab a garden hoe when he found one and "send it back to the fiery abyss from whence it came" as he used to tell Lena.

With that in mind, Bill asked, "So how are you going to kill it?"

Greg stopped and turned around to look at Bill. "Kill it? No, I'm not going to kill it, mate. It hasn't done anything to me. It's only doing what it needs to do to survive. I'll catch him and call a snake removal specialist out here. They'll relocate him to a better place more snake friendly."

"You're going to catch it?" asked Bill who was suddenly very nervous. "How are you gonna do that?"

"Well, mate, I reckon I'm gonna do it with your help," said Greg with a smile.

"No, no, no, no, no," said Bill as he sat his plate down on the glass coffee table in front of him. "I don't do snake grabbing."

"I'm not asking you to grab it, mate," said Greg with a slight chuckle. "I just need you to move the chair away so I can get to him."

Bill froze momentarily at the thought of being within a few feet of such a poisonous snake. Greg, sensing Bill's nervousness, said, "Well don't soil your pants, mate. C'mon, let's get this done."

Giving in, Bill rose slowly and began to walk closer to the poisonous reptile. As he approached, he put his hands on the very edge of the chair while trying to stay as far away as possible.

"Alright, then," whispered Greg. "Go ahead and lift it up slowly."

Bill began to pick up the chair, which he discovered was much heavier than it looked. As he was lifting, he glanced over to see the look on Greg's face. With the chair in his arms, he couldn't see the snake anymore and now had to rely on Greg's expressions to tell him if something was happening.

He began to slowly back up with the chair in his grasp when Greg's face suddenly became fearful.

"It's moving! Back up! Back up!" shouted Greg.

Bill moved backwards as fast as he could while carrying the heavy chair. Still slightly light-headed from the earlier incident, the weight of the chair caused him to fall backwards towards the glass coffee table. At the last second, Greg caught him with a solid hand on his upper back to keep Bill from falling.

"I've got ya, mate," said Greg with a smile. "No more dives tonight, alright?"

Setting the chair down on the ground, Bill simply nodded up and down as he sighed.

They both turned to look at the snake that was now in a corner of the room but facing out towards the two men.

"Well this is gonna be more difficult than I thought," said Greg. "I can't grab him because of the way he's sitting so I need you to distract him."

"You want me to distract a venomous snake?" asked Bill.

"Yeah, just get him to look at you. You've got him nice and pissed now so it shouldn't be too hard," said Greg who was now breathing a little heavy. "Just walk up to him from the side, get him to look at you and I'll grab him from the other side."

Another long pause ensued as Bill closed his eyes and took a long but deep breath.

"Alright," said Bill as he tried to psych himself up. "Just walk up to it." He began to take small baby steps toward the snake from the left side of the wall as Greg approached from the right. "Just walk up to the snake." He was now within five feet of it. "Just walk up to the super poisonous snake."

The snake was still stretched out and appeared to be staring between Bill and Greg. Suddenly, it turned its attention toward Greg. Stopping, Greg said, "This is it for me, Bill. I need you to move closer. If I back up, I won't be able to grab him."

Slowly, Bill inched his way closer to the snake but the snake didn't take its eyes off of Greg.

"I think he likes you, Greg," said Bill.

At that second, the snake turned to look at Bill and raised a quarter of its body up and flattened its neck.

"Be careful, Bill. These bastards are very quick," said Greg who could no longer hide his fear behind a veil of humor.

"Just one more step," said Greg.

Bill took a deep breath and lifted his left foot. Before he even had a chance to move it forward and put it down, however, the snake moved towards Bill who, at the sight of the movement, jumped backwards and fell up against the wall behind him. With its mouth open and neck coiled up and ready to strike, the snake pursued. Bill had nowhere to go as he was trapped between the wall and the sofa where he was previously sitting. The impact of landing on his butt along with the continued dizziness from earlier caused his world to spin. The only thing he could do was curl up as tight as he could and await the venomous bite.

The snake was only inches away when, all of the sudden, Greg flew into view with his left arm fully extended. He landed flat on the ground, grabbed the snake by its tail with his extended hand and pulled. With one swift motion, Greg shot up from being face down to being on his feet and brought the snake along with him. He stood up tall with a large smile on his face as he held the snake up in the air by its tail.

"Good job, mate! You did great!" said Greg.

"Are you kidding? I almost got bit!"

"Oh I wasn't going to let that happen to you. You'll be alright," said Greg with a smile.

Holding the squirming snake with his left hand, Greg extended his right hand and helped Bill up to his feet. "I'll go put this guy somewhere he can't get out of," said Greg as he slapped Bill on the shoulder.

Bill, still shocked at his close encounter with one of the most venomous snakes in the world, stood motionless with his mouth hanging open.

"Oh, I almost forgot," said Greg as he walked away. "What your dad wanted me to tell you…"

Stopping, Greg turned to Bill.

CHAPTER 8

"Welcome to Straya."

Chapter 9

The initial weeks after making the move to Australia passed by quickly for Bill as Chad began his physical therapy routines with Greg. Although fairly simple to the eye, Greg informed Bill that these "passive range of motion exercises", as Greg called them, also worked hand in hand with the electrical stimulation therapy which he said would, "begin the healing process for the spinal cord."

Although he was there for every one of Chad's therapy sessions, the days soon began to wear upon Bill. He was still able to do some work remotely for his business, but the time zone difference meant that Bill was only able to work at night in Australia which was morning in Texas. This meant during the day, Bill oftentimes had nothing to do other than respond to the occasional email.

At first, Bill enjoyed the quiet of the day as well the opportunity he had to share this time with his son. As the days went by, however, he began getting restless. In all of his professional years as an adult, Bill had never had a break like this and, quite frankly, he didn't know what to do with himself.

After about a week, Bill began looking around the house for things to do. This was quickly dismissed, however, as Greg kept his house in excellent condition. Eventually, Bill began wandering around the outside of Greg's house hoping that maybe he could at least cut the man's grass or something to that effect. That, too, was frivolous as Greg had a landscaping company which regularly visited his house and maintained his property.

One evening, Bill decided he would vent the restlessness he was having by going for a run. Surely that was something he was still able to do. Greg, however, advised against this idea.

"It's not safe to be running about at night around here, mate," said Greg. "A lot of trouble makers are wandering around the roads at this hour."

Dismayed, Bill finally resorted to doing something which he always got on his father's case for doing; parking himself on a couch and watching television. This was amusing at first to see all of the different shows and news stations in Australia. As the days dragged on, however, this too became wearisome.

One particular Sunday, however, Bill was flipping through the channels and he stumbled upon a highlight reel from an auto race. He didn't immediately recognize the cars being used or the track they were racing on. One thing was for sure, though; Bill couldn't take his eyes off of it.

Never being a big fan of watching races on television, Bill had always said he'd rather be at the race and experience the atmosphere. This race, however, was something else. These were large sedans which resembled the American NASCAR vehicles except that these cars were on a road course as opposed to the ovals typically associated with NASCAR. Eventually, Bill caught wind of what he was watching. The feeling took him back to his childhood.

"So I see you've found our national sport," said Greg as he entered the room from behind where Bill was sitting. "The Virgin Australia Supercars Series; the greatest show on four wheels, as some say."

"I haven't seen one of these races since I was a kid," said Bill. "They don't really air these overseas." Still fascinated by the race, Bill added, "These cars look so different from the ones I saw growing up."

"Yeah the cars your old man used to race are probably stashed away in some museum somewhere," said Greg. "I don't watch the races as much as I'd like to so I couldn't give you any specifics about the cars—but one thing's for sure; they're still very fast."

Bill kept his eyes glued to the TV as the commentator briefly recapped the race which was apparently held the week prior. "It looks like it's not just Ford and Holden out there anymore," said Bill referencing the addition of the Nissan Altima Supercars. "Is the Ford and Holden rivalry still raging on?"

Although he wasn't up to date with the current events of the sport, Bill knew enough about it from his dad to remember the oftentimes bitter rivalry between the manufacturers of Ford, represented by the blue oval, and Holden, represented by the red lion.

Greg didn't immediately answer the question which prompted Bill to turn around to see what was happening. He was met by the stare of a man who looked as if someone had just slapped him across the face.

"There never was a rivalry, mate," said Greg annoyingly. "That's because there's no competition against a Holden."

"Oh don't tell me you're a Holden guy," said Bill with a smile.

"Born and raised, mate. You won't find a blue fabric in this house. Well except for some of your rubbish, I suppose," said Greg.

Bill had a number of Ford shirts which he had collected over the years, and they'd become a part of his regular wardrobe.

"Hey, I'm a guest," said Bill. "You can make an exception, right?"

"I suppose so, mate. Even the losing team needs its cheerleaders, I reckon."

Gesturing back towards the events on the TV which was currently focused on the winning car, Greg said, "Take this guy; Derek Renshaw. He used to be a Ford driver; could hardly ever crack the top-ten in a race. Now he's in a Holden and he practically wins every race. He's an ass and a poor sportsman, but he's a helluva Holden driver."

"Why do you say that about him?" asked Bill.

"Oh it's just little things he does that makes the sport look bad," said Greg. Turning to look at Bill, he added, "Speaking of looking bad, have you looked in the mirror lately? You look like a bloody caveman's pet orangutan."

It had been several weeks since Bill had shaved, and his beard had now turned into an unruly mess. On top of that, it had been much longer since he had gotten a haircut.

"Yeah I'm just kind of…bored," said Bill reluctantly. "I don't mean to sound disrespectful because I'm very thankful to be here for Chad's sake, but I just don't have anything to do."

Greg lowered his brow slightly and looked off to the side as if he was thinking. "Tell you what, mate. You've been cooped up in here for quite a bit now. I'm surprised you haven't lost your mind. Why don't you take the car tonight and get out for a bit," said Greg.

"I appreciate it, Greg, but I need to stay here with Chad. He's the reason I'm here," said Bill.

"For one, I wasn't asking you. I'm telling you to take my car and get out for a bit," said Greg as he threw the keys to Bill. "Secondly, I'm the reason you're here. You need me to help take care of your son and that's what I'm going to do. You can't take care of him if you can't take care of yourself. I know he still isn't speaking but if he was, he'd probably tell you to get out for a bit, too."

"Alright, alright," said Bill. "I won't fight you on this one. I could use some time to myself."

"If you're interested, there's a bar a little ways from here called Bear Knuckles. The owner's a friend of mine from a good ways back and I believe he knows your dad. His name's Tubbs."

"Tubbs?" echoed Bill.

"You'll figure it out, mate," said Greg with a smile. "Tell him who your dad is and he'll probably give you a drink on the house or something."

"Thanks for the heads up. I might just do that," said Bill.

"Oh and do be careful, mate," said Greg. "There's a reason they call it Bear Knuckles. Some of the patrons can sometimes be quite…lively."

* * *

It had been quite some time since Bill had been able to take a breather and simply go out. In fact, he hadn't done so since Lena's death. So much time had been spent in mourning the loss of Lena, realizing his new way of life with Chad, planning the move to Australia and adapting to yet another new way of life that he honestly could not remember the last time he was able to have what is affectionately known as 'man time.'

As he prepared for a night on the town, he took Greg's advice and trimmed his beard to look more presentable and styled his hair—which was longer than he'd ever had it—so that it looked cleaner. Just as he was about to leave the house, however, Bill felt as if he was missing something. He did a quick equipment check to ensure that he had everything he needed.

"Phone, wallet, keys…" said Bill as he patted down each item with his hand as he named them off.

"Ring…"

That was it. He wasn't wearing his wedding ring. Immediately—and more so out of habit—Bill started towards the bathroom where he kept his ring but stopped short. In his mind, he argued whether or not he should put it on since, technically, he was no longer married. He had worn the ring everywhere he went since his wedding day. Even since the accident which claimed Lena's life, Bill had continued to wear the ring. More out of a fear of abandonment that if he stopped wearing it that Lena would truly be gone, Bill had never bothered to entertain the thought of *not* wearing the ring. Until now. Indeed, it had become almost an automatic process for him; something he would normally do without even thinking about it. He always put the ring on before he left to go anywhere and took it off when he went to bed.

As he stood in the hallway of Greg's house halfway between the bathroom and the door to freedom, however, Bill stared down at his empty ring finger which, over the years, had developed a slight tan line around where his ring would normally be. As he continued to contemplate which decision he should make, he remembered why he came here.

"As much as you're going there primarily for Chad, you need a fresh start, Bill," said William before their departure from home.

A fresh start.

Those words hung in Bill's mind for several seconds as he stood motionless in the hallway. Deep inside, Bill knew what he needed to do. But there was something else; some sinister feeling he could sense inside of him that if he didn't put that ring on, he'd truly be alone.

It had been nearly three months since Lena's death.

No. It's too soon.

He felt frozen, unable to move or leave this train of thought which seemed to hijack his mind. A thousand different memories, words and thoughts seemed to be storming through his head at once and he found it impossible to shake it loose. With this feeling came the sensation that he was being pulled underwater. Unable to breathe or move, he felt as if he was choking on indecisiveness.

"A fresh start," Bill whispered to himself. "Or should I? This is all I have left…"

All of a sudden, he was pulled to the surface and away from the storm of his mind by the heavy hand of Greg landing on his shoulder from behind. "Just don't forget to fill the car back up before you bring her back. That big V8 is thirsty!" said Greg as he walked by.

"Uh, yeah. Will do," said Bill as he was still trying to come to his senses.

With his mind suddenly free, he took a deep breath followed by a step forward.

* * *

Bear Knuckles was not at all what Bill had expected. As he pulled up, he noticed a giant grizzly bear standing above the doorway of the building. At first glance, he didn't think anything of the heinous-sized grizzly bear—which stood over 20 feet in height—until he took a second look. As Bill did a double-take, he noticed that the giant bear had human fists and it appeared to be in a classic fighting stance. As Bill walked between its legs which led to the front door of the establishment, he said to himself, "Where did you send me, Greg? Crocodile Dundee's house?"

Entering the bar, Bill did a quick survey of the area before he walked any further. At first, he noticed the typical style bar one would expect to see, which featured a wooden counter top, vinyl wrapped bar stools which had bear faces on the seats, an assortment of drinks lining the wall on the other side of the bar and numerous televisions which were all airing various sporting events.

A good sized crowd was huddled around the largest of the televisions but what was being shown was hidden from Bill because of the angle he was currently standing. As he turned his gaze, he noticed that the bar extended much further back and he could see tables and booths which he guessed were for sit-down meals.

It was what Bill saw next which captivated his gaze. As he looked past the tables and the booths, he could see what looked like a tube chassis from a car sitting on the ground in the back of the bar. In front of it was a large curved screen which seemed to wrap 180 degrees around the front of the frame. Above it were three video projectors which, when combined, appeared to create one solid image. What the entire contraption was, however, was unknown to Bill as an even larger crowd was gathered around it. The only thing he could hear coming from that direction was a rowdy crowd giving off a few cheers and the occasional choice word.

Bill walked in and grabbed a seat at the bar close to the large TV which still had about 8-10 people sitting around it. As he looked to see what they were watching, he was very surprised to see that it was an American NASCAR race. Bill couldn't help but chuckle at the irony.

A sudden roar from the back where the roll cage contraption was located caused Bill to turn his head to the left to see what was going on.

"What'll it be, mate?" said a female voice.

Bill turned back to notice a woman standing behind the bar with an almost annoyed look on her face as she held an empty glass in her hand.

Bill thought the woman, who was stunningly beautiful, couldn't have been any older than 25, although her tan skin and long, curly blonde hair made it difficult to accurately guess her age. Wearing a name tag which read, "Abby", she seemed taller than her figure would allow. Still, her green eyes appeared tired as she tried to smile. It was obvious she'd been at work all day. Wearing a brown shirt with an apron around her waist, she stood waiting on Bill's response.

"Hi, there," said Bill with a smile. "I was told to ask for Tubbs."

At that, several of the patrons who were watching the NASCAR race on TV turned to look at Bill.

"Tubbs, huh? Who wants to know?" she asked suspiciously.

Before Bill could even answer, Bill heard a loud voice coming from the crowd around the TV.

"You new here? Where you from, mate?" asked one of the men.

"I guess it's hard to hide an American accent around here. I'm from Texas," said Bill.

"Texas?!" shouted the man as he stood up. "What brings a man from Texas into this bar?"

"I'm in town," Bill said as he tried to act calm. "A friend of mine recommended this place. Thought I'd come by and have a look around."

"A look around, huh?" said the man in a husky voice as he slowly began to walk towards Bill.

Once the man cleared the crowd which was still watching the race, Bill was able to get a look at him unobscured.

The man was a giant to say the least. With a short military-type haircut and a clean-shaven appearance, the man's intimidating face appeared to be made of leather, which led Bill to believe that he'd spent a large amount of time in the sun. Slightly older than he first appeared, it seemed that every ounce of him was pure muscle with arms which looked as if they could suffocate a wild boar. He wore a tight black t-shirt tucked into black jeans which further illustrated his physical form. Bill could hear the *thud* of heavy boots with every step the man took.

And this mountain of a man was walking towards Bill...

"Maybe your friend's not too wise, huh? Maybe your friend thought it'd be funny to send an American into a bar...that doesn't like Americans," said the man in a low but eerie voice.

Greg, I'm going to kill you.

He felt a lump grow in his throat but he stood his ground.

"Well, friend, I'm just here for a drink. I don't want any trouble," said Bill. He knew he'd set himself up as soon as the words left his mouth.

"Sometimes trouble finds you whether you're looking for it or not. Maybe you're just in the wrong place at the wrong time...friend," said the man as he stopped mere inches away from Bill.

Bill knew he had nowhere to go. If this guy was indeed looking to cause a fight, Bill was in for it. He had nothing around him he could use as a weapon that would do any harm to a man of this size. He couldn't run because he was sitting on a bar stool which was drilled to the ground. The man would be all over him in less than a second if Bill decided to flee. Knowing that he had no options, Bill played along.

"Maybe I go wherever I want to go," said Bill with as much authority as he could muster up as he looked the much larger man directly in the eyes.

The man took a step closer and slammed his heavy fist down hard on the bar next to Bill. "Maybe I'll rip off your head and take a massive shit down your neck!"

"Go right ahead," said Bill as he sniffed with his nose, "By the smell of your breath, I'm guessing you've already practiced on yourself."

The two stood only a few inches apart as they stared each other down. Finally, after a few seconds, the massive man burst into laughter along with the entire group which was watching the race behind him.

"That's a good one, mate!" said the man as he continued laughing. Bill, who could tell that he had a slightly shocked look on his face, glanced at the female bartender who was now smiling as she shook her head side-to-side.

"He does that to as many new people as he can," said Abby.

"And he didn't back down!" barked the man. "What's your name, mate?"

"Bill Watson. And you?"

"Watson, huh? And you say you're from Texas, right? You don't say. Abby, I reckon I'm seeing a ghost of some sort," said the man.

"I reckon you're right, Tubbs," said Abby with a smile.

"Tubbs?" said Bill, surprised.

"The only Watson I've ever heard of who would have the balls to come into this bar is also in Texas, last I heard," said Tubbs.

"That would probably be my dad..."

"William Watson," Tubbs said as he finished Bill's sentence. "That's a name I haven't heard in a long time and a name I'll never forget. Like some damn Highlander's name, or something. That bloody bastard is why I hate Americans. I lost a lot of money on him!"

"How so?" asked Bill.

"The man wins the championship in his debut season. Practically unheard of," said Tubbs. "So I bet that if a rookie can do it once on his first season, he could do it again the next season. And when I say 'I bet', I mean I bet a lot, which means I lost a lot after he decided to leave us all behind to become an American."

Bill smiled. "Well if this is your place, you seem to be doing very well for yourself."

"Yeah, that was a long time ago and a lot has changed," said Tubbs. He looked at Bill with a sinister smile. "Maybe I shake you down, huh? Take back what I lost on your father!"

"Well the way I see it, you owe me about $30," said Bill.

"How do you figure?" asked Tubbs curiously.

"Let's just say that I'm going to need a new pair of pants after what you just pulled on me," said Bill.

Everyone in earshot distance burst into laughter at the comment.

"You're alright in my book," said Tubbs. "Abby, give the man a drink on the house."

* * *

For the next half-hour or so, Bill and Tubbs relayed information and stories pertaining to Bill's dad as well as Bill's own racing experience and what brought him to Australia to begin with. Tubbs humbly listened and only stopped to ask a question once every few minutes. Exchanging stories, Tubbs relayed to Bill how he got started in business after serving in the Australian army. Bill was also surprised to learn that Tubbs was a nickname given to him by his dad, William.

"He was a bit older than me when we first met, and let's just say I was a bit large for my age," said Tubbs. "And by 'large' I don't mean Australian-large, I mean American-large if you catch my drift."

Bill could only smile and nod at the comment.

"Anyways," continued Tubbs, "I was with all of my friends when I got to meet the driver who was taking the—at that time—Australian

Touring Car Series by storm in his debut season: William Watson. He was signing autographs and my friends and I were up next."

Tubbs took another long gulp of his beer and continued. "Finally, I walk up to him and couldn't even find my words, mate. I mean, this guy was my bloody hero. So he looks at me and says, 'You're a big boy, aren't ya? What do they call ya, mate?'

"I was completely tongue-tied. Finally, he grabs the hat I had for him to sign, autographs it and says to me, 'Alright, Tubbs. You hold on to that.' Ever since then, the name kinda stuck."

"Where's that hat now?" asked Bill.

"In some box somewhere," answered Tubbs. "I don't really follow racing too much anymore, but a lot of the patrons here do."

Just then, a roar of applause came from the back of the room where the giant car frame was located. "And that, mate, is the only reason why I keep that debauchery in here," explained Tubbs as he pointed behind him towards the large device.

Bill looked over Tubbs' shoulder to get a better look. "What is it?"

"Some big video game or 'driving simulator' as the boys call it," said Tubbs sounding slightly irritated. "People come from all over to have a go on that thing."

Bill, still fixated on the simulator, asked, "So is it just an arcade game or something?"

"Oh no, mate," exclaimed Tubbs as he turned to look at the simulator.

"This thing is as close as you can get to the real deal without actually costing you money when you bin it into a wall," explained Tubbs. "It about cost me my left nut to get it, but ever since I did, it's hardly ever gone unused."

Through the crowds, Bill could just make out the scene. There were about 15-20 people all crowded around it and, above the constant cheering which was often mixed with vulgar insults, taunts and general negative comments, Bill could hear the roar of an engine broadcast over the loudspeakers set up around the simulator chassis.

The sound of the engine sent chills down Bill's spine. It was the first time he had heard the all too familiar sound in quite some time, and there was no denying that he missed it.

There was something else, as well. As whoever was in the simulator finished and exited it—similar to how one would exit a real racecar—Bill saw the driver and felt that he had seen him before from somewhere. As much as he tried to pin it, the thought of the person's identity eluded him.

A hard and sudden slap on the shoulder from Tubbs snapped Bill out of his daze.

"Well are you just gonna sit there and shit yourself again or are you gonna go back there and show those arses how they do it in America?" asked Tubbs who laughed as Bill jumped upon the physical contact.

"The driver who just got out, I feel like I've seen him before. Who is he?" asked Bill.

"That guy? Well you're pretty well informed for only being in-country for a short period of time. That's Derek Renshaw. He's a..."

"A Supercars driver," said Bill. "What's he doing in here?"

"Him and his mates usually come in here if they're around after a race weekend," said Tubbs. "He's part of the reason why I have to stay in shape. I've had to throw his sorry arse out on a number of occasions. That only pisses his mates off and then a fight usually breaks out."

"Why don't you kick him out permanently?" asked Bill.

"He has his uses, mate. He's good for business, and he brings a good crowd more oftentimes than not," said Tubbs. "So are you going to race him or not?"

Bill, who was initially stunned by the question, said, "I...uh...I don't really race anymore."

"The hell you don't!" exclaimed Tubbs. "Your father is a racing legend in this country, and from what you told me, you've got the same blood running through your veins."

"Yeah but I just don't..."

"I don't care what you think you don't do anymore. You're in my bar and your drinks have been on me. So unless you want to repay me for all of the beer you and I just drank..."

"Your beer, too!?" exclaimed Bill.

"You're going to take your Yankee ass back there and race," finished Tubbs.

"You're going to be that like, huh?"

"You're damn right I'm going to be like that. Don't bring some sympathy shit sob story to my table," said Tubbs, alluding to the story Bill had told him about Lena's accident. "I'm sorry to hear about it, but right now, I'm not taking 'no' for an answer."

"What, am I in fifth grade again? Are you gonna flick a booger at me or something if I don't?" asked Bill sarcastically.

Tubbs stood up to full height and looked down on Bill as he said, "No, but I'll wring your sorry little neck and toss you back there myself!"

Holding his open palms toward the larger man in defeat, Bill conceded. "Alright, alright. At least if I make a fool of myself, I never have to come back."

Standing up and stepping away from the table, he was half tempted to simply walk out of the bar. However, another part of him was curious to try the contraption, even if he didn't want to admit it.

"This is your fault, you know," said Bill.

"My fault? You haven't even done anything yet, mate. Where's your pride?" said Tubbs as Bill turned and walked towards the simulator.

From behind Tubbs, Abby appeared. Holding a glass in one hand and a cleaning towel in another, she asked, "Why'd you make him do that? The man came in here for a drink and you've gone and thrown him into the lion's den."

Sitting back down, Tubbs chuckled to himself. "Honestly? I just wanna see what's gonna happen."

"You're impossible," said Abby. Shrugging her shoulders, she added,

"Still, let me know what happens."

Laughing to himself, Tubbs said, "Believe me, Abbs. I'm sure you'll see it for yourself."

* * *

Bill felt like a kindergartner who was walking toward the monkey bars which were surrounded by the bigger kids as he walked towards the rear of the bar. Approaching the simulator, the first person who noticed Bill began spreading murmurs about the approaching stranger.

"Hey, look at this," Bill heard one man whisper to another.

"That's the yank that came in earlier," he heard another say.

His presence began spreading like a wildfire as head after head began turning to notice Bill. Before long, Derek Renshaw had his eyes fixed on him as he approached.

Derek Renshaw was a man of small stature and build. Although he appeared to be physically fit and roughly around Bill's age, he was more of the *beanpole* physique. He had short but spikey dark hair, olive skin and wore a white t-shirt that read "I'm with loser," which had arrows pointing both left and right. A five-o'clock shadow peppered his face and, as he approached Bill, perfect white teeth filled his modeled smile.

Walking forward to meet Bill, Derek extended his hand in greeting. "You're the new guy here," said Renshaw. "I'm Derek and these are my mates. Well most of 'em anyways."

Bill extended his hand and met Derek's handshake. At once, several of the people standing alongside of him began snickering and whispering amongst themselves.

Through all of the childish and drunken talk, Bill finally made out what someone had said.

"Derek's just rubbed his balls and shook this yank's hand!"

Still shaking Derek's hand, Bill had to fight to not recoil once he heard what was happening. He didn't want to appear weak in front of this crowd.

"Bill," was all he could get out.

Although Bill didn't have an accent, his single word was enough for some of the people who didn't know his origins to pick up that he was from America. Some began mimicking his voice with a southern accent, which was quite humorous when combined with their native Australian tongue.

"You lost, mate?" asked Derek with a sinister smirk as he released his hand.

"Nope. Just thought I'd come back here and give this thing a try," said Bill as he began looking the simulator over. "So, where do you put the quarters in?"

Several of the people standing around chuckled as Derek flashed a grin. "You done any racing before, mate?" asked Derek.

"I've done a few laps," countered Bill.

"A few laps," echoed Derek. "The man's done a few laps, he says."

A few of the people began a taunting "Ohhh" as if in deep suspense.

Bill couldn't help but smile at the antics.

A lone voice from amongst the crowd emerged and said, "I've heard he's done more than a few laps."

Here it comes, thought Bill.

"This yank is William Watson's son," said the voice.

There was a brief moment of silence as everyone in the immediate area seemed to suddenly gain an ounce of respect for Bill. Derek was the one who finally broke the silence.

"Old Watson's son, huh?"

"Heard him talking with Tubbs earlier," said the man in the crowd. "Said he gave up racing, too."

"Like father, like son," said Derek as some of the men in the crowd laughed. "The old man just took the money and ran. Afraid to lose it, is what I'd say."

Bill had had enough of the antics. "It's a good thing I didn't come back here to hear what you had to say. I'm here to try this little toy out," said Bill as he brushed past Derek towards the simulator.

Built into a roll cage like that of an actual race car, the inside of the simulator looked almost identical to that of a real car including the one minor detail of the seat being on the right hand side which put the shifter to the left of the driver.

As Bill was about to climb into the simulator, he cast a glance back to Tubbs whom was standing and watching all of the action with his massive arms crossed.

Taking a seat inside the cockpit, Bill suddenly felt out of place. He had never been one to play computer games before and could feel a touch of anxiety sweep over him.

He had no idea what to do to get the thing going.

Like a real race car, there was a five-point harness which Bill strapped himself into. Once the final harness strap clicked together, he was firmly secured into the seat.

"All of the cars and tracks in this simulator are laser scanned from their respective real-life counterparts," said a new voice coming from behind him. "That means everything is accurate down to the smallest detail. It's already setup up to run, but I don't think it's exactly fair to pit you up against the Mountain on your first go..."

"The hell with you, Lathan," said Derek. "The man's the son of a Bathurst winner. I'd love to see him have a go at the Mountain in our car."

The crowd behind Bill cheered in approval.

"He's setting you up for failure," said the voice only identified as Lathan. He spoke much quieter now but was closer to Bill's ear so that only he could hear him.

"This is one of the most challenging circuits in the world. Have you ever even seen a race here before?"

"When I was younger but it's been awhile," answered Bill.

"Just take it slow at first. You'll be in a Ford Falcon Supercar and they're not overly polite to foreigners or beginners," said Lathan. "I'll do my best to walk you through it."

A hand reached up to the mouse and keyboard which were off to the side. After a few clicks, the screen in front of Bill showed the view from inside of a race car parked in pit lane.

Bill's heart began to race.

"The shifter is sequential," said Lathan. "Pull it towards you to up-shift and away to downshift. The footwork is the same as your h-pattern transmission but you have the option of not using the clutch on the downshifts. In that case, you just blip the throttle when shifting."

"Dog box transmission?" asked Bill.

"That's right," said Lathan who sounded impressed. "These cars have a lot of power but the tires which feel like they're from a small highway car. The back end will want to jump out on you just like the real car does. Avoid slamming the throttle down when exiting the turns and just ease her into it. Be smooth and mind your braking distances. She's a lot of car to stop and the wheels will want to lock up on you."

Bill soaked all of the information in but in a moment of sarcasm asked, "Anything else?"

"Yeah," said Lathan. "Don't crash unless you love hearing you name said in vain."

Bill chuckled to himself. "Thanks."

"Don't thank me yet, mate. You haven't done anything," said Lathan. "Just pretend that you're in a real car and ease her out of the pits."

Putting his hands on the wheel, the sensation instantly revived a dormant hunger in Bill. He could feel a surge of energy rush through him but he fought to contain it. He knew that he would need to stay calm in order to avoid embarrassing himself in front of everyone.

* * *

Although it was only a computer simulation, Bill couldn't help but feel impressed with how realistic it was. Additionally, Bill received the surprise of a lifetime when he hit the first bump on the virtual track and realized that the simulator's chassis actually moved. The people who had come to watch got a bit of a laugh as the chassis jerked and startled Bill who was not expecting it.

The driving, much to Bill's amazement, was actually very enjoyable, but he knew he was taking it easy and not wanting to make a fool of himself in front of everyone. As he strolled around a virtual Mount Panorama in a virtual Ford Falcon Supercar, Bill was all but lost in the moment. At first, it was an information overload as his senses seemed to be overwhelmed. It had been several months since he had been in a race car and he knew he was a bit rusty. His saving grace, however, was the voice of Lathan in his ear.

Guiding him through the twists and turns of the treacherous circuit, Lathan advised Bill on the racing lane and braking points. After three complete laps of taking it easy, however, Bill was ready to get after it.

"Alright," said Bill. "Training wheels off."

"You pick things up quick but you're still well off the pace, mate," said Lathan. "You've got some extra room on your approaches so try braking a bit later and harder before the turns."

"Will do," said Bill.

As he began his fourth lap on the circuit, the crowd behind him was getting antsy.

"C'mon, have a solid go at it," someone shouted. "Do your father proud."

"It's no use, mate," said the voice of Derek. "All that Americans know how to do is turn left."

The crowd laughed loudly, but Bill wasn't fazed by it. He could hear audible voices behind him but he was so locked into the zone that he had no idea as to what they were saying.

Full throttle across the start/finish line, Bill charged in deep into the infamous Turn One of *Hell Corner*. Clipping the left side apex and using the rumble strip on the right side at the exit of the turn, Bill put his foot down and began his climb up the Mountain.

"That turn was spot on, mate," said Lathan. "You'll have good pace heading into *Griffins Bend*."

"I'm guessing that's the name of the next turn?" asked Bill.

"You guessed right. Eyes forward now and stay focused."

Braking hard and late for the uphill right turn, Bill eased onto the throttle and carried the momentum towards the next set off corners called *The Cutting*.

"A little wide but still good and clean," commented Lathan. "Keep it up."

"Yes, keep it up," said the sarcastic voice of Derek. "We're all watching you. No pressure, yank."

Winding his way through the digital circuit, Bill was still taking it easy on some parts as he was still very unfamiliar with the intricacies of the course. As he crossed the finish line, however, the crowd which had gathered behind him began to cheer.

"That's a 2:10.4, mate. Great job for a first full-on lap," said the voice of Lathan.

"But still several seconds off my pace, sweetie," said Derek only a few inches from Bill's ear.

Not expecting the close proximity of Derek's comment, Bill had to fight not to flinch. If Derek had been trying to distract Bill, however, it didn't work.

Pushing on, Bill decided he'd go for one final lap and give it his all.

* * *

"It looks like they haven't eaten him alive back there yet, Tubbs," said Abby with a smile. "The man's doing as good as some of the amateur drivers do. Maybe even some pro's, too."

"He's definitely got it in his blood, that's for sure," said Tubbs as he watched from a distance. "Reminds me of his old man..."

* * *

The small crowd behind the simulator began to cheer as Bill tackled *Hell Corner* and raced up *Mountain Straight*. He seemed to be carrying more speed this time and Bill could feel his adrenaline pumping.

As he approached *Griffins Bend,* he braked a bit later than on his previous lap and compensated by braking a bit harder. As he turned the virtual car in, Bill was rewarded with the sight and feel of a car running the ideal line on the edge of the grip limit. The crowd, now excited for the newcomer's success, began to cheer even louder. Some even began yelling to "Stick it to him, mate! Stick it to Renshaw!"

Derek stood silent with his arms crossed and an intrigued smirk on his face as he watched the action unfold.

Climbing the Mountain even more, Bill had a smooth and flawless run as he raced through *The Cutting.*

Lathan, who was still standing behind Bill, was amazed at the progress the American was making. "You've got this, mate! Great j..."

"Just let me race!" shouted Bill, trying to stay focused. He was briefly snapped back into reality as he heard the crowd cheering behind him. He smelt the scent of cigarettes and alcohol as he looked at his hands on the fake racing wheel. He also sensed the feeling of Derek's eyes boring strongly into the back of his head.

Shaking it off, Bill crossed over *Skyline* and into *The Esses*; a downhill labyrinth which can deceive even the more experienced of drivers. Bill almost fell for its tricks as he had to brake a little earlier going into *The Dipper* to scrub some speed. Back on pace, Bill rounded *Forrest's Elbow* and went full-throttle down *Conrod Straight.*

Mind your braking.

Bill shook the thought loose as he braked hard and downshifted through the gears while going into *The Chase*. The crowd behind him cheered even louder as Bill rounded the final few corners of the lap.

Completing the final corner, the excitement got to Bill as he lay on the throttle too hard which caused the back end of the car to shake loose for a moment. Although it was a mistake, it did little to quell the crowd as Bill crossed the start/finish line and brought the car to a stop.

"You're bloody kidding me," said Lathan. "A 2:07.4 on your fifth lap. I've never seen that before in my life. Hell, I've never even heard of that from a beginner; not on this mountain, at least."

Climbing out of the cockpit, Bill's back was soaked in sweat as Derek approached.

"You look like you've just ran a marathon, mate. I guess it's true when they say that Americans don't work out much," said Derek. "Not bad though, mate…for an empty track. Try doing that with a full field of *real* cars and then come talk to me."

Wiping the sweat from his forehead, Bill smiled as he replied. "Maybe I will."

Turning to walk away, Derek chuckled.

"No, mate. You won't."

* * *

"You're a bloody Rembrandt, mate!" exclaimed Tubbs. "I've never seen someone tackle that track like that after only a few laps. You did your name proud, mate."

"And you shut Renshaw's mouth, too," said Abby. "That's reason enough for me to thank you."

Still fanning his sweaty shirt, Bill replied, "I'll admit, that was more fun than I thought it'd be."

"What did you think it was going to be?" said Tubbs. "A bloody arcade game?"

"Actually, yeah I did," answered Bill with a smile. "If I was still into racing, I'd probably get one of those things for my house." Bill's words caused an awkward pause as a moment of silence came over the small group.

"What do you mean if you were still into racing? How could you even say something like that after what you just did?" asked Tubbs.

"As much fun as I had, I didn't come to Australia to race. I came here to take care of my son," said Bill. "Speaking of my son, it's getting a bit late. I'd better…"

"Not before I buy you a drink, mate," said a familiar voice from behind.

Bill turned to see a slender, medium-built man about his size walking towards him with his hand extended. "Nick Lathan," said the man as Bill met his handshake.

"What you just did there; I've never seen anything like it," said Nick. "What other driving have you done?"

"I ran in the SCCA Trans-Am Series back in the States," said Bill. "Did some karting when I was younger, too."

"Before we go any further," said Nick as he held both hands up in front of him, "Ford or Holden?"

The question was so absolute and matter-of-fact that it caught Bill off guard. He hesitated before he answered as his eyes wandered to see the expression of not only Nick, but also that of Abby and Tubbs. Their eyes were open with expectation as they awaited his answer.

"Well since it's what I drove back in the States, I'd have to say Ford," answered Bill.

Nick's head dropped as he let out a sigh. Abby and Tubbs, on the other hand, were beside themselves.

"That's the correct and ONLY correct answer to that question!" exclaimed Tubbs.

"If only ol' Nick here thought the same," said Abby. "Isn't that right, Nick?"

"Ah shut up, Abby," said Nick as he fired back. "You make me sick sometimes, you sook."

Bill, who had an upbringing of always treating woman with respect, didn't take to kindly of Nick's words. "Look, I appreciate your help on the simulator, but you shouldn't talk to the lady like that."

"It isn't the worst of what I've said to her, and I'm bound to say even worse things if she keeps talking like this," said Nick.

Bill, slightly confused, asked, "Did I miss something? All she did was make a comment on how you're apparently not a Ford fan."

"Yeah, mate. And I've been hearing these *comments* for as long as I can remember," said Nick.

Bill, feeling a little out of the loop, looked at both of them and asked,

"Are you two…um…"

"Related? Unfortunately, yes," answered Abby. "This here's my esteemed brother."

Tubbs chuckled to himself. "You may as well get it all out into the open, Abby."

"Oh please do," said Nick sarcastically.

Abby didn't waste any time. "We were born and raised into a Ford family, you see. Mum and Dad both drove them and so did Nick when he first started driving," said Abby. "He got into racing as a kid and eventually went on to win the Australian Formula Ford Championship. When a shot came to race in what's now called the Super2 Series…"

"That's a step below the big time," added Tubbs as he put two beers down in front of both Nick and Bill.

"...we all but knew he'd be going after the first door that came open for a Ford ride," continued Abby. "But what does he do? He goes after the *very* first offer that came on the table..."

"Which was a Holden," said Tubbs as he chimed in again.

"...and my family was crushed. Turns out, so was the car. That thing was a lemon, and his team was good for nothing, as well."

"Look, it really wasn't that bad, mate," added Nick. "She's exaggerating. We had a number of top-five finishes and the team was good to me."

"Was?" asked Bill.

"Like many who came before me and many more who will come after, we eventually ran out of money," said Nick. "Sponsors said they weren't seeing a payoff and some of them pulled the plug on the whole operation."

"So you don't race anymore?" asked Bill.

"Oh I still do, mate. Just not at a full-time level. We've had to downsize the team and we only run a few races a season, but we still get out there and run strong thanks to a few private sponsors. I've even been a co-driver for the big time series a few times," said Nick.

"So how do you know Derek Renshaw?" asked Bill.

"Aside from him being the current 'golden boy' of the Supercars Series, you mean? We both raced in Formula Ford together when we were younger," said Nick. "I was always faster than him but he always got the most attention because of his antics. People said it was good for Australian motorsports to have 'racing personalities' as they called it. Regardless, it was a great feeling to beat him in the championship way back when.

"We both raced in the Super2 Series together back when it was called the Development Series. He, however, attracted the bigger sponsors, got a strong car and eventually won the championship. He got a drive and moved up to the main series and—although he had a rough start—he made some good decisions and now he's on top," said Nick.

"Mind your words, mate," said Tubbs in a low but stern voice.

"I'm guessing his 'rough start' was in a Ford?" asked Bill.

"You guessed right," answered Nick. "He never really favored one manufacturer over the other and just went with whoever paid the most. At first, it was a Ford."

Tubbs cut in and said, "And the blessed Ford just couldn't stand hauling around that colossal pile of s…"

"Tubbs!" exclaimed Abby. "Calm down, mate!"

"Anyway," continued Nick, "a Holden team made him an offer he couldn't refuse and the rest is history. He's not untouchable and he may not be the classiest guy in the sport, but the man's got pace and his team's got the money and a strong car to back it up. In this sport, that means everything."

"Not everything," said Tubbs. Pointing at Bill, he said, "Your old man accomplished everything with a small team that didn't exactly have piles of money lying around."

"Yeah but times have changed, Tubbs," said Nick. "With all of the manufacturers, cameras and big time sponsors, the competition is so close that if you're even slightly off the pace, you'll never have a chance." Bill, although enjoying the small talk, felt a little out of place again. He knew it was getting late and he felt as if he had already gotten more than he had bargained for by coming here.

"Well, I must say that this has been a night worth remembering," said Bill. Taking the final sip of his drink, he put the empty bottle on the bar and said, "It was a true pleasure meeting all of you, but I really do have to get going. It's getting late and I need to get back to my son."

"Before you go, mate," said Nick, "I figure a man of your experience wouldn't mind at least visiting a race around here. Could I somehow convince you to come by the track next week? I've actually got a Super2 race coming up soon and the team and I will be doing some testing in Winton along with a few other teams. I figured I could at least show you a proper Aussie race track if you're up for it."

Bill felt his lips tense up as he debated the offer in his head. He couldn't help but feel the pull back into racing but he also felt the pull inside of him which was a keen reminder of what the sport has cost him already. As much as he wanted to accept the offer, he knew that going to a race track would only cause him to be sucked back into the insatiable hunger which he knew racing to be. Knowing where it would eventually lead him, he didn't feel the need to go down that path again.

With as much sincerity as he could muster up, Bill said, "Thanks, Nick, but I'm going to have to pass. As much as I appreciate the hospitality that you guys have shown me in here, I really didn't come all the way across the world to get back into racing again."

The shared expressions on the faces of Nick, Abby and Tubbs were all disappointed.

Extending his hand again, Nick said, "Well, no hard feelings, mate," as Bill extended his own hand to meet the handshake. "If you change your mind, you know where to find me."

With that, Bill shook hands with Abby and Tubbs, thanked them for the drinks and exited the bar.

* * *

A few moments had passed since Bill had departed and the three continued to sit in silence. Thinking about all that they had just witnessed, one person seemed to be more disturbed than the rest.

"I can't believe it," a disappointed Nick finally said as he slapped the bar. "So much talent gone to waste."

Wiping the bar down, Abby interjected. "I don't know about you but he seems scared, almost."

"The guy's been through a lot recently," said Tubbs who was peeling the label off his bottle. Recalling the earlier conversation he had with Bill where he was informed of the younger man's recent events, Tubbs wasn't too shocked at Bill's sudden exit.

"Told me his tale, he did. Said the last time he raced, he was so upset with his performance that his wife had to drive him home. Along the way, they were in an accident and the poor woman was killed. His son's beaten up pretty bad, too."

The information floated around the three of them in silence for what felt like several minutes. Letting the newfound details on the man they just met sink in, things began clicking together for the trio.

"He *is* scared," said Nick. "That much is for certain. So what was he going on about how he came to Australia to take care of his son? Couldn't he just do that in the States?"

Tubbs relayed the information about the connection Bill's father had made with renowned Physiatrist, Greg Foster, several years ago.

Bringing the three up to speed with how Foster was looking after Chad, it was Abby who suddenly felt chagrined about the last conversation the group had shared with Bill.

"You should've said something, Tubbs. And you shouldn't have pressured him like that. If I had known this beforehand..."

"If he's anything like his father, he's stronger than he looks," said Tubbs. "To be honest, I'm not giving up on him."

"Neither am I," cut in Nick. "Did you see his face when he was in the simulator? He had total concentration and was hitting his marks. He wasn't stumbling his way around like most of the amateurs who come here and give it a go. You only see that kind of dedication from experienced drivers."

Still cleaning from behind the bar, Abby stopped in front of both Nick and Tubbs. "Well, I would hope that you two wouldn't give up on him so easily. Plus, I think he'll need some support in this life," said Abby.

The two men looked at each other with coy smiles.

"What?!" exclaimed Abby.

Nick and Tubbs chuckled briefly before the latter said, "Yeah, I'm sure you'd love to give him some *support*, Abbs."

"No, not like that," Abby quickly said. "I mean, he is kind of cute…for an American."

Nick took a long swig from his drink and slammed it down on the bar. "Now I've seen it all," he said as he rose and walked away from the bar. "My little sister going after William Watson's son. What a world, what a world."

Chapter 10

"It could be something worth checking into. You never know what may come of it," said the voice on the other end of the phone.

"Yeah but that's the thing. I'm not sure if I *want* to know what may come of it," replied Bill as he paced back and forth in the waiting room at Greg's clinic. "I didn't give it all up and come all the way over here to just jump back into it again."

"Look, son. I know you're there for Chad. We can both agree on that. But why not at least entertain the idea? It's not like they're asking you to sign contracts, jump in a car and race. You'd just be going to watch a few teams practice and you could possibly meet a few other people along the way. What harm could come of it?"

"I know that, Dad, but I just don't want to be sucked into that life again. I mean, look where it got me," explained Bill.

"Racing didn't get you there, son. Life did," said William calmly. "You've got to learn to either roll with the life's punches or you'll get carried away by the waves. Judging by what Greg's told me about how bored you've been, you seem to be down to your last paddle."

"I just…" Bill hesitated as he began rubbing his temples with his free hand. He could feel yet another headache coming. "I don't know, Dad. I think I just need something to do."

"Well it sounds to me like that *something to do* has just been placed in front of you," said William. "You're your own man, Bill, and I can't make decisions for you. But I will say that opportunities like this don't come around very often. When they do, it's wise to jump on them."

Bill, still holding his cell phone up to his ear, put his free hand into his pocket and allowed his head to drop slightly. Pondering this idea, he let his thoughts take him away to the unknown avenues of what the possibilities could be.

"Watson? Mr. Bill Watson?"

A female voice called from behind him. Turning to look, he noticed that it was one of the nurses from Greg's office.

"Yes ma'am. That's me," said Bill.

"Ah. We're ready for you now," said the older nurse.

Turning back around briefly, Bill said, "Dad, I've got to go. They're about to start Chad's next therapy session."

"Give him a kiss for me and tell him I'm praying for him."

"I will, Dad. And thanks for talking to me. I really appreciate it."

"Any time. And son…remember that I'm behind you no matter what you choose to do."

"Thanks again, Dad. I'll talk to you later," said Bill as he hung up the phone. At that, Bill approached the nurse who was patiently waiting for him.

Leading him down a short hallway which resembled more of an office building than a physical therapy center, Bill asked, "How's he been doing so far?"

"He's a little fighter, he is," replied the nurse. "He's made leaps and bounds since you and Dr. Foster first brought him in but he still has a long road ahead of him to recovery."

The nurse led Bill to the room he had been coming to for the past few weeks. Inside, Greg was there filling out some paperwork, and Chad was laid out on the exam table with his head resting on a pillow. Turning to look at his father as he entered the room, Chad gave a slight smile.

Bill couldn't help but feel touched at the sight and the high spirits Chad had been showing lately. Walking up to his son on the table, he knelt down and kissed him on the forehead.

"That's from grandpa," said Bill.

"Good arvo to you, Bill. Did you get to talk to the old man before you came in?" asked Greg without looking up from his paperwork.

"Yeah and I heard that you did, too," said Bill with a coy smile. Greg smiled back at the comment, "Well, mate. Your father is certainly interested in how you're doing." Putting the clipboard down, Greg turned his attention to Chad. "Well, Chaddy, let's get you fixed up, shall we?"

Bill took his usual seat alongside the bed which allowed him to be out of the way and gave Greg the freedom to move about the exam table.

"You know, I've been thinking about flying your dad out here sometime. I haven't seen him in years and I reckon he owes me a stubby…or three," said Greg as he slowly began to lift Chad's left leg through a range of motions.

"Have we been that bad of guests?" asked Bill.

"Oh no, mate. I just haven't seen the old bast…I mean old man in a long time," said Greg as he bit his tongue for Chad's sake. "I've actually been enjoying having you and Chaddy around. It's been good to have some company in the house. It can get quite lonely if you don't keep yourself busy."

"Yeah, tell me about it," said Bill.

Greg smiled with a small chuckle as he continued his work on Chad. "Just try to relax," said Greg to Chad.

As Bill watched, he saw Chad close his eyes as he heeded Greg's words. Curiously, Bill often wondered what his son was thinking about in these moments. He imagined that it would be quite easy to wonder about the future and think about despair as he lay partially paralyzed on a doctor's table but Bill didn't sense that about Chad. He could tell by the expression on his face that he felt at peace with it. Whether by confidence in his progress or simply acknowledging his condition, he knew Chad was on the road to recovery.

It had been nearly two months since they arrived in their new home with Greg in Australia, and it seemed that Chad had taken to it quite well. At times, he seemed to have a calmness about him which Bill found to be soothing.

There were moments, however, when he knew Chad was still hurting. Whether from the injury he sustained from the accident, the sudden loss of his mother or both tragic events combined, Bill could oftentimes still see the despair in his son's face—and in his own.

But Bill knew that he had to remain strong for Chad. They were both in this together, and Bill was fully aware that his son was depending on him to be by his side during this difficult time in his life. What Bill was also becoming aware of, though, was how *he* was coming to depend on Chad more and more throughout this journey.

With the sheer amount of downtime Bill currently found at his disposal, he often wondered about what the future held for them. After much thought, however, he still wasn't able to answer some of his own questions such as how long they were going to be in Australia, what he was going to do if they had to stay here, what was he going to do with his company back in Texas and, most importantly, would his son ever walk again?

As Greg continued with the physical therapy exercises with Chad, the young patient slowly opened his eyes and turned to look his dad directly in the eyes. Strangely, it was almost as if Chad could sense the thoughts running through his father's mind. Although he still wasn't speaking, Bill could somehow sense that Chad was non-verbally saying, *It's okay, Dad. We'll make it through this.*

Bill felt his eyes begin to tear up. Throughout his life, he had gone to great lengths to ensure that his family had everything they needed to be successful in life. From private schools to professional instructors for recreational sports, Bill knew that every investment he made into his son was an investment into his son's future.

Now, he felt differently. It was almost as if his idleness was causing him to see things in a new light. Even though Chad had everything he needed to overcome this condition with time, it wasn't by Bill's doing. A passenger of sorts, Bill felt that by him doing nothing, he was becoming nothing. Nothing but a moral support figure, anyway.

"Can you feel any of this, Chad?" asked Greg as he massaged the bottom of Chad's feet to stimulate blood flow.

Shaking his head from side to side, Greg continued. "That's alright. I can feel the muscles in your legs getting stronger. We'll get through this. I promise."

As he went on with the treatment, Greg said, "You'd be surprised at how much power your mind has over your body, Chad. Always keep a positive outlook no matter how bad things get."

As Greg finished up the session after some time, the two lifted Chad and gently placed him back into his wheelchair. "Well, Chaddy," said Greg, "we're making progress with every session."

As Greg went back to his clipboard to make notes and document the day's session, Bill knelt down in front of Chad.

"You did a great job, son," said Bill as he took Chad's hand. "We're going to get through this."

As Greg finished up his notes, he sat the clipboard down, reached into his pocket and fished out his car keys. Tossing them to Bill, he said, "You two can head out. Just don't forget about me," as he slapped Bill hard on the shoulder. "I've got to run to my next appointment but it was good to see ya, mate!" Approaching Chad on his way out, Greg said, "Chaddy, you take care of this bloke, okay?"

* * *

After Bill had loaded both Chad and his wheelchair into Greg's car, they set out to head back home. Since Greg only had the one car, there was a standing agreement between both Bill and Greg that he was free to use his car whenever he liked so long as Bill picked him up from work in the evening.

It was a more than generous offer, which Bill appreciated. Additionally, Greg grew to like the "curbside service" as he called it which allowed him to be chauffeured around.

As father and son drove together, Bill rolled the windows down to enjoy what was a beautiful Australian day. Cruising along through downtown Sydney, it wasn't long, before their nice drive was cut short due to a traffic jam.

"Of course," said Bill with a hint of frustration in his voice.

After a few minutes of sitting still, Bill finally said, "How about some music?" Turning on the radio, they were immediately met with a political talk show, which Greg was last listening to. Not a fan of politics and really having no vested interest in the Australian version, Bill changed the channel using the presets which were programmed into the radio. Once again, he was met with another political talk show.

"C'mon, Greg," said Bill as he shut the radio off.

As the two continued to sit in silence in the traffic, Chad reached his hand into his pocket and pulled out what appeared to be a small metallic object. Grabbing Bill's hand, Chad placed the object into his father's open palm. Inspecting it, Bill saw that it was a toy die-cast race car.

"Where'd you get this?" asked Bill. "Did Dr. Foster give this to you?" Chad answered Bill's question by nodding up and down. Examining it in his hand as they waited in traffic, Bill stared at the red and white car, which featured a black hood with a single white stripe down the center. With the number 28 circled in black with *Holden Dealer Team* written along its side, Bill recognized this car from somewhere.

"It looks so familiar," said Bill. "Chad, I think you've got a little piece of history right here. If my memory serves me right, I think this is Peter Brock's car from his first win at Bathurst in…oh…1972, I think…"

Awestruck by what he held in his hand, Bill couldn't take his eyes off the small race car. "You know," he said, "that race was one of the first races your granddad and I watched together. He had it saved on tape and when I was old enough to understand racing, he put it on to show me."

Taken back to memory lane, Bill continued. "The *Hardie Ferodo 500* was what it was called. Granddad and I watched this car go around that track for hours. It's kind of ironic, really. I'm a Ford guy who honestly got into racing because of this Holden."

Although Bill normally tried to stay reserved and strong around his son, the sight of this small piece of history seemed to open up a portal of thoughts and feelings which Bill was containing all this time.

"I'll be honest with you, Chad. Sometimes I do miss it. The sensation of being behind the wheel, the vibrations, the noise, the adrenaline...the rush; it's really hard to compare that to anything else in life.

"After the...you know...the accident, I thought that I gave up racing because it never took me anywhere. Looking back, though, I think I gave it up more out of fear. I was afraid of what would happen if I ever got behind the wheel of a race car again. And to be honest, I still am.

"I gave it so much. Especially when I was younger. But no matter how hard I pushed, I was still never able to win a race. If I had a nickel for every podium finish, though..."

Bill looked over at Chad who was staring right back at his father with the utmost interest.

"When you're racing, everything else seems to sail right out the window. Worries, fears and life in general are gone. All you're left with is a hunger to win."

Bill fumbled the toy car around in his hand as he sighed. "I just don't know, Chad. It's almost as if there's something inside telling me to never get involved with racing again. But then there's that other side that is hungry to do it. It's that feeling that you get when you know you still have so much potential left in you and so much more that you want to accomplish. The problem is that I don't know which side to listen to. Because of that, sometimes I feel like I just wanna burst."

As the traffic began to move slightly, Bill was brought back to reality. Continuing to fumble the small car in his hand with his fingers, Bill turned and smiled at his son.

Handing the car back to Chad, Bill said, "I'm surprised Greg gave this up. This is quite a catch. Probably worth a lot of money, too. Make sure you take care..."

Bill was stopped short as Chad shook his head at him.

Instead of receiving the car back, Chad grabbed his father's hand and closed his fingers around the car. Looking up into his father's eyes, Chad squeezed his father's hands tighter around it. They held each other's gaze for several seconds as Chad tried to relay the meaning of this to Bill.

Bill could feel his own emotions about to pour over as he received the message from his son.

"Son, I don't think..." said Bill as he was cut short again. This time, it was caused by Chad gently pushing his father's hand which held the car back towards him.

Longing to communicate with his son, Bill so wished that Chad could speak his mind. "What do you think I should do?" asked Bill.

At that, Chad extended his right arm and pointed towards the car in Bill's hand. "That's what I was afraid of," said Bill.

As traffic continued to crawl all around them, Bill once again became fixated on the small toy car. The sight of it caused him to think about all of the highs and lows he's had in his foray into motorsports. He remembered the joy of just participating in his first race and bringing the car home in one piece. He thought about the memories of seeing his son cheering for him in the stands alongside Lena...

Lena.

How he missed his beloved wife. Although he himself had come to grips with what had happened on that terrible day, he truly had no idea how Chad was feeling about the fact that he'd never see his mother again. Alone in that car together, each other is all they had left.

Remembering the events like they happened yesterday, Bill tried to stay strong but could feel the pull of grief upon him once again.

Turning to look at Chad, a single tear ran down Bill's face as he quietly and softly said, "I'm sorry, Chad. I'm sorry that you have to go through with this. I never wanted this for you."

Still looking over at his father, Chad reached over and put his hand on top of Bill's. It was the touch of his son's hand which seemed to bring Bill back to reality. Once again, it was like Chad was saying, *I miss her too, Dad. But we still have each other.*

Indeed, Bill now knew how much he had come to depend on his son. Although they had taken a heavy blow during the accident, it didn't change the fact that they were still family. Wiping the tear from his face, Bill held the small car out in front of him as he turned to Chad.

"You know what this means, right?" asked Bill. "Are you sure?"

Nodding his head up and down, Chad smiled as he knew that his message was finally received.

"Well, alright then," said Bill as he felt a sudden surge of confidence. "Let's see where we can go."

Chapter 11

Although it was only a Wednesday night, it was still proving to be quite busy. Wiping the bar surface down when people left, making sure the new customers had drinks served promptly and ensuring the existing customers' glasses stayed filled, Abby more often than not had her hands full.

She'd been working at Bear Knuckles Bar for several years now and it had taken nearly that long for most of the regular customers to finally stop making the typical crude gestures towards her. Despite the fact that Tubbs was keen on throwing anyone out of his bar for doing anything he even slightly disagreed with, he oftentimes left Abby to deal with these types of problems on her own.

A military man through and through who served in the Australian Army, Tubbs was always telling Abby when she first started that she'll have to learn the "lay of the land" around the bar if she hoped to survive. That included learning how to deal with customers who were oftentimes in various stages of drunkenness.

More often than not, they were harmless, and she'd sometimes even call a cab to take them back home. There were times, however, when certain customers were simply beside themselves as they saw an attractive woman walking towards them asking them if she could serve them another drink.

"Well, pretty lady. Maybe you could come back to my place and I could serve *you* something!" said one such customer who looked young enough to be straight out of high school.

Normally, Abby would simply walk away and go on to helping

other patrons. Over the years, however, she'd learn to be just as quick witted as some of the customers in her comebacks.

"How you gonna do that, mate? You going to take me to your bedroom in your mum's basement and show me your little light switch?"

Usually, the other person would back off after the brief verbal volley. There were a few occasions, however, when the comebacks insulted more than the other person's ego, and they wanted to get physical. Unfortunately for the other person, that's when Tubbs would step in. The sheer sight of a tank-like human marching towards them was oftentimes enough to deter any type of further escalation. But if things did get rough, Tubbs was more than ready to hold his own.

Today, though, there were no such customers. Many of the patrons were, instead, glued to the television as they watched a pre-recorded Sydney Football Club game which Tubbs typically played throughout the week after a match.

Abby knew most of the regulars who came in during the week. She would often even greet them by name as they walked in and serve them their drink of choice as they took their seat. Lost in the rhythm of her work, she would have been lying if she later stated that her heart didn't skip a beat when Bill Watson walked in.

Handsome as ever with his slicked back dark hair and trimmed beard, he smiled as he made eye contact with Abby and walked towards her.

She instantly hoped that she hadn't looked *too* shocked to see him. "Well, mate. I didn't think I'd be seeing you around here for some time," she said.

"Hey, Abby. Good to see you again," said Bill as he took a seat at the bar.

"Likewise," said Abby as she inwardly hoped that she wasn't blushing. "What'll it be?"

"Well," began Bill, "I'm actually looking for..."

"Yank!" A loud voice shouted from above the crowd. As Bill turned towards the direction of the shout, he was met by the colossal figure of Tubbs steaming towards him with a huge smile on his face.

"Oh no," said Bill under his breath.

As Tubbs approached, he grabbed Bill as if he were a ragdoll, put him into a bear hug and lifted him off the ground. "How are ya, mate?!" exclaimed Tubbs.

Unable to answer because of the sheer amount of force being pressed against his ribs and lungs as he was shaken about, all that Bill could do was moan as his feet dangled above the ground beneath him.

Finally releasing the much smaller man from his ginormous grasp, Tubbs let out a loud bellowing laugh as his face continued to be filled with a smile.

Now able to catch his breath, Bill was at last able to get the simple but now exhausted words of, "Hey, Tubbs," out of his mouth.

"Oh, Tubbs," said Abby as she shook her head. "Leave the man be."

"Sorry, mate," said Tubbs. "Just didn't think I'd be seeing ya around here again."

Stumbling his way back into his chair, Bill said, "Well, let's not make a habit of doing that every time we see each other."

Abby chuckled a bit as she said, "There aren't many people who come here that he actually looks forward to seeing."

"Ah, you'll get used to it, mate," said Tubbs as he slapped Bill hard on the shoulder. The jolt nearly knocked Bill off of his seat.

"So," said Tubbs, "you here for the game?"

Rubbing his shoulder which most likely had a large hand print on it, Bill answered, "No, I'm actually looking for someone."

Abby and Tubbs both quickly exchanged glances.

"Who you looking for, mate?" asked Tubbs suspiciously. "You need me to bust someone's skull or something?"

Chuckling as he turned to face Abby, Bill said, "Your brother, Nick. I was thinking about taking him up on his offer of going to the track."

At that point, the look on the faces of both Abby and Tubbs was priceless. As their imaginations simultaneously burst with expectation, their faces failed to hide their joy. As such, Bill couldn't help but comment on it.

"Are you guys okay? You look like I just gave you both a golden ticket to Willy Wonka's chocolate factory."

"Mate," said Tubbs, "are you really gonna do it?"

"I just want to take him up on his offer to visit him and his crew at the track," said Bill. "I think he said they were doing some testing or something."

"Yeah," said Abby. "They'll be testing along with a few other teams this weekend at Winton."

Tubbs, who now had his lips pursed together with a satisfied smile, began nodding his head up and down. "You're gonna do us proud, mate," said Tubbs.

"I'm not gonna do anything," said Bill. "I'm just going to the track to see the cars and meet some of his team."

"So what was it?" asked Abby.

Confused, Bill replied by asking, "What was what?"

"Oh c'mon, mate. What was it that made you change your mind? When we last saw you, you were practically dead-set on never seeing a race car again."

Bill, letting a smile slip onto his face, said, "My son, actually."

At that, Bill pulled from his pocket the small die-cast car which Chad had handed to him in the car ride home from his physical therapy session earlier in the day. "He gave me this," said Bill as he held up the miniature Peter Brock car for both Abby and Tubbs to see. "Although he's still not speaking right now, I'm pretty sure he spoke directly to me with this."

Allowing Tubbs to handle the small car, the larger man said, "Wow. That's deep, mate. Sounds like your boy's got a good head on his shoulders," as he gave the car back to Bill.

"I know that you probably don't want to bring him in here, but I'd certainly like to meet him someday. I've heard a lot about him," said Abby.

Bill replied, "Well, I'll be taking him to the track this weekend so if you're free..."

Bill stopped short as he soon realized what it sounded like he had just said. He hoped Abby didn't think he was asking her out on a date.

"Well," Abby thought, "I'm scheduled to work this weekend..." "Not anymore you're not!" exclaimed Tubbs as he openly flashed Bill a wink. At that, Abby could no longer hide her blush.

"Well who's going to work the bar, Tubbs? You?" asked Abby.

"What do you think I was doing before you came along?" answered Tubbs. "I'm just as pretty as you so I'll keep things moving over here. You two kids go and have fun."

Bill couldn't help but smile as Tubbs gave him a slight poke in the ribs with his elbow.

"You're impossible, Tubbs," said Abby. Reaching beneath the bar, she grabbed a small business card and wrote down Nick's number on it.

"I'll let him know you're coming, but you should probably give him a call and get the where's and when's," said Abby.

Taking the card, Bill put it in his pocket as he said, "I appreciate it. I guess I'll see you this weekend."

"I guess you will," said Abby with a coy smile.

Flashing a grin towards Abby, Bill turned and said, "Take it easy, Tubbs," and turned to exit the bar.

As the two watched Bill walk away, Tubbs was met with a hard slap on his muscular arm from Abby.

Giving Abby a confused look, he asked, "What's flown up your arse all the sudden?"

"Sometimes I don't know which is worse," said Abby as she tried to hide her frustration from nearby patrons. "The gawking customers or your lack of discretion."

"Discretion?" repeated Tubbs. "That's William Watson's kid! C'mon, Abbs. You haven't been in a relationship ever since you ran over that one bloke..."

"And that's what happens when you jump in front of a moving vehicle," said Abby cutting off Tubbs as she began gathering up a few empty glasses on the bar.

"Rumors are that nobody saw brake lights, either."

"Yeah? And they also say that boys with big hands are big in other places too," said Abby as she was clearly upset and began to walk off.

"Abby!" shouted Tubbs which succeeded in stopping her. "All I'm saying is to just give the man a chance. You never know what will happen," said Tubbs with as much sincerity as he could muster up.

Turning to face Tubbs, Abby quickly marched back towards him and got close enough to where she could whisper.

"Alright, listen to me," said Abby quietly. "The man's a widow, Tubbs. A bloody widow. I'm sure he's a nice guy but the last thing I want is for someone to constantly be comparing me to someone I'm not. I don't know how long he was married for but I reckon it was long enough to raise a child. You just don't forget someone like that overnight and I'll be damned if I'm going to be someone's rebound girl again."

With that, Abby slammed all of the empty glasses she had collected down onto the bar in front of Tubbs and stormed off.

Now sitting alone at the bar, Tubbs turned towards the door and gave a solemn salute in Bill's general direction.

"Good luck, mate. And stay away from moving vehicles when she's around."

* * *

Later that evening, Bill mapped out the distance to Winton Motor

Raceway and found that it was close to six hours away from Greg's house in Sydney. As such, this would certainly require Bill to borrow the car for the weekend. Although he'd yet to call Nick to confirm his arrival, he began making small preparation the following morning such as gathering some overnight materials.

As Bill drove Greg home from work that evening with Chad in the backseat, Bill relayed the new information about Chad, Tubbs, Abby, Nick and the testing event at Winton to Greg and awaited a reaction.

"Well, mate, I can't exactly say 'no' when you've been a bloody saint around the house and to your son," said Greg. "Plus, I know you've been wanting to get away for a bit, so this'll be a good little holiday for you and Chaddy."

"Are you gonna be okay without a car?" asked Bill.

"Don't worry about me, mate," replied Greg. "To be honest, it'll be good to stay in one spot for a bit. It's been frantically busy at the office lately. I could use the downtime."

After a short pause, Greg continued. "So I'm going to ask the question I think even you may be asking yourself: What are you planning to accomplish down there?"

Initially caught off guard by the question, Bill took several moments before he answered. "To be honest, I don't know," Bill finally answered. "Spend some time out of the house with Chad, see some race cars, meet some interesting people..."

"You gonna do any driving?" asked Greg as he yawned.

"I seriously doubt that," answered Bill. "Nobody in their right mind is going to let me—a complete stranger—just jump into their race car on a track I've never been on before."

"You never know, mate," said Greg as he closed his eyes. "Don't close any doors before they get a chance to fully open."

"What do you mean by that?" asked Bill.

"I mean that you should think of this as an opportunity," said Greg. "I've never been invited to a race track to meet a race team; at least not since your father's day. Most people haven't had that chance. But here you are, new to Australia, and you're already churning up opportunity. The door is opening for you, Bill. Even if ever so slightly, it's opening. You'd be wiser for it if you let the situation develop more and, like I said, don't close any doors before they get a chance to fully open.

"Above all, always remember this: Let the situation develop."

Bill, nodding his head in agreement, said, "Very well said."

"Yeah well that's about it for my moonlight wisdom. Now hurry up and get me home before I fall asleep and start drooling all over myself." When Bill turned the car into Greg's driveway, he knew that he had one more thing he needed to take care of tonight.

After helping Chad out of the car and situated into his wheelchair, the three made their way inside. Once there, Greg immediately stated that he was turning in and went to his room for the night.

Bill, after assisting Chad with his nightly routines, laid Chad down in bed and knelt down beside him. "Well, Chad, it looks like we're going to be going to a racetrack this weekend," said Bill softly. "It feels like it's been forever since we last went to..."

Bill stopped short as his mind recalled the memory of his last visit to a track. The race which was an utter embarrassment to him, the argument, the ride home...

The crash.

Feeling like he'd suddenly been punched in the stomach, Bill laid his forehead down on Chad's bed.

"What am I doing, Chad?" asked Bill. He immediately regretted saying that in front of his son.

As he sat there with his head down pondering what he would say next, Bill heard the sound of a small sniffle coming from Chad. Looking up, Bill noticed small tears building in Chad's eye which the low amount of light in the room reflected off of. He too recalled that fateful day and the subsequent aftershock of their current situation.

"Hey, it's okay, Chad," said Bill. "I think we both know it's all still pretty fresh on our minds."

Reaching up and wiping the tears from Chad's eyes, Bill could almost feel tears beginning to build inside of him. "Let's not think about this and get some sleep, Chad."

After saying a brief prayer, Bill, telling Chad that he loved him, turned off the light to Chad's room and closed the door. Returning to his own room, Bill immediately sank to the base of the door after closing it behind him. Putting his head in his hands, he couldn't believe he was going through this sudden influx of emotions. Having been so initially excited to make the trip to Winton, now he wasn't so sure it was such a good idea.

Do I really want to drag Chad and myself back into this?

He closed his eyes and remembered all of the memories he had cherished of Chad and Lena being at the track with him on race day.

The memory alone made him choke up.

"God, I miss her," Bill said softly.

With his head still in his hands, Bill suddenly remembered that he was planning to call Nick tonight and arrange the meeting at Winton.

Pulling the business card that Abby gave him from his pocket, he studied it in his hands as he examined Abby's handwriting. While examining the card, he noticed a small smiley face which Abby had drawn on the card after Nick's number.

Bill couldn't help but chuckle at the thought behind the simple image. If anything, a part of him still wanted to go to Winton now just for the chance to see Abby again, but he quickly dismissed that as a plausible reason to attend. He simply wasn't ready to get himself into a relationship.

In his heart and mind, Bill was still married to Lena. Although he briefly entertained the idea and knew that one day he would eventually get into a relationship, his memories betrayed him as he remembered that maybe he wouldn't have to.

His mind traveled back to when he was still in the hospital. He remembered the visit he received from the doctor just before he went to see Chad for the first time after the accident. He recalled the words of Dr. Owens…

What would Lena do? She'd tell me to press on no matter what. Shaking free from the memory, he focused once again on the business card in his hands. If anything, the memory which had just surfaced proved to be the deciding factor for Bill.

Making up his mind, he pulled his phone from his pocket and dialed.

Chapter 12

The following day seemed to go by fast as Bill and Chad spent the majority of the afternoon getting the things they would need for what would be a long journey to Winton.

The two loaded up and by the time the evening came, they had their bags packed and were ready to hit the open road first thing in the morning.

Having communicated with Nick on the previous night, Bill was invited to stay in the same hotel as Nick and his crew. However, due to budgeting, Bill would have to pay for his own room. This suited Bill, as he didn't want to impose. He maintained to both Nick, Greg and Chad that he was simply going to meet the team and see the car in action.

When Bill woke the following morning, he felt like a kid waking up on Christmas day. Although it wasn't yet dawn, Bill breezed through the room like he'd been up for hours as he got ready for the day ahead of him.

After showering and getting dressed, he woke Chad up and, as quietly as possible, made breakfast for the two. Despite their efforts, however, Greg soon appeared from his room.

"Think you could sneak off in the night, huh?" Greg said with a smile.

"Just stealing the car, is all. No big deal," said Bill in kind. "I didn't mean to wake you."

"No, you didn't wake me, mate," said Greg. "I set my alarm to make sure I could see you two off. Maybe help you get loaded up.

"I appreciate it," said Bill.

After having a cup of coffee Bill had prepared, Greg assisted with getting Chad ready as Bill began loading their items in the car. Although it was only a short weekend trip, Bill was notorious for forgetting things when he packed. As such, he checked, double-checked and re-checked everything to ensure he had what he needed.

Satisfied, he zipped up his bag and loaded his and Chad's into the car.

"Anything else?" asked Greg from the doorway to the garage.

Closing the trunk of the car, Bill answered, "Yeah, there's a box inside the pantry but I'll get it."

"No, don't worry, mate," answered Greg. "I'll grab it."

Bill, now smiling, waited for the reaction. Coming from the kitchen, Bill heard Greg's voice say, "You've got to be kidding me!"

Several seconds later, Greg appeared in the garage doorway with a small cardboard box filled with junk-food. "You're gonna be dragging the bottom of the car against the road if you eat all of this shit, mate!" exclaimed Greg. "Is this what they do in the States?"

Unable to hide his smile, Bill stated, "Junk food and road trips kind of go hand-in-hand back home. You learn to appreciate it."

"I don't think I could learn to appreciate looking like I was a pregnant man," said Greg as he handed the box to Greg.

"And don't worry, I'll clean the car up when we get back," said Bill as he loaded the box into the back seat of the car. "No crumbs, I promise."

Chuckling, Greg replied, "If you end up eating all of that, you may not be able to bend over to clean under the seats."

The two men assisted Chad in getting into the passenger seat along with getting his wheelchair loaded into the trunk. After that, they were all set.

"Well, mate. Not what I was expecting when you first got here," said Greg as he extended his hand. "It's honestly really good to see the two of you getting out and away for a bit. You both deserve it."

Meeting Greg's hand with his own, the two shook hands as Bill said, "I can't tell you enough how much I appreciate you letting us use the car, Greg. Thank you."

"No worries, mate," said Greg. "Have fun, let your hair down and all that stuff. But above all, just remember what I told you: Let the situation develop. No need to rush into anything but no need to be a mere passerby either."

"Duly noted," said Bill.

As Bill turned to look to see if Chad was comfortable in the car, he noticed that his young son was already asleep in the passenger seat.

"At least he'll have his energy later," said Bill with a smile.

"You'd best be going if you want to beat the traffic, mate," said Greg as he slapped Bill on the shoulder. "Take care and let me know if you need anything."

"Will do," answered Bill as he opened the garage door.

Backing the car out slowly, Bill waived to Greg as the garage door closed behind him. Putting the car into gear, Bill and Chad drove off into the early morning darkness.

* * *

"That's great news!" said Bill.

"Yeah, you're telling me," said Bill's longtime friend and co-business owner, Pat Henderson. "At first, I wasn't so sure if he was going to pull the trigger on the deal or not. But after a nice dinner and some of my magic business mojo, it all came together. However, it's going to be a bit before he signs the papers."

"How long are we talking and why?"

"He said it could be another few months," said Pat. "Something about 'tying up some loose ends back home'. I didn't really press him on the issue. I'm sure that we'll be talking more soon."

Despite the fact that months had passed since Bill first learned of a potential client which Pat had been working on a business deal with, things were developing slowly on both sides of the fence. The client, a wealthy businessman from Greece, wasn't willing to rush into a major business deal without first making absolute sure that this was for the best.

If signed, the deal would be the largest in the history of *Dynamis Engineering*.

"Well don't let him slip away," said Bill. "This'll be huge for us if we can get the deal worked out."

"Bill, I'm offended," said Pat as he tried to act shocked. "Have I ever let a business deal slip by?"

Bill smiled as he imagined his friend's merry face glowing with confidence. "Not once, Pat. I have complete faith in you that you'll do the right thing. Thank you again for all of the hard work you've put in while I've been away."

"It's not a problem, Bill. Remember, I live for this stuff!"

"That's something I'll never forget," said Bill.

The two exchanged further details on the deal with the potential client as well as on personal matters such as the current progress of Chad. Bill was also pleased to learn that his father had also visited Pat at the office on several occasions and was even doing some work around there to help the staff with their paperwork.

"He's a real trooper and the ladies love him," said Pat.

"Yeah, he's a charmer all right. Don't work him too hard, though," said Bill. "If you don't stop him, he'll stay there and work all night."

After concluding his phone call with Pat, Bill looked over at Chad to see that he was just starting to wake up. "Wakey wakey, sunshine," said Bill. "You've pretty much slept through the majority of it. We'll be there in less than an hour."

The night sky, which was present when they had first departed from Greg's house in Sydney, had been vanquished by the rising sun which gave way to what looked to be the start of a beautiful day.

With the landscape now visible in the light, the two were mesmerized by the beauty of the Australian countryside. With the sweeping plains and the rolling hills on either side of them, driving at highway speeds seemed to do the nature around them an injustice as there was simply so much to see and appreciate.

Having only heard stories from his father of the beauty of what William referred to as "Wild Australia", Bill couldn't deny the peaceful serenity which came along with giving witness to country's great beauty.

"Pictures and movies just don't do it justice," said Bill.

Although Bill had already dug into the box of junk food as the empty wrappers around him indicated, Chad had yet to eat anything since their departure.

"You must be hungry." Reaching back into the box, Bill grabbed a few items and placed them on Chad's lap.

"Here you go. How about some music to get the day started off right?" Having updated his playlist on his phone, Bill began playing one of his favorite road-trip songs: *Roadhouse Blues* by *The Doors*. The tune seemed to carry them on as they continued their long drive down Hume Highway. As they drove along, they soon began seeing signs for Winton Motor Raceway. Bill could feel the butterflies begin to churn in his stomach as each passing second brought them closer to their destination.

As the music carried on, they soon located the exit for Glenrowan-Winton Road and, shortly thereafter, arrived at the track. After finding a parking spot and bringing the car to a stop, Bill took a deep breath and looked over at Chad.

"You ready?"

Chad, still loading up on junk food, turned to his dad and smiled ear to ear as he nodded his head up and down.

"No time like the present, then," said Bill.

Turning the car off, Bill saw the various teams out and about as they made their preparations for the day of testing. Due to the cost of renting a facility for testing purposes, many motorsports teams will oftentimes pitch in together to cover the price. This allows for several teams to get the benefit of testing their equipment for a fraction of the cost to the individual team. And with the constant strain which is on the various racing teams and their finances, many were keen to take advantage of whatever savings they could get.

As previously discussed with Nick, Bill sent him a text message indicating that he had arrived. After a few moments, Bill received a reply with instructions for where to go and who to ask for. With that, they exited the vehicle and set off.

* * *

"Bill! Good to see you again, mate!" said Nick as he came out to greet Bill and Chad. "Welcome to Winton! I'm glad you guys could make it. Hopefully it was a pleasant drive through the bush."

Extending his hand in greeting, his was met in kind by Bill's hand. "It was," replied Bill. "I can't tell you how much we both appreciate you inviting us out, Nick. On that note," said Bill as he gestured towards his son, "I'd like for you to meet my son, Chad."

Kneeling down in front of Chad's wheelchair, Nick reached out to shake hands with Chad.

"It's very nice to meet you, Chad. I'm Nick and I'll be your tour guide this arvo. I think I speak for the team when I say we're all very glad you could make it out." Standing back up, Nick led the way into the facility as he said "C'mon, I'll introduce you all to the boys."

Following Nick through the various garages, Bill was taken back in time as he navigated his way through the environment of his old life. The smell of racing fuel, the revving of V8 engines, the sound of air guns and the various teams wearing their appropriate race suits were more than enough to put a smile on Bill's face as he pushed

Chad along in his wheelchair.

The sight of a child in a wheelchair certainly drew the attention of some wandering eyes, but just about everyone was courteous about it. Although there were a few whose stares made them feel uncomfortable and out of place, many of the people scurrying about simply smiled in return. A few friendly pit crew members even gave a friendly "G'day, mate," to Chad as they hurried about the tasks they were attending to.

However, all of the pleasantries seemed to end once they arrived at the pit stall where Nick's team was housed for the day.

"What the hell's the matter with you?! Do you think we paid all of this money to test here just so you could sit on your arses all day?! Get back to work!" shouted a very tall and stalky man with curly grey hair and a thick British accent.

"And you!" he continued as he singled out an unfortunate pit crew member, "You'd better start changing tires faster, now! And by now, I mean yesterday! I'm tired of seeing you out there being the slowest one! The faster you do it, the faster you can crawl back to the hole you came out of."

Watching and listening from a distance, Bill felt slightly uncomfortable at the sight of the man—who stood well over six feet in height—as he berated his troops from above.

Leaning over towards Nick, Bill quietly asked, "Why's he so angry?"

"He's not angry, mate. He's British," answered Nick as if he'd come to this conclusion long ago. "He's like this all the time so you might as well get used to it."

"Who is he?" asked Bill.

"His name's Richard Mayfield and he's the Team Principal," answered Nick as he led them forward into the garage. "He's a colossal prick most of the time and you can hear his mouth all the way down pit lane. But he does have his moments of pure genius. Although his name's Richard, amongst the team and I, he's affectionately known as 'The Dick.'"

"Lathan!" shouted Mayfield as he became aware of his driver's presence. "What's this? More guests? Are we running a race team here or a bloody soup kitchen?"

Ignoring the question, Nick introduced Bill. "Richard, I'd like for you to meet Bill Watson and his son…"

"Bill Watson, huh?" asked Richard interrupting Nick. "Yes, sir," answered Bill. "And this is my son, Chad."

Completely ignoring Chad, Richard continued. "I heard you were in Australia but I didn't think I'd actually see you at a track," said Richard.

Curious, Bill asked, "Where did you hear I was in Australia?"

"Oh it was that bloody Derek Renshaw character. I guess you two have already met."

Bill scowled at the mention of Derek's name as Richard continued. "He was on the telly the other day saying something about how he ran into you at some bar in Sydney. He said…oh, how did he word it," wondered Richard as he looked up in deep thought.

"Ah! He said seeing you made him think that America needs to work on their plumbing if a lone turd can float all the way over from the U.S. and land on our shores," said Richard as he briefly chuckled. "Quite funny if you ask me."

The sound of the air guns seemed to snap Richard's attention elsewhere as he briefly turned around to face the crew.

"Chewy! If I have to tell to you one more time to zip up your bloody firesuit to hide that furry creature sticking out of your body, I'm going to pull out all of your disgusting chest hair, create another Yowie costume and make you wear it on race day."

With Richard turned away, Nick turned towards Bill, pointed at Richard and quietly said, "The Dick".

Turning around in time to see Nick's antics, Richard turned his attention towards the driver. "And why the hell aren't you suited up and ready to go?!" barked Richard. "Get your bloody lid onto that head of yours and get your scrawny arse in that car! We've got work to do!"

Raising his eyebrows with a surprised but guilty look, Nick said, "I'll see you in a bit, mate," as he turned towards the direction that his gear was located.

"Ah, she's a beauty, isn't she?" said Richard as he motioned towards the car, which was up on jacks in the garage.

"The Holden Commodore. It's a shame they don't sell these to you yanks back in the Colonies. 635 horsepower, V8 engine, sequential gearbox and a top speed of about 300 kilometers per hour. If the sound of one of these ladies doesn't send shivers down your sausage, I don't know what will."

Curious, Bill asked, "Are these the same cars used in the Supercars Series?"

"No, no, no. This is the Super2 Series or what used to be the Dunlop Development Series. These cars are just the hand-me-downs; the old cars the main-game drivers used to drive before the series upgraded to the newest generation of cars."

Now standing with Richard, Bill realized that the taller British man had yet to recognize Chad.

"Richard," said Bill as he tried to get the man's attention once again. "This is my son, Chad."

Staring down towards Bill's wheelchair-bound son, Richard face went blank as if he was unsure of what to say or even how to react. He asked a simple question.

"What the hell happened to you?"

There was a brief moment of silence as Bill felt a sudden surge of anger come to the surface. He contemplated punching the larger man in his nose for asking such an insensitive question to his wheelchair-bound child. Knowing that no good would come from it, as it surely wouldn't teach someone who has the desire to ask a crippled child that kind of a question a lesson, Bill looked the much taller man dead in the eyes and simply said, "Car accident."

There was no response from Richard as he unlocked his gaze.

Remorseless or just plain arrogant, he responded flatly, "Tough luck."

Bill could feel his heartbeat rising as the anger began to surge through him. Who could say something so disrespectful to a child?

"You heartless bastard!"

A sudden voice rose over the noise and commotion. Bill, Chad and Richard turned to see Abby standing there with her hand on her hip and a fresh dose of her own anger on her face. "How much of a dick do you have to be to say something so disrespectful to a child in a wheelchair?" asked Abby as she marched towards Richard.

Before the tall Brit could respond, Abby continued by sticking her finger in his face and saying, "You can run your racing team with an iron fist and you can talk to my brother any bloody way you'd like, but how dare you talk like that to him!" as she gestured to Chad. "Did he ever do anything to you? Or are you so heartless now that you just don't even care anymore?"

"Look," replied Richard as he appeared to have been punched in the gut by the verbal barrage he just endured, "this is a racing team. You need more than heart, you need balls and that's why I'm in charge. If you don't like it, get the hell out my garage."

The two held each other's gaze momentarily before Richard turned to Bill and quietly said, "Nice meeting you," before walking off.

Strangely, Bill could almost make out a tear in the taller man's eye before he donned his aviator sunglasses and walked off.

"Meats! Get this damn car on the ground! Lathan! Why are you not in the bloody car yet?!" shouted Richard as he returned to business.

"Well that's quite the entrance," said Bill as he turned and greeted Abby.

Smiling and giving a slight shrug of her shoulders, Abby replied, "I don't mind putting that brute in his place every now and again. It keeps the senses sharp."

Smiling, Bill turned down towards his son and said, "Chad, I'd like for you to meet Nick's sister, Abby."

Kneeling down in front of Chad just as Nick had previously done,

Abby extended her hand to greet Chad, who unabashedly had a smile on his face from ear to ear.

"It's very nice to meet you, Chaddy. Sorry that you had to hear me go off like that," said Abby.

"Unfortunately, that's not the first time he's heard a conversation like that," replied Bill as he thought of all of the arguments he previously had with Helen.

"Regardless, I'm glad both of you guys could make it out. They should be getting started any minute now," said Abby as she rose to her feet.

"I take it you know all of these guys pretty well?" asked Bill.

"Oh yeah. I've known these boys for several years now. You've obviously met Richard already," said Abby.

With the crew members all suited up in their appropriate fire suits, they were identical in appearance aside from their physical traits which made them stand out from one another. Pointing to another very tall crewman, Abby said, "That's Chewy. He's as strong as a mule, tall as a tree and as hairy as a wallaby. Hence the nickname.

"Then there's Meats," said Abby as she pointed towards a shorter and very thin crewmember. "He used to work in a butchers shop before he found his way over here. Scrawny as a twig, he is. You'd think he'd have a little more meat on his bones by now…"

"Hence the nickname," said Bill as he finished Abby's sentence.

"Exactly!" said Abby as she chuckled.

Pointing to a slender man wearing large framed glasses who was seated at a desk with all of his attention focused on some sort of worksheet, Abby said, "And that's Gadget. He's the team's engineer, and he's a bloody genius. He's a bit of an introvert so he doesn't say much. Single, no kids and runs numbers all of the time; even on his days off. Could probably be making millions doing something else but he loves his racing."

The sound of the engine firing up in the garage caused Bill, Chad and Abby to cover their ears as Chewy and another crew member pushed the car out onto pit lane.

As the three of them were talking, Nick had slipped into the car, strapped himself in and was ready to begin testing.

Once the car had left the garage and began moving down pit lane to enter onto the track, Abby said, “C'mon. Let's go find some seats where we can see everything.”

As they headed towards a sitting area, Bill couldn't help but feel a surge of adrenaline run through him as he heard Nick hit the throttle once he exited the pits.

***

Only a few cars dotted the 1.86 mile circuit as the various teams got their testing underway. Featuring 12 turns of various complexity, Winton Motor Raceway excelled at keeping a driver busy.

Sitting with Abby in one of the grandstand seats, both Bill and Chad were enjoying their first look at an Australian race track. With Chad sitting on his father's lap after leaving the wheelchair at the bottom of the grandstands and being carried up to the top step on Bill's shoulders, the three visitors had a great view of the entire track.

Together, they had witnessed Nick make several runs over the course of an hour or so as the team tested out different configurations on the car. Still, being a newcomer to the track, Bill still couldn't believe how narrow the track appeared at certain points.

“I can't even imagine what it must be like to race on a track like this with a pack of cars all around you,” said Bill as a small line of cars drove past them. “It seems like a very tight course.”

“It's definitely not one of the fastest circuits they come to, but it's certainly challenging and full of action,” said Abby as she pulled a stopwatch out from her pocket. “Did you ever race anything like this back in the States?”

"Not even close," said Bill as he shook his head. "I've only raced at a few circuits, to be fair, but none of them were like this. Tracks like The Circuit of The Americas, Road Atlanta, Sebring; they all had their challenging bits but they're high speed tracks."

As Nick crossed the start/finish line, Abby clicked the start button on her stopwatch. "He's looking good so far but let's see how fast he is."

Taking notice, Bill couldn't help but be slightly amazed at Abby's level of interest. "I didn't realize you were so into racing," said Bill.

"Racing's in my blood, mate. It's in my family's blood," said Abby without taking her eyes off of Nick's car as he maneuvered it around the corners on the track. "You above all should know about that. Plus, he's my brother. It's one thing to see your older sibling out there racing cars but someone's got to crack the whip every once and awhile. I like to think the feedback that comes from family holds a bit more water than most. Plus, Nick's learned by now to take my advice seriously."

"What kinds of advice do you normally give?" asked Bill.

"Mostly for him to just race harder," said Abby. "He can be a bit gun-shy sometimes because he doesn't want to damage the car. He'll lay back instead of fighting for a position. The team's on a tight budget and anything that happens to the car can have serious implications down the line."

As Abby finished talking, Nick crossed the line as Abby hit the stop button on her stopwatch. Turning to see her reaction, Bill saw Abby's lips pucker up as she shrugged her shoulders and tilted her head slightly to the right.

"It's decent enough for the car he's driving but there's still room for improvement," said Abby as she put the stopwatch down.

As Nick slowed the car down for what appeared to be a cooldown lap which, among other things, allowed air to flow through the brake ducts which cool the brakes before coming to a stop, Bill couldn't help but ask what was on his mind.

"So why isn't Nick driving for a Supercars team? He certainly looks to have the talent for it."

"He does, and five or so years ago that would've been all he needed," said Abby. "Nowadays, teams are going after the younger stars and there's certainly plenty to pick from. Nick's a great driver but he's not getting any younger, and with the team's budget, he's getting fewer and fewer races in. At 31-years old, teams and big sponsors want someone who will be sticking around. Plus, the big teams want someone who can push a car to its limit and who isn't afraid to bang doors for position. It's like what I always tell Nick: 'You won't win any races by being a gentleman out on the track.'"

Curious, Bill asked, "Is that why Derek Renshaw's in it?"

Abby turned to Bill with a look of disgust. "No, mate. Just no. Don't get me wrong, though. Renshaw can drive but so can everyone else at his level. Right now, he just happens to be on the best team with the most money that has the best crew and the best car. I don't think he's as fast as Nick but my brother's a bit more conservative on and off the track."

"Unlike Derek?"

"You've met him once, mate, and that's all it usually takes to understand what kind of a person he is. He's loud, he's crude and he's obnoxious. His team tries to keep him on a leash so that he stays out of trouble but for some reason, the fans still love him. He's what you yanks would call a *cowboy*."

Chuckling at the comment, the memory of his encounter with Derek after he had gotten off the simulator at Tubbs' bar surfaced to Bill's mind.

"Not bad though, mate...for an empty track. Try doing that with a full field of real cars and then come talk to me."

"Maybe I will."

"No, mate. You won't."

The words seemed to hang over Bill. Not sure of whether it was a challenge, a dare or simply Derek informing Bill that he was beneath his notice. Regardless, the words seemed to resonate within Bill.

"Well it's pretty obvious that the guy doesn't like me," said Bill.

"That's because he sees you as a threat," said Abby. "Even though it was only a simulator in the back of a bar, you did very well in front of him and all of his friends despite his best efforts to throw you off. Plus, you're the son of a legend around here. That's why he's trying to discredit you now with his antics in the news about you."

As they spoke, a loud booming voice echoed from the garage up to where they were sitting.

"Why is the car just sitting there!? Get the fans on it and get it into the garage! NOW!"

Knowing the British accented voice of the team principal, Bill and Abby couldn't help but laugh.

"So what's his story," asked Bill.

"Who, Richard? Don't really know, to be honest," answered Abby. "He's never really opened up about his past to either myself or Nick, and that's perfectly fine by me. The less I know about him, the better. All I know is that he came over here from the U.K. to manage a few drivers in the Formula Ford program and ended up staying here. The rest is history."

Recounting his previous conversation with Richard, Bill said, "Well he certainly isn't short for words, that's for sure."

"Don't take it personal, mate. He's just an ass," said Abby. "I'm not really sure why he is the way he is but I figure it's none of my business." From where they were sitting, they soon observed the car being pushed into the garage. Standing to her feet, Abby said, "Let's head back down there and see what's going on."

* * *

"It's a bit too loose through the corners. The back end wants to step out on exit and it's a bit squirrelly under braking."

As Abby, Bill and Chad entered the garage, they witnessed Nick, who was still in the car, giving the last of his feedback to both Richard and the engineer, Gadget. As the taller British man simply listened, Gadget was feverishly taking notes.

"We'll get it all sorted out. Good work out there," said Richard. Turning towards the car, Richard patted the hood softly as he leaned up against it.

"It never gets old seeing her out there," said Richard loud enough for everyone in the garage to hear. "This thing works the corners better than a prostitute."

Somewhat instinctively, Abby reached down and covered Chad's ears. "Richard! Can you at least watch your mouth around the kid!" said Abby.

"Just the man I was looking for!" shouted Richard in Bill's direction as he completely ignored both Abby and Chad. Bill, who was now standing beside Nick who had just exited the car, was perplexed as to why Richard would be looking for him.

"Me?" asked Bill feeling silly for even asking that out loud.

Approaching both Nick and Bill, Richard stopped short and appeared to be looking them both over from head to toe.

"Yep, that looks about right," said Richard as he continued to analyze them both. "Stand still."

Walking beside them, he continued to study both of them in a very odd manner.

"Have you finally fallen off the wagon, mate?" asked Nick who looked just as confused as Bill.

"Shut it!" shouted Richard. Several moments passed as Richard walked around the two of them again and again. Finally, Richard stood in front of both men and crossed his arms.

"I've looked you up, Mr. Watson," said Richard with very suspicious eyes. "The cars you raced in the colonies are fairly similar to what we race here."

"They share a few aspects," replied Bill who was still curious as to the sudden interest from Richard.

Richard's face turned into a large smile which revealed his yellow teeth. "Get in."

"Wh...what? Me?"

Rolling his eyes and dropping his folded arms, Richard's smile turned into a face of frustration. "Well of course you! Nick! You two look to be about the same size so get that fire suit off, give it to our esteemed guest here and put him in the car," said Richard as he turned to walk away.

"No!"

The sharp voice caught Richard by surprise. Everyone in the garage suddenly stopped what they were doing to observe the scene unfolding in front of them.

Chewy, who was standing about two feet away from Bill, whispered, "What have you done, mate?"

Nobody in their right mind answered Richard in such a manner. The look now on Richard's face was evident of the fact.

"What in the hell did you just say to me, Watson?" asked Richard calmly.

There was a moment of silence before Bill responded sarcastically. "I'm pretty sure you heard me."

Locking eyes with the smaller American, Richard slowly walked up to him. "You know, I could blow up on you right now but I won't. I could yell so loud that my ancestors would do backflips but I won't," said Richard calmly. "I'm giving you one chance; just one chance to take this opportunity. If you say no again, I won't hold it against you. The crew and I will finish the day out and you can stay as long as you'd like. Then, once we're done, you can crawl back under the rock you came from."

"Why?" asked Bill. It wasn't so much of a question but more of a demand as to the reasoning behind this request.

"Look. I've never met your dad but around here, your name is bloody royalty. I won't give you my reasoning behind it but just trust me when I say I'm up to something. Now what's it going to be, Watson? In or out?"

Sensing the eyeballs of everyone around him burning into him, Bill could feel his face turning red.

"Why would I trust you? I don't know you."

Richard held his ground and spoke calmly as he flashed a grin back at Bill. "Last chance."

Now faced with a decision which he never wanted to face again, Bill's life seemed to come to a crossroads at this very point. His mind wandered for a brief moment as he remembered his very first race in a go-kart from when he was just eight years old. He thought of the moments he shared with his father preparing the kart and how special they were to him. Recounting the time when he started his own business which sponsored his latest racing endeavor, Bill remembered when he purchased his own Trans Am Series TA2 Ford Mustang race car and how Chad and Lena...

There it was again.

He remembered the argument which he provoked which ultimately led to the crash. He remembered the cold headstone which carried her name, the year of her birth followed by the year of her death.

His wife was dead.

He remembered the accident which claimed her life. He thought of the aftermath that left him scarred with the life-altering knowledge which changed everything followed by coming to grips with the knowledge that the accident had paralyzed his son. And for what? Racing cars around a track?

It had brought him nothing during his brief stint in auto racing except for pain, ruin and emptiness. If there was one thing he could take away from it all, however, it was the great memories he had shared with Chad.

The thought of his son caused him to turn down and meet his stare. Bill remembered that it was Chad who had inadvertently brought him out here. He knew, however, that he would do anything for his son. Like himself, Chad was an only child.

After the death of Lena, all they had left was each other. Knowing that he had never gotten anything from racing, Bill knew that his son had indeed been influenced by the sport over the years. Like Bill and his father, racing is what brought Bill and Chad closer together.

Bill remembered the smiles from both Chad and Lena when he downed the entire bottle of champagne after earning his first professional podium finish. The thought alone made him smile.

They were great memories which he would always carry with him. More importantly, they were memories which Chad would always have with him. Even after he grows up and Bill was gone, the memories Chad shared with his father will be there to guide and inspire him for the rest of his life.

Turning again to Chad who was sitting in his wheelchair with Abby standing directly behind him, all that Bill could see was the smiling eyes and the excited face of expectation from his son.

Bill needed no further encouragement.

Meeting Richard's eyes with his own, a smile slipped onto Bill's face. "Alright."

Chapter 13

Although it was a bit snug, Nick's fire suit fit comfortably enough, along with his gloves, shoes and a spare balaclava. It was the first time Bill had put on any sort of race suit in several months but the feeling was one which a driver never truly forgets. Like a knight who puts on his armor before going into battle or a firefighter who puts on his suit before charging into the flames, a driver putting on a race suit transforms them into someone ready to become the next world champion.

As Bill walked out from the restroom, everyone in the garage seemed to stop what they were doing to look. As it so happens, it's not every day that people see the son of an Australian racing legend walk into a garage ready to hit the track for the first time in Australia.

"Well I never thought I'd see the day, mate," said Nick who was sitting with Abby and Chad off to the side of the garage. "A Watson in my race suit. I must say, you look good, mate. Or rather, I look good."

As Bill walked towards the car, he'd suddenly had enough of the stares. "Seriously, guys. I'm not Jesus," said Bill. "Enough with this nostalgic crap and let's get moving."

As everyone chuckled and got back to making their final preparations to get the car on the track again, Bill noticed Richard speaking quietly to some of the crew. The meeting only lasted for a few seconds before the crew broke away and began changing the tires. "I'm surprised," exclaimed Richard as he walked towards Bill. "I didn't think you Americans came in that size anymore," said Richard as he patted Bill on the stomach. "You all set?"

"As ready as I'll ever be considering the circumstances," replied Bill.

"Let's get you in the car."

Slipping into old habits, Bill instinctively walked to the left side of the car which, in the U.S., would've been correct. Knowing what he had done as soon as he arrived at the wrong door, he tried to play it off by continuing his walk around to the other side of the car.

It didn't work.

"Lost already, mate?" asked the short bean-poled figure named Meats.

"I guess I forgot what country I was in," replied Bill. "Old habits die hard, I suppose."

"Fair enough," said Meats. "Just don't turn left when you're supposed to turn right on the track. We all know how you yanks love your left turns."

Like I haven't heard that one before.

Opening the door to the car and slipping into the driver's seat, Bill was surprised at how well the seat insert—which was designed to fit Nick's body—fit that of Bill's. Extending his feet towards the pedals and putting his hands on the wheel and left-handed gear lever, it was almost as if the car had been built around him. It fit him perfectly.

As he sat waiting, Bill was met by the face of Richard in the window area since the window net had yet to be raised. Richard's face looked like that of a stone as he bore his eyes into Bill's. "Three rules," said Richard as he held up his three large fingers. "Rule number one: Don't crash my car or I'll rip your Yankee balls off."

"That'll be an easy one to remember," said Bill sarcastically. He wasn't sure if the taller British man was simply toying with him.

"Number two: Don't crash my car or I'll toss what's left of your Yankee ass in front of a moving bus."

Bill was suddenly silent as all doubt was removed concerning his previous thought. He had a brief idea as to what the next rule would most likely be.

"And rule number three: Have fun!" said Richard with a painted-on smile which revealed his yellow teeth. "Oh and do make sure you smile for the cameras. The world's watching, and after this, everyone is Australia will know that William Watson's son is in the country," said Richard as he added, "No pressure."

Suddenly feeling the butterflies in his stomach as if he were about to be racing in front of the largest crowd he had never seen, Bill replied, "You know, you're not very good at this pep-talk thing."

Still smiling as he closed the window net, Richard rose to his full height and began to walk away but stopped short as he knelt his head back into the car.

"Oh, and did I mention for your sake and mine: Don't crash!"

As Richard walked away, Nick appeared in the same area and gave Bill some advice. "Just remember the simulator and you'll be fine," said Nick. "The power will creep up on you if you're not careful so just take it easy until you feel you've got the hang of it."

"Are you sure this is a good idea?" asked Bill.

Nick laughed at the question and didn't answer.

I guess he thinks I'm joking, thought Bill.

"There'll be a few other cars out there but just remember; we're testing, not racing."

Bill could feel the nervousness building as he looked over past Nick to see Chad sitting with Abby. The smile on his son's face seemed to calm him down.

Noticing Bill's attention was elsewhere, Nick smiled as he turned towards Chad and back to Bill as he said, "Don't worry, mate. We'll look after him while you're gone."

Bill took the meaning of those words to heart but in a different way than they were most likely intended. Talking Bill through some of the controls and switches, Nick did his best to make sure Bill was prepared for whatever the track—and the car—had in store for the American. From behind him, Bill could see the flash of cameras as they snapped photos of Nick leaning into the driver's seat.

"That didn't take long," said Nick of the quick media response. "Just forget about them while you're out there and have fun, mate."

What in the hell am I doing in this car?

Bill couldn't believe the series of events which had led him to being in the driver's seat of an Australian race car.

You really can't make this stuff up.

"Drop the car!" yelled the booming voice of Richard.

Just then, Bill felt as if he had just been slammed to the ground as the car came back onto the earth. With the car still in neutral, the pit crew began pushing the car out onto pit lane with Gadget standing in plain view and showing him when to turn the wheel and when to straighten it up.

With the car on pit lane, Bill closed his eyes for a split second and said a silent prayer.

Protection, Lord.

"Whenever you're ready, hit the ignition and fire her up," said Nick as he took a step back.

Opening his eyes, Bill flipped the *ignition* switch followed by the *start* switch which caused the V8 engine to roar to life. The sound sent chills down Bill's spine and he could suddenly feel goosebumps up his arms. Knowing that he couldn't suppress his smile if he tried, the feeling of excitement suddenly overtook him as he revved the engine.

A voice coming from his helmet barked into his ear.

"Pit lane speed limiter. Turn it on. And make bloody well sure you turn it off once you leave the pits."

The voice of Richard only added to the euphoria Bill currently found himself in. He was a kid in a candy store with a pocket full of quarters right now, and he planned to savor every moment of it.

Pulling the sequential shifter once to put the car into *first* gear, Bill eased onto the throttle with his right foot as his left foot lifted off of the clutch pedal. As the car began to move, Bill gave a casual wave to everyone as he drove down pit lane towards the track entrance.

* * *

With the pit exit leading directly out towards a quick left and right called the *Motorsport News Esses,* Bill let the car glide its way through as he slowly came to grips with the unfamiliar track.

Accelerating slightly down the next straight which leads to the right turn of *Honda Corner,* Bill could already feel himself getting back into the groove of driving as the familiar feeling of the vibrations and the noise put him into the zone.

A short straight led to another right turn at *Nissan Corner* and after that, another short straight called *Foott Waste Straight* followed by a sweeping left turn which led Bill onto Turn 6 of *Roll-over Corner.*

The next part was a relatively slow section but the temptation to push harder was there. Bill resisted and maintained a slower speed as he learned the track. Going through Turns 7, 8 and 9, Bill eased onto the throttle and shot down *Shannon's Straight* towards the right turn of *NorthernBM Corner—a* long straight which gives drivers a chance to open the throttle and leads to the final two turns of the track. Coming out of the final corner, Bill passed by the pits which were on his left as he began his first flying lap.

Although he had already visited the first section of the track when he exited pit lane, this was his first time entering it at speed, so he was cautious under braking. Clipping the apexes of each turn, Bill got on the power after Turn 2 but did so a little too hard which caused the rear wheels to spin as the back end kicked out slightly.

"Whoa there, lady!" said Bill aloud as he lifted off the throttle slightly to regain traction. Now comfortably back in control for the time being, Bill pitched the car into the right turns of *Honda* and *Nissan Corners.* Still learning the track, Bill noticed that one of the other cars which was also on the track was coming up behind him. Maintaining his line and pace as they approached *Shannon's Straight,* Bill rolled off the throttle to indicate to the other driver that he knew he was there and that he was letting him by.

As the other car drove past, Bill was now in an ideal situation to learn the track at speed by following the overtaking car.

A classic learning technique used in many driving schools all over the world, lead-follow exercises allow new drivers to follow someone who is familiar with both the car and the track to get up to speed much quicker. This teaches where the braking points are and how hard you can push the car through the corners.

At first, Bill had trouble keeping up with the car he was following. Compared to his former TA2 car, this car had a lot more oversteer than Bill was used to, the balance felt off since he was sitting on the right side and the rear of the car was very loose. It felt as if the tires were worn out but Bill did his best to maintain his pace. As the laps rolled on, however, Bill began getting more and more comfortable with the car as he was able to maintain pace. Within a few laps, the gap between himself and the car he was following began to shrink.

Before long, Bill was only a few car lengths behind the other car as they sprinted down the front *Kitome Straight.* Heading into the Esses, Bill began setting up the other driver for a pass. Seeing an opening heading into *Honda Corner,* Bill moved to the inside, braked later and harder than the other driver and completed the pass before heading into *Nissan Corner.*

Bill was beside himself with excitement. On the outside, he may have appeared calm and collected but inside he was smiling from ear to ear as he fixed his gaze upon the next car up the road. He was now completely in the zone. Despite the apparent looseness of the car, Bill felt connected to the road and now felt confident enough to be able to carry a decent pace around the track.

As he continued to navigate the corners, Bill was heading towards *Northern BM Corner* when the voice of Richard came on the radio.

"Box this lap, Bill. Box this lap."

Entering pit lane, Bill decelerated and hit the pit lane speed limiter button on the steering wheel which allowed him to maintain the designated pit lane speed while going down the long straight.

Seeing as there were only a handful of teams testing today, it was relatively easy for Bill to spot the pit stall as he turned the car in and brought it to a perfect stop inside the lane.

***

"The way you were driving, you'd think you were gunning for my job," said Nick as he slapped Bill on the back. "Great run, mate. How'd the car feel?"

After exiting the car and removing the helmet, HANS device and balaclava, Bill knew that there was no way to hide his smile now.

"It was great," answered Bill. "It was a bit more slippery than I thought it'd be which surprised me a few times. It almost felt like the tires were already used up."

"You can thank me for that," said the booming voice of Richard coming from behind. "We put on older rubber before you set off."

"Why'd you do that?" asked Nick.

"Firstly," explained Richard to Bill, "because you're not worth the cost of a new set of green tires and we also need to save those," explained Richard. "Secondly, I wanted to see if you could even *tell* that you were on used rubber. And third, I wanted to see what your times would be once you got up to speed on the used rubber."

There was a long pause as the three men stood there staring at each other. Bill could see Abby in the background standing alongside Chad as the two watched and listened to what was going to happen.

"Well?" asked Richard.

Confused, Bill looked to Nick for a brief second before asking the obvious, "Well, what?"

"Are you going to bloody ask me how you did or are we just going to stand here and look at each other like cattle?" exclaimed Richard.

Bill was definitely curious as to what his times were, but it was Nick who had finally had enough of the games. "C'mon, out with it, mate. How did he fare?"

Smiling all of the sudden, Richard snapped his fingers and extended his arm. Just then, Gadget came running over and put a clipboard into Richard's extended hand.

Looking down at it, Richard asked, "Are you sure you two aren't long lost twins or something? You wear the same size suit, have the same size head, fit into the same seat perfectly..." Handing the clipboard to Bill, Richard added, "and now you're running nearly identical lap times."

As Bill inspected the details on the clipboard, Nick eagerly moved to look over his shoulder so he could see the results.

Nick Lathan—1:24.969
Bill Watson—1:25.128

"Bloody hell, mate," said Nick. "On old tires, at that. Are you sure you're not gunning for my seat?"

Bill chuckled a bit at the idea. "Don't worry about me. I'm just thankful for the opportunity to give your car a steer," he said.

"Don't thank me, mate. Thank this bloke," said Nick as he pointed to Richard. "He kept me in the dark about this. I had no idea what he was planning and, to be honest, I still don't."

"I'll explain everything to you later, Nick. We're about done here for the day so let's get everything wrapped up," said Richard.

Stepping towards Bill, Richard extended his hand and said, "Mr. Watson, it's been a pleasure."

Meeting Richard's handshake, Bill replied, "The pleasure was all mine, Mr. Mayfield."

Chapter 14

After returning the gear he had borrowed, thanking everyone again for the chance to participate and giving a special thank-you to Abby for watching Chad while he was out on track, Bill and his son loaded up and departed from Winton. Electing to stay the night at the local hotel which Nick's team was also using, Bill and Chad hit the road back to Sydney early the next morning.

The drive home went by quicker for Bill since Chad was awake for the entire trip. Despite his current inability to speak, Chad smiled as he listened to his father go on and on about the experience and how lucky he felt to be able to drive an Australian race car. Bill went on for hours about the whole ordeal and before long, they found themselves pulling into the garage back at Greg's house.

Coming out of the house to greet them, Greg was dressed in the most relaxed manner in which both Bill and Chad had ever seen him. Wearing loose fitting workout shorts, an old Holden t-shirt and flip-flops while sporting a weekend beard, Greg was almost unrecognizable.

"Welcome back!" shouted Greg as Bill turned the car off and opened the door. "How was the drive?"

"Better than I could've hoped," replied Bill. "Thanks again for letting us use your car."

"It's not a problem at all," said Greg. "I would ask how everything went but I already know."

"What do you mean by that?" asked Bill as he moved to the other side of the car to help Chad exit the vehicle.

"I'm not sure if you saw the photographers and cameramen but they certainly saw you," replied Greg as he assisted Bill by getting Chad's wheelchair out of the trunk of the car. "There were stories all over the place about how the son of an Australian racing legend is in the country and at a race track."

Bill recalled seeing a photographer or two but was certainly surprised to find that the news had traveled so far and so quickly.

"I think they're just making a big deal out of nothing," said Bill. "I was just there for the experience and it was very gracious of the team to let me take their car for a spin."

"Regardless, mate, you certainly woke up a bit of a sleeping monster in me," said Greg. "All of this talk about racing inspired me to do some catching up on the Supercars Series. I must've watched five or six races while you boys were gone."

"Yeah? Did it bring back any memories from your own racing days?" asked Bill.

"Bill, those days are long behind me," answered Greg. "Although I certainly had fun with it, your father was the real racer. Now, however, the guys racing in our top category are extremely competitive. It was really nice just to kick back, relax and watch them go at it."

Smiling at the thought of Greg—who could hardly ever be found in the same spot for more than a few minutes—lying on a couch watching TV all day, Bill said, "Well you look very…relaxed."

Taking a deep breath and exhaling it slowly, Greg replied by saying, "I certainly feel very refreshed, that's for sure. I think I really needed this."

"So did this guy," said Bill as he opened the door for Chad. "Did we have fun or what?"

Chad, still smiling, gave a thumbs up with both hands as he extended his arms forward.

As the two men assisted Chad in getting out of the vehicle and into his wheelchair, Bill began explaining to Greg how the event unfolded and how shocked he was at how well everything turned out.

"I'm just glad that I didn't stuff the car into the wall. I haven't driven a race car in several months," said Bill as the three of them sat at the kitchen table.

As Bill continued explaining the details from the trip, Greg got up and prepared lunch for the three of them.

"From the footage they showed during the stories they were running about you, it looked like you at least knew what you were doing out there," said Greg.

After they had eaten and Bill had finished telling all of the details, Greg asked, "So what's next?"

Caught off guard by the question, Bill wasn't sure. He had been so swept up with what had just happened that he hadn't bothered to ask himself what might transpire after the fact.

Shrugging his shoulders, Bill replied, "I don't know. Maybe get some race tickets and go watch the team race. To be honest, I don't even know when or where they race next."

Grabbing their plates and carrying them to the kitchen, Greg said, "I know that the Great Race is coming up in the next few months. Maybe you could score some tickets to it. Just remember your old friend here if you do," said Greg as he pointed to himself.

"The Great Race?" asked Bill.

"The Bathurst 1000. C'mon, mate. Surely you've heard about that," replied Greg.

"I have. I've just never heard it called that before," said Bill. "Mount Panorama...where my dad won, right?

"That's right. And in his debut year, at that," said Greg. "I don't think I'll ever forget it and neither will Australia. Doing something like that is unheard of nowadays."

"If it's coming up soon, I'll ask Nick and see if he'll be able to get us all in," said Bill. "It'd be great to see the place where my dad..."

A sudden pain surged through Bill's head, causing him to cut his words short. Losing himself mid-sentence, he did all he could to maintain his composure as he put his fingers against the temples of his head to try to subdue the pain.

A few seconds of silence passed as Greg realized that Bill was in fact in pain. "Are you alright, mate?"

"Yeah," replied Bill. "It's just a headache. I'm probably just dehydrated. It's been a long drive," said Bill.

Looking up at Greg, Bill could see in his eyes that the man was suspicious of something. There would be no fooling him, however, as one didn't earn as many accolades as Greg has without possessing a fair bit of common sense.

"If you don't mind, I'm just going to lie down for a bit. Hopefully it'll wear off in time," said Bill as he headed towards his room.

"You go right ahead, mate," replied Greg as he continued to look suspicious. "I'll take care of everything here."

* * *

It was initially difficult to fall asleep when Bill first laid down on his bed. Being that it was only two in the afternoon, he lay there motionless for several moments until his body and mind finally dozed off. Despite the fact that he had just returned from an action-packed adventure, it was a dreamless sleep. However, it was much needed. Bill was only expecting to sleep for a few hours or so but it turns out that his body had other plans.

Nine hours later, Bill woke up. It was now 11 pm and he found himself wide awake.

"Well this sucks," said Bill quietly to himself as he sat up in bed. Standing up slowly, Bill felt that the effects of his massive headache were gone. Confident that he could move about without fear of tumbling down and waking up everyone in the house, Bill opened the door of his room and walked out into the darkness of the hallway.

As he walked down the hall, Bill peered into Chad's bedroom through the partially cracked door to see him sound asleep. Turning back towards his own room, Bill suddenly remembered that he had promised Greg he would clean out his car of any junk food remnants from his trip. With everyone else asleep and Bill wide awake, this seemed like the perfect time to do it.

Tip-toeing down the stairs without making so much as a sound, Bill now had to get across the living room and kitchen as the door to the garage was on the far end of the latter.

Bill was about halfway across the living room when a small lamp suddenly clicked on.

"Trying to sneak out, are we?"

Jumping at the sudden voice, Bill turned to see Greg seated on the couch. "You scared me there, Greg," said Bill. "My nap went a little longer than I thought. I was just gonna clean your car out like I'd promised." Bill noticed that Greg had a bottle of scotch on the coffee table in front of him with a small glass about a quarter full in his left hand. His cell phone also lay on the table in front of him.

Sitting motionless, Greg didn't seem his usual happy self. There was no smile on his face even as he held Bill's stare with a fierce intensity.

Bill couldn't help but notice. "Are you alright?" asked Bill.

A few long seconds passed before Greg responded. "I am, but what about you?"

Shrugging his shoulders at the odd question, Bill replied by saying, "I'm not sure I know what you mean."

Closing his eyes and exhaling slowly, Greg waited several seconds before he spoke again. "Your little *headache* incident earlier got me thinking about something," said Greg as he opened his eyes and met Bill's stare again. "I distinctly remember someone talking to me about something very similar a few years ago but I just couldn't put my finger on who it was. I couldn't recall if it was a patient, a family member or a friend. Then out of the blue, I got a phone call from your father."

Lifting the glass of scotch to his lips, Greg finished off the drink in one swig and continued.

"Aside from catching up on things and our normal banter, I decided to go out on a whim and tell him about what happened to you earlier with your *headache*. Turns out he was as shocked as I was and had quite a lot to say about a similar scenario that affected someone you both knew."

Greg let the words hang in the air for several seconds. He could already see from Bill's face that he knew what he was referring to.

"It doesn't take a rocket scientist or someone with a PhD in brain surgery to put two and two together, Bill," said Greg.

Bill suddenly felt as if he had been punched in the stomach. "When were you going to tell me, mate?" asked Greg as his voice began to rise.

Sighing deeply, Bill knew there was no hiding it now.

Greg continued. "And not just me, but your dad. And Chad! When were you planning on telling them?!"

"It's not that simple," said Bill softly.

"Bullshit!" shouted Greg as he stood to his feet. "You're not only disregarding yourself but you're disregarding your family!"

"Chad comes first," said Bill. "I'm only here for him and he's come too far only to be hit again."

"It doesn't need to be this way, Bill. There's other ways to go about…"

"I can't, Greg," said Bill cutting Greg off. "I just can't."

The two men stood in the dimly lit room for several moments before Greg motioned to the other couch for Bill to have a seat. As the two sat down, Bill still felt like there was an elephant in the room which was being ignored.

It was Greg who finally took the shot. "When did you find out?"

Bill gathered his thoughts and told his friend all of the details.

* * *

Several days had now passed since Bill and Chad's trip to Winton. During that time, the two had returned to their normal routines.

Over the course of their time in Australia, Chad had learned to take his new way of life in stride as he was now able to practically do everything by himself. Although Bill always supervised, Chad had grown into a very capable boy considering his condition. Although he still required assistance with certain physical actions such as going down the stairs, Chad needed little help with mundane tasks such as getting out of bed, climbing in and out of the car and making his way around in the wheelchair.

Still, it was Bill's fatherly duties to make sure that Chad was okay. Despite how well Chad had adapted to his condition, Bill hadn't yet come to the point where he felt comfortable leaving Chad on his own to navigate the obstacles of his daily life.

As Bill was sitting with his son on a Saturday morning, there was a knock on the front door of the house. Still attending to Chad upstairs, Bill knew that Greg would attend to whoever was there.

Not paying much attention to the knock anymore, Bill returned his focus to his son. With all of their physical therapy appointments with Greg completed for the week, Saturdays were normally the days when Chad enjoyed just staying inside and hanging out with his dad.

"So what's on the agenda today, Mr. Watson?" asked Bill as he smiled at his son. "Do you want to catch up on our TV shows, go see a movie, go to the..."

Bill was cut-off mid sentence as Chad pointed towards something. It was his video game console.

One of the few items Chad brought with him during the journey from the U.S. to Australia, Chad's video game console was often seen by Bill as an escape for his son. Plus, Bill knew that very few kids (and a some adults) could ever be separated from their video games.

"Hey, I got back into this racing stuff because of a big video game. Seems only fair that you get to have fun too, right?"

Chad nodded his head up and down in the childish manner which he never seemed to lose.

"Alright," said Bill. "Let's get you set up."

Just then, Bill heard Greg's voice coming from downstairs. "Bill, you've got company."

Furrowing his brow as he thought about who it could be, his answer came from downstairs via the sound of a booming voice with a heavy British accent. "And hurry it up, Watson! I haven't got all day!"

Chapter 15

"Well you look fresh," said the towering figure of Richard Mayfield as Bill made his way down the stairs.

"Richard," said Bill as he acknowledged the older man. "I'm surprised to see you here. What brings you out today?"

As Bill made his way into Greg's foyer where he saw Richard standing, he was also surprised to see both Nick and Abby there as well.

"Nick, Abby," said Bill, genuinely shocked to see them. "What a surprise!"

Extending his hand, Nick greeted Bill with a handshake. "Good to see you too, mate. Sorry about the unannounced visit but we were kind of hoping you'd have a moment to chat with us a bit."

"Hi, Bill," said Abby with a cheerful smile on her face. "Where's Chaddy?"

"Oh he's upstairs playing video games," replied Bill. "You know how kids are."

"Yeah," said Abby as she nudged her brother. "We know how kids love their video games. Don't we, Nick?"

"Oh, can it, Abby," said an embarrassed Nick.

Popping his head around the corner, Greg, who had stepped away as Bill came down the stairs, said, "Why don't you all come in and have a seat."

As the three guests followed Greg and Bill into the living room, Greg pointed them towards the sitting area where they all found a seat.

"Can I get you all anything to drink?" asked Greg.

Nick and Abby each asked for a glass of water, but Richard seemed content. "Not for me, thanks," he said with a smile. Reaching into his jacket, the Brit pulled a silver flask from his coat pocket. "I've brought my own refreshments."

In unisom, Nick and Abby both rolled their eyes.

Taking a seat across from the three guests, Bill's curiosity could take no more. "So what brings you guys out here?"

"Down to business," said Richard in his typical booming voice. "I like it! Nick?"

As if taking a cue, Nick spoke up. "You impressed a lot of people with your run at Winton last week. Even though it was only a few laps, you got the media stirring with rumors and whatnot."

"Rumors? What kind of rumors?" asked Bill with a slight chuckle.

"We'll get there," replied Richard just as Nick was about to speak. "Please continue."

Giving Richard an annoyed look, Nick turned back to Bill and continued. "Apparently, you touched a chord in the heart of many Aussies. Whether it be memories of your dad or the story of how you ended up out here or..."

Bill interrupted. "Of how I ended up here? Who would know why I'm here?"

"Word gets around, Bill. When video of you started going around, people started coming forward who saw you at certain places and the media starting putting pieces together," said Nick.

"It wasn't going to stay a secret forever," said Richard. "Your name and heritage are too great to keep hidden." He added, "Since your time on the track, we've been bombarded with calls from people and businesses who want to support us because they think you're on our team."

"Except that I'm not," said Bill flatly.

Speaking sharply, Nick said, "Look, mate, I told you a while ago that our team doesn't have the money to run full-time anymore.

It's just not there. However, we've recently been approached by a major financier. They've agreed to sponsor the team for a full season starting next year."

"That's great news," said Bill, truly excited about the great news for his friend. "That's exactly what you were looking for, right?"

There was a brief moment of silence and Bill could almost pick up that there was more that was waiting to be said. "Why do I get the feeling that you three didn't come out here just to tell me that?"

"We didn't," said Richard in a flat monotone voice. "There was a condition with this agreement," said Nick.

Bill chuckled. "Of course there is."

"The company, which is called *Higgins Financial,* is all over the world but is new to Australia. They're some capital management firm which caters towards people who make a lot more money than you and I do. They're backed by some serious heavy hitters," said Nick.

"Sports stars, celebrities, real estate moguls..." said Richard.

"They're wanting to get their name out there in Australia but they want to do it in a big way and with a figurative bang. So they've made us a proposition," said Nick. "After seeing the reaction *you* caused, they did their homework on you and liked what they found. They want our team to bring you on board. And in doing so, they'll enter us as a wild card entry into the race."

"What are you talking about? What race?" asked Bill.

The question hung in the air for a brief moment. Richard, who had allowed a slight grin to slip onto his face which slightly exposed his yellow teeth, looked the American who was sitting in front of him in the eye and uttered one word.

"Bathurst."

Bill was speechless and felt like he'd just been punched in the gut as the heaviness of that single word sunk in. The look on his face seemed to mirror his internal feelings.

"It'd be a one race deal," said Nick. "If we run strong and finish well, they've agreed to foot the bill for the team next season."

Bill was already shaking his head. "I don't understand. Why me? There are dozens of other drivers who are more experienced that you could pick from and..."

"They don't want any other driver, mate. They want you," replied Nick. "They saw you on the screen and they saw an opportunity. They remembered how your dad set this country ablaze with his actions and became a legend at Bathurst. Then he vanished and now all these years later, his son returns and is now in a race car as well. It's nostalgic stuff like that which made them reach out to us."

Bill wasn't convinced. "So you're asking me to race in the Bathurst 1000."

"Yes we are," replied Nick smiling. "This is the big time, mate."

"That would mean we'd be racing against Derek Renshaw, too. Right?" asked Bill

"The one and only," said Richard with a smile on his face.

"So I'm guessing that since this is the 'big time' Supercars series, we'd also be switching to one of the newer cars, right?" asked Bill.

"You would be correct," answered Richard. "We'll be running the newer Gen2 cars, which are the ones that replaced the cars we're currently driving in the Super2 Series."

"Have any of you guys driven or so much as worked on the newer cars?"

"Nope," replied Richard again.

"So what chance do you have to begin with?"

"None," answered Richard flatly.

Bill lowered his head and chuckled.

"We'd be getting the chassis from an established team," said Nick. "They'd set the car up for us and share their data but obviously their priorities will be their own cars. Don't worry, though. Our boys know enough about this sort of thing to take it from there."

"Plus," added Richard, "nobody's expecting us to show up and set the world on fire with speed. We'll have expectations for the race but they'll be reasonable given that it's a new car and chassis for us."

"Speaking of chassis," said Abby, "I think you'll prefer the marque which we'd be using."

A heavy sigh came from Nick. "The man signing the checks at Higgins Financial likes his Fords, so the deal says we have to drive the Ford Falcon. It looks like I've come full circle."

Bill glanced over at Richard to see if the comment would invoke some sort of reaction from the British man.

"Don't look at me," said Richard. "I couldn't care less about that sort of thing. I'd put Nick here in a shopping cart if these blokes paid for it."

"Guys," said Bill with his head hung low, "I really appreciate you coming out here, but I have to wholeheartedly decline the offer."

"What? Why?!" demanded Nick.

"Look, I've entertained the idea of driving a car and maybe even doing a race here and there if the chance came up in a lower series, but Bathurst? In the Supercars Series? For 1000 kilometers in a car neither of us have ever driven on a track I've never even seen? I haven't been in a race in months and on top of that, I've never been in an endurance race either. I really appreciate the offer but I don't really have an interest in going on international television and making a fool of myself."

"Bill, this is Bathurst!" said Abby. "Do you know how many people would give anything to get a chance like this? This is the race which made your dad a bloody legend in this country."

"I understand that, but I'm not my dad," said Bill who was getting visibly irritated. "Do you guys want me to call him up and have him come down here to race? It seems I can't escape his shadow and everyone expects me to be William Watson all over again."

Standing up, Bill continued. "I've got news for you guys. I'm not my dad!"

"Bill, please," said Nick. "Do it for me. Do it for the team. If only to help us out next season. Nobody's expecting us to blitz the field or anything like that. We just need to go out there and have a race. That's all."

"Nick, you're not really putting me in an ideal situation, you know," said Bill. "If I say no, what's that make me look like? I end up not only ruining your deal but your season as well. Can't you find someone else to do this?"

"I know it's not ideal but to be honest, they're more interested in you at the moment," said Nick. "Who knows, if we put on a good showing, maybe they could get you in a car next year racing full-time as well."

That was exactly what Bill didn't want to hear. The comment from Nick seemed to snap Bill back to his original priorities.

"I don't want to be in a full-time ride next season," said Bill sternly. "I'm here in this country because my son is paralyzed and can't walk and still won't speak. As soon as he's better, we're leaving."

"Bill, what's the matter with you?" asked Abby. "We're not asking you to give up your son. We're not asking you to give up anything. We're asking you to just do what seems to come naturally to you, and that's to drive a race car. You're being handed a fully-funded car to run in Australia's greatest race. How could you say no to that?"

Bill could feel his face turning red. As he stood there in front of the three guests, he turned to see Greg standing in the kitchen.

Greg, meeting his stare, could knowingly sense why Bill was so uncomfortable all of the sudden.

Returning his gaze to Nick, Bill answered his friends request flatly. "Look, I didn't come to this country for fame and glory or to chase a dream that's long gone. What I need is for my son to get better. Having cameras and fully-funded race cars around isn't going to help. I wanna help my son and enjoy the time I have…".

Bill stopped short. He had said enough on the topic. An awkward silence fell over the room as Bill began to feel the stares of the three guests digging into him.

"I'm sorry. I just can't."

As Bill turned and began to walk away, Nick quickly rose to his feet.

"Why the hell not?! What are you so afraid of? Is there some reason for all of this nonsense?!"

Bill stopped in his tracks as he felt the weight of what he was about to say bear down upon his shoulder. It was time to let go of the burden of secrecy.

"Yeah, there is," he said softly.

Turning to face Nick, Abby and Richard, Bill took a deep breath before revealing his darkest secret.

"I have cancer."

* * *

"Mr...Watson," said the man as he looked for Bill's last name on his clipboard. "I'm Dr. Owens. How are you feeling?"

"Still a little dizzy but I'm just wanting to go see my son," said Bill as he was hoping to keep the visit—which he assumed was simply a routine check-up—as short as possible.

"I understand," said Dr. Owens. "I won't keep you any longer than I have to but there are a few things which I'm needing to talk to you about."

Suddenly alert and sitting up as straight as he could, Bill asked, "Is this about my son, Chad?"

Taking a seat on a chair across from the bed, Dr. Owens exhaled softly. "No, Mr. Watson. This is about you."

"Me?"

"Yes. While you were unconscious, we performed a CT scan which is somewhat routine after any sort of traumatic brain injury. We were initially wanting to see the extent of the damage caused by the accident but we found something else along the way."

Bill could feel his heart sink further into his chest.

"After speaking with your father, he informed us that your mother recently passed away from a very rare form of brain cancer, correct?

"Uh, yeah that...that's right," stuttered Bill.

"I know that this is a lot to take in at the moment with everything going on, but we pulled her file and read that she suffered from a variation of what's called Pleomorphic Xanthroastrocytoma. Although it is treatable, her case was extremely aggressive. Tell me, have you experienced any severe headaches recently?"

"I...I don't think so. No, sir."

"Any seizures, unexplained sickness or sudden drowsiness?"

"No," said Bill. "Why are you asking me all of this?"

* * *

Bill recalled the fateful meeting he had with his doctor while he was still in the hospital recovering from his concussion after the accident. Relaying the information to Richard, Nick and Abby, the three guests sat speechless as Bill explained the sudden headaches and how they'd progressively been getting worse.

"The doctors said that I have the same type of cancer that killed my mom," said Bill. "The only difference is that the knock I took to the head during the accident seems to have irritated it somehow. It caused some inflammation which is making it spread faster. If it wasn't for the accident, though, I never would've known until it was too late."

Silence enveloped the room, but it was Abby who finally spoke up. Still shocked, her eyes were as open as Bill had ever seen as she asked, "Can't they operate or give you a treatment of some sort?"

"They can operate but because of where it is and how much it's spread, it'd be extremely risky. Since I'm the only one Chad has left, I can't risk being an immobile vegetable in a hospital bed especially with how much he needs me right now."

Wiping the tears she was trying to hide from her eyes, Abby's questions continued. "How long do…I mean…how much time…"

"Eighteen months, two years," said Bill. "Three at the most. Right now it's just showing as headaches but it'll get worse over time."

"How worse?" asked Abby.

Bill sighed deeply. "It'll get to the point where I won't even remember any of your names."

Nick, feeling like he'd been kicked in the stomach, finally spoke up. "I'm sorry, mate. I didn't mean to pressure you like that."

"You didn't know, Nick. Don't worry about it. I probably should've told you guys sooner," said Bill.

"Who knows so far?" asked Abby.

Looking around, Bill said, "Just the people in this room," motioning to Greg who was now standing off to the side in the living room. "I haven't told Chad or my dad yet."

Taking a deep sigh, Nick slapped his knees as he stood up. "Alright. We'll work something else out. I'll call up the people at *Higgins* and let them know…"

"No," interrupted Bill. "You're not going to mention this to anyone outside of this room. This can't get out. Not until I tell my son."

"So what do you propose we do then?" asked Nick. "I can't exactly keep them on the line forever."

Bill said, "Here's what I have in mind."

He was about to speak when the sound of a silly chuckle emanated from the corner of the room. It came from the one person who'd yet to speak up since Bill had made his revelation. Everyone in the room turned to look at Richard.

"You have a problem, Richard?" asked Bill sharply.

Before answering, the tall British man chuckled again. This time it was louder. "Yeah, I do have a problem," said Richard. "And it's not new race cars, big-dollar contracts or corporate sponsorships."

Richard stopped laughing and turned to face Bill, suddenly serious.

"It's you."

Recalling the time when Bill first met Richard at the track in Winton and felt like he was about to punch the taller British man in the face for demeaning his son, a similar burst of adrenaline kicked into Bill's system. "And what problem is that, huh? That I won't drive your race car?" asked Bill as he made no effort to hide his anger.

"No. My problem is that I can't believe I ever wasted my time on a loser like you."

"Richard!" said a shocked Abby. "After what he just told us, how could you say..."

"I don't care if he told us he had one more day left to live," said Richard interrupting Abby. "If that were true, Mr. Bill Watson, you'd just go off and hide in a hole and wait to die because that's exactly what you're doing now. You're the son of a legend but you're nothing like your father. Hell, you're not even half the man your father was."

Having enough of the Brit's mouth, Bill advanced on Richard ready to strike, but Nick stepped between the two and held the angry American back.

Richard went on. "From the moment I first met you, you've been some sort of a recluse; always afraid to put yourself out there because the truth is that you're afraid. And what do people do when they're afraid? They hide. In your case, you're hiding behind your illness and you're hiding behind your son."

"You sonofabitch!" shouted Bill as he lunged toward Richard. Nick and Greg both jumped in to hold Bill back as Bill tried to break free from their grasps.

The sudden display of force startled Abby as she voiced her protest. "Oh, my God! Bill, stop!"

Richard didn't so much as flinch. "Am I supposed to be afraid of you?" asked Richard as he remained seated.

The words caused Bill to stop struggling for the moment but he kept his furious eyes locked sharply on Richard as Greg and Nick maintained their hold.

Pointing his long index finger at Bill, Richard continued. "Is your rage and anger towards me for saying what you already know supposed to make me frightened? Oh, I know. You think because you've got death and misery in your life that you've got some right to be angry with me simply for pointing that out to you."

Standing up, Richard continued. "Allow me to fill you in on a little secret. Not too many people know this, but I think you need to hear it."

Released from the grasps of Nick and Greg, Bill calmed momentarily as he listened. "I originally came to this country decades ago with *my* son. He was about 17-years old at the time and he was already a fantastic driver. We came here because he just loved Australian touring cars. I mean, he wouldn't shut up about them. He had done so well in karting back in England that when he got a chance to test drive for a team here in Australia, we were on the first flight out."

Pausing for a moment, Richard let his head drop towards the ground as he recalled the memory. "I was at the track with him when it happened."

Reaching into his jacket, Richard pulled the silver flask from his breast pocket, unscrewed the lid and took a swig. "I was there doing what I did best for my son—shaking hands, making connections and meeting potential sponsors while he was out on track living his dream."

Tightening the lid on his flask, he held it in his hands as he fixed his eyes upon it. "When I heard the squeal of the tires followed by the sound of the crash, I felt a pain like I'd never felt before and haven't felt since. In my heart, I knew what had just happened but I didn't want to believe it. My son was too good of a driver."

Richard continued. "Brake failure? Blown out tire? Nobody knows. His car ended up rolling half a dozen times before it came to a rest shiny side down. That's when the fire started. By the time safety crews got out to the crash, it was nothing more than an enormous fireball."

Abby, who had long suspected that there was more to the man that Richard was, began to weep softly.

"I went back to England only to remember that I was divorced and Ty was my only child. I fell into such a deep state of depression that I lost my job and eventually lost my house."

A moment of silence fell over the room. Richard, continuing to stare at the shiny silver flask in his hand, seemed to be lost in thought as the memories of old flooded over him.

Standing there lost in the moment as well, Bill finally spoke. "What changed?" he asked calmly.

Lifting his head to look up at Bill, Richard smiled and spoke softly. "I did."

He continued. "Years passed by and I was just scraping a living as I went from job to job. I ended up selling everything I had except for the clothes on my back just to buy more drink to drown myself away. I had nothing. Finally, I had had enough of nothing. I decided that I was going to end my life."

Holding up his flask, Richard went on.

"So there I was with this flask and a bottle of pills in my one bedroom flat ready to do the deed. I had drank myself into such a state that I wouldn't feel a thing.

"That's when I heard him."

"Heard who?" asked Bill.

Richard paused momentarily before answering. "My son, Ty. You all probably think I'm delusional, and I'm sure I was at the time, but I heard his voice as clear as you hear mine.

"It was just a few short words but they changed my life from that moment on. He said 'We're not done yet, Dad'."

Richard smiled at the memory as he continued. "It was something he used to say to me after every one of his races. He was such a smart kid. Always looking towards the bigger picture and always knowing that there was more out there for him than what was in front of him at the time. That was the first time someone had called me 'dad' since the accident years ago. After that, I knew I had to turn my life around and start living for something.

"I decided right then and there that I would live such a life that's worthy of my son's memory. I wouldn't let my son's legacy die with me. I wouldn't be so selfish as to let him be forgotten like that. I vowed that I would live on and live my life as if he were with me everywhere I went. So I came back to Australia, and I began helping young drivers who didn't have the money to get into racing find a way to chase their dreams. Isn't that right, Nick?"

Nick, touched by the story, could only nod his head up and down in agreement.

"And that, Bill Watson, is why I'm standing here today. I decided that I wouldn't run from my ghosts anymore. I would live."

Bill, who was now free from the grasps of Nick and Greg, stood motionless as he listened to the older British man.

"The only question I have for you is this," said Richard. "What's your story going to be? Will you rise to live a life worthy of celebration and remembrance? Will you be someone known for standing up every time he's knocked down? Or will you fall, become forgotten and let the legacy of your family die with you?"

Everyone in the room fell still as if awaiting for a certain sound to pull them from their motionless state. Bill, who could feel the eyes of everyone in the room on him, felt as if he was standing on the brink of something huge. It was almost as if his life were being torn just as two masses of land are torn apart during a violent earthquake.

As it stood now, he was trying to bridge the gap with one foot on each side, unable to decide which side to choose. One choice defied all logic and explanation while the other, although safer, would seem to cause him to do just as Richard said and become forgotten. He didn't want that. Bill needed to know that his son would remember the man that his father was and not the man he could've been. He had to make a decision and he couldn't run from it any longer.

Lifting his head and looking Richard in the eye, Bill finally spoke.

"It must feel good."

A perplexed look came on Richard's face as a result of the unexpected comment. "What do you mean?" he asked.

"Knowing that if your career in racing ever falls short, you could always pick up a gig as a motivational speaker."

A large smile surfaced from Richard's face as Nick, Abby and Greg laughed at the comment.

Richard was still smiling when he softly asked, "So what do you say?" Nodding his head slowly up and down, Bill looked Richard in the eyes as a smile slipped across his face.

"Alright."

"Yeah, mate? We're doing this?!" said Nick.

"Yeah," said Bill who was now smiling himself. "We're doing this."

Nick couldn't contain his excitement as he began to cheer. Embracing Bill, Nick picked the American up off the ground and began swinging him around as the others in the room laughed.

"We're racing at Bathurst!" shouted Nick. "The bloody Bathurst 1000!"

Still smiling from ear to ear, Nick dropped Bill and was already breathing heavily.

Slapping the young man in his stomach, Richard said, "If you're already out of breath after that, we've got a lot of work to do to get you two ready."

Undeterred, Nick said, "Well, it's time we let the world know."

"Not yet," said Bill. "Before we announce anything, I need to have a little talk with two very important people."

Richard nodded in approval. "Fair enough."

Caught by surprise, Richard about had the wind knocked out of him as Nick slammed into him and embraced him. "Get your greasy hands off of me, you mongrel!" said Richard as he tried to contain his laughter. The more he struggled, however, the tighter Nick seemed to squeeze the British man.

While Nick and Richard were caught in their own moment, Bill noticed Abby walking towards him. Before he could even say a word, however, she embraced him. It was the first time Bill had felt the embrace of a woman since before Lena was killed in the accident.

For a while, Bill was simply lost in the moment. He felt his arms lifting as he wrapped them around Abby and he rested his chin on the top of her blonde head.

Finally, he spoke. "What's this for?"

Bill could feel Abby take a deep breath before she spoke. "You're a brave man, Bill Watson. Not for jumping into a race car or racing at Bathurst, but because of what you're willing to do for your son. He'll never forget this as long as he lives, and neither will I."

Closing his eyes, Bill could feel the dread in his own words as he spoke. "I'm going to need all of the bravery I can get when I go tell my son that in a few years, his dad will be dead."

Chapter 16

Bill could feel his arms shake as the strain began to set it. His core muscles felt as if they were on fire, and he so badly wanted to stop—but he wouldn't. He had to keep going if he wanted to reach his goal…lest he suffer the consequences of failure.

"Keep it up! Don't you quit on me now, yank!" said a growling raspy voice coming from the right side of Bill.

Another drop of sweat rolled off of Bill's nose and landed on the ground, which was only an arm's length away. His mind was focused on the task at hand, however, which at the moment sounded simple enough. He just needed to maintain the push-up position for as long as he could. The fact that he had just completed a rigorous exercise routine, however, seemed to compound the effects of the situation he now found himself in.

Looking over to his left, Bill noticed that Nick was in the same world of pain as their brutal taskmaster pushed them even harder.

"Raise the right leg!"

Bill could hardly believe the request. Both he and Nick had been holding this position for several minutes, and they were already weary from the torturous day of physical training. Still, Bill complied with the request, which was more like a demand.

Lifting his right leg, Bill had to adjust his body so he could maintain his balance.

"Keep that arse down, yank!"

Noticing that his butt was lifting into the air, Bill received the rebuke and adjusted his stance once again. At this point, the pain was almost unbearable.

"Ten more seconds!"

The words were a light at the end of a tunnel for both Bill and Nick. The seconds seemed to last an eternity until the instructor began counting down from five.

"Five, four, three, two…SWITCH LEGS!"

The simultaneous groan from Bill and Nick only stirred their trainer on. "When your mind is willing to quit, it will cause your body to shut down too. That's why you *always* have to be ready to give it everything you have and never quit! You have to dig deep!"

Bill could feel his entire body shaking with exertion. The pool of sweat under his nose had turned into a small pond, and it almost seemed as if there was a faucet turned on over his head as sweat continued to pour down his face.

"Never quit!"

Despite being outside, the shouting voice of the trainer echoed throughout the area. It came again but louder this time.

"NEVER QUIT!"

Bill knew that he was only seconds away from collapsing. It seemed that his trainer picked up on that as well as he knelt down beside Bill.

"You tired, mate?"

Bill looked to his right and glared at his taskmaster, who just so happened to be the bar owner who had almost destroyed him the first time they met and who eventually became the team's personal trainer.

Tubbs had no sympathy on them.

"I asked you a question, yank," said Tubbs. "Are you tired?"

The question hung in the air as Bill was unable to answer. With his body shaking as it was pushed to the limit, the lack of a reply from Bill seemed to answer the question.

"It's all in your mind, Watson. Let your heart take over!"

Bill felt a brief but sharp pain on his left leg as Tubbs slapped it.

"Get that leg up higher!"

Gritting his teeth, Bill used every bit of strength left as he strained to lift his leg as high as he could.

"Keep it up, up, up, up…and relax."

Both Bill and Nick collapsed face down onto the ground.

"Good job, Gents. One minute break. Make sure you're drinking plenty of water."

Tubbs walked off to give Nick and Bill their full minute to collect themselves. It had been several weeks since Nick, Richard and Abby first approached Bill about racing a wildcard entry at the Bathurst 1000. Since that time, the media had been stirred into a frenzy. Everywhere Bill went, he was surrounded by fans and reporters alike.

Although their primary sponsor, Higgins Financial, was fronting the money for the car and the entry into the Great Race, Bill and the team soon learned that the deal wasn't all what it was cracked up to be. During the negotiation and contract signing process, Bill was made aware of just how political the realm of professional motorsports had become. Although *Higgins Financial* was an extremely wealthy company, they weren't too eager to hand out too much of their wealth to a racing team.

"Look," said the small Italian man who was the lawyer for Higgins Financial. "My client wants their name on the car, and they want you two in the car. They've agreed to sponsor Mr. Lathan to race next year in the Super2 Series on the basis that you, Mr. Watson, agree to participate as a driver in the Bathurst 1000."

It all sounded pretty decent to the team until they got into the fine details of the contract. Aside from the normal sponsorship requirements such as speaking well of the company (which the team would need to become subject matter experts on) as well as maintaining a professional appearance throughout the event, the lawyer elaborated on a few details which the team was not too happy about.

"Higgins Financial reserves the right to pull their support from the team at any time and for any reason," said the lawyer. "Additionally, you will be responsible for covering the costs of any and all damages to the car. If for some reason the car is involved in an incident and is deemed a total loss, we will not cover the cost of a replacement."

"This is outrageous!" yelled Richard.

"If you don't like it, find another sponsor," said the lawyer as he slid the forms across his desk for the team members who were present to sign. "We're here for the promotional opportunity only. To my client, the car is nothing more than a moving billboard which they want their name on."

"What about training facilities for the team and the drivers?" asked Richard.

"As covered in the contract, the drivers and crew will be responsible for arriving at the event in good physical condition. Higgins Financial, however, will not cover the costs for training facilities so each member will be responsible for their own personal fitness."

Even though the conditions were less than ideal, the end product involved them getting into the biggest race in Australia. So, after signing the forms, the team had to make arrangements for certain things—a physical trainer being one of them.

It was Abby who posed the question nobody had thought of: "What about Tubbs?"

The mountain of a man was certainly in peak physical condition, and his own workout regimen was borderline insanity to most people. It seemed to be a natural choice…at first. More than happy to inflict pain and despair on two of his closest friends, Tubbs took the position as the team's personal trainer for free in return for access to the garage on race day.

From that moment on, the lives of Bill and Nick had been made into a living hell. Immediately after they shook hands on the deal, Tubbs had them on their faces doing push-ups. After that, he made them run with him until *he* got tired. Unfortunately for Bill and

Nick, that didn't happen for almost eight miles. Then it was back to Tubbs' house where, come to find out, he had a full obstacle course set up in his backyard.

"This is what I use to train, mates. It's hell on earth but you'll build stamina and strength—both of which you'll need in the car. When I'm done with you two, I'll be able to slap both of you on your arses and not be able to tell which one of you is an American." said Tubbs.

Bill and Nick both stood in awe at the sights which lay before them. A full military-style obstacle course fit with items which would require them to climb over, crawl under, balance, hang and jump, the two drivers could only dread doing such a thing after what they'd already been through on the first day.

Still, Tubbs pushed them both into the late hours of the night. This pattern continued for the next several weeks as Bill and Nick arrived at Tubbs' house every morning.

During the evenings, if both men were still able to stand, Tubbs would open his bar up just for the three of them so that Nick and Bill could get practice on the driving simulator. Since the simulator used an exact laser scan of Mount Panorama Circuit, the practice laps Bill and Nick put in would hopefully prove to be invaluable. After weeks of practice, they were able to memorize the racing line as well as their braking and turn-in points before they ever actually turned a lap on the real track.

That became their routine as the duo prepared for the fast approaching race day. Now less than two weeks away, the training under Tubbs seemed to have intensified.

On this particular morning, however, Tubbs was feeling extra spry, and the physical improvements the two drivers had made over the past few weeks almost seemed to void out as the larger man inflicted punishment.

Finally able to stand up after the strenuous workout, Bill walked over to help Nick up.

"Make it stop, mate. Make it stop," replied Nick as he rolled onto his back.

"It'll stop when we're in that car," said Bill as he grabbed Nick by his arm and pulled him up.

"No it won't," said Nick. "Tubbs will just find a way to muscle himself into the car and make us curl dumbbells while we're driving."

The two men had no time to laugh, however, as they gulped down water in preparation for whatever the next workout would hold.

Aside from Bill, Nick, and Tubbs, Abby and Richard were there as well as Chad. Getting his mind ready for the next workout which Tubbs had in store, Bill's eyes locked with Chad's. They both stared in silence for a moment before Chad's face gave off such a smile which only his son could make.

Bill felt his heart being pulled.

It had been several weeks since Bill had made the difficult phone call to his father to explain what was going on. Upon hearing the words that his only son was going to die of cancer, William quickly broke down.

However, Bill had yet to make the revelation to his son. *If only you knew, Chad. If only I had the guts to tell you.*

"Watson!" Bill turned to see Tubbs marching towards him.

"Get your head out of your arse and give me 40 push-ups!"

Bill sighed as he dropped down and began his punishment. Beside him, however, Nick chuckled.

"Oh you think that's funny?" yelled Tubbs.

"No, I was just…" Nick soon came to the realization that history wasn't on his side. That history was a brief mental reminder that every time he had tried to talk his way out of one of Tubbs' punishments, it only made it worse.

"Never mind," said Nick as he hung his head down low.

"Good," said Tubbs. "Now why don't you take Earl for his morning walk."

Earl, a 45-pound rock which Tubbs affectionately referred to as his pet, soon found itself in Nick's arms as he carried it all the way down to the end of the road and back. Nick knew better than to protest at this point.

While the two were working, Richard called Tubbs to his side. "Don't kill them too badly today, Tubbs," said Richard. "They've got to be in decent form when we reveal the car to the public."

"The car? Really?" asked Abby. "It's about bloody time. Do they realize that the first practice sessions start in less than two weeks?"

"It's been a task getting the car ready since it's being prepared by another team," replied Richard. "Let's just say that we're not their top priority, but better late than never. They said it's all ready to go so we're expected there this afternoon for the big reveal before it ships off to the track."

"Unless they delay it again," sneered Abby.

Their big public reveal had been scheduled for last week, and the team and their sponsors had planned a very elaborate ceremony. In a venue loaded with press and fans who had thrown in their support early on, the plan had been simple enough: someone would be inside the car while Bill and Nick would be on either side of it. When lights on the stage went out, the car would start, the engine would rev a few times to build up suspense, and then the lights would come on. At that point, the curtain would rise and the car would pull out onto the smoked filled stage flanked by both drivers on either side. It would've been a stellar photo opportunity with the hopes of it making motorsports headlines all over the world.

Unfortunately, things didn't quite go as planned.

When the lights had dimmed and the person in the car was supposed to fire up the engine, the car didn't start. After several attempts and moments of delay, Richard suggested that they push it out.

"Just wheel the bitch out there!"

They were just about to deploy Richard's method when they were stopped by a representative from Higgins Financial.

"No, no, no!" said the man quietly. The crowd was waiting in hushed suspense for the big reveal but the darkness they sat in during that moment was going on for far too long.

"How silly will it look pushing a dead car out there for our big reveal. You may as well push a shopping cart full of groceries out there with you. I'll make the announcement that we've had technical difficulties and we'll be postponing it."

"We're going to look like idiots rain-checking our own reveal while the reveal is going on," said Nick.

Despite Nick's future racing endeavors being on the line with this deal, he was often vocal with his objections towards Higgins.

"We won't reveal the company's car in this manner," said the representative in a British accent. "The integrity of Higgins must be preserved. The reveal is postponed." Needless to say, the crowd which had been there to show their support was greatly disappointed at the sudden announcement.

It wasn't the first setback and it more than likely wouldn't be the last. Bill, who was too busy straining to knock out his remaining push-ups after a grueling morning of workouts, didn't hear what was being discussed behind him. As he finished however, he rolled over onto his back and lay there momentarily.

"Good job, mate," shouted Tubbs. "You've done a hell of a job today. Thanks to our buddy Richard here, it looks like you're all done for the day."

Still lying on his back and breathing heavily, Bill was barely able to get his arm in the air as he waived in the general direction of Richard as a show of thanks.

Chuckling a bit, Tubbs turned back to Richard and said, "He'll be alright."

Right about that time, Nick was coming around the corner after carrying Earl up and down the street. He was about to set the rock down in the location where he had first picked it up, but Tubbs intercepted him.

"You can set Earl down over there," chuckled Tubbs as he pointed to the other side of his backyard. "He likes that side better. More sunlight."

"Oh for the love of..." muttered Nick under his breath.

* * *

Since Nick and Bill needed to freshen up before their meeting later in the day, Abby offered to give Bill and Chad a ride back to Greg's house in her vehicle. As they rode, Bill couldn't help but notice how Abby had rolled her window down, while Chad plugged his nose due to the odor which was emanating from Bill.

It was a short ride but Bill couldn't help but notice everyone's silence. "Look, it's not my fault I smell bad. Blame Tubbs," said Bill as he sniffed his own armpits. The only reaction which it invoked was an audible "Ugh" from Bill as he rolled down his own window.

"I just hope you're not stinking up the seat too badly," replied Abby. "I'll have you in here shampooing this beast if that's the case. This here's my baby." Abby gently caressed the dashboard of her blue Ford Ranger as she smiled at Bill. "This truck and I have been through alot together."

"Is this the truck you used to run over an ex-boyfriend?" asked Bill. It was an odd question to ask but he was curious nonetheless.

"Nick likes to talk behind my back apparently," replied Abby with a somewhat guilty look on her face. "Yeah, this is the one. Luckily that bastard's thick head didn't leave a dent in the bodywork."

"Do you make a habit of running over your ex's?" asked Bill.

"Only if they make a habit of cheating on me," said Abby. "Why? You curious to see how fast you can run?"

Bill laughed. "No. Something tells me I wouldn't get very far."

"No you wouldn't," said Abby. "The Ford would catch you or I'd just follow your smell. Either way, you wouldn't escape."

"I'm guessing no one ever has?"

"And no one ever will," said Abby with a sinister smile.

The two laughed as Bill cast a glance in the back seat to see Chad smiling. Seeing his son smile seemed to pierce his heart as his face hardened.

Abby could notice the sudden change as she pulled up to Greg's house. After passing through the gate, they were met on the driveway by Greg as Abby turned the car off. With the windows rolled down, Greg approached the car and leaned inside the window.

"Well how are ya, Abby? Good to see you again."

"I'm good, Greg," said Abby. "How have you been?"

"I'm about to head out to work in a bit but figured I'd help get Chaddy inside," said Greg. "Abby, you're more than welcome to come in for a bit if you'd like."

"Thanks Greg, but I've got to have a brief chat with Bill here," said Abby. "Maybe after?"

"The door's open to you at any time," said Greg as he opened the back door to Abby's Ranger and started getting Chad out.

"Here, Greg," said Bill. "Let me give you a hand."

"No, no, no. You sit tight," said Greg. "It's not an issue at all."

After getting the wheelchair out from the bed of the truck, Greg had Chad unloaded in about 30-seconds.

"See? All set. I'll get him inside while you two have your little chat." said Greg as he and Chad started for the door. As they made their way to the house, Chad turned and waived at Abby as they headed inside.

The silence was deafening inside the truck as the two sat motionless for a moment. It was Abby who finally broke the silence. "When are you going to tell him?" she asked but it sounded more like a demand.

Bill sighed. "It's not *when* but *how*," replied Bill. "I just don't think now is the best time. He's been doing so well and Greg told me he thinks Chad will start talking again soon. I don't want to throw it all away."

"You're not throwing anything away, Bill," replied Abby. "You're his dad, and this is something that he deserves to know."

"He does deserve to know but how will he take it, Abby? How would *you* take it if Nick came to you and said he'll be dead in a year or so? It's not that simple to tell him especially since..."

"Since he's lost his mum," said Abby.

"Yes. Right now I plan to tell him after Bathurst. I've spoken with my dad and he agrees. I just can't imagine what it'll do to him when he realizes that I'll ... you know ... be gone too."

The words hung in the air for a long while as Bill could sense Abby's uneasiness.

Believe me, Abby. It doesn't get any easier to realize that I'll be gone soon. She had to fight to hold back her tears but it was a fight she couldn't win.

"Bill," said Abby as her eyes watered, "I'm so sorry. I'm sorry that you have to go through this. I'm sorry that you won't be around to see your son grow up."

Bill resisted the urge to cry but he knew that he was on the verge as well. He had given his share of tears already, though. For his wife, Lena, for Chad and now, for himself.

He turned to Abby and smiled. "Abby, you don't need to be sorry. I've made my peace with this and I know that Chad will be in good hands. These past few months have been nothing short of amazing, and I've met some incredible people along the way. Yourself included. I'm really thankful for all that you've done not just for the team but for Chad as well. I know that he really enjoys it when you're around."

Abby smiled at his words. They seemed to give her hope whereas before, it felt as if a piece of her were being ripped out. "Thank you, Bill. I really enjoy being around him, too."

She turned and looked at Bill. "And you're not so bad to be around either," she said with a grin.

Bill smiled, and he could feel his face blush from the words.

"Maybe I should wear this fragrance more often," said Bill.

Abby laughed as Bill opened the door to exit the vehicle.

"So after Bathurst then? That's when you're going to tell him?" asked Abby.

"After Bathurst."

"Alright. I'll pick you up in a few hours."

Stepping his foot out of the truck, Bill had his back to Abby as he turned his head and replied, "Please and thank you."

"Hey," said Abby.

Bill was about to step out of the truck when he stopped. Turning back to Abby, he was caught off guard when Abby leaned across his seat and kissed him on his cheek.

"Now get out of here before you make my truck smell like a laundry basket."

* * *

Bill entered Greg's house to see Chad in front of the television in the family room watching a race. Right away, Bill recognized it as one of the Supercars Series races—the same series he would be racing in at Bathurst.

"They're in Sandown this week," said Greg who was coming down the stairs. "First leg of the endurance season before Bathurst. Your mate Derek Renshaw is doing fairly well."

Gesturing to the screen, Greg indicated Derek's car—a red and gold Holden Commodore—currently leading the race. He was in a close battle at the moment but he looked as if he was in control of the situation with his pace.

"He's quick," said Bill.

"His car's quick," snapped back Greg. "And I'm not just saying that because I'm a Holden fan. You have to look at the details. When you see him get put under a lot of pressure, he'll buckle a bit. Not a lot, but enough to see it if you know what to look for."

The two men watched the race for a few moments as they both observed Renshaw in action. The second placed car was beginning to pressure him and as they were heading down the long front stretch which led to a left-handed Turn 1, the car behind Derek showed its nose at the last second. Bill noticed just briefly how Derek overshot his brake marker as a result of the sudden distraction.

"You see?" asked Greg. "Missed his mark by just a fraction."

Although it was a mistake, Renshaw was able to adjust and closed the gap which the second placed car was about to take. Retaining the lead, Derek continued on.

"It's little things like that which you need to keep in your arsenal. He's good, but he's not bulletproof. You'd do well to remember that," said Greg.

Bill looked at the race on the screen which showed tens of thousands of fans at the track and which was being broadcast to dozens of different countries all over the world. He suddenly felt despair take over.

"Greg, what the hell am I doing?" asked Bill. "Sometimes I think that I'm just getting in over my head with this but I just go with the flow. People have invested a lot of money into me and the team. I mean, look at all of those people! I've never raced in front of a crowd like that and it isn't even Bathurst."

Bill let his head drop. "Should I even be doing this, Greg?"

Greg sighed as he looked at Bill. "Unlike your father, I got out of motorsport when I was young," said Greg. "I'm not mad that I did, though. I'm happy with my life and I'm proud of the things I've accomplished. But there's always that voice in the back of my mind asking me the same thing over and over again: What if? What if I had stayed in the game and continued racing? Would I have ended up like your father and became a champion as well? Could I have seen more of the world? Would I be more happy with myself?

"It's things like that which can haunt a man if he's not careful. I've moved past motorsports for the most part but for you, I fear that if you turn your back on this, you'll never escape from that giant *what if* question."

"It won't be that bad," said Bill. "It's not like I'd have to deal with that for long."

"True, but think about your son. His father has been invited to race in the greatest spectacle in Australian motorsports. And he's an American at that. How do you think he'd feel explaining for the rest of his life that his father backed out? It would destroy him, Bill. I mean, look at him. You're his bloody hero."

Looking towards his son who was locked into the race unfolding on the screen in front of him, Bill couldn't help but melt at the sight of his son totally engaged with what was happening on the screen.

"He's been my biggest supporter ever since I got into racing several years ago," said Bill as he smiled. "From cheering in the stands with his mom as I raced to helping me work on my old race car in our garage back home, he's been by my side through it all."

Smiling at the thought of the fond memory, Greg softly replied, "It would seem that the journey isn't quite over yet. Don't you think?"

Bill locked eyes with the television screen which had the image of Derek's car as the main focus. Greg was right. Although this seemed to be a constant struggle in his mind, Bill now knew with 100 percent certainty *why* he was doing this.

Not for fame. Not for fortune.

For Chad.

Chapter 17

"From our simple beginnings in London to our first expansion in Turin, Italy, Higgins Financial has now stretched across the globe with offices in Beijing, Los Angeles, Chicago, Munich and Tokyo. Now, we are pleased to announce the grand opening of our newest location here in Sydney, Australia!"

The small group of press and fans which had gathered outside the new location of Higgins Financial in Sydney applauded at the words of the CEO and Founder of Higgins Financial, Jonathan Higgins. An older man of small stature, Higgins wore a dark grey suit with a white dress shirt unbuttoned at the collar. His white hair waved in the slight breeze which was present and it seemed to match his white goatee. Although he was Caucasian, his skin tone stood in stark contrast as it seemed to be an unnatural mixture of yellow and orange.

Still, the billionaire-businessman stood behind the podium and spoke confidently as someone who had given similar speeches hundreds of times before. His accent was tough to pin down, however, as it had a mix of British and American.

Higgins continued. "Unlike our previous locations, however, we plan to enter into the Australian marketplace with a bit of style and flair. Behind me is the car and the two drivers which we have entered into Australia's great race, the Bathurst 1000. It's my great honor to introduce Australia's own Nick Lathan and, all the way from Austin, TX, Bill Watson!"

The crowd erupted in cheers as Bill and Nick took a few steps forward to stand on either side of Higgins. Wearing their custom-fitted driver's suits, Bill and Nick couldn't help but feel a bit awkward in the color choice. In Nick's words, the two of them looked like escaped prison inmates as they flanked the CEO of Higgins Financial in their orange racing suits.

"Bringing a plethora of experience to the table, Mr. Lathan and Mr. Watson will be piloting the very first Higgins Financial race car with the hope of bringing home the grand prize," said Higgins.

What in the world is he talking about? He never said anything about winning it.

Casting a quick glance over at Nick, Bill could tell that his counterpart was thinking similar thoughts.

"Without further delay, I would now like to present you with the #528 Ford Falcon FG X which will bear the name of Higgins Financial at the Bathurst 1000!"

The crowd cheered again as Bill and Nick walked respectively to the left and right side of the car. Just like they had practiced before the event started, Bill and Nick simultaneously pulled off the cover to reveal the race car to the crowd.

Although the initial art sketches had been revealed to the team way beforehand, Bill and Nick were both hoping that the actual car would look better than what the artwork had shown.

They were wrong.

A combination of bright orange with white highlights which resembled paint splatter, it was loud, obnoxious, and in the eyes of Bill and Nick, ugly. The two drivers did their best to hide their disdain.

After the cover was pulled back, Bill walked over and took his place beside Nick on the left side of the car where they stood as Higgins continued his speech.

Leaning over to Nick's ear, Bill whispered, "It looks like a traffic cone that had an orgasm."

Nick about choked on his own laughter as he tried to maintain a professional appearance. This caught the attention of more than one of the associates from Higgins Financial who were also present for the reveal. As if on cue, both Bill and Nick smiled and nodded to the seemingly disgruntled associates.

"Without further ado," said Higgins, "we'll now open up the forum for anyone with questions for the drivers."

Nick and Bill took their places along either side of Higgins who stood in front of the podium. Several reporters stood up and Higgins pointed at one older man to ask his question.

"Yes, my question is for Bill. Will your father be present at the race?" Bill stepped closer to the microphone to answer.

"At this time, I'm not aware of any plans for dad to be here. However, he's an old rascal who's still full of surprises so never count him out."

A young female reporter stood up. "Bill, do you really think your team has a chance of winning the race?"

Bill chuckled. "We've got a good car, we're backed by a good company and we've got a good team. To me, that means we've got just as good of a chance as anyone. We certainly plan to be competitive."

There were a few chuckles in the crowd as the female reporter sat down. Then a young man stood up and asked Nick a question.

"Nick, how does it feel to be going against your old rival Derek Renshaw once again and do you think both you and Bill have a chance against him and the other established teams?"

Bill stepped aside so that Nick could answer the question. "We certainly look forward to mixing it up with the best of them," said Nick. "Derek's obviously a good driver and he's been in the game for a while now but with Bill's Trans-Am experience in the States and my experience in the Super2 series as well as co-driving with a few drivers in Supercars series, I feel that we've got a lot of experience to fall back on."

As Nick took a step back, several members of the press jumped at once to ask the next question. One voice overpowered the others which came from a woman who was small in stature and who had a very high pitched voice.

"Bill, how does it feel knowing that your son is in a wheelchair while you're out driving race cars?"

A few murmurs came from the crowd as they expressed their disdain for such a question.

Bill didn't hesitate with his answer. "Ma'am, I'm a race car driver which means I drive race cars. That's what I do and I like to think that I do it well. My son is my greatest fan and I can assure you that no one is more excited that I'll be racing in the Bathurst 1000 than he is."

A few claps came from the crowd at Bill's response.

Leaning into the microphone, Nick added, "To be fair, I'm pretty excited too."

There were a few isolated laughs in the crowd as the next person stood up to ask a question. "Bill, do you really think you should be racing given your condition?"

A sudden hush fell over the crowd, and Bill felt a kick in his stomach but tried not to show it.

There's no way he could possibly know. I haven't told anyone in the media yet.

Bill tried to say something but it was clear that he had been caught off guard by the question. "Um…I'm not…"

"Our sources confirm that you were diagnosed with brain cancer. Is this true, Bill? And how does your son feel about this, especially after the accident which led to your wife's death?"

Bill felt stunned and frozen. Too stunned, in fact, to notice that every eye in the vicinity was fixed on him. He had been caught completely off guard by the comment about his cancer, Lena and Chad.

Chad!

Bill looked over to the side to see Abby standing alongside Richard as they too looked down at the face of the small wheelchair-bound child who had just found out in an unimaginable way that his father had cancer.

The look on Chad's face was one of complete hopelessness. As Bill looked his son in the eyes even from a distance, he knew that the haunted look on his son's face would stay with him for his remaining days.

Bill so wanted to say he was sorry to his son but he couldn't. He felt as if he was completely frozen in place.

Seeing that things had gone too far, Higgins cut in.

"Mr. Watson has been medically cleared by CAMS to race at the Bathurst 1000," said Higgins. "There will be no more questions today. That is all."

* * *

As the minutes passed and the small crowd dispersed, only a few people now remained. Among them was Abby who was sitting on the steps leading up to the front door of the new Higgins Financial building with Chad in front of her. Chad looked as if he'd been crying. As Bill and Nick approached, it was obvious that Abby had been trying to talk to him and possibly cheer him up. They noticed that there were tears in her eyes as well.

"Hey," was all that she could say to the two men.

Bill took a deep breath and spoke up. "Would you guys mind giving us a minute or two?"

Nick walked forward and extended his hand to Abby to help her up onto her feet. "Sure, mate," said Nick. "Take all the time you need."

As Nick and Abby walked away, Bill slowly sat down in front of Chad. He wasn't sure where to begin but he knew what he had to say.

As he began, Bill grabbed his son's hand.

"I'm sorry, Chad. I'm so sorry I didn't tell you sooner. I planned to tell you after the race. I didn't want it to happen like this."

Chad's eyes began to fill up with tears again as his head lowered. Bill took note that Chad's fists were also balled up.

Bill continued. "You're probably mad at me and I totally understand if you are. It's just with everything that's happened with us…with mom…I didn't want to drop this on you just yet.

"Can you forgive me?"

Chad sniffled as tears continued to fall from his eyes. Although he was still not speaking, it could be argued that Chad didn't need to in order to communicate his emotions to his father. The look in his eyes were words as unto themselves, and Bill could almost hear the sound of his son's voice—a sound he hadn't heard in many months now.

What Bill saw in that moment was a look similar to that which he saw when the reporter first asked him the question regarding his cancer; the look of hopelessness. But deep down, there was something else. It didn't take Bill very long to figure it out as it was something he himself battles during difficult times.

Anger.

In Chad's mind, he would soon become an orphan. His mother had died a horrible death in a car accident and now his father would die a slow death from cancer. Deep inside, Chad felt the bars of his prison cell closing in around him tighter than ever. The past few months had been good to him, and he felt he would be escaping this dungeon he was in very soon. But as this revelation surfaced, the bars of his cage seemed to thicken, the light became darkness and the room seemed to become even smaller.

He felt like he was being suffocated from the inside out. His father, his best friend, would soon be dead.

As Chad sat in the wheelchair he'd been bound to for the past several months, he felt like the life inside of him was fading. Losing not one but both of his parents was too much for him to handle.

"We'll get through this, Chad," said Bill. "We've got good people here with us too. We're not alone."

The words only seemed to intensify Chad, who was now on the verge of a complete breakdown.

"Chad, please."

The balled up fists of his son soon began slamming against the armrests on his wheelchair. Suddenly, Chad reached into his pocket and retrieved an item he'd been carrying with him ever since it was given to him: the small die-cast Peter Brock race car.

As he clutched it in his hand, he used all of his anger to toss it down the stone stairs in front of him. The tears were streaming down his face as Nick and Abby came back to Bill's side.

"Chaddy, it's okay," said Abby as she kneeled down in front of him and put her hand on his shoulder.

Chad, shaking his head, pushed her hand away in protest.

Nick put a hand on Bill's shoulder to try to console his friend, but the image of his son in such a state had shaken him to his core. Bill simply sat there just as frozen as he felt on the day his father had told him that Lena was dead.

How could it have come to this?

* * *

"How in the hell did this get out! God help you if you work in this company and you're the one who leaked this to the press!"

The sharp and professional looking man who had just been standing on the podium giving a speech was gone. In his place, another side of Higgins was showing his face as he paced back and forth from behind the large desk in his office.

Bill, Nick and Richard sat in chairs in front of Higgins' desk as they watched the businessman stew in his anger.

"It was only a matter of time before this got out," said Richard as he tried to calm Higgins down. "We just have to find a way to turn this around."

Throwing his hands into the air, Higgins shouted, "And just how do you plan to turn it around?"

"Yeah, Richard," commented Bill. His words seemed gutted and deflated even as he spoke them. "How do you plan to turn it around?"

"We turn this into a sympathy vote," said Richard.

"What are you on about now," asked Nick. "You don't win races with sympathy."

"No," said Richard, "but you win loyalty. This was a cheap shot but we can turn it around. Bill, you'll make a full statement explaining your situation. Then we'll invite all kinds of cancer survivors and what have you. We'll turn this into a good thing which we can use."

"Not a bad start," admitted Higgins. "What else can we do?"

Bill, however, was disgusted. "You do realize that I'm sitting right here, right?"

Richard looked at Bill, and the contempt in his eyes was easily viewable.

"You want me to make a statement? I'll make a statement. But we're not taking this and turning it into a dog and pony show. I'm not some damned politician who's trying to win votes. This is my life we're talking about."

"We know that Bill," said Higgins, "but we also have to look at this from a business standpoint so that..."

"No, you need to look at this from *my* standpoint, sir. I have a son who's in a wheelchair and he just found out that his dad has cancer. He doesn't know how long I have, he doesn't know how bad it is, he doesn't know anything. He just knows that someday and probably soon, he'll be all alone. I have to fix my family before I can worry about your company."

There was a long silence in the room as Higgins looked to be in deep thought.

"Very well," Higgins said at last. "Everyone, take some time and we'll work this out while Bill takes care of his family. I'll prepare a press meeting where Bill can make a statement on the issue. Does that sound good to you, Mr. Watson?"

"That'll work," replied Bill nodding in approval. "Thank you, sir."

Everyone got up to leave as Higgins spoke up once more. "Richard, please stay a moment."

Bill and Nick shuffled out of Higgins' office as they exchanged looks of displeasure. After closing the door behind them, Nick finally opened up.

"Look Bill, I know this has suddenly put you in a tough spot. I honestly don't know how you're even keeping yourself together. But don't feel like you're obligated to do this. If you've been waiting for a way out, this is your best chance. Nobody will fault you for it or think any less of you."

As the two were walking, Bill stopped and leaned up against the wall with his head down. "I'd be lying if I said that it didn't cross my mind," he conceded. "I could disappear and enjoy what time I have left with my son. But you, Chad and myself know that I can't do that. I can't run from this."

"You wouldn't be running, Bill. You'd be doing the smart thing."

Bill just shook his head. "The smart thing isn't to jump ship as soon as there's a hole. We're a team and we'll work through this."

"It's not the team I'm worried about. We'll be just fine. It's you. Bill, you've got bloody brain cancer and you're signed up to race in one of the most grueling races in the world!"

The words hit home for both of them. It was a blunt realization that sometimes, one just can't muscle their way through every obstacle despite having the best of intentions. Even though he knew deep inside that he would be willing to give it his all, he had no guarantees that his body would be willing to make the same commitment.

"Alright," said Bill. "I'll think about it."

"It's not that I don't want you on the team, mate. It's that I want you to make sure you're happy with where you're at and to enjoy the relationship you have with your son. Please don't take this the wrong way."

"I'm not," said Bill. "And thanks for being honest with me. It looks like I've got a lot to think about."

***

Back inside the office, Higgins had yet to cease his pacing.

"Richard, we've got a serious problem," said Higgins. "We're just days away from the start of the race week and we've got a driver whom I suspect isn't 100 percent on-board."

"Don't kid yourself," replied Richard. "He's just a little shaken up at the moment. Give him some time and he'll be back in the game."

"Yes, but do we really need him at this point?" asked Higgins. "That's what I want to know. We've already made the announcement that we're entering the race and ever since we announced that we'd be sponsoring a team, we've seen an increase in the number of clients at Higgins Financial. We haven't even turned a damn lap yet and we're already making money off of this."

"So what are you proposing?" asked Richard bluntly.

"I'm proposing that we dump the American and find someone who doesn't have bloody brain cancer. Is that so difficult to imagine? You're connected in this industry, so I'm sure that you could find us a replacement driver. I think we should just cut our losses and the potential for an embarrassment."

"Yes, but you're talking about abandoning a driver who..."

"What I'm *thinking* about is abandoning this entire deal! We've essentially already gotten what we came here to do and that was to get ourselves established in the Australian market. I need *you* to tell me why *we* should stay," said Higgins.

"Because this race and this series represents the heart and soul of Australian motorsport. If you pull out support now, you'll suffer a backlash like you wouldn't believe. I say we stay the course and let this play itself out.

"What's more is that he'd already told you he had cancer," Richard continued. "Why do you suddenly want to change the plan and pull him out?"

"Let's just say that I'm seeing things from a different light now. When the press started questioning his ability to finish the race, I suppose I began to as well. We're dumping a lot of money into this venture and I want to make sure it's money well spent."

"Yes, but how will it look if you give the boot to Bill Watson? The man just got shell shocked on international television in front of his handicapped son and now you want to dump him from the team?"

"Oh, not me. You. You'd be the one dumping him," said Higgins.

Richard, who had been leaning forward in his chair, sat back and sighed. "That way, it doesn't make you look bad," said Richard as he finally saw the full picture from Higgins' point of view. "It makes you look like you're just the one with the name on the car and it makes us—me—look like the villain."

"You're beginning to see what it takes to make it in the corporate world," said Higgins as he finally sat down. "I want you to have another driver ready."

"Look, John, you need to trust me. The man can drive, and I promise you that his condition won't be a factor in the race. Please just trust me on this. I can have another driver ready but give the man a chance. At least let him turn some laps during the practice sessions before you make a final decision on him. Please, John."

Higgins sat back in his chair and considered. His gaze went upward as he appeared to be staring off into space. Finally, he snapped back into reality.

"Alright. I'll evaluate his performance during the practice sessions.

But let me be clear about this: I'm giving him one chance. Just one. That was the nature of our contract together. You gave me control of the team in return for me providing funding for this race and for your driver next season. The next time we have the discussion, Watson's out. Do you understand me?"

Richard didn't like it but he knew that he'd been backed into a corner. "And what happens if I say 'no'?"

"Then you can find someone else to sign the checks."

Chapter 18

Two days had passed since Chad had found out about his father's condition. Since that time, Chad had regressed back to the initial state from when Bill and his father first brought him home from the hospital after the accident. He showed no emotion or reaction and looked as if he were locked inside of a shell which was that of a human figure. He was simply gone. There were times, however, when Chad's emotions would rise to the surface, but this often happened in the form of anger.

Bill and Greg tried their best to work with Chad but the news of his father's condition had taken a toll on him—one which Greg feared may have long-term psychological side effects.

"I've done all I can, mate," said Greg as the two men talked at home. "I'd just give him some time."

"How much time are we talking about?" asked Bill.

"It's hard to say. It could be a week, a few weeks, a month or more. The truth is that it's completely up to him."

"So what can I do to help?" asked Bill who was desperate to take some sort of action to make things right.

"Well, it's coming up on evening now so obviously not much today. You're only a few days away from the start of practice at Bathurst, so I'd advise you to go and clear your head after he sets in for the night."

Bill couldn't even think about racing right now.

"How in the world am I going to clear my mind from this, Greg?"

"You've got to become bigger than your obstacle. That's how.

You've come too far to give up now. Remember that what you do right now will be what Chad remembers for the rest of his life. And the only way you're going to be able to do anything is if you go and clear your head."

Bill considered for a moment and then conceded. "Alright. But first, I'll go make sure Chad's in bed."

Bill turned to walk toward the stairs which led up to Chad's bedroom but stopped just short.

"Greg, thanks for everything. I don't think I can ever tell you enough."

Greg smiled at the remark. "It's the least I can do for what your father did for me and my family all those years ago. But we're beyond personal debts now and I'm just glad that you could be here and that I can help Chad."

Bill nodded in appreciation of the comment and headed upstairs. As he climbed and began walking down the hall, he stopped just outside of Chad's room and peered inside the door which was slightly cracked open. Still seated in his wheelchair but with his pajamas on, Chad was motionless except for his eyes, as he was reading a magazine. As Bill opened the door and stepped in, Chad casually looked up to acknowledge him.

"Whatcha reading?" asked Bill.

Immediately closing the magazine, Chad tossed it onto the ground in front of his wheelchair.

Walking further into Chad's room, Bill retrieved the magazine which had landed with the cover facing down. Flipping it over Bill saw the front page of a motorsports magazine which featured a picture of the *Mount Panorama* logo written on the side of The Mountain along with a picture of Bill off to the side. Above Bill's picture were the words 'American Invasion!'

Bill chuckled at the cover. "You know, your old man's been having his picture taken so much these past few weeks it's a wonder I can still see straight from all of that flashing."

Chad simply stared down onto the ground and folded his arms across his chest as his father spoke.

Bill, however, remembered that like himself, Chad often turned to his passions when he just needed things to make sense.

"You're a lot like me, you know that?" said Bill. "We live in such a crazy world where terrible things happen all the time and sometimes it just doesn't make sense. But when I slip that helmet on, it all goes away. There's no sickness, no tears, no politics; it's just you and your team battling against other drivers and their teams: man and machine in harmony together. It helps me to make sense of everything, Chad. When you're in the car, you're not thinking about anything else other than what's going on around you. You're so focused on what you're doing that when you're done and you get out of the car, you realize that you miss it. You miss the noise, the chaos, the adrenaline, the heat and the sense of competition.

"One day, you'll get to experience it, Chad. You won't be in this wheelchair forever. I promise. One day, racing will be more than just words and pictures in a magazine or on a television. It'll be a sensation that you'll experience and that you'll never forget."

Kneeling down beside Chad, Bill placed his hand on his son's head. "I love you, Chad. I don't want you to ever forget that. You're the best of your mother and me, and I know that she'd be proud of you just like I am. We have hardships that come up in our lives but it's how we deal with them that defines who we are. You're a strong young man, Chad. Don't ever let your present circumstance dictate your future. I don't and nor should you."

Bill could see that Chad was holding back tears in his eyes. The memory of his mother was still fresh on both of their minds.

"I miss her too, Chad," said Bill. "Every morning, every evening, and every moment of every day, I miss your mother. She was my best friend and sometimes I feel like I'm lost without her."

Bill could feel his own eyes watering up. He didn't need to cry in front of his son right now, however. Enough tears had been shed already.

"We have to stay strong for her and for each other, Chad," said Bill as he stood up. "Stay strong, Chad. Just like your dad does. Stay strong."

Lifting his son and carrying him to his bed, Bill tucked Chad in and knelt beside him once again. Bill said a quick prayer with his son and then stood up to leave.

Standing in the doorway with still enough light coming from the hallway to see Chad's face, Bill said goodnight to his son.

Chad made no response. His face was void of both emotion and expression as he stared off blankly into space.

"I love you", said Bill as he closed the door.

Heading back downstairs, Bill found Greg in his study room reading. Stopping just outside the doorway, Bill leaned up against the wall and sighed.

"I've got a lot of thinking to do," said Bill.

"You and me both," said Greg. "I just got word that I'll be getting a few new patients starting next week. Things are likely to get pretty busy around here and at the office."

Bill stopped and thought for a second before responding. "Greg, I think you may have just answered one of my questions."

"Yeah? And what question was that?" asked Greg.

Bill was silent for a moment. He was still in deep thought, which soon became obvious to Greg.

"It looks like you still have some thinking to do. Here," said Greg as he tossed Bill his car keys. "Driving seems to help me clear my head and I reckon it'll help you, as well."

Bill caught the keys and held them in his hand. He stared at them for a moment as if they also sparked some sort of thought about what he was needing to do.

"Are you alright, mate?" asked Greg.

Snapping out of it, Bill replied, "Yeah, I'm good. Thanks for this, Greg."

Holding up the keys, Bill spoke up again. "Does it ever get old having us around? I mean, would you ever tell me if we were getting in the way?"

Lifting his eyes from what he was reading, Greg seemed shocked at the question. "Now why on earth would you ask me that?"

"More out of curiosity," said Bill. "You've shown a lot of hospitality since we've been here and I sometimes wonder if..."

"Don't," said Greg abruptly. "Don't ever think that you're an inconvenience to me at all. I've enjoyed having both you and Chad around. It's certainly nice having someone to chat with around the house and I'm grateful to have had a hand in Chad's recovery process, but..."

A moment of silence filled the air before Greg spoke again.

"Bill, I think you and I both know that there's only so much I can do for him. With what's happened with Chad finding out about, you know, your cancer, it's had a very obvious negative effect on him. I can continue offering him as much physical therapy as I can but I think he may need someone else who specializes in child psychology."

Nodding in approval, Bill said, "I've been thinking about that as well."

"And?"

Holding up the keys, Bill said, "Hopefully when I get back, I'll know what I'm supposed to do."

* * *

Bill drove around town for about thirty minutes in an effort to clear his head. It was evening now and the lights of Sydney lit up the sky. It was a beautiful city but there always seemed to be something going on. With all of the activity which ultimately led to traffic, Bill found it hard to concentrate on other things.

Realizing that he was now fairly close to Tubbs' bar, Bill decided to stop by for a bit. As he pulled up, Bill noticed that there were only a few cars in the parking lot. He parked close to the front and after exiting from Greg's car, he walked towards the entrance of the bar.

Bill immediately noticed that there was someone standing off to the side of the building who was smoking. The person was close enough so Bill gave a cordial nod and a quick "Hey" as he continued towards to the entrance of the bar.

"Hey yourself," said the man.

Bill stopped dead in his tracks. He knew that voice.

"Pretty shocked seeing you here, Billy Watson," said Derek Renshaw. "I thought you'd be in full damage control mode after your botched car reveal a few days ago."

Bill was speechless from being caught off guard.

Derek continued. "You know, it's always tough when the press find out things they shouldn't know. I swear, sometimes it feels like someone's just feeding them the information just to piss you off. Say, how's your boy doing?"

Bill had had enough. He charged forward and grabbed Derek by the collar of his shirt and slammed him against the wall.

"You sonofabitch! It was you, wasn't it?!" said Bill. "You found out and told the press, didn't you?"

A smug smile crept onto Derek's face. "It's about time you showed this side of yourself, Watson," said Derek. "This must be the real *you*. All of this well-behaved nonsense we do in front of the cameras is such a waste. I think you're finally starting to see how the game is played."

"What are you talking about?" snarled Bill.

"People think that racing is just cars going around a track. It's not," said Derek. "It's just as mental as it is physical. When you learn that the race doesn't begin at the green light but at the first shot that one competitor takes against another, then you'll start to understand how the game is played."

Tightening his grip around his collar, Bill only got more angry. "So you mean to tell me that you leaked this news which led to my son falling back into a psychological coffin so you could gain some sort of advantage over me?"

"You'll be surprised at how easy it is to control people and completely rattle their world once you learn what it is that makes them tick," said Derek. "In your case, it was your dark secret. A secret, by the way, that someone at Higgins was more than willing to share with my team and I…for the right price."

"Oh, so you think you can control me now?" asked Bill.

"Of course I do. That's why your hands are around my neck and that's why you'll be thinking about this moment while you're on the track instead of focusing on what you're needing to do."

Bill knew then that he had been goaded into a confrontation. He had let his emotions get the better of him, and he had just been beaten by the man whose neck he had in his hands.

Bill wanted so badly to squeeze down tightly but he knew that's exactly what Derek would want. He wasn't going to play his game anymore. However, he wasn't about to let him off the hook that easily.

Bill cocked his right arm back and punched Derek hard in the stomach. The feel of the impact sent jolts of adrenaline and satisfaction through Bill. He wanted to land another blow on Derek but thought better of it.

Instead, he tossed him aside onto the sidewalk which ran alongside the bar.

Adjusting his shirt as he stood up, Derek said, "You'd better hope that doesn't leave a mark. Imagine what the press would say if they found out that the son of the great William Watson just attacked the current Supercars championship leader."

Bill started towards him once again but Derek didn't budge. He knew that Bill couldn't do anything to him. Stopping just short of him, Bill stuck his finger in his face and lowered his voice.

"You think you're protected by your fans, your cameras and your bullshit games? That won't stop me forever. If I were you, I'd grow eyes in the back of my head."

"I reckon I should because that's exactly where you'll be the entire race—behind me. Let's face it, Watson. You know this just as well as I do: you don't have a prayer of winning that race. You're a field filler. Nothing more."

Turning to walk away, Derek looked over his shoulder at Bill as he lit another cigarette.

"See you at Bathurst, yank."

* * *

Bill stayed outside for a few minutes to let his blood cool down before entering the bar. As he paced back and forth outside, a few patrons who were either entering or exiting *Bear Knuckles* shot Bill a suspicious look. Either they recognized his face from the news or they were suspicious of the man who was pacing outside of a bar at night.

Knowing that he didn't want to have another confrontation with anyone, Bill decided that he'd better go inside. As he entered the bar, he was immediately greeted by Tubbs who was sitting on a bar stool by the entrance. Even though he and Tubbs were friends by now, Bill could never get over just how imposing it was to see someone Tubbs' size walking towards him. The man was simply a tank.

"Yank!" shouted Tubbs loud enough that everyone in the bar stopped and stared. Getting up from his seat, Tubbs rushed over to greet Bill, and the young American knew exactly what that meant: a giant bear hug.

Wrapping his massive arms around Bill, Tubbs lifted the smaller man off the ground and shook him side to side.

"Alright, alright, Tubbs," said Bill. "Give my ribs a break."

Dropping Bill, a giant smile formed on Tubbs' face as he took Bill's words literally.

"I can do that for ya!" shouted Tubbs as he cocked his arm back as if readying to deliver a massive punch to Bill's ribs. Holding his hands out in front of him in a feeble form of defense, Bill could only chuckle.

"No, no. You know what I mean, Tubbs," said Bill. His voice seemed to carry the weight of his worries.

The larger man changed his expression as he picked up on the fact that Bill wasn't in the mood for games.

"What's the matter with you?" asked Tubbs in his typical non-sensitive tone. "Oh, and you just missed that bastard Renshaw. He was here a few minutes ago."

Bill huffed at the sound of that name. "Yeah, we met outside," he said with a scowl.

"Did you knock his block off, mate?" asked Tubbs with a smile. "We all know he's got it coming."

Bill was silent as his mind replayed the events which just occurred. He was still kicking himself for falling into Renshaw's trap.

"That would be exactly what he would've wanted me to do, Tubbs. But it's exactly what I wanted to do, nonetheless."

"Don't let him get in your head, yank. We're not too far away from the race so you know he's going to be coming after you."

"Yeah, he's coming after me, alright," said Bill. "Did you know he's the one who leaked the information about me to the press?"

Half expecting some sort of sympathy, Bill was taken back by Tubbs' response. "And let me guess: You're just going to sit there and cry about it now, aren't you?"

Bill, who had taken Greg's advice and made the trip to help clear his head, was finding that it was having the opposite effect. He was getting sick of all of it.

"No, Tubbs. I'm not going to sit here and cry about it and I don't expect you to offer any sympathy. None of this makes sense to me. There's over twenty-five other cars in this race but for some reason, he sees me as a threat. Why?"

Tubbs was about to snap back with an inappropriate comment when he was interrupted.

"Because he sees you as a threat, Bill."

Turning around, Bill noticed Abby standing behind him wearing her usual work apron.

"Remember when you first came into this bar a few months back and you stood your ground against him? Nobody does that. Renshaw goes around just shy of pissing on about every other driver and they don't do anything about it because they're scared they might lose their sponsor if they start getting into trouble. But in walks this American—the son of a legend—who isn't bound by the same rules Derek has to play by, and he fears that. He may act like he's big and tough but believe me, he's genuinely afraid of you, Bill."

"Why would he need to be afraid of me?" asked Bill. "I've never even been in a Supercars race before."

"That doesn't matter at all, Bill," said Abby. "You're stealing the spotlight from him, and you're now just as popular as he is because of your father. That's put him on the defensive."

Bill shook his head. "I don't know why everyone's getting so worked up. It's only one race and I'll be leaving after…"

The words came before Bill had fully realized the magnitude of them. They had been on his mind ever since he put Chad in bed for the night but in truth, he had been considering it for some time. Now they were out and there was no going back.

"Wait, you're leaving?" asked Tubbs. The shocked look on his face was one which Bill had never seen on the colossal man.

"I wasn't planning to tell anyone until after the race but yes, we're leaving."

"But why? Where are you going?" asked Abby who was just as shocked.

"Back home. Back to Texas. I think that with all that's happened, Chad would benefit from being home with me and his Grandfather."

Shaking his head, Tubbs made no attempt to hide the disappointment from his voice. "I guess I thought you liked it here. Enough to stay, that is."

"It was never about staying and finding a new place to live," replied Bill. "This was always meant to be a temporary deal."

"But what about his therapy with Greg?" asked Abby.

"We'll continue it for as long as we're here, but then Greg will recommend someone who can pick it back up when we get back home," answered Bill.

There was an awkward pause in the conversation as the three seemed puzzled by what to say next. Although Tubbs looked genuinely upset, it was Abby who appeared to be both sad and angry at the same time. Bill knew he had to say something to her.

"Tubbs," said Bill as he addressed the larger man. "Would you mind if I had a moment with Abby."

Expecting some sort of snappy comment, Bill was surprised when Tubbs simply rose from his seat and walked off. That alone gave Bill a sinking feeling inside.

Turning his attention to Abby, Bill could sense that Tubbs' sudden exit had a similar effect on her as well.

"Abby," said Bill, "I know you and I have gotten close over these past few months, and I certainly appreciate how you've looked after my son. But…"

"But you never intended to stay here," said Abby cutting in. "Did you?"

"No. I never did, Abby," said Bill. "I only came here for Chad."

Abby chuckled but it was more of a sign of regret as she shook her head.

"I guess it's my fault then," said Abby. "It's my fault for allowing myself to get so close to you but all along you already knew."

"Abby, I never expected any of this when I got here. I never expected to meet someone like you or your brother or even Tubbs, and I certainly never thought I'd be racing ever again. I just..."

"Look, Watson. Don't give me that 'It's not you, it's me' story. If you've made your decision, so be it. You're man enough to make that decision, so be man enough to tell me like it is and let's just be done with it."

Abby was going on the offensive. He had briefly seen this side of her before when they had first met several months ago, and he perceived that this was her way of letting go. She preferred a cold break instead of letting emotions linger. As much as Bill wished he and Abby could continue to talk it out and reach some sort of middle ground, he knew she would have none of it.

"So that's it then," said Bill.

Shrugging her shoulders as if she couldn't care less, Abby replied, "Yeah. I suppose that's it."

With nothing else to say, Bill rose from his seat and walked out the door. A night which was supposed to bring clarity and some sort of call to action to help him push forward proved to be quite the opposite.

As he entered the car and started the engine, Bill stopped before he put it in gear. Sitting there in the driver's seat, Bill felt anger begin to rise up within him once again. He thought about his son who was unable to walk or speak, and his wife Lena who he missed so much. He thought about his father whom he had invited to live with him back in Texas so he wouldn't be lonely—only to leave the country to come to Australia. But what burned in him the most was how for the first time in his life, he felt as if he wasn't in control. It was almost as if Bill was simply floating in an ocean as he was tossed here and there by the waves. The ride had led him many places but he couldn't say with confidence that they were places he wanted to go.

He thought about the impending mountain he now had before him.

Bathurst.

It was a mountain he was expected to climb, but not one which he truly wanted to climb. In his heart, Bill simply wanted to be there for his son.

Feeling as if things were falling apart around him, he struck the steering wheel hard with his palm.

"Dammit!" shouted Bill. "Dammit all!"

Putting the car into gear, Bill drove off into the night.

Chapter 19

A place renowned for birthing legends while also handing out crushing defeats to those it deemed unworthy, Mount Panorama is regarded by many as one of the most demanding race tracks in the world. Whether it's the 23 various turns, the nearly four-mile length, or the 570-foot difference between its highest and lowest points, the Bathurst 1000—a one thousand kilometer race which often spans over six and a half hours—is revered as one of the great motor racing events in the world.

When a driver is turning laps on the Mountain, they're not only competing against their fellow drivers but also against the Mountain itself. With challenging corners surrounded by concrete walls, one momentary loss in concentration can end your day...or worse. Additionally, drivers are also competing against the elements of mother nature herself. Aside from being an historic race track, Bathurst is the home to several species of local wildlife which have interrupted previous races on more than one occasion. Due to the length of the race, the weather can also change from a beautiful and sunny day to an utter downpour of rain. And unlike American oval racing, the Supercars series doesn't stop when the weather turns ill.

The week of the Bathurst 1000 approached quickly and before long, Bill, Nick, and the team had arrived at the historic Mount Panorama Motor Racing Circuit. The team rode in by RV and even from a distance, Bill could see the white letters which spelt MOUNT PANORAMA on the side of the Mountain. The sight of it caused

Bill to get slightly wheezy in his stomach. Although many fans and even a few drivers were excited to see the son of a legend at Bathurst again, Bill couldn't help but remember that this would be his first race since the accident which changed his life forever.

With practice not getting underway until Thursday, the team's arrival on a Tuesday gave them plenty of time to get settled in—unless you were a driver, that is. For Bill, Nick, and the various other drivers, these next few days would be filled with interviews, sponsorship commitments, meet-and-greet sessions with fans, technical briefings with the team, parades, photo sessions and still more interviews.

To most drivers, they were just eager to put the helmet on and get the race going. For Bill, however, all of this was a welcome distraction from everything else that was going on in his head.

In the days leading up to Bathurst, Bill felt as if he had been stretched thin. Between Chad's complications, his sponsorship commitments, tech briefings, and his falling out with Abby, Bill couldn't exactly say that he was mentally prepared for what he was going to be attempting to tackle in the next few days. He wasn't sleeping and he often found himself dozing off during interviews and briefings.

Although he often used the excuse that he was simply under a lot of pressure, many who were close to him, including his team, had the distinct feeling that he wasn't all in for the race.

As for Chad, there hadn't been much improvement. The only progress was that Chad was actually showing something that could be construed as emotion now. He would chuckle at the occasional joke or comment, but that was it. Although it was progress, it was nothing compared to the efforts he had made up until he found out about his father's condition. At that point, Chad had been so close to his former self that both Bill and Greg were confident he would soon be speaking again.

All of that was now gone.

After the array of various commitments on Tuesday, Wednesday started off with more of the same. Fans from all over Australia and New Zealand were pouring in by the tens of thousands now and it wasn't until mid-afternoon that Bill finally found himself standing alone with Nick in the team's garage. They both stood for several moments simply staring at the car as the team was busy making various adjustments.

It was Nick who finally broke the silence. "God, this thing is ugly."

Bill chuckled as he stared at the bright orange and white Ford Falcon which stood before them.

"How come all of the other cars on pit lane look like proper race cars and ours looks like it's come out of some amateur series painted by some bloke in his shed?" asked Nick.

"Are you just saying that because it's a Ford?" asked Bill.

"No…well, not entirely," replied Nick. "Look, mate. I'm just happy to have a drive in the main game so Ford, Holden, Nissan, or whoever. They're all the same to me at this point."

"Unless it looks like this," said Bill as he gestured towards the car they'd be sharing for the 1000 kilometer race in a few days' time.

"At least we don't have to see it from the inside," replied Nick.

As the two were talking, Richard approached while carrying a clipboard. "What are you two bumbling on about?" asked Richard in his usual sarcastic tone.

Bill chuckled. "Modern art," as he gestured towards the car.

Richard turned to look at the car and tried to suppress his laughter.

Against his best efforts, however, he soon found himself laughing with the two drivers.

"Alright," said Richard changing to a serious tone. "Down to business. Thursday is the first day of practice and from then on it's a mix of sessions dedicated to both the main drivers and co-drivers followed by qualifying. We've got a pretty good grasp of what we're after thanks to the data provided to us by the factory Ford team who supplied us with the car. Once we get a good idea of your pace around here, we'll take a closer look at strategy."

"It'll also give us a chance to see how well this thing handles around the Mountain," said Nick.

"And you'd best not stuff it up either," replied Richard sharply. "The boys at Higgins were clear when they said that. If we bend these fenders up a bit we can get it repaired, but put the shiny side down somehow, that'll be it for us."

"What kind of an organization hamstrings a team like that?" asked Bill.

Richard looked both ways before answering and took a step closer to Bill and Nick as he did. "The kind that doesn't care two bits about motorsport and only cares about profit," said Richard in a lowered voice. "Yes, this is a shady deal but so long as you don't go out there trying to set the world on fire, we should be fine.

"And speaking of Higgins," said Richard turning his focus to Bill, "they've requested your presence in their very expensive executive trailer at your earliest convenience."

Bill raised his brow and lowered his chin. "Just me?"

"Just you I'm afraid," replied Richard.

"Did they say what it was about?"

"Yes they did," said Richard.

There was an awkward pause in the conversation as both Bill and Nick waited to hear from Richard what the cause of the summons was about. Richard, on the other hand, had fixed his attention back towards the information on the clipboard he was holding.

"Well?" asked Bill.

Looking up as if he was suddenly surprised by the question, Richard asked, "Well, what?"

"Aren't you going to tell me what this is about?"

"Why would I do that?" asked a confused Richard.

"Because you're my Head Engineer and you're supposed to tell me these things," said Bill who was partly joking.

Richard wasn't buying it. "Well, Mr. Watson," he said, "As your 'Head Engineer', I'm advising you to walk your scrawny arse over to that very expensive executive trailer, poke your head in there, and ask the ones who've summoned you."

Bill knew he wasn't getting anywhere. Letting the issue drop, Bill headed that way as he said, "You're hopeless."

Nick waited a while to make sure that Bill was no longer in earshot distance before he finally spoke up. "They're sacking him, aren't they? Because of his condition."

Richard dropped the clipboard to his side and dropped his head.

Taking a deep sigh, he lifted his head towards Nick and replied, "Time will tell."

* * *

Bill began making his way towards the RV he was summoned to. It wasn't difficult to miss. The larger camper was essentially a house on wheels with fully extending sides to add to the square footage. The gold and black pearl RV was cleaned daily by a team which followed the Higgins Financial executive team around and today was no exception to that.

As Bill approached, he could see two men outside washing it and, as ridiculous as it seemed to have someone wash a stationary RV everyday, the work they did certainly paid off as the camper glistened in the sunlight.

Bill was about 20 meters away as he walked down the row of RV's and busses when all of the sudden, his head felt as it were caught in a vice grip. The pain gripped his scalp and traveled down into his eyes which caused them to feel as if they were going to burst out of his head. All that he could do was try to act as normal as he could as he suddenly turned to hide behind the closest RV. Once there, Bill gripped his head in his hands and closed his eyes as he waited for the pain to dissipate. Putting his back up against the RV and squatting down, Bill breathed deeply, which he found helpful when dealing with these sudden attacks. Although the seconds ticking by felt like an eternity, the pain eventually ceased and Bill was able to open his eyes once again. As he sat squatting there behind someone's RV, he couldn't help but think about how these attacks were getting worse and more frequent.

At first, they were several weeks apart. Initially, the pain was equivalent to a minor headache but as time progressed, it only seemed to intensify. Unsure if it had anything to do with the stress he was being put under or not, Bill was hesitant to visit the hospital. He had come so far that he'd never forgive himself if he simply threw in the towel at this point.

"Not long now," Bill morbidly reminded himself.

Picking himself back up, Bill waited a few moments before emerging from behind the RV. He got back onto the road leading to Higgins' RV until he found himself knocking on the door in a moment's time.

The door opened and Bill recognized the person standing on the other side as one of the executive team's many administrative assistants. Not sure of her name, however, Bill gave a cordial "Hello" as the assistant smiled and stepped out of the way to allow him to enter.

Once Bill had boarded, he noticed that there was another female assistant in the RV as well. As Bill took a step in, he saw both of the ladies exit the camper and close the door behind them without so much as saying a word.

Before Bill had a moment to ponder the reasoning behind such an exit, he noticed Jonathan Higgins seated at the kitchen table in the center of the RV along with someone sitting across from him that Bill didn't recognize. A younger man who was presumably in his mid to early twenties with messy brown hair, a scruffy attempt at a makeshift beard, and a relatively small figure, the unknown figure wore the team's orange polo shirt with neatly pressed black slacks. This combination struck Bill as odd given the duality of the appearance of the young man from the shoulders up.

"Bill, please join us," said Higgins as he stood to greet the new arrival. Pulling a chair out and gesturing towards Bill, he said, "Make yourself at home."

Bill moved further into the RV and couldn't help but realize just how spacious it was.

Higgins picked up on Bill's intrigue. "Yes, this is my home away from home," he said proudly. "This serves as a fully functional center of operations for me while I'm away from the office. When combined with our mobile team who go with us while we're on the road, we lose no efficiency while we're traveling."

Bill could tell that Higgins was trying to impress him. Not really in the mood for pleasantries due to his recent incident while en route to the RV, Bill simply smiled and nodded.

In previous discussions during the weeks leading up to Bathurst, Bill and Higgins often butted heads on several occasions, and it was no secret that the two didn't like each other. Although Bill was grateful for the opportunity he had before him, he was none too thrilled in the manner in which it was being done. Between the shady contract, the constant disagreements on how the operation was run, and to what Bill oftentimes considered disrespectful remarks towards himself and his American heritage, both Bill and Jonathan Higgins would not be walking away from this event as mutual acquaintances.

One thing Bill had to remember throughout all of this, however, was that Nick would potentially be getting a full-time ride next year in the Super2 Series—with Higgins footing the bill. That knowledge alone caused Bill to scale back his often vocal disagreements with Higgins or with any of his executives. In fact, one of the *only* reasons Bill had even agreed to this deal was for the simple fact he would be helping Nick out. Bill made a mental note to not destroy what was truly the only shot at a ride that his friend Nick had.

As Bill took a seat at the end of the table with Higgins to his left and the mysterious young man to his right, Higgins took a deep sigh as he normally did when he was about to say something which he knew Bill wouldn't like.

"I'm sure you're curious as to why I've called you here, Bill, so let's get right to it," said Higgins.

"I'm all ears," replied Bill.

"After speaking with the Board of Directors, we've decided that we want to give you an out."

A perplexed look came upon Bill's face. "An out?" he asked. "What are you talking about?"

"Bill, let's be honest with each other. You've been out of racing for a while now and we know the enormity of what you're being asked to do," said Higgins. "Given your condition and how it was previously unknown to us when we initially offered you the job, we want you to bow out gracefully."

"You want me to quit," said Bill harshly. "Let's not dance around the issue, John."

"No, Bill. We want you to publicly withdraw," replied Higgins in a calming tone. "The public is aware of your condition, and there'll be no disgrace on your part."

"So you don't think I can do this. Is that what this is about?"

"No, this is about a calculated business risk. It's not that we don't think you *could*, it's more of an issue of us wondering if you *should*. So here's what we're proposing: You make a public statement and gracefully bow out of the race. Your friend Nick still gets to keep his shot at a full-time drive next year. In addition, you'll still be a full-time member of the team and will be financially treated as such. Additionally, the Board has authorized me to provide you with a 'hardship bonus' in the amount of $25,000, which you can use as you see fit. We know that you were planning to move back to the U.S. after Bathurst so this money will be enough to get you home and situated again. The only thing you have to do is accept the offer and all of this will be over."

"Wait," said Bill, "So you're pulling out of Bathurst?"

"Not at all," replied Higgins. "My nephew here, Marcus, has agreed to assume your role as co-driver."

Looking over at the young man sitting to his right, Bill noticed a smug smile upon his face.

"Your nephew," replied Bill with a decent amount of vocal disgust. "Are you kidding me? Does he even have any racing experience?"

"I've raced Formula Fords in Europe for two years now," said Marcus in a scratchy voice.

"So you've never even raced a sports car or sedan?"

"No, but I've had a lot of time on the simulator," replied the younger man.

Bill did a full facepalm as a visual testament to his utter disgust. "So let me get this straight," said Bill. "You want me to bow out of a team that I signed a contract with so I can be replaced by an inexperienced kid who's gonna crash the car."

Turning to Marcus, Bill said, "Yes, kid. You're gonna crash the car."

"Mr. Watson," said Higgins as he cut in. "I didn't bring you in here to harass my nephew. What I need from you is an answer."

"What happens if I say no?" asked Bill.

There was a long pause in the conversation as Higgins began to show visible signs that he was getting frustrated.

And there's that vein popping out of your forehead like it always does when you get mad.

"Bill, we both know that I can legally fire you and be done with it. In order to avoid a public backlash, however, I'd prefer if you..."

"Fell on my own sword," said Bill cutting in.

It was hard to tell at first but as the conversation progressed and Bill began seeing the corner he was being pushed into, he felt something reignite inside of him. It was a feeling he'd not felt in quite some time but one which he knew quite fondly.

It was a passion to succeed.

It was not something that could be bought or manufactured. One simply had it or they didn't. The last time Bill felt this type of passion was his last race at the Circuit of the Americas in Austin, TX. That fateful race which saw him skid off the track and get stuck in a sand trap which inevitably led to the car ride home that ultimately claimed the life of his wife, Lena, and also put his son in a wheelchair unable to walk or even speak. It also led to him learning of his own dark secret which will eventually claim his life.

Knowing that this was truly his last chance to do something great in his life, Bill wasn't about to be cornered by some business executive and a spoiled kid who just happened to choose the right parents. Even if his decision was partly made to merely spite the aforementioned people, the major reasoning behind it was simply because he felt that the fire had finally returned to him.

"Well, I've got an answer for you, Jonathan," said Bill.

Sitting back in his chair and crossing his leg in front of him, Bill uttered one word. "No."

The single word seemed to levitate in the room between the three of them. Bill could sense the anger rising in Higgins as well as the disappointment in his nephew.

"What do you mean 'no'?" asked Higgins.

"I'm pretty sure it's self-explanatory."

"Do you have any idea what I could do to you, Watson? You don't come in here and turn me down! You think that just because your dad was some legend here that I'm supposed to care? I don't know who you think you are but..."

Holding up his hand in front of him, the gesture from Bill seemed to stop Higgins from progressing in his anger any further. Bill knew that he could argue and make snarky remarks to the man all day long but that would get him nowhere. He needed to seal the deal and move on. Due to his experience in dealing with businessmen from his time at his company back home in Austin, TX, Bill knew he had to speak Higgins' language. Ultimately, it all came down to money.

"Look, Mr. Higgins. You need a driver with experience and you also need to put on a good show for your debut in Australia. We can sit here and squabble back and forth all day but in the end, the people are the ultimate decider. They've come all the way out here and expect me to be in that car, so don't you think people will be a bit skeptical if I all of the sudden throw in the towel only to be replaced by the CEO's nephew? You'll face a companywide backlash for sure. We can make this better for both of us if we just maintain our original plans."

Higgins sat still but maintained eye contact with Bill. Appearing to be in deep thought, a sudden grin came upon the man's face.

"Alright, Bill. We'll play your way," said Higgins as he leaned back in his chair. "I'm gonna give you one chance. Just *one*," said Higgins. "If you screw up, if I see something I don't like, or if I see you having some seizure and you start convulsing all over the ground, you're done. And not just you, but your buddy Nick, too. Screw this up and I'll pull the plug on his entire plan."

"Leave Nick out of this, Higgins," replied Bill as he extended his index finger towards the business executive.

Higgins simply smiled at the gesture. "No, Bill. You don't get to make those demands to me," said Higgins with a sly voice. Bill knew that this was Higgins' ace in the deck and now he was playing it.

"If this is so important to you, then so be it. Be aware, however, that the consequences will be on you."

Rising from his seat, Higgins turned and walked towards the kitchen sink behind him and appeared to be staring out the window. A few seconds passed and when he finally spoke again, he addressed Bill firmly.

"We're done here. Get out."

Bill was happy to oblige.

Chapter 20

The week of the Bathurst 1000 is much more than just a showcase for the premier racing category in Australian motorsports. It's a rolling circus with practice sessions, qualifying and races from several different series all going on under a tight schedule. From Ute racing to the Porsche Carrera Cup, Touring Car Masters as well as the Super2 Series, it's nothing short of organized chaos.

In the days leading up to arriving at Bathurst, Bill was in a constant contemplative state of mind. He wasn't sure why he was even racing despite the fact that he'd told others on numerous occasions his reason for doing so. Regardless, Bill knew that his heart was not fully invested in it at that point.

Now, however, things had changed. Bill felt alive with the spirit of competition again. He wasn't just competing against the other drivers in the Supercars category, he was now competing for his seat. After being told by the head of Higgins Financial that he was essentially getting benched in order to have his seat taken by an adolescent, Bill felt something reignite inside of him that he hadn't felt in some time.

The crew back at the garage were none too happy with the decision by upper management for Bill to sideline himself, and they fully supported his decision to essentially stick it to the man.

"What kind of a flog hires and fires a driver before there's even been any racing?" asked one crew member.

Bill felt encouraged to see the team coming together to support him. Additionally, the team could sense that something was different about Bill. As the various crew members went about their business of preparing for the upcoming practice session, there was talk of Bill's sudden awakening.

"It's like the yank got a swift kick in the arse and it woke him up." There was still the duty of racing that needed to be done, and the clock was now approaching the very first practice session.

As the race week officially kicked off on Thursday, the various categories took to the track to practice first before the main series.

As the hours ticked by, both drivers were chomping at the bit to get out on track. Since Nick was listed as the primary driver, he would be hitting the track before Bill in the first one-hour practice session taking place on Thursday morning. Both drivers were suited up at this point and going over some last minute data with Richard as the team prepared the car for the session.

"Don't worry too much about all-out pace during this session," said Richard. "Use this time to get acclimated with the car. We'll obviously send Nick out first since he's the primary driver and has experience at the track. After a few laps, we'll bring him back in so he can give Bill some information on the state of the track."

Richard turned to Bill and looked him straight in the eyes.

"Then it's all up to you, my American friend," said Richard. The eyes of the entire team were upon him at that moment, and Bill could certainly feel every one of them.

Bill smiled.

"Not too many Americans around these parts, are there?" asked Bill. In just about every interview and conversation he had done, Bill was oftentimes referred to simply as *the American.*

"No," answered Richard flatly. "In fact, you may very well be the only American to have ever raced in the Bathurst 1000. Well, to my knowledge, at least. So go forth and represent the Colonies well."

The whole team laughed at the gesture.

"I guess it doesn't help that I'm half Australian, does it?" asked Bill.

"No," said the entire team in unison.

As they were about to break for the meeting, Richard stopped both drivers to issue one last remark. "Good luck, have fun and for the love of all things holy, don't hit anything."

Smiles were everywhere as the excitement of finally getting out on track was taking hold. The team had now pushed the car out into pit lane as the time for the first practice inched closer. Just before things got going, the two drivers exchanged words.

"Well, here we are," said Nick. His face was electric with energy and, just as he'd been doing ever since the team arrived at Bathurst, Nick was smiling from ear to ear. "I can't believe it's here. I can't believe we're going to actually race."

"You know, I don't think I ever thanked you," said Bill. "My mind's been all over the place but overall, I'm happy to be here and to have this opportunity. Thanks for inviting me along."

"Well, you can thank me when it's over," said Nick as he pulled his helmet over his head. "This place has a habit of taking your good feelings, chewing them up, blowing them out the back tailpipe and right into the toilet."

The sound of various engines igniting broke up their conversation.

"I guess it's time, huh?" said Nick.

"Time indeed," replied Bill as he slapped Nick on the helmet. "Good luck out there."

"Alright, mate. See you in a few."

Grabbing his helmet but staying behind in the garage, Bill watched as Nick climbed into the car and fired it up. For a brief second, Nick closed his eyes and let the sound of the motor run through his veins.

The euphoria of hearing a racing engine fire up never got old to Bill, and if he had any doubts about his decision to not step down, the sound of the engine cast it away.

After some time, a loud horn sounded that indicated the practice session had officially begun. Starting with the first pit box on pit lane, each car filed into a single line as they moved to exit the pits.

When the time came for Nick to join the cue, Bill watched as their car pulled away, exited the pits and pulled onto Mount Panorama for the first time.

* * *

Out on track, Nick was sure to give some space to the car in front of him during the out-lap, just as the car behind had given him a bit of a gap. Crossing the line to start the first flying lap, the smile on Nick's face he had earlier was now gone. Instead, it was replaced with pure concentration and focus. He needed every bit of focus due to the nature of how the car was handling.

It was skittish in that the rear of the car was very loose while heading up the Mountain. This was to be expected, however, as it was a cool morning and the tires were still warming up. Easing it through the next few laps, Nick was finally able to get into a rhythm and focus on knocking out solid laps.

Making mental notes of things that needed to be changed about the car as he drove, he relayed them over the radio to the team once he got to either the long backstretch of *Conrod Straight* or the front straight just before *Hell Corner*.

Some parts of the car's handling needed work but this was also to be expected. One of the reasons why there were six different practice sessions before the actual race was to have the time to not only make appropriate changes to the car but to also test those changes. Oftentimes, turning a wrench in one spot threw off the settings on another spot which would cause the car to feel even worse.

Additionally, one had to consider that the track itself would be changing over the course of the race weekend due to the amount of rubber which would be laid down by the various events taking place. Depending on the weather, more rubber on the track meant more grip. Drivers and engineers were forced to keep that in mind before they made too many changes to the car early on.

Despite it being a practice session, drivers were still doing what they do best and setting the fastest times they could get. Not only was it a measure of where the car was in terms of reliability and handling, but it also showed the fans all over the world who was looking quick early on.

As the car started settling in and Nick was able to get into a consistent groove, his lap times began improving each time he crossed the start/finish line.

Even as he crossed the line for the last time before beginning a cool down lap, however, Nick couldn't help but shake his head. Looking at the lap time on his digital dash, he had posted a time of 2:08.971.

"How's she feel?" asked a voice over the radio.

"Like a brick sliding on ice," replied Nick sharply. "She's all over the place and there's a bit of a strange vibration going on."

"Bring the car in and we'll take a look and make a few changes based on your feedback," said the voice who Nick could now tell was Richard. "Then we'll put Bill in the car and see how his feedback lines up."

"How's the rest of the field on time?"

A single word from the other end of the radio said it all. "Ahead."

Nick could sense the anguish in the tone of Richard's voice but had to remember it was still early in the race weekend.

Several other drivers were following a similar strategy during the one-hour practice session by doing a few flying laps and then bringing the car back into the pits. As such, Nick was part of a five-car pack which all headed into pit lane together.

Approaching the pit box, Nick pulled the car into the garage so the team could make the necessary adjustments. The clock was still ticking on the practice sessions and every second was vital for the wild card team.

Nick brought the car to a halt with Bill standing by. As previously discussed, the two drivers would be practicing driver swaps even during practice sessions. It was a bit of a ballet of sorts. As the exiting driver unbuckled the belts, disconnected the drink straw, cool suit and radio and then climbed out of the car, the exiting driver then turned around and helped the entering driver get into the car by buckling some of the belts of the five-point harness that the driver sometimes couldn't see due to the vision restrictions of their helmet. Not all driver combinations worked like this, as some teams prefer to have someone else assist the entering driver who hasn't been in a hot race car for an hour or more.

The Mount Panorama two-step went just as smoothly as they'd practiced, ending with Bill strapped into the car and ready to go. Once Bill was set, Nick kneeled down by the door to give Bathurst's newest driver a quick rundown.

"The track is starting to warm up a bit but it's still rather slick at some places," said Nick. "Back your braking points up until you're comfortable with the car."

"Copy that," replied Bill. "What's wrong with the car? I heard something about a vibration over the radio."

"The crew's looking into it now. They're also looking to make a few changes to help the car be a bit more stable on top of the Mountain. It's a bit of a handful at the moment but the track will change over the course of the weekend. Let's just hope we can follow those changes in the right direction."

Nick slapped Bill on the top of the helmet. "This is it, mate; your first laps at Bathurst in a Supercar!"

Bill could feel the adrenaline pumping through his veins and he was ready to get out there and give it a go. But just as Nick was finishing their impromptu meeting with Bill, Richard approached with ill news.

"We're done for now, Gents," said the Brit. "It looks like we've got a tailshaft that's out of balance which is causing the vibrations. We won't be able to get you out in this session, Bill."

Bill lowered his head as the sudden news sank his ambitions. "Don't worry, mate," said Nick trying to cheer Bill up. "It's a new car and it's better to find these things out now rather than later. Plus, the next session is less than two-hours from now and that's for co-drivers only. You'll get plenty of time to get behind the wheel."

Disappointed by being grounded but encouraged that the problem was identified and was being corrected, Bill climbed out of the car.

Immediately upon exiting, a camera was there in Bill's face along with a pit lane reporter who began asking him questions.

Off to the side, Nick and Richard were having a discussion of their own.

"Can we get this fixed in time before the next practice?" asked Nick.

"The boys'll get it taken care of. I wouldn't worry about that too much," said Richard.

Gesturing towards a monitor which showed live timing and scoring, Richard inhaled deeply before saying, "That's what you should be worried about."

As Nick stepped closer, he couldn't believe his eyes.

Topping the times so far was Derek Renshaw with a lap of 2:05.971. "How in the hell are we nearly three seconds off of his pace?" asked Nick, who was visibly astonished.

"Mind yourself," replied Richard quietly as he gestured towards a camera that was now pointed right at the two of them.

All Nick could do was smile at the camera.

Richard rolled his eyes at the failed attempt to play it off.

"Well, I'm sure Renshaw will get a chuckle over it. At least it'll make the highlight reel."

* * *

As the first practice session ended, the results didn't lie: Renshaw was on fire. His co-driver, a man by the name of Marty Osborne, was on a similar pace as well.

A former full-time driver, Osborne had a drive in the main series several years ago before running into sponsorship problems, which ultimately forced him out. Luckily, he was soon picked up as a co-driver for the main series by Renshaw's team and they'd been a successful pair ever since. With multiple wins to their names along with several more podiums in the Enduro Cup—a championship within the season consisting of all three endurance races on the Supercars calendar—the duo was certainly a force to be reckoned with and so far, they were proving that point once again.

Practice 2 was approaching, and Bill and Nick's team were just finishing up their work on the car. With only a few minutes remaining until the pit lane opened, Bill was already strapped in the driver's seat and ready to go. Unfortunately, the car wasn't quite ready.

"Just a few more minutes," came a voice from under the car.

For a moment, Bill closed his eyes and put himself on the track. Over the course of his training which led up to this moment, Bill had spent countless hours on the simulator in preparation for the race. Right now, his mind was climbing the hill up *Mountain Straight*. He braked late and tipped the car to the right to make *Griffins Bend*, which led to *The Cutting*. Maneuvering his way through *Reid Park* and onto *McPhillamy*, Bill's mind looked ahead to his braking point and timed it perfectly as he plunged down *The Dipper* and onto *Forrest's Elbow*. From there, it was a long downhill charge along *Conrod Straight* and into *The Chase*. Mashing the brake pedal down, Bill envisioned his turn-in point as he...

"Let's go!"

Startled back into reality, Bill opened his eyes to see bodies moving out from under the car and fresh tires going on.

As he saw the crew jump into action, Bill felt the car drop down from the jacks as he heard the horn sound which signaled the start of Practice 2.

"Not bad timing, Chewy," said Richard.

Bill checked the tightness of the straps on his harness for good measure. He could hear the cars rolling off of pit lane behind him. Firing the engine up, the team pushed the car out onto a now empty pit lane. Putting the car in first gear and hitting the pit lane speed limiter, Bill accelerated away.

"You'll have a clear track ahead of you since the field is already away," said a voice over the radio.

"Copy," replied Bill.

As Bill approached the pit lane exit, a smile slipped onto his face as he disengaged the pit lane speed limiter and, for the first time in what now seemed like forever, hit the accelerator on his V8 powered race car.

The euphoria Bill felt was exhilarating. The g-forces, the scream of the engine, the vibrations running through his body; it was like a door had swung open and had welcomed him back home.

As he powered up *Mountain Straight* for the very first time and began shifting through the gears, Bill thought of his vision from moments ago. He knew when to brake but also knew that the car and tires were not up to temperature, so he resisted the urge to brake hard and late.

"It's just the out-lap, Bill. Don't get yourself all worked up," Bill said to himself out loud.

Cruising up the Mountain for the first time ever was a surreal feeling. It was here on this mountain that his father had become a legend. Now here he was, albeit many decades later, on the same track, racing in the same race.

Oh, the irony.

Making it to *Conrod Straight,* Bill once again had to resist the urge to charge full throttle down the hill at race pace. He lifted off the accelerator, braked early and turned the car in at just the right time as he took a bit of the inside curb on the left.

Now heading towards the downhill *Murrays Corner*, Bill completed the left-handed turn and powered on to start his first flying lap in an Australian Supercar.

Whatever vibration issues that had been present before were gone. Additionally, the car didn't seem nearly as unstable as Nick had described it.

As Bill drove into *The Cutting*, a little wiggle from the back end was all he felt, which was mostly due to the tires still getting up to temperature.

As the track drops away heading into *Frog Hollow* and *Sulman Park*, the outside wall on the right gets close very quickly but Bill charged on. Once a driver passes over *Skyline*, they're effectively going down the Mountain for the rest of the lap. Through *Skyline*, *The Esses* and *The Dipper*, Bill then plunged the car down towards *Forrest's Elbow* and down *Conrod*.

Feeling much more confident with the brakes now, Bill braked later this time and was rewarded with a feeling that there was still room left in the braking zone to take it even further in. Clipping the apex at Turn 21, Bill continued his descent until making the final turn at *Murrays* and crossed the line. Glancing down at the digital dash, Bill couldn't believe it.

2:07.963—a full second faster than Nick.

Feeling that the car was now up to temp, Bill went for another lap. Crossing the line again, the dash read 2:07.655.

After six laps, Bill had further reduced his time to a 2:07.358. "Alright, Bill," said Richard over the radio. "You're in fifth at the moment. Box this lap, please. Box this lap."

"Copy that. The car feels great," replied Bill.

"We're going to make it feel better. Track's clear behind you at the moment so give the car a good cooldown lap."

As Bill made his way back around the circuit on his cooldown lap, his mind was reeling at what had just happened. Despite the fact that the other cars out on track were being driven by the co-drivers, Bill's pace gave him confidence.

Although still running at a high rate of speed but not quite that of his previous laps, Bill proceeded along his path as he continued to allow the car's engine and brakes to cool as best as he could.

About halfway through his cooldown lap, Richard came on the radio. "Bill, you've got three cars coming up behind you. They're at race pace so you'll want to just let them by. They won't have room to pass between *The Dipper* and *Forrest's Elbow* so get up to speed and let them by on *Conrod*."

"Copy," replied Bill.

Accelerating again, Bill was able to maintain pace over the cars approaching from behind him. As he approached *Forrest's Elbow*, Bill completed the left turn which led to *Conrod Straight* and glanced up into his rearview mirror to see how far back the other cars now were. When he brought his attention back to the front, his stomach suddenly sank as Bill caught a glimpse of something darting out in front of his car. It happened so fast that Bill didn't even have time to hit the brakes before smashing directly into the creature.

The impact was a mess of violence and carnage. Bill's visibility became completely obscured as the creature rolled over the hood and smashed into the front windscreen with enough force for it to become lodged in place. With no way to see around the mass of brown fur which obscured his vision and even less control due to the damage from the impact, Bill was nothing more than a passenger as the car careened off to the right side of the track and smashed hard against the wall, which caused the creature to roll off of the windscreen. Due to the momentum Bill had upon impact into the side barrier, the car bounced off of the wall several times until it finally came to a halt.

When it was all over, Bill couldn't even comprehend what had just happened. One moment he was driving and the next he was parked in a crumbled mess on the side of the track.

With grass shavings all over the inside of what was left of the car and blood smeared on the now smashed and caved-in windscreen, Bill felt completely defeated as he dropped his head back into the headrest.

* * *

Richard, Nick, the crew and the majority of the worldwide motor-sports community watched with horror as the accident unfolded on television.

Both Richard and Nick stood motionless, fearing the worst until they saw Bill moving inside the car. They waited until the trackside emergency crew arrived and pulled Bill out of the car before they finally breathed again. Exiting the car and standing on his own power, they watched Bill walk around the car to see the extent of the damage.

"Kangaroo?" asked Nick.

"Yeah," replied Richard. "A bloody Kangaroo."

Richard took his headset off and gently placed it onto the table in front of him. Slowly turning around, he saw the entire crew huddled together behind him watching the incident unfold. Off to the side, Richard saw the look on the face of Bill's son, who was watching from a distance with Abby by his side.

Taking a deep breath, Richard's next words were simple but absolute as he shrugged his shoulders.

"We're done."

Chapter 21

"We're reporting live from pit lane at the Bathurst 1000, and as many in Australia and indeed across the world have just witnessed, Bill Watson has just had an unfortunate but devastating incident involving some of the area's local wildlife while on his cool down lap during Practice 2. This isn't the first time a kangaroo has interrupted a race at the Mountain but this is certainly one such instance which will go down in history.

"Trying to follow in the footsteps of his father—the great William Watson who conquered both the Mountain and the championship in his debut season all those years ago—it would appear that the historic drive for Bill Watson at Mount Panorama just wasn't meant to be.

"It's been no secret in the days and in fact weeks leading up to the Great Race that the relationship between the Lathan/Watson duo and their primary sponsor, Higgins Financial, has been rocky at best. We've now been hearing reports that due to the level of damage to the car, Higgins Financial has in fact pulled the plug on the entire operation. With no sponsor and a car in shambles, it looks as if the wildcard entry of both Lathan and Watson are without a ride and effectively grounded. A sad ending to a team which was showing so much promise just days before the start of the Bathurst 1000."

* * *

CHAPTER 21

Bill sat on the floor of his hotel room as the evening sky crept in through the windows. With no lights on, Bill simply sat in silence as Chad slept in one of the two twin beds in the room. His mind was in a constant state of flux as it periodically switched between a state of utter paranoia and then back to that of complete numbness.

After the accident, Bill was immediately assessed by the medical staff and was found to have escaped the incident with no injuries whatsoever.

No injuries that were visible, at least.

Within moments, Nick, Richard and Bill were summoned to the trailer of Jonathan Higgins. It was a short meeting with only the CEO speaking.

"Gentlemen, I'm afraid that this parade has come to an end," said Higgins. Sitting with the three men in front of him, he leaned back in his chair with his hands folded in front of him on his stomach and spoke the words as if he didn't have a care in the world.

"We came, we saw, and we failed. I understand that this is racing and things like this happen, but given our budget for this event and the overall damage to the car, I'm hereby terminating our contract and severing all ties with the team."

Turning his attention towards Nick, Higgins continued. "Mr. Lathan, I know we had a deal but unfortunately, it looks like you won't be able to live up to your end of the bargain. I'm afraid that we won't be sponsoring you next year in the Super2 Series. I'm sorry, but a deal is a deal."

Nick sat motionless looking both infuriated and disappointed. "Bill," said Higgins as he turned his gaze towards the American, "I must say that I admire your passion. Not many people in your shoes would deny the offer I made you to simply take the money and walk away. Instead, you decided to be difficult and now it would appear that everyone involved with the team will suffer for it. You had me going there for a bit once your lap times starting coming in, so I can't argue with your racing skills. It would seem, however, that fate has aligned itself against you. Your father was a great man who did many great things. You, however, will be remembered not for the battles you fought but by the method in which you fell for the last time."

Standing up as to hover over the three men in front of him, Higgins concluded the meeting by saying, "We're done here. I wish you all a safe journey to wherever you call home. Get out."

The meeting played over and over in Bill's head as he sat in silence. Darkness had now enveloped the entire room and the only illumination came from the lights of the buildings outside and from various cars which were driving by on the streets below. Bill sat and watched the light dance upon the wall as he sat in darkness.

Still motionless, Bill couldn't help but wonder what he would do next. Move back to America with Chad? Go back to work? Live out the rest of his days until he can no longer remember who he is or what he'd done? He simply didn't know.

A soft knock on the door pulled Bill from his trance. Standing up, Bill walked towards the door and looked through the tiny peep hole in the center. He had to do a double take because he couldn't truly believe who it was.

Unlocking the door quietly, Bill slowly opened the door letting the light shine in which caused him to initially squint. The two stared at each other for a brief moment before the visitor finally spoke.

"I thought you could use some company," said Abby. "I hope you don't mind."

Bill smiled as he held a finger up to his lips and then pointed inside, referring to Chad. Abby took the hint.

Inviting her in, Bill and Abby tiptoed past the slumbering Chad and slipped out onto the back patio which overlooked the city below. Closing the door behind them, they both took a seat side-by-side.

Abby breathed the fresh air in deeply. "It's a nice night."

"Yeah," replied Bill. "It's nice. I think this is the one time of year that the weather is about the same here in Australia as it is back home in Texas."

Abby turned to Bill. "You miss home, don't you?" she asked.

Bill took a moment to think before he answered. "Sometimes I do. Other times, not so much."

Abby turned back to face the city lights.

"I've never left Australia," she said. "I was born and raised here and I don't have any plans to ever leave. But I'm sure you said the same thing about America."

"To be honest, I never thought about leaving until my dad brought it up," replied Bill. "I had no reason to leave."

"What's it like over there in America?" asked Abby. "The only thing I ever hear about the U. S. is either about your politics from the news or from Tubbs always shouting about how fat he thinks Americans are."

Bill chuckled at the comment.

"It's not too different from here. I mean there are a few differences in the culture but for the most part, our lives are the same. We both have families, jobs, hobbies, good food, social events, people we care about…"

Bill paused.

"You miss her," said Abby who instantly picked up on Bill's reaction.

"Not a day goes by that I don't think of her," said Bill of his wife.

"I just," Abby began to choke up as she continued. "I can't imagine what it must be like to have gone through what you did; What you *still* go through. Losing your wife? Seeing your son in a wheelchair? Finding out you have brain cancer?"

"Crashing into a kangaroo with a perfectly good race car…" added Bill.

Abby chuckled slightly at the comment. "Believe me, Bill. You're not the first person to do that and you certainly won't be the last."

"I really wish I could say that comforts me," replied Bill.

"How do you do it?" asked Abby abruptly.

"Do what?"

"Stay strong. How do you stay so strong and determined after all of these things have happened around you?"

"What makes you think that I'm strong and determined? Right now I'm the laughing stock of Australia and I feel every bit as much."

"It's not your fault, Bill. It's just..."

"It's just racing, I know. That's all I've been hearing from people. But what nobody seems to understand is that's it for me. That's how my story ends, Abby. No great battle up the hill fighting with all diligence. No epic struggle worthy of remembrance. I'll just be remembered as someone who had *potential*; someone who had all the makings to do great things in this world but didn't."

"That's not how your son will remember you," said Abby.

"No, but I can only hope he's not ridiculed because of it for the rest of his life. You know, I still can't believe that I got talked into this. I just can't believe it. How in the world did I let myself get talked back into racing again? I'll tell you how. Because racing is nothing more than an addiction. A life-sucking, money-draining, soul-destroying addiction that's never done anything good..."

Abby placed her hand on top of Bill's. The immediate sensation caused Bill to pause. All of the heartache he was going through, all of the troubles, trials and tribulations, it all seemed to fly off the edge of the balcony with her simple touch.

Bill felt his soul come to peace. It was the first time in a long while that he had felt this type of relief. With the weight of his burdens momentarily lifted, it seemed that all of the built up emotion masked by the weight of his worries suddenly began to pour out.

"I'm so sorry, Abby."

"You have nothing to be sorry for," replied Abby. "You're one of the strongest people I've ever met, but everyone has a breaking point. I'm just glad that I could be here for you."

Abby laid her head on Bill's shoulder. The seemingly innocent gesture caused Bill to close his eyes. Comforted by her presence, Bill in turn laid his head on top of hers. At that very moment in time, all felt as if it were right in the world. Time seemed to stand still and Bill could only hope that it would. He closed his eyes and embraced the moment as he placed his other hand on top of Abby's.

"*One* of the strongest people, huh? Not *the* strongest person you know?" asked Bill.

Abby chuckled slightly. "Once you work for a guy like Tubbs, you'll understand."

Bill laughed. "I don't doubt that for a second."

They both sat as the cool air of the evening swept across the balcony. Bill felt it tingle against his skin, and for the first time in a long time, he felt glad to be alive.

* * *

After receiving a small kiss from Abby just before she left his hotel room the night before, Bill had fallen into a deep sleep but still managed to wake up before dawn.

He looked over to notice that Chad was also awake in the bed next to his.

"Morning, sunshine," said Bill. "I hope you slept as good as I did."

Chad smiled and nodded his head up and down. It was a soothing sight to see.

Just then, Bill's phone rang. Looking at the caller ID, Bill saw that it was Richard calling.

"You're up early, sweetheart," Bill answered jokingly.

"Glad to see you've got your sense of humor back," answered Richard.

Right away the fatigue in his voice was noticeable.

"You sound tired," said Bill. "Long night?"

"You have no idea," responded Richard.

Although Bill had found a restful night of sleep, he could only assume that Richard had taken to the bottle once again.

"Look, I'm sorry to bug you this early in the morning but it seems that we're not quite done."

"What do you mean?"

"It would appear that there's a bit of paperwork you have to sign before you go off to … I don't know … wherever it is you're off to next," said Richard.

"What are you talking about?" asked Bill. "What kind of paperwork?"

"Contract terminations or something. Look, I'm not exactly in the position to be explaining things right now," said a very tired Richard. "Just swing by the garage at the track so we can get this over with and move on."

"Alright," said Bill who was still slightly confused. "When do I need to be there?"

"Five minutes ago," replied Richard. "Let me know when you get here and I'll meet you."

Before Bill could acknowledge, Richard had hung up.

"Such a pleasant man," said Bill to himself. He turned to Chad who was listening intently. "Well, it looks like we've got one more trip up to the track we need to take care of. After that, we head back to Greg's in Sydney and get ready to go home."

Even as the words left his mouth, Bill could hardly believe them.

Jumping out of bed, Bill prepared to finish the final chapter of his racing career.

* * *

With Bill and Chad taking a cab to the track, Bill messaged Richard to let him know that he was en route.

No response.

As they arrived at the track, Bill tried again but this time by calling and messaging. Still nothing.

"Okay, now I'm getting annoyed," said Bill as he stood by an entrance waiting for Richard.

Bill could see teams working and people milling about in the background. Not wanting to be recognized, he slipped a hat over his head.

A car drove past the entrance where Bill and his son were. It slowed as it drove by.

"Keep going. Keep going," mumbled Bill under his breath.

The car then stopped, did a U-turn and drove into the parking lot.

"Great," was all Bill could say.

The car drove up to the pair and came to a stop with the driver's side of the vehicle facing them. Bill felt a mix of disgust and anger as the window rolled down. "Hey there, Yank. I hear you're looking for a ride," said Derek Renshaw. "You don't mind if I drive, do you? I've heard that you're not too friendly to our local wildlife when you get behind the wheel."

Bill could only laugh.

"I'm glad to see you're in good spirits. Bad luck though, Watson. Look on the bright side: Now you get to watch the entire race on TV without worrying about hitting anything."

Out of the corner of his eye, Bill could see a few fans standing on the other side of a fence recording the exchange with their phones.

Keep your head on your shoulders, Bill.

"It looks like this is it, Derek," said Bill. "It's been nice meeting you." Bill extended his hand to shake Derek's but the latter simply smiled.

"This isn't *it* because it never *was*," said Derek as he began rolling his window back up. "Good riddance, Yank."

Getting the final word in, Derek spun the tires as he sped off towards his destination.

"Well, that's over," said Bill to Chad.

All of the sudden, the sound of hundreds of camera shutters

erupted at once. Bill looked toward the sound source and noticed dozens of photographers taking pictures of Bill.

"What in the world are they doing? It's not like they've never seen me before." said Bill.

Turning to look at his son, Bill did a double-take as he realized that it was Chad, not him, that they were taking pictures of. There he was, the son of Bill Watson and grandson of William Watson, fully extending his right arm in the direction of the fleeing Derek Renshaw while elevating his middle finger in a symbolic gesture which made Bill both proud and shameful, but leaning more towards the former.

"Chad!" said Bill as he pulled his son's arm back down to his side, but it was all an act for the cameras. Leaning in to whisper into his ear, however, Bill said, "That's my boy."

Finally, a door behind Bill swung open and standing there in the doorway was a soggy-eyed Richard. Bill was initially taken back by the sight of his former teammate.

"Wow," said Bill. "You look like hell."

"I'm sorry, Bill," said Richard. "I dozed off for a bit right after you called me."

"After I...No, Richard. You called me. Remember?"

Richard looked perplexed and embarrassed. "I did, didn't I? No matter. Come on. Let's get this done with."

Leading Bill and his son through the various buildings and outside alleyways, Richard's pace was surprisingly quick for a man who claimed to be as tired as he was. Bill noticed, however, that Richard was leading them the long way around as to avoid any nosey fans or media personnel.

"Richard, what in the world is the hurry?"

No answer came from the Brit. He simply maintained his pace and continued on. "Why couldn't this paperwork wait another day? How is it that..."

Bill stopped dead in his tracks.

Richard had led Bill and Chad back into their old team's garage.

Instead of there being a heap of the race car Bill had totaled, there was instead a fully rebuilt Ford Falcon FG X parked in the garage. Sporting a different livery which was black supplemented by a mix of white and red highlight colors along with black wheels, the car bore the name of Bill's company, *Dynamis Engineering*, on the hood. Along the sides, the red NASCAR-style numbers on the doors reading *528*—the number from Bill's former race car—gave the car an aggressive appearance.

Bill was completely awestruck and speechless.

"How?" he asked. "How is this possible?"

"Because I do business for business because business is good," said a familiar voice.

Bill turned around to see his old friend and business partner, Pat Henderson, standing behind him. The large man approached Bill with his signature smile while wearing his all too familiar dress shirt and necktie, which still looked like it was choking him to death.

"Hi, Bill," said Pat. "I heard that you were having some car trouble."

"Pat!" said Bill as he embraced his friend.

"What are you doing in Australia?" asked Bill. "And how did you get the money for this from the company?"

"Well, all of the money you used to use to sponsor your old car was just adding up as the months went by. That and the big deal I'd been working on finally came through with our new client from Greece. When I heard about what happened, I had to step in."

"I can't believe it," said Bill.

Even as he stood there looking the car over, Bill was running the figures through his head.

"How did you convince Higgins to repair the car?"

"I didn't," said Pat.

"Did...did you buy the car from Higgins?" asked Bill.

"I did," answered Pat with a smug grin.

"I didn't know that the car was for sale."

"Neither did he. But I'm a hell of a salesman," said Pat.

"But even then, there's no way that the company had enough money lying around to not only buy the car but to repair it as well. How did you do it?" asked Bill.

"Oh I had some help," said Pat.

"From who?"

"From me," said a new but familiar voice.

Walking into the garage, William Watson was smiling with joy as he looked upon his son and grandson for the first time in several months.

"Dad!"

Bill ran over and embraced his father.

"Good to see you, son," said William softly into his son's ear.

"How did you do this?" asked Bill.

"My old house finally sold and I couldn't think of a better way to celebrate than to put it toward a race car for my son. It's not everyday I get to come to Australia and watch my son race at Bathurst with my grandson by my side."

William walked over to Chad and knelt down in front of him. "You've gotten big!"

Chad smiled at the comment and extended his arms outward to hug his grandfather. Just then, a few other familiar faces entered the garage.

"Sorry we're late, mate!" said the booming voice of Tubbs. "This place isn't very easy to get to."

"No, it's not. Especially when you're driving like a bat outta hell. I think these two got sick in the back," said Greg gesturing towards Nick and Abby who were also with them.

Turning to acknowledge Bill, Greg said, "What, you didn't think I'd miss your race at Bathurst, did you?"

Bill and Greg embraced as Tubbs chimed in. "I hope you don't mind, mate," said Tubbs, "but I've taken the liberty of doing a bit of advertising on the car."

As everyone in the room turned to look at the car, they all noticed the giant image on the roof of the car of a bear with human hands balled up into fists with the words *Bear Knuckles* layered in front of the creature.

"Not at all, Tubbs," replied Bill with a smile as he greeted his friend. "Not at all. Guys, I can't thank you enough."

"Oh don't thank us," said Pat. "Thank the crew who put this thing back together overnight."

"Overnight..." Bill put two and two together. "Richard?" Bill turned to see Richard fast asleep in a chair by the door.

"He and the crew were here all night working," said Nick. "Don't worry, mate. He sent the rest of the crew back to the hotel to get a few hours of sleep before we get to it."

"Wait," said Bill. "You knew?"

"I only found out about it late last night," said Nick, "from her."

Bill was even more puzzled than before. "You did this?" asked Bill to Abby.

"You're damn right I did, Bill Watson," said Abby. "To be honest, I had this in mind as soon as I saw that hideous car that Higgins had you driving. After the accident, I put the plan into action and started making phone calls."

"So all last night, you knew," said Bill in utter disbelief.

Abby shrugged her shoulders and smiled. "Surprise."

"From the bottom of my heart, thank all of you," said Bill.

"We all believe in you, mate," said Tubbs. "You too, Nick."

"Enough of the warm and fuzzies, though," said William. "You guys had better get this thing ready for the track. I won't be far behind."

"Where are you off to?" asked Bill.

"Your father's off to meet with the press," said William with a beam of pride in his smile. Bill looked surprised.

"Hey, when you return to your home country all these years after you've accomplished what I did, it's okay to let everyone know you're in town for a few days."

"You bloody legend, you," said Tubbs with a childish starstruck look in his eyes.

Just then, Greg moved to greet his old friend. “How are ya, you old bastard?” asked Greg to William as he extended his hand in greeting. “How many times has the nurse had to change your diaper so far today?”

“I was hoping you’d give me a hand with that,” replied William as he met Greg’s handshake. “My old ass could use a good powdering.”

“Let’s get this thing ready to roll!” shouted Nick. “We’ve got a race to make!”

Chapter 22

Although it took a bit of explaining to the officials from a barely conscious Richard to get the car back onto the grid for the main race, the team was able to get it done. At first, however, it became apparent that Richard was in no condition to be speaking in such an important situation…or at all. Luckily, Pat was there and was more than eager to step in and get the deal squared away with haste. Despite this small victory, however, both Bill and Nick knew they were now at a serious disadvantage.

Because of the earlier accident and the amount of time it took to repair the car, the team had missed valuable practice time: time which would've been used to tune and further prep the car for race conditions. Additionally, they were also starting from a relatively clean slate again with a fresh car after the rebuild. That meant that all of the work the team had previously put into the old car was gone.

Luckily, the factory Ford team which had previously agreed to share their data with what was now the former Higgins Financial team upheld their agreement. This was a huge plus to Bill's team, which now had a monumental task of preparing the car for the upcoming qualifying session.

Once the car was brought back into the garage, the sleep deprived team—now powered by energy drinks—got to work. With the team busy behind them, both Bill and Nick met with Richard to go over the logistics of the day.

"Before the qualifying session later today, we'll have a chance to get the car back on the track for a brief practice session," said Richard.

"That will be our one and only chance to get a reading on the car before qualifying. There was a practice session earlier today for co-drivers only but between making the final preparations on the car, transporting the car, to handling the logistics of getting it back onto the grid, we missed our shot. The last session before qualifying is for both primary and co-drivers. We'll have the car ready to go by then."

Turning his attention to Nick, Richard continued.

"You'll obviously be driving for the qualifying session since you're the primary driver. We'll have you in the car for the majority of the practice session. We'll be relying on your feedback to get the car in proper shape for the race."

"No worries, mate," said Nick. "Maybe we'll get lucky and get a spot in the Shootout."

Richard raised his eyebrows and lowered his chin. "Let's not get our hopes up."

Although many Motorsports events have the standard qualifying format where each car is given a set amount of time or laps to lay down their best lap time, the Bathurst 1000 adds another factor in with the Top Ten Shootout. After the initial qualifying session, the drivers who posted the ten fastest times advance into the Shootout. They're then given another opportunity to post a fast lap. The results from the Shootout then determine the starting order for the top ten drivers for the race. The remaining drivers who didn't make the Shootout (11th to last) start according to their qualifying times from the initial session.

The significance of making the Shootout is that even if a driver only makes it into the top-ten by the skin of their teeth, they have another opportunity to improve and potentially grab pole position. Additionally, it ensures that the team that starts on the pointy end of the field is more than just lucky. Even if a driver posts the fastest lap during qualifying, they then need to repeat that pace or top it if they hope to make it official during the Shootout.

Only the best teams make it into the Shootout, and Richard was quick to remind them of their place.

"Look, Gents. If you thought we were down before all of this happened, we're even further down now," said Richard. "We've got an underdeveloped car, a crew that's half asleep and not enough time to work out the kinks that are certainly waiting for us."

Bill sighed. "So what's the good news?"

"The good news, Mr. Watson, is that we have the data that we need to set a good baseline," said Richard. "While we were rebuilding our car, the factory Ford team were able to get their car into top shape. After the deal fell through with Higgins, they were technically off the hook with sharing their data with us."

Pointing his finger towards Bill's friend standing at the entrance of the garage, Richard continued. "Your friend Pat is one hell of a negotiator."

Bill chuckled. "That he is."

"I don't know how, but he managed to revive the deal with the Ford team. That alone could be the difference between us being competitive versus being a backmarker."

"You be sure to buy that bloke a beer or something, mate," said Nick.

"He prefers Greek pastries," replied Bill.

The three men laughed as they parted ways to get ready for the upcoming practice session.

As both Nick and Bill suited up in their driving gear, the crew worked feverishly to get the car ready in addition to completing any last-minute repair work on the car. The clock ticked away and with only five minutes remaining until the start of the practice session, the car was finally wheeled out of the garage.

The crowd outside in the stands erupted with cheers as the sight of the car that was once destroyed but now rebuilt and freshly sponsored came into view. Television crews and photographers surrounded the car as Nick waived to the crowd and climbed inside.

As clock was winding down, the final practice session before qualifying began and the cars pulled out of pit lane onto the track. As the freshly completed car rolled out of its pit stall, the entire crew came out of the garage and applauded. It was a monumental effort which they had successfully completed. The rest was now in the hands of Nick who was driving a car which had been rebuilt in a matter of hours.

Bill would be lying if he said he didn't see more than half of the crew cross their fingers as the car rolled away down pit lane.

* * *

For the first fifteen minutes of the practice session, Nick was absolutely quiet on the radio. In the garage, Richard and the crew were looking over the data coming back from the car to get a reading on the overall telemetry. Additionally, they were watching the times that Nick was posting each time he crossed that start/finish line.

The crew was simply astonished. The lap times coming in were very quick. Right away, Nick was sitting inside the top-five.

Richard made the call out to Nick over the radio. "How's she treating you?"

Several seconds passed with no response.

"Nick?"

After several more seconds, a reply finally came from Nick. "You're not going to believe this."

"What is it? What's wrong?" asked Richard.

"Nothing!" said Nick. "The car feels bloody fantastic, mate!"

As if that wasn't enough, Nick crossed the line and set a lap time which put them in third for the practice session. The crew behind Richard began to cheer.

"Don't get too excited just yet," said Richard over the radio. "You're quick, but it's mostly co-drivers out there right now. Plus, Renshaw is sitting P1 at the moment. He put a quick lap in early on and now his co-driver is out there. We'll see where we are at the end of the session. Go ahead and bring it in so we can get Bill in the car."

Bill stood by at the entrance of the garage ready to go. With his helmet on, he watched as the car came into view as it entered pit lane. Just then, a hand slapped Bill on the shoulder. Turning around, Bill was surprised to see his dad standing behind him.

Nothing was said between the two men. William was smiling from ear to ear as he extended his hand. Bill met his father's handshake and patted him on his shoulder. William stepped away as the car pulled into the pit stall.

It was a full-speed pit stop despite it only being a practice session. Every person on pit lane knew that races were won and lost by pit stops, so practice was essential.

As the crew hurried to add a bit of fuel and change the tires, Bill assisted Nick with exiting the car. In turn, Nick assisted Bill with entering. Making sure that the radio connection, cool suit, and drink hose were connected, Nick then closed the door to the car and walked back into the garage to give his briefing to the crew.

Bill, now tightening the harness straps, felt the car come down from the jacks. Pulling away from his pit stall and heading down pit lane towards the entrance of the track, Bill began setting his focus only to have it momentarily distracted by their rival team who were in the first pit stall.

Standing at the entrance of his team's garage holding a large cardboard sign which read "Save the Kangaroos!" complete with a drawing of one of the local inhabitants with a tear rolling down its face was the unmistakable grin of Derek Renshaw. He was accompanied by a few members of his crew who were on their knees as they wept before a stuffed kangaroo which was lying on the ground in front of them. Derek waved the sign at Bill as he drove by.

Bill chuckled briefly and wondered if Derek had stayed up all night making his poster.

"I'm surprised he even knows how to spell 'kangaroo'," said Bill.

Immediately, however, Bill set his mind back into gear as he pulled out onto the track. With only 15 minutes now remaining in the session, Bill wanted to make the most of it.

Although his first few laps were a bit reserved, Bill chomped down on the bit with less than ten minutes remaining. He was now out there with many of the primary drivers but since it was just a practice session, they gave each other space and let the faster drivers go through as to not hold them up.

As Bill laid into it, he could tell right away how different the car felt to him. It was hard to describe, but it just felt *right*. He felt connected and was able to slip into a grove as he ran lap after lap. The car simply felt hooked up as he tipped it into *The Cutting*. It was confidence-inspiring to know that everything was working as it should including his mind. As he navigated the twists and bends leading up the Mountain, it was almost as if he and the car were dancing.

He wasn't tense, but focused; not reacting to the car's actions, but planning them.

"It feels like I've grown this car out of my ass!" shouted Bill over the radio as he plunged down *Conrod Straight*. It was the sensation Bill had been waiting for. Crossing the line for the final time as the practice session concluded, Bill was actually disappointed with the fact that he now had to get out of the car.

"Great job, Bill," said Richard over the radio. "You didn't improve on Nick's time but you were off by less than a tenth. We were the eighth fastest overall."

"Thanks to you and the crew for getting this thing out here, Richard. You and the boys did an amazing job."

Eighth.

Bill knew that it was cutting it close in terms of making the Shootout. Eighth in practice was great but he also knew that all of the teams would be bringing their A-game to qualifying.

Still, Bill felt a deep sense of pride in all the work his team had put into the car. Not only was it an improvement on the eyes with the new livery, but it ran like a dream.

Now, however, the car would be in the hands of Nick for the upcoming qualifying session.

* * *

A few hours had passed since the conclusion of the final practice session before qualifying. This allowed for the other categories, which were also present at the track, to race in various events. While it was popular with the fans, the drivers in the Supercars series knew one thing was for certain: all of the racing going on would change the condition of the track. With more rubber being laid down from tire wear and the temperature steadily rising, the track was bound to be more slippery during qualifying.

Teams up and down pit lane were working hard to ensure not only that their cars were prepared, but their drivers as well. They knew full well that one could turn a wrench until they were blue in the face but it wouldn't matter one bit if the nut behind the wheel wasn't mentally prepared.

Nick was pacing back and forth in the garage. With the car essentially ready to go, the crew were making a few last minute changes while a small crowd consisting of Richard, Bill, Chad, Abby, Tubbs, Greg and William watched the nervous Nick pace from one side of the garage to the next.

"Does he normally do this?" asked Bill to Abby.

"No. At least I've never seen him like this before a race."

Bill sighed. "We can't let him go out like this," he replied.

Overhearing the conversation, Tubbs took it upon himself to

remedy the situation in the only way he knew how.

"Hey!" shouted Tubbs. "Get your head outta your arse and screw it back onto your shoulders where it belongs!"

Shaking his head, William intervened. "Shut up, you," he said as he brushed past Tubbs.

Walking up to the nervous driver, William stood directly in front of him and stopped. "You nervous, son?" he asked.

"That could be argued," replied Nick.

"Why? Why are you nervous?"

"Just look around," answered Nick. "Cameras, tens of thousands of people, a race car that only survived after several people dumped a fortune into it and the crew worked overnight to repair, and now William Watson is standing in front of me. Yeah, I'm bloody nervous!"

William chuckled. "This is fun. Isn't it? All of this racing business. I mean, can you believe you get to drive a race car for a living? We're some of the most envied people in the world. Both young and old from all over the planet want to be doing what you're about to do. But at the end of the day, we do what we do because we not only love it, but because it's fun. Speeding down straights, clipping apexes, out-braking our opponents, feeling the crush of the g-forces on our bodies—it's the exhilaration of it all that pushes us to press on even if we don't have a prayer of winning. You and Bill, however, are in a purpose-built machine whose lot in life is to do your bidding. That's your office, mate, and your business is racing and to have fun doing it. So go out there and do just that—have fun. No pressure, no fear, and no bloody cameras. When you slip that helmet on, close your mind and open your eyes. Your body will handle the rest."

Nick smiled at the words from the legend standing before him. The look in his eyes indicated that he was both honored and humbled to have received a talk from a man such as William Watson. Indeed, no one else on pit lane would be able to say the same thing, and Nick felt better because of it.

"Has anyone ever told you that you have a very soothing voice?" asked Nick half jokingly.

The group laughed.

"My wife used to tell me that," said William. "She would've liked you. You've got a good head on your shoulders. But like Tubbs said, it does in fact belong on your shoulders."

Slapping Nick on the back, William turned and faced the entire crew. "I just want to say that I'm proud of all of you. You didn't give up when many others would've. You stuck with it and most importantly, you stuck with your drivers when they needed you most. You're all exactly what any decent driver wants: A solid foundation. You've got guts, diligence and perseverance. I'd be proud to call you my team if I were still racing so I know I speak for both Bill and Nick when I say that I'm proud of each and every one of you.

"This team has what it takes to be a winning team, but a lot stands between us and victory. Most notably is this big damn mountain. But if everyone stays focused, keeps a calm mindset and works aggressively, I feel that this small team will punch way above its weight. We're a wild card entry so nobody's expecting great things from us. Let's show these teams that we can go punch for punch with the big dogs. Should we falter in the process, we'll go down with our heads held high knowing that everyone here gave it their absolute best and left nothing on the table. This is who we are and this is what we were born to do. Go fast, work hard, and never...ever...quit."

The crew applauded the encouraging words of William. Bill, stepping forward to give his dad a hug, noticed that a camera crew had slipped in when they weren't looking and were filming his father's entire speech.

William, noticing the cameras, turned towards them and said, "For public motivational speaking inquiries, please contact my agent."

Everyone in the garage—camera crew included—erupted in laughter. Bill stood in amazement at what had just happened. Only moments ago, the garage was silent with the suppressed frustration and anxiety from Nick. A few encouraging words from his father had changed all of that. Bill was glad that his son was here to witness this. Even though his time remaining in this life was short, Bill could only hope that his example, along with that of his father, would leave such an impression that Chad would live a life of honor and integrity just as he had tried to do—and as his father had done.

"Get her ready and parked outside, boys," said Richard. "Qualifying is upon us."

* * *

Similar to practice, qualifying saw all of the cars hit the track together for the forty-minute session. With thirty-one cars on the entry list for the Bathurst 1000, the track would surely fill up in a hurry.

With Nick strapped into the car, he waited patiently to be released from pit lane. Although several thoughts were running through his head, he quietly meditated on the words previously spoken by William.

No pressure. No fear. There's no reason to fear anything. I've been in this situation more times than I can count. This one's no different.

Closing his eyes, Nick uttered the words slowly to himself. "No pressure. No fear."

He knew that every driver up and down pit lane would be having a similar feeling of butterflies in their stomachs, including Derek Renshaw. Although Renshaw was quite the character in front of the camera, he was still human.

A loud horn blasted in the background which woke Nick from his trance. Signifying that the qualifying session had begun, Nick waited to be released from his pit stall. The cars pulled out one-by-one. With the team's pit stall towards the rear, Nick watched and waited as he saw the cars pull away one at a time. When it was his turn, he made sure the car was in gear as he applied some throttle while lifting his foot off the clutch. As the car began to move, Nick engaged the pit lane speed limiter as he followed the car in front of him out of the long pit lane and onto the racing surface.

Taking his time on the out lap, Nick began warming up the tires and brakes while also doing his best to get a feel for the track conditions. Much had changed since his previous outing in the earlier practice session, and with the sun shining brightly without a cloud in sight, the heat ultimately caused the track temperature to rise.

As Nick weaved his way through the twists and turns of Mount Panorama, he felt confident enough that he'd be able to replicate his previous session and get into the Top Ten Shootout. It was just a matter of making the car stick and not making any mistakes. It wasn't a small order considering the reign of terror this mountain has been known to dish out on unsuspecting drivers. It was indeed because of this mountain that they had a newly sponsored car to begin with.

With the tires now warm and Nick ready to give it a go, he completed the final corner of his out lap and powered away to start his first flying lap.

After negotiating *Hell Corner,* Nick set his sights up the hill which led to *Griffins Bend.* Braking late, Nick tipped the car in and gave it some throttle. Right away, the back end began to come unglued. It was a bit of a wrestling match between himself and the car as it bobbled mid-corner, but Nick was able to keep it together and carry on despite the obvious loss in time.

As he carried his speed into *The Cutting,* Nick kept the thought in the back of his head that if he was struggling with grip, so was everyone else in the field.

Onward and upward, Nick continued his climb up the Mountain as he navigated through *Reid Park.* There was no doubt at this point that Nick was dealing with a different car. It was loose but that was to be expected. Pressing on was all he could do at this point, so he did just that.

Approaching *Skyline,* Nick had to adjust his braking point ever so slightly to compensate for the slick conditions. At first, he carried too much speed and almost smacked the wall on the right leading into *The Dipper*. It felt like a sloppy lap thus far but he knew that he had time to get a few more good ones in.

Approaching *Forrest's Elbow,* Nick completed the left turn and got on the power. The long downhill stretch of *Conrod Straight* was a brief chance to get your mind right for the upcoming hard braking zone. One couldn't get too comfortable, however, since the long straight went by quickly while traveling at speeds in excess of 180 mph.

Mashing hard on the brakes and tipping the car into *The Chase,* Nick was eager to see the time of the lap. Completing *Murrays Corner* and crossing the start/finish line, the readout on the dash showed a time of 2:07.251.

"You're currently in 9th at the moment," said Richard over the radio. "P9."

"Copy that," replied Nick. "It's slick out here but I'm doing the best I can."

"You're doing great. Just keep it pointed forward and bring it home in one piece."

As Nick was on his next lap, he caught up to slower traffic and was forced to abandon the lap due to the amount of time he had lost trying to get around the slower car. With 31 other cars on the track, various strategies from the different teams were all at play and sometimes those strategies conflicted with those from other teams.

Still, Nick did all he could to not spend the tires on a lap which didn't count, but he also needed to stay out of the way of faster cars.

After completing the lap, Nick powered off towards another. On his next lap, Nick was able to improve upon his previous time with a 2:06.927.

"We're down to thirteenth at the moment," said Richard on the radio. "The quick times are starting to come in from other drivers. We've got enough time for about two more laps. See if you can make the most of them."

Nick wasn't shocked by this news one bit. With the session coming to an end soon, all of the drivers would be throwing everything they had at the track in an effort to make it into the Shootout.

As Nick raced up *Mountain Straight,* he asked, "What's the current pole time?"

"2:06.5 set by Renshaw but it probably won't stand for long," said Richard. "Several drivers are about to come around now. Head down, eyes forward."

That was Richard's way of telling Nick to shut up and focus. Pressing on, Nick was determined to squeeze every bit of speed that he could out of the car. With the tires now at optimal temperature, he found himself sliding around a lot less.

This was evident as Nick came around to the start/finish line to complete his lap. The digital dashboard showed his time as a 2:06.802.

"We're on the bubble in tenth at the moment," said Richard over the radio. "Give me one more fast one and that should secure us a spot in the shootout."

"Copy," replied Nick.

No pressure. No fear.

The words replayed in Nick's mind as he raced up *Mountain Straight* for the last time this session. He was well aware that his lap had to be perfect and that he was needing to hit all of his marks on the track.

As he made the elevated left turn up *The Cutting,* Nick modulated the throttle and short-shifted to third gear just before reaching *Quarry Corner.* The car felt settled all the way through *Reid Park* even as he nearly kissed the right side wall at *Sulman Park.*

Making the plunge down *Skyline,* Nick was calm and collected all the way through and the car was a visual representation of it. Navigating *The Dipper,* the #528 Ford Falcon looked to be in good form as it made the downhill left-turn at *Forrest's Elbow*.

Now it was a final chance to breathe before going into one of the hardest braking zones in the series. Taking one last gulp of oxygen, Nick went hard on the brakes as he headed into *The Chase*.

Making the left turn out of *The Chase*, Nick took too much of the inside curb which unsettled the car slightly and caused it to wobble. Forced to lift off the throttle momentarily to regain stabilization, Nick was able to gather it back together—but in his heart, he knew it was over. He had just blown the lap.

"I'm sorry, boys," said Nick over the radio before he had even taken *Murrays Corner*. "I stuffed it up."

As Nick crossed the line, the time on his dashboard read 2:06.788. Surprised to see that it was still an improvement over his previous lap, it made Nick feel even worse to think of what the time could've been had he not made the error.

"Did we make it?"

There was a long pause over the radio.

"Hey! Did we..."

"I heard you the first time," snapped Richard over the radio. "We're still waiting for the rest of the cars to finish. Cool it down—the car and yourself—and bring it back in."

The slow lap to cool the engine and brakes down was horrible for Nick. The long wait to see if they had done what was seemingly impossible made him drive a bit faster to get to the pit stall. Still, it was a good chance for Nick to catch his breath after the intense forty-minute session. It's not every day that one is racing laps at one of the most challenging race tracks in the world while driving at the absolute limit. He just wished that he hadn't gone slightly over that limit.

Pulling back into the pit stall, the crew was standing by to get the car wheeled back into the garage. As Nick finally exited the car, he couldn't wait anymore. Running up to Richard, he asked again.

"Did we make it?"

Standing with his head buried in his clipboard, Richard simply pointed to the monitor off to the side which displayed the event results. As he started from the top, he noticed that Derek Reshaw had managed to secure provisional pole.

"Big surprise," Nick muttered under his breath.

As his eyes continued to scroll down, his stomach sank. There he was—the #528 Dynamis Engineering Ford Falcon—in 11th. He had just missed the 10th position, and a spot in the Shootout, by a mere five thousandths of a second.

He wanted to drop to his knees in anguish but the slap on his shoulder caused him to turn to see who it was. It was followed by another slap and still another. Turning, Nick noticed it was the entire crew coming over to congratulate him.

"Great drive, mate," said one crew member. "We're starting in 11th at the Bathurst 1000."

Another approached and said, "You made all of our hard work pay off. Fantastic job, mate."

Approaching at the tail end of it all was Richard, Abby, Greg, Tubbs, and William followed by Bill who was pushing Chad's wheelchair around the garage on the back two wheels as the latter smiled.

Stopping the wheelchair in front of Nick with an "Errrrr!" sound mimicking tires squealing, Bill said, "Well here he is, Chad! The man who just put us in the front half of the grid of the Bathurst 1000!"

Sticking out his hand to shake Nick's hand, Chad's smile was enough to melt Nick's heart despite his bruised ego.

"Thanks, little buddy," said Nick to Chad. "And thanks to everyone here. You all did a tremendous job on the car. It felt great out there despite the conditions."

Even Richard had a smile on his face after Nick's performance. "You really drove the tires off of it, Nick. Excellent work and great hustle out there."

"Even though we didn't make the Shootout?" asked Nick.

"Damn the Shootout," replied Richard. "Just one more chance to stuff up the car before the race."

Bill, giving Nick a hug, said, "Great job out there. You put on a good show, too."

"Glad I could be of service," replied Nick. "So what do we do now?"

"Now," said Richard, "we can all finally get some rest."

Chapter 23

Back at the hotel, there was no rest to be found for Bill during the night. Arriving at the hotel later in the evening after getting dinner with the team and his friends, Bill was initially eager to get some sleep after the day's events. Settling Chad down for the night, Bill couldn't help but be impressed by his son's ability to seemingly go to sleep as soon as his head hit the pillow.

"He certainly didn't get that from me," said Bill after he checked on Chad before preparing for bed himself.

A soft knock on the door changed all of that.

Opening the door, Bill was happy to see his dad standing there. Carrying a medium-sized brown cardboard box which was about ten inches wide, over a foot long but only a few inches thick, Bill initially thought it was simply a gift from some people back home in Texas.

He was greatly mistaken.

"I was cleaning up the house one day and I stumbled across this," said William softly after noticing Chad was fast asleep. "I knew what it was the moment I opened it, but I promise I didn't go through it. It's certainly not my place to do that. But it is something that I think you should have with you."

As William removed the item from the box, Bill instantly knew what it was. His heart sank into his stomach as his father handed him Lena's journal.

It was a simple book in appearance: a brown leather cover with Lena's name embroidered in gold print onto the bottom right hand side. Bill had bought this journal for Lena after they had gotten married, but they had agreed to both write in it from time to time. Although Bill occasionally wrote in it at first, it soon became mostly Lena's penmanship.

As Bill took a seat on his hotel bed and flipped through the pages, he had to fight back tears as he glanced at the beautiful handwriting of his now deceased wife. He found the story Lena had written about their first wedding anniversary and how Bill had planned this elaborate evening only to run out of gas while in route to their destination. Flipping through a few more pages, a small ultrasound picture fell out from when they first found out that they were having Chad. Entry after entry, Bill's mind was taken back to some of the best years of his life.

As Bill glanced over the pages, he had to stop himself from choking up. They would not be tears of sadness, however, but of joy. Indeed, Bill counted himself as one who was blessed to have lived a life such as this. Although things certainly didn't turn out the way he had hoped or planned for, he knew that few things in life ever did.

As Bill flipped towards the end of the journal, he noticed several empty pages still remaining to be filled.

"There's still room in there," said William gesturing to the blank pages. "Room to share some of your thoughts. You don't have to do it now but I think Chad would appreciate it when he grows up."

It was an image which was still hard to grasp: knowing that Chad, his son who currently couldn't walk and who was still not speaking, would soon be an orphan.

Even though Bill had thought he had made peace with the idea, the thought was suddenly so alarming that he had to stand up. Walking over to Chad, Bill once again checked to make sure he was asleep. Noticing that he was making his usual light whistling sound which he typically did when he slept, Bill knew that Chad would be oblivious to what was about to be spoken.

As he began pacing back and forth, he soon realized that there was a hard question he needed to ask his dad—one he had been putting off for a long time.

Unable to even make eye contact with his father because of how difficult of a question it was to ask, Bill decided to simply be out with it.

"Dad?" asked Bill.

William, studying the movements of his son, remained silent.

"I've still got time...*some* time left...but I...I need to know that Chad will be looked after ... when I'm gone."

Despite the fact that William was fully ready and willing to assume the responsibilities of being Chad's guardian, hearing those words coming from his only son sent him over the edge.

Barely able to hold himself together, William somehow managed to get the words out which he needed to say. "Of course, son. I'd be honored."

Bill could no longer fight back the tears.

"Thank you, Dad. For everything. There's one thing I need to give you, though."

Reaching over towards one of his bags, Bill retrieved a small envelope from it and handed it to his father.

"I know you weren't expecting this when you walked in here, but I need you to hold onto this."

Taking the envelope in his hand, William examined it and asked, "What is it?"

Bill took a deep breath. "It's my will and several other legal and financial documents. Not just because of...you know...my condition, but also just in case something happens in the race."

Able to hold off the wave of emotion up until this point, the older man began to weep as well as he sat down and held his face in his hand.

Sitting down beside his father, Bill put his arm around him and embraced him. He could feel his father shuddering as he wept and Bill realized that he had never seen his dad like this before, even when his mother had passed away.

In that moment, Bill reaffirmed why he was racing at Bathurst. It wasn't for fame or fortune or for one last thrill. It was for his son and now, for his father as well. It was to make them proud and to honor them.

He wanted to honor his father because of how selfless he had been all throughout his life. He would correct and discipline at times but he would also use those situations to encourage and inspire. It was because of William's dedication as a father that Bill was the man he was today. And because of that, Bill had been able to apply those same principles to his own son. Despite the circumstances now surrounding Chad's life, the foundation of his family was something he would always be able to fall back on for the rest of his days.

As if suddenly realizing that his emotions were on full display, William wiped his eyes and gave a slight grunt. Gathering himself back together, William stood and said, "Get some rest tonight, son. You'll need a clear mind for the days ahead."

As William turned and headed towards the door, Bill said, "I love you, Dad."

Taking in a deep breath, William stopped in his tracks but didn't turn around as he replied, "I love you too, son," before exiting.

After his father had left the room, Bill spent the remainder of the night reading Lena's journal from cover to cover. As he read her words, he could almost hear her voice speaking to him in his ear. The glimpse into her mind followed by the memories of her voice were soothing to him. Like before, he wasn't sad as he read through the journal of his now deceased wife. Instead, he smiled as he continued through the pages. He oftentimes found himself laughing at some of the memories which he himself had almost forgotten.

Bill had mourned Lena's death for the past several months, but if there's one thing he'd learned from his own circumstances, it's that life should be celebrated. With this book in his hand, every entry was a celebration of their life together. It was a life they had built from the ground up and one which they were happy to have been able to be a part of. Most importantly, they had been able to raise such an amazing young man like Chad.

As Bill got to the end of Lena's journal, he came across her final entry:

"Well, tomorrow is another race for Bill. I get so worried seeing him out there but I wouldn't ever tell him that. The last thing I want him to be thinking about out there is that I'm worrying about him. As much as I don't get this race car stuff, I'm glad that Bill has something like this in his life. I just remember how my dad was when I was growing up. He would just sit on the back patio all day arguing about politics with his neighbors and cowering to my demanding mother. I'm so glad Bill will never be like that.

"Seeing how involved he is in Chad's life and vice versa is something I really cherish. Even though I secretly dread the day that Chad will want to get into a race car as well, I trust Bill enough to know when he'll be ready and I know that he'll use every safety precaution available. Plus, I think if he were perfectly honest, Bill's most likely dreading that day as well.

"It's funny when you stop and think about it. Most parents are fine watching their kids put on a helmet and smash their skulls together on a football field. They think it somehow makes them tough. Even though the team element is something I think Chad would enjoy, deep down I think Chad likes the individual accomplishments much like his dad and granddad do. Plus, I can already see it in his eyes. It's the same look that both Bill and his father have as soon as someone brings up racing: The look of hunger.

"It's one thing to see a man pursue his passions with a hunger. Hell, I think it's downright sexy. But to see your son developing that same drive is exciting and scary. At the same time, I know that Chad is a very smart kid. Whether he wants to race, go into the engineering business with his dad or branch off to do his own thing, I can rest assured that he'll be successful

regardless of what he does because he's simply driven to succeed...like his dad.

"Call it stubborn ambition or a never quit mentality, I'm thankful to be surrounded by my boys. I'm a very blessed woman to have a family with such a strong core foundation. I know that regardless of life's circumstances and whatever trials and tribulations come our way, we'll always stick together. Even my nutty Australian father-in-law who manages to get Bill in and out of far too much trouble is an important part of our family. It's who we are and how we've grown together as a family. There's never truly a dull moment in the Watson household and I wouldn't change this life for anything.

-Prayers for my boys-

"To my dearest son, Chad. I pray that God's favor shines upon you in all that you do. As your mother, I always try to protect you but I know that one of these days, you'll be all grown up and on your own and you'll realize just how challenging life can be. It won't always be easy but remember that it's not meant to be easy. You will stumble at times and you will fall, but I pray that you always remember to get back up. I thank God for you every day and I look forward to watching you grow up and succeed in life.

"To my husband, Bill. I pray God's grace and protection upon you during your race. Not just your race at the track, but your race in life. Regardless of where you finish, you'll always be my knight in shining armor, my rock, my hero, my best friend and my one true love. I know that you're wanting to win this race but know that you're already a winner in my heart. Still, I know that you're going to go out there and give your absolute all. That's why I love you...because you don't know how to do 'just good enough'. Be the relentless warrior both Chad and I know that you are and you go make us proud. God bless you, Bill Watson.

"Until next time."

Bill had to wipe a tear from his eye as he finished the final passage.

He knew that the words he just read would resonate with him for the remainder of his life.

As Bill put the book on his nightstand, laid down and closed his eyes in an attempt to get at least a few hours of sleep, he had one last thought before his mind faded for the evening.

For Chad. For William.

For Lena...

* * *

After a night of much needed rest, the team was fully recharged and ready to go the following day. Although qualifying was officially behind them now, there was still plenty of work which was needing to be done on the car as well as testing to ensure that the fuel strategy for the race tomorrow would keep them in a competitive spot.

As usual, the team got an early start on the day and met at the garage before sunrise. Despite the early hours, there was plenty of activity in and around the paddock as various categories prepared to go racing on the Mountain.

Additionally, today was also the all-important Top-Ten Shootout. Although Bill and the team wouldn't be participating due to their 11th place qualifying position, the team still had a vested interest in the results, especially in regard to Derek Renshaw.

With Renshaw taking provisional pole position in the earlier qualifying session, he now had to make the best run possible in order to take official pole position for the race.

The weather was ideal for qualifying. Although the sun was out, the air was cool and pleasant without a cloud in the sky. With the tens of thousands of fans lining the way around the infamous track and enjoying the beautiful day, they all stood to their feet as the first car began rolling out of pit lane.

Starting with the 10th placed car, each driver would get one flying lap around an empty track in an effort to post their quickest time. In theory, the driver who barely made it into the top-ten could potentially still walk away with a pole position, although such a feat was rare. Despite the odds, however, all of the drivers were without a doubt ready to give it their all.

As car after car went by, the leaderboard started to fill up with times.

Everything was going smoothly until the seventh car out smacked the wall hard while coming out of *The Cutting*. It was one of the factory Ford cars which Bill's team had been receiving data from. It was a hard shunt, which instantly ended their Shootout run and possibly their race.

As Nick and Bill watched, they both turned to each other and said the same thing without actually uttering any words.

That may have just killed our chances.

They both knew that the track was ferocious in its own right and demanded respect. Even for those who made the Shootout—the best of the best drivers—they still had to tread carefully on the Mountain.

Eventually, the wounded car was able to make its way back into the pit lane and into its respective garage stall. The two knew that they would be feeling the repercussions of this later on due to the amount of data which was being shared between the two teams. But for now, the show rolled on.

As the cars continued to streak past the front stretch where Bill and Nick both watched from the team's garage, they waited patiently. Although everyone who was in the Shootout was their direct competition, the two men were eager to see where their rival, Derek Renshaw, would slot in.

With only a two cars remaining who needed to put in a qualifying time, Bill turned to notice that Richard was off in a corner speaking very quietly into his phone.

Maybe it's a personal call.

Bill recalled that he had never seen Richard take a personal call while at the track, so it struck him as odd. Additionally, Richard was doing his best to look inconspicuous. By doing so, however, he made himself look even more suspicious.

Realizing that it could just be one of the many quirks of the older British man, he paid it no further mind and fixed his attention back onto the timing and scoring screen.

Renshaw was up next.

As their rival pulled out onto the track to start his warm up lap, there was a mix of cheering and booing from the crowd. Both Bill and Nick couldn't help but smile.

Taking a brief glance over his shoulder, Bill noticed that Richard was now pacing back and forth and speaking even softer into the phone. Bill could only shake his head as he wondered what the man was up to but once again, he turned his attention back to the screen as Renshaw started his hot lap.

Making a perfect entry and exit out of *Hell Corner,* Renshaw raced up *Mountain Straight* as he began his ascent up the Mountain. Through *Griffins Bend* and *The Cutting,* Renshaw's form was perfect.

"He's looking good," admitted Bill.

"It's a long lap," rebutted Nick. "There's still a long way to go."

As Renshaw completed the first sector, his time thus far was .05s quicker than the previous driver who had taken provisional pole. It wasn't much, but whether by a second or a thousandth of a second, a faster time is a faster time. Sometimes that's all the difference between starting first or much further back.

As he raced up to *Sulman Park,* Renshaw flung his car across the left hander and was only millimeters away from scraping the wall on the right side. He was completely committed at this point and both Bill and Nick knew there was little that could stop a leading Supercars driver once they were fully in the zone.

As Renshaw headed towards *Forrest's Elbow,* however, he unexpectedly slowed all of the sudden. Just as quickly as he slowed, he mashed the throttle and raced down *Conrod Straight*.

Bill looked at Nick with a perplexed look and the latter's face showed a similar expression?

"What the hell just happened?" asked Nick.

As they watched the video from the broadcast go through the replay from inside Renshaw's car, they soon found their answer. It appeared that a large man who was standing close to the track was wearing a bright yellow shirt which, apparently, Renshaw mistook for a caution flag. As is standard protocol, he slowed. As he made the turn which showed a clear track in front of him, he realized that he had slowed in error and sped off. His lap, however, was useless at that point. He had no chance of taking pole position and as he crossed the line, his time slotted him back into eighth.

"Would you look at that," said the voice of Richard who was now standing behind them. "What a shame that must be for our friend Mr. Renshaw. I'm sure he's very displeased with himself."

Bill suddenly put two and two together.

"Richard," said Bill, "Did you…"

The British man cut him off as he put his index finger over both of his lips and quietly mouthed, "Shhhh…"

Bill could only smile and assume that the incident which had just happened was Richard's doing, but he doubted he would ever get a straight answer from him.

The fallout, however, was enormous. Replays of the incident were being broadcast on the television and the announcers were quick to point out that very little of Derek's radio transmission after the incident occurred could be used due to the high level of vulgarity. Needless to say, he was not happy.

Up until that point, Derek was on target to put his car on pole position at one of the biggest races in the world. That chance was now gone—and in quite humiliating fashion to boot.

The media were all over Derek as he brought his car back to pit lane. Standing outside of his car, the reporters and photographers waited patiently for the driver to exit the vehicle. He sat in the car for a long moment before exiting. Immediately, he was rushed with questions.

"Derek, can you tell us what happened?" asked one reporter.

He had nothing to say, however, as he quickly exited the car and walked into his team's garage. The photographers were snapping away as the driver stormed off.

Back in their garage, Bill and Nick watched the entire debacle unfold. "Well," said Nick. "It looks like we'll be a little closer to Derek than we thought."

"Let's hope so," said Richard. "He's fast, though, so I wouldn't expect him to be there for very long. Just remember this: we're in this to get a good result. We'll always aim for the win but we're going to be realistic as well. Let's run our own race and not do anything stupid."

Bill and Nick both nodded in agreement.

"Of course," said Bill. "We're punching above our weight as it is but we've got a good car. We'll do what we can tomorrow."

Richard put a hand on a shoulder of both Bill and Nick. "That's all I can ask from you two."

As Richard walked away, Bill and Nick turned to face each other. "I don't care what he says. We're gonna give this place all we've got and then some," said Nick.

Bill smiled. "You bet your ass we are."

Chapter 24

Race day.

It was days such as this that Bill loved waking up to. Feeling the excitement coursing through his veins even as he lay in bed, Bill was surprised he was even able to sleep given the enormity of what he was about to attempt.

Despite the need to wake up early to get a head start with the various race day preparations and sponsorship commitments, Bill felt rejuvenated—very similar to how he remembered feeling as a kid on Christmas morning. Just before he rose from the bed, however, Bill looked over to see Chad already awake and in his wheelchair. He was sitting by the back sliding glass door looking out over the city.

Initially shocked at the idea of Chad getting into the wheelchair by himself, Bill knew that, like him, his son was resourceful when the situation called for it.

As Bill sat up in bed, Bill got a better view of Chad and noticed that he had his helmet on his lap with his hands resting on top of it. Bill sat motionless and simply absorbed the moment as he allowed the image before him to etch itself into his memory.

Taking it one step further, Bill reached over to the nightstand beside his bed and grabbed his phone. Holding it up to Chad, Bill snapped a picture. The sound caused Chad to turn around.

"Well I see you're already up," said Bill as he sat up in bed. "You ready for today?"

Turning the wheelchair around to face his dad, Chad simply smiled and nodded his head up and down.

As Bill stood up from bed, Chad wheeled himself over to his dad. Stopping just in front of him, Chad handed the racing helmet to his dad.

"Thank you, Chad," said Bill. "You know, I couldn't do this without you."

Chad smiled as he placed his hand on top of his father's.

"Nor would I want to."

Although the change in his son was gradual, it was there nonetheless. As the race week had progressed, Bill had noticed the demeanor of his son take a few cautious but optimistic steps in the right direction. Additionally, he had felt it in himself too: the breath of change.

Once motivated by anger and a foolhardy desire to live up to some self-imposed reputation, Bill wasn't sure if it was the presence of both his family and his new friends all together to support him which was causing him to feel a divine sort of peace. Regardless, the change in him was as evident as it was refreshing. Although tempers were sure to flare in a racing situation, Bill was now dedicated to making sure it wasn't anger that was driving him as it had done in the past. It was his passion along with the mindset that he now knew who he was racing for.

The two got ready for the day and were out of the hotel within the hour. Although the race was the main draw for the fans, the drivers had various commitments throughout the day such as interviews, autograph sessions, team briefings and more. And at the end of all that, drivers were fully expected to get into the car and drive for 1,000 kilometers.

As both Bill and Chad arrived at the track, they were greeted by Richard.

"Look at this," said Richard as he approached the two with a childish grin on his face. Pulling a yellow caution flag out from his jacket, he waved it around to reveal that it had the image of

Derek Renshaw's face on it.

"I had a bunch of these made up last night," said the British man. "Had to pay express pricing but I think they'll fetch a handsome amount of beer money."

Bill could only smile and shake his head. "You're a brilliant mess."

Richard laughed as he ushered both Bill and his son into the team's garage. Once there, Bill noticed that everyone was exceptionally quiet as they worked about. Although a radio in the background played some music to break up the silence, the crew spoke very little to each other or to anyone.

Off in the corner, Bill noticed that Nick was already dressed in his race suit as he sat quietly by himself.

Bill approached. "Dressed in your Sunday best, I see."

"You know it, mate," said Nick quietly.

Bill couldn't resist asking."What's going on? Why is everyone so quiet?"

Nick smiled as he sat up in his chair. "It's kind of surreal to be honest," he said. "The crew and I have been together for so long and here we are—at the Bathurst 1000. The team's never done a race like this before. In a few hours, it'll be chaos all over the track. I guess we're all just soaking it all in before the real fun begins."

Bill understood. Many of the team members working on the car had been involved in motorsport for the entire lives. Slowly but surely, they've all been working hard to get to where they were today—on a team entered into one of the biggest racing events in the world—the Bathurst 1000.

Bill felt honored to be a part of such a sacred moment in the lives of so many people.

"I mean this when I say it," said Nick. "We wouldn't be here without you, mate."

Bill chuckled at the idea. "And the same thing goes for you. Had you guys never given me the opportunity to test your car at Winton, I wouldn't be here either."

"That almost feels like another lifetime ago when you think about it," said Nick. "So much has happened since then."

Smiling as he reflected on what this day meant to everyone on the team, Bill noticed that everyone was calm and collected as they made their preparations for the day ahead. Everyone, that is, except for Richard.

Smiling from ear to ear, the towering Brit had already begun walking up and down pitlane showing his latest creation to many of the teams who had no love for anything related to Derek Renshaw. Bill noticed that he was indeed selling a fair amount of his Renshaw-inspired yellow flags as he went along. When Richard finally reached the team's garage, his pockets were stuffed with money.

"Win it or bin it, drinks are on me tonight!"

The crew could only laugh as Richard hurried past them and towards the team's trailer. Suddenly stopping, Richard turned to look back at both Nick and Bill with a very confused look on his face.

"What the hell are you two waiting for? Let's go! We've got a lot to discuss!"

Bill and Nick fell into step behind the tall Brit. Almost immediately, fans began to recognize the now famous driver duo, and many stopped them for autographs and pictures along their route. Richard went along with it but after seeing that they were making slow progress and the crowd was growing more and more with each passing moment, he stepped in.

"Alright, alright," said Richard as he began stepping in between his drivers and the fans. "We've got work to do. You'll see them at the autograph session."

Looking at the two drivers, Richard simply said, "Go." Making it the rest of the way to the team's trailer, Richard breathed a sigh of relief when he finally stepped in.

"My word. You boys have suddenly become so very famous."

Bill and Nick only chuckled as they took a seat around what had been designated the *discussion* table.

"Alright Gents," said Richard as he slumped into a chair in front of the two drivers. "Let's talk driver order."

Because there were two drivers sharing the driving duties over the course of the race, the order in which they started was an important decision to make. Each driver would be required to complete a minimum of 54 laps, but no more than 107 laps of the 161-lap race. Additionally, there would be seven compulsory pit stops, which every team would be required to complete.

"The fans want to see Bill start," said Richard. "From a strategy standpoint, this works since we're getting word that many of the teams will be starting with their co-drivers as well. That way, Bill can get his minimum lap requirements taken care of early on so that Nick can finish the race."

As the co-driver, Bill was fully aware that, although his driving was equally important to the team, he was mostly there to support Nick, since he was still aiming for a full-time drive next year. Although their deal with Higgins Financial had fallen through, a strong showing for Nick during the race would certainly draw the attention of teams who may be looking for a full-time driver next year.

"We'll obviously have to roll with the punches that come with the flow of the race but for now, the basic strategy we'll move forward with is Bill starting the race, keeping the car clean, doing some clean laps and then we'll switch you out to give you a break depending on how you're doing. We've got seven pit stops to fill so while the crew is working, that'll give us plenty of time to do a driver change.

"Also, it would be important to point out that we are expecting a bit of weather this afternoon, so get your umbrellas out, gentlemen."

The thought of racing in the rain sent Bill back to the Circuit of the Americas in Austin, TX. The day he embarrassingly spun off the track.

The day Lena died.

Bill shook the memory from his mind. Perhaps he'd be lucky and miss the rain. As the three men continued, the team's head engineer, Gadget, stepped in and joined them. For the next several moments, the four men went over every detail of the car, the race, the conditions, the competitors and strategy. Nothing would be left on the table before anyone stepped foot onto the grid.

An ever-in-motion puzzle, motorsport was, is, and always will be a game of predicting the future. Although many see racing as a contest between the greatest drivers, it's the great minds behind the scenes which give those drivers the tools they need to be successful. In many regards, the real battle takes place between the engineers and the various crew members who work on the cars.

Although the driver is often the face of the team, it's the crew who play one of the most vital roles in motorsport. With someone responsible for fueling the car as well as the various crew who change the tires, each person added into the equation uses tools which also represent a possible point of failure.

Should a wheel gun fail during a pit stop, that's valuable time lost. And in a race such as the Bathurst 1000, every second counts. When you also factor in all of the information and telemetry data being sent from the car to the garage which then needs to be translated into strategy by various engineers and ultimately implemented by the crew, it makes for exciting and oftentimes predictably unpredictable racing.

As the men finished up their meeting, Richard stood up first.

"I don't need to tell you so I'll tell you anyway," said Richard. "Stay hydrated, stay away from American food and..."

"And don't get an STD before the race. I know the drill," said Nick who's had to hear that line from Richard before the start of every race.

"I'll stay alert for rain," said Richard as he moved to leave the team's trailer. "You boys just keep your head down and your eyes forward and we'll all wind up having a pleasant day at the track."

As Richard exited the trailer, Gadget followed closely behind which left both Nick and Bill alone.

"I don't think I've ever mentioned this to you," said Nick, "but Richard is an absolute wizard when it comes to predicting the rain. I've never seen anything like it. He can literally step outside and predict when the rain is going to start falling sometimes within the minute. The man is a freak of nature."

Bill smiled at the image in his mind of Richard as a weatherman. "I'm guessing he's saved your skin on a few occasions with that ability."

"He has," replied Nick. "But there have honestly only been a few occasions that I've raced in the rain, and it's been several years since. How about you, mate? What's your wet weather experience like?"

Bill momentarily froze at the question. He wasn't sure if he should delve into the entire story of what happened during his previous wet race—and the subsequent aftermath—or just give a generic answer.

He never got a chance as a knock on the trailer door interrupted them.

"Who is it!?" shouted Nick.

"Unlock this bloody door before I save you the trouble and do it for you!" shouted a voice from the other end. There was only one person who could say something so ridiculous but sound so frightening at the same time.

Nick opened the door to reveal Tubbs standing there looking as intimidating as ever. "Are you going to bloody invite me in or what?" asked Tubbs.

"Come on in, Tubbs," shouted Bill still seated at the table.

As Tubbs stepped in, he turned back around and bent over as if lifting something from the outside.

"Up you go, mate," said Tubbs.

As he turned around and walked into the trailer, Tubbs carried Chad along with him. The young child carried a smile on his face which brought joy to Bill's heart.

Behind them, Abby and William also stepped in.

"Not a bad setup you boys have here," said William as he looked around the team's trailer. "Much nicer than what I had back in my day."

Turning his attention to Bill and Nick, William asked, "You boys ready?"

It was a simple question but one that carried much weight. There was so much that went into getting ready for a race such as the Bathurst 1000 but at the end of the day, both of the drivers knew they had to trust that the team had made all of the preparations and that they were as ready as they could be.

To Bill, that seemed like a good answer.

"As ready as I'll ever be."

"Good," replied William.

Bill could tell that his father was in full competition mode. He had seen these characteristics before whenever a big race came on TV and when he'd share one of his personal racing stories. His entire demeanor would change to a serious and slightly on-edge William Watson.

"Always remember to stay focused on the big picture and don't get distracted by the small things. You boys do your jobs, trust that your team will do their jobs and you've got a good chance of a strong result. Racing is nothing new for you guys so don't get swept away in the nostalgia of this track. At the end of the day, it's just another race track that you have to maneuver around."

The words hit both Bill and Nick strangely considering that they were coming from an actual Bathurst winner. Oddly enough, however, William was right. It was easy for drivers to get caught up in the lore of how the Mountain was alive and how it had a mind of its own. The circuit was, in fact, just how William had described it.

"I'd honestly never thought of it like that but I'll be sure to keep that in mind throughout the day," replied Nick.

Abby finally spoke up. "We just wanted to come by and wish you guys good luck. I'm sure things are about to get crazy for you both so we were hoping to catch you beforehand."

"Yeah," said Tubbs. "You should see the crowd out there supporting you guys. Never thought I'd see that for a wildcard team."

"We've got just as good of a chance as the rest of them," replied Bill. The comment brought about a proud smile from William. He slapped his son on the back and shook Bill from side to side.

"Your mother would be proud."

Bill couldn't help but think, *So would Lena.*

"Well, we'll leave you to it then," said William. "The team was kind enough to offer us a spot in the garage to watch the race, so you know we'll be pulling for you boys from there."

Bill stood up. "Chad, how do you feel about coming to my interviews and autograph sessions with me?" he asked.

Hoping to see his son become excited at the prospect of joining his father in the pre-race activities, Bill was slightly shocked to see Chad with a less than enthusiastic look on his face.

Taking the cue, the others stood up to take their leave. "C'mon, fellas," said Tubbs. "Let's give these two some space." Nick, Tubbs and William all stood to exit but Abby stayed put. "These three I mean," said Tubbs while a sly smile.

As the three men exited the trailer, Bill, Chad and Abby sat in silence for a moment. Turning towards his son who sat with his head lowered, Bill spoke.

"For a while, I questioned myself. I kept asking 'Why are you getting back into a race car? After all that's happened to you, why go down this path again?' It took a long time for me to be able to answer those questions but in the end, I realized that racing is just like life:

"We all start out not knowing anything. We grow and work our way up, fight the battles and endure the wars. Along the way, we make some lifelong friends and create some amazing memories. Sometimes we win, and many more times we lose. Good things happen, bad things happen, but it's how we react to these situations that defines who we are as individuals and as drivers. In the end, we can look back and either smile at the things we've accomplished or weep at what we wished we had accomplished. Either way, we run our race. Each and every one of us, from every walk of life, we run our race."

Bill knelt down in front of his son.

"This is my race, son. And I'm not just talking about the race that's about to happen. I'm talking about watching you grow into a great young man. Being there for you for all of your victories and your defeats. Regardless of what happens today or tomorrow, nothing will ever take that from you or me. I love you with all of my heart, Chad. But always remember that your race is going on too. Don't ever let circumstance dictate what you can or can't do. You forge your own path and don't let anything or anyone get in your way and tell you what you can't do…"

Bill stood up.

"…just like your dad. Can you do that, Chad?"

Chad lifted his head to look his father in the eyes. Bill could see the sense of resolve in his son as he nodded his head up and down.

"Good," said Bill. "Speaking of races, how about we get going." A smile crept onto Chad's face.

Turning to face Abby, Bill wanted to tell her that he cared for her and that he didn't want what they had to end.

"Abby…"

Before he could continue, Abby stood up and embraced him. Feeling her arms around him sent shivers down his spine as he embraced her as well. They stood there together for a while before a knock on the door startled them. The door swung open.

"What did I tell you!" said the resounding voice of Richard. "No STDs before the race!"

Abby and Bill laughed at the comment as Richard closed the door.

Looking each other in the eyes, Bill simply said, "Thank you."

"For what?" asked Abby.

"For being here."

"Oh, don't get all mushy on me, Bill Watson, " replied Abby as she blushed slightly.

Bill took a deep breath and exhaled slowly.

"Shall we?"

* * *

After a plethora of TV and various media interviews, autograph sessions, parade laps and other activities, Bill was now standing on the grid of the Bathurst 1000. The cars had now been rolled out of pit lane and parked in their starting order for The Great Race. Once there, the drivers exited the vehicles for what was typically the final round of interviews done by the sports broadcasters from the grid.

Suited up and ready to go, Bill now had to put his gameface on. Although he was happy to have had Chad accompany him on his many pre-race engagements, he now had to center himself and focus on the task ahead of him. He'd be lying if he said he wasn't a little tired already.

Richard along with William, Greg, Tubbs, Abby and Chad were all there on the grid standing beside the car with Bill and Nick. Flooded with spectators, crew members and various TV personalities, the grid looked similar to a circus due to the amount of people. Given that the Bathurst 1000 is one of the great motorsports spectacles on the planet, however, this was to be expected.

William, seeing that his son was a bit taken aback by the enormity of what he was able to attempt, approached Bill.

"Remember what I told you once: when you put that visor down, put all of this behind you. The spectacle, the crowds, the cameras, even us. Tune it all out."

Bill didn't speak. He simply smiled and put a hand on his dad's shoulder.

"I never thought I'd see the day when my son would be standing on the starting grid at Bathurst," said William as he smiled. "I'm so proud of you, son. Win, lose or draw."

The two men embraced and just then, a swarm of photographers and camera crews surrounded them. The snapping of pictures distracted them and they both turned to face the sea of paparazzi.

"I guess we're giving them a good photo op," said William with a chuckle.

"Alright, alright, that's enough," said Richard as he waved his arms at the media crews as if dusting a swarm of flies away from his face. "Let's get our man in the car, shall we?"

William extended his hand towards Bill and the latter met his handshake. "Good luck," said William.

"Thanks, Dad."

As William walked off of the grid and headed towards the team's garage, Bill walked over to Abby who was accompanying Chad.

Kneeling down in front of his son, Bill spoke.

"Can you do a favor for me and watch after Abby while I'm on track?" Bill looked up to see Abby smile as Chad nodded his head up and down in agreement. Mimicking his grandad, Chad reached out to shake Bill's hand. Bill couldn't help but smile as he shook his son's hand and then picked him up to hug him.

"Thank you for all of the encouragement. I couldn't have done this without you."

Bill lowered Chad back down into his wheelchair and then turned towards Abby.

At first they simply smiled at each other until Abby spoke first. "Take care of yourself, Bill Watson," said Abby as she planted a kiss on his cheek.

"Come on, Chaddy," said Abby. "Let's head over to the garage to see the start of the race."

As Abby and Chad strolled away, Bill looked one last time to see his son waving at him. As all of that was going on, Bill was oblivious to the fact that Richard had snuck up behind him.

"Bill," whispered Richard into Bill's ear.

Bill turned to see Richard standing incredibly close to him. The taller British man smiled as he whispered once again into Bill's ear.

"No…S…T…Ds…"

Bill could only chuckle.

Richard laughed it off as well but soon set his attention to the business at hand. "Get your damn lid on and your Yankee ass in the car."

Putting his helmet on and climbing into the car, Bill strapped himself into the safety harness, attached the radio, drink, and cool-suit connections to his helmet and suit. Then he waited. He watched as camera crews, sports broadcasters and photographers swarmed his car. Thinking of his father's advice, Bill centered himself and closed his eyes momentarily.

"When you put that visor down, put all of this behind you. The spectacle, the crowds, the cameras, even us. Tune it all out."

Slowly but surely, the grid began to clear as spectators, team members and reporters exited the track. As he started the car, Bill watched as the grid slowly began to empty until it was just the cars.

Starting from the left side of the sixth row, Bill would be on the inside for the first left-handed turn called *Hell Corner*. Before that, however, there was a formation lap which involved the entire field taking a slow lap around the track to warm up their tires, brakes and engines. They would then return to their starting positions on the grid where they would perform a standing start for the race.

"Thirty seconds," said a voice on the radio.

Bill could sense his heart rate starting to climb. For a brief moment, he closed his eyes again and tried to center himself. He placed his hands on the steering wheel to feel the vibrations of over 600hp. Putting his foot on the clutch, he waited.

"Formation lap commencing," said Richard over the radio.

The field all moved at once as Bill launched the car just as he had practiced. It was a smooth getaway off the line and it gave Bill confidence that he would do it right when it counted in a few moments.

The field swept through the turns and bendy bits of Mount Panorama as they weaved from side-to-side to warm up their tires. Progressing down the long *Conrod Straight*, drivers were accelerating and then braking heavy. This was to get their engines and brakes as close to operating temperature as possible for the start of the 161 lap race around the nearly 3.9 mile circuit.

One by one, the cars filed back onto the front stretch and stopped at their respective starting positions. As Bill brought his car closer to his spot on the grid, Richard's voice came over the radio directing him on where to stop so he didn't move too far forward.

"Keep coming. Keeeeep coming," said Richard. "Annnnd stop. Alright, Watson. Take it easy on the start and bring it back in one piece. Good luck and eyes forward."

Bill didn't respond. He was now completely and totally in the moment.

Each passing second felt like an eternity as Bill waited for the remaining cars to file into their starting grid positions. Although more familiar with the rolling starts which were featured in the Trans Am series he formerly raced within the U.S., Bill had been practicing his standing starts for this very moment. Simply by looking at the telemetry data from Nick's previous starts along with data provided by the factory Ford team, Bill was able to see precisely the amount of throttle to apply and how much to let off the clutch to get an ideal launch. From then on, it was a matter of practicing through repetition.

After the remaining cars reached their respective starting positions, a track marshal ran out to the rear of the field and waved the green flag which signaled that the race was now ready to start.

The sound of nearly 20,000 hp erupted as thirty-one V8 engines redlined to prepare for the standing start. The red light at the start line became illuminated to indicate that start was only seconds away. Once the lights went out, the race would officially begin.

Bill waited with his left foot on the clutch and his right foot partly on the accelerator.

Get ready, Bill. Get ready for it.

The lights turned off and Bill slowly let off the clutch which caused the car to roar into motion with little to no rear wheel spin. It was a near perfect launch. The drivers in the front of the field had a similar launch as they all piled into *Hell Corner* two abreast.

The Bathurst 1000 had begun.

Chapter 25

As Bill charged out of *Hell Corner* on the opening lap, the field had yet to file itself into a single line. As such, Bill remained on the left side as he headed into the right turn of *Griffins Bend.* Now on the outside, his cold tires protested as the rear of the car began to swerve a bit as it searched for grip. This cost Bill a position which shuffled him back to 12th.

He wasn't out of the woods yet, however, as he was still side-by-side with another car while heading into *The Cutting*. This time, Bill found himself on the inside of the left turn. The driver to Bill's right soon filed back behind him which was the smart thing to do this early in the race. The last thing someone wants to do is crash out of a 1000 kilometer race on the first lap.

As Bill wound his Ford Falcon through *Reid Park, Skyline* and *The Dipper,* he was starting to find his rhythm and get into a groove as he stayed on the back bumper of the car in front of him.

Although Bill had now had his share of practice laps around Mount Panorama, nothing could fully prepare him for what it was now like navigating the course while also mere inches away from both the car in front and behind.

Heading into the downhill braking zone at *Forrest's Elbow,* however, Bill carried too much speed and locked up the brakes only slightly. It proved to be costly as Bill had to scrub speed off his car lest he smack the right side wall at the exit of the turn. This again hurt Bill as he lost momentum while heading down the longest straight of the track.

Since the field was so condensed with it being the start of the race, the closest driver behind Bill made passing the American look easy as he got a better drive out of the corner than Bill did. That wasn't the end of it, however, as the next driver behind him was able to pull up alongside Bill as they headed towards *The Chase*—a fast sweeping right-handed turn which leads to a hard downhill braking zone.

The other driver fully expected Bill to back out, but the American held his ground. Instead, they went two-wide through *The Chase* on the opening lap. Still side-by-side, Bill now had the inside line heading into the next left-hander which he made the most of. Clearing the other car, it was a simple run from that point down to *Murrays Corner*, another downhill braking zone which led to a 90-degree left-handed turn with a harsh curb at the apex of the corner. Hitting it too hard would unsettle the car and most likely lead to an unfortunate incident.

Bill navigated through the final turn successfully and crossed the line to finish the first lap of the Great Race. In all, he had fallen from 11th to 13th in just one lap.

Only 160 laps to go.

* * *

"He's certainly not making our lives easier, that's for sure," mumbled Richard as he stood staring at the television screen in the team's garage. The race was now only five laps in and Bill had dropped another spot down to 14th.

Standing next to him, Nick voiced his support.

"He just needs to find his groove. It's his first race in quite a while so once he settles in and gets in the zone, he'll start making up some spots. Early days, mate. Early days."

"I hope you're right," said Richard. "The camera crews seem to have an infatuation with our car at the moment as that's all they seem to be focusing on."

"That's because there's not much going on up front," said Nick. "That won't last for long, though. Once Renshaw settles in, he'll be making a move early to get out front in the clean air."

Richard, closing his eyes and leaning his head back slightly, furrowed his brow as he breathed in and out slowly.

"Not if the rain gets here first," said Richard.

"How much time do you think we have?" asked Nick.

Richard paused for a moment with his eyes still closed.

"It's still unclear," said the Brit. "I'll be able to tell more accurately as it gets closer."

The two men turned their attention to the weather radar screen in their garage and saw a small system moving directly towards them.

"Nothing crazy," said Richard. "Just rain. Nothing bad enough that they'll stop the race. How good do you think our man out there is in the wet?"

Nick raises his eyebrows and sighed. "We'll find out soon enough."

* * *

As the laps began to tick away, Bill began finding his form. He had allowed himself to settle down after dropping several spots at the start of the race. Now thirteen laps in, Bill was driving defensively at the moment as the car behind him was trying to make a move for position. So far, Bill had been successful in holding off the challenging driver and maintained his position in 14th but he didn't want to hold anyone up this early in the race. Two cars fighting together are slower than one car by itself and the last thing Bill wanted to do was waste time in a meaningless battle. At the same time, however, Bill wasn't about to hand over another position if he could help it.

Bill decided to press on, but he didn't have to fight hard for long.

Upon starting lap 14 and heading into *Hell Corner,* the driver behind Bill drove in too deep under brakes and went wide into the grass. Barely missing the sand trap which would've beached his car, the driver was able to get going albeit after losing several seconds in the process.

It was exactly what Bill needed. With his tail clear at the moment and the next car about a second and a half in front of him, Bill took this opportunity to breathe for what felt like the first time since the race began. He was able to get more settled in now and began to set his sights on the car in front. Although he had lost some ground, Bill certainly felt like he had the ability to get a few of those spots back before he eventually handed the car over to Nick for his stint.

Keeping a sharply focused mind, Bill shut out any and all distractions as he fixed his gaze upon the car in front which was now getting closer with each passing lap. At the start of lap 17, Bill was now right on the rear bumper of the car in front. As the two raced up *Mountain Straight,* Bill moved his car over to the right side as they approached the braking zone. Getting on the brakes just a fraction of a second later than the other driver, Bill was able to slip past him and reclaim one of his lost positions.

Now up to 13th, Bill made it a point to not get caught up with what the car behind him was now doing. Instead, he took Richard's advice, "eyes forward," and looked up the road to the next turn and on to the next car.

As he navigated through *Forrest's Elbow* and down *Conrod Straight,* Richard came over the radio.

"You're two seconds behind the car in front and currently gaining roughly two tenths per lap on their position. Good job and stay focused."

Although the advice was well-meaning, Bill was actually taken out of his zone of concentration for a brief moment after the comment from Richard. He was so focused on what he was doing but he still had to realize that there was an entire crew back in the garage watching and analyzing everything which was going on.

Shaking off the pull of distraction, Bill replied simply by saying, "Copy."

After a few more laps had passed, Bill was now on the back of the 12th placed car. Wanting to make his move soon as to do so before the upcoming pit stop, Bill saw an opening on the final corner and gave it a go down the inside. Knowing that it was a risk to make a move like that this late into a stint, Bill was nonetheless able to make it stick to complete the pass. Now in 12th, Richard came over the radio as Bill was heading up *Mountain Straight* on lap 21.

"Box this lap, Bill. Box this lap," said Richard. "Tires and fuel only. No driver change."

A bit of a gap had opened up between Bill and the next car ahead of him as he continued to wind his way through the circuit.

Regardless, Bill set his focus towards the next car even though it appeared to only be a small dot about five seconds up the road as he raced down *Conrod Straight*.

Bill was so focused, in fact, that he was on the verge of driving past the entrance to pit lane which was on the left side of the track. It was Richard, however, who was happy to remind him.

"Box the damned car!" shouted Richard over the radio.

Bill didn't even get a chance to verbally respond as he flung the car onto the pit lane entrance at the last possible moment. Hard on the brakes, Bill locked the wheels up and just barely got the car slowed down in time before getting to the entrance to pit lane. The last thing he needed was a pit lane speeding penalty after all of the work he'd just done to reclaim those lost positions.

Hitting the pit lane speed limiter button on his steering wheel, Bill took a deep breath as he looked ahead for his team's pit stall.

Seeing one of the crew waving him in, Bill proceeded down pit lane, turned into his pit stall and brought the car to a stop on the appropriate marks.

Right away, the air compressor plugged into the left side of the car which caused the jacks at the bottom of the vehicle to drop and lift the car off the ground. The crew went to work with changing tires and refueling the car.

Unlike NASCAR, tire changes in the Supercars series are done much faster since all four tires can be changed at once. There are also no lug nuts used on the wheels in the Supercars series but rather a single large wheel nut in the center which is faster to secure. However, fuel is pumped via a hose in Supercars and not large fuel cans which are used in NASCAR. With the refueling of 110 liters (about 29 gallons) taking roughly 30 seconds, NASCAR race cars are able to receive 12 gallons of fuel in about five seconds.

As Bill sat and waited for the pit servicing to complete, he took a deep breath and a drink from the in-car water dispenser.

"Ten seconds," said a voice over the radio. "Pit lane is clear. No wheel spin, please."

Another quick way to receive a penalty was to cause the tires to spin while the car was off the ground. A major safety issue, that was a sure way of ruining your race with a minimal amount of effort.

Bill had both hands on the wheel as the car dropped down to the ground.

"Go, go, go!"

Bill eased back onto the throttle as to prevent burning the tires up. A flawless pit stop. Bill cruised towards pit exit, disengaged the pit lane speed limiter and rejoined the race.

Although he was now a few positions back from when he had entered the pits, that would soon shuffle itself out as other cars took their respective stops. After completing two laps, Bill saw the car which had previously been five seconds up the road from him rejoin the track from the pits.

"Next car is now less than two and a half seconds ahead," said the voice of Richard over the radio. "Good hustle."

Although the car in front of Bill had fresher tires, they had yet to come up to full operating temperature and as such, the driver didn't have the desired grip levels, which Bill had since he'd been out for two laps already. As the driver in front of Bill continued his out lap, Bill closed in.

As the two reached *Forrest's Elbow,* Bill was now on the back of his target and was ready to go on the attack. Plunging down *Conrod Straight,* Bill got a better run and was able to maneuver himself to the left side of the track alongside the driver he was chasing. As the two headed into *The Chase,* the other driver backed out and decided not to run the risk of going side-by-side on cold tires. Completing the pass, Bill had now worked his way back up to his original starting position of 11th.

It had just taken him twenty-five laps to do so.

***

Back in the pits, the crew of the number #528 Ford Falcon cheered as they witnessed Bill complete the daring pass for 11th while heading into *The Chase.* The applause could be heard all the way outside and drew the attention of the media teams which were constantly roaming around looking for additional video to use in their broadcast.

"Everything from this point on is a gain," said one of the crew members.

Richard, noticing how the crew was in high spirits, couldn't help but shake his head slightly. Although it was a gutsy move by his driver to get the position, it made him feel uneasy.

William, who had been standing behind the engineers analyzing the plethora of data coming from the car and back into the garage, noticed the gesture from Richard and approached.

"What's the matter?" asked William.

Richard sighed. "Your son's doing a stellar job but it's way too early in the race for him to be making kamikaze moves like this," said Richard in reference to what he and the crew had just witnessed. "Sooner or later, one of those are going to bite us bad if he keeps it up."

William scoffed at the comment. "Playing it safe never won any races," he said. "He's out there to win it, not to cruise around and try to get meaningless points. You forget that this is it for him; there's no next race or next season. Once this race is over, he'll probably never turn another lap on a track in his life. He's giving it his all out there, so you need to trust him."

Richard turned to William with a slightly annoyed look on his face. "What I need, Mr. Watson, is for him to bring that car back in one piece. He's running lap times which are currently faster than the leaders but I want to make sure we can *finish* the race. Everyone in this garage is depending on him to make the right judgement calls out there."

"He is," replied William. "He's not doing anything that I wouldn't do or that anyone who wants to win this race wouldn't do. Just let the man race."

With that, William turned and walked away.

About to mumble some comment under his breath in regard to receiving free wisdom from the great William Watson, the opportunity was stolen from Richard as the pit crew suddenly became frantic.

"Tire! Get ready!" someone called out.

Turning toward the commotion, Richard saw the pit crew scrambling about as they quickly rose from their seats. He turned back toward the monitor to figure out what was going on.

"What the bloody hell just happened?"

* * *

Maintaining his gap over the car he had previously passed for 11th, Bill hadn't been able to stretch away like he had hoped. If anything, he felt that he was pushing too hard in order to keep the contending car behind him.

As the laps ticked away, Bill could feel his car getting more loose. Although he still had good straight line speed, his corner exit speed was beginning to wane. Bill had another eight laps until the next pit stop and he was determined to not drop another spot before then. He would do everything he could to maintain his track position.

Crossing the line to start another lap, Bill tipped the car into *Hell Corner* and proceeded up *Mountain Straight* with the challenging car still hot on his tail. As he hit his braking point and began to make the right turn into *Griffins Bend* however, Bill suddenly heard the unmistakable sound of a delaminated tire coming from the front left side of the car.

A byproduct of belt separation within the compound of the tire, delamination causes the tire to degrade at an extremely high rate. When a tire begins to delaminate on a race track, it becomes a serious issue for both the driver and the cars around them.

"Tire!" shouted Bill over the radio. "Delaminated tire!" A few seconds passed before a reply came.

"Copy," replied Richard. "We see it."

"Sonofabitch," Bill mumbled under his breath.

This was indeed a worst-case scenario. Having just started a lap, Bill would now have to navigate all the way around one of the most notorious race tracks in the world while driving a car with only three good tires and one which was quickly falling apart. And because of the delaminated tire, Bill was forced to drive at a much slower rate than the normal race pace. The last thing he wanted was to lose control of the car and send it into one of the many walls located around the track.

As car after car began to pass him, Bill could see bits of rubber flying from the front left side of his car as he tried to stay off the racing line. The yellow of the local caution flags waved around him as Richard came over the radio.

"Don't stop. Whatever you do, don't stop," said Richard over the radio. "We're ready for you in the pits. When you bring it in, Nick will jump in the car once the crew gets it patched up."

Nursing the car through *The Dipper,* Bill had a sinking feeling in his stomach. All of the hard work the team had done to get the car ready for the race would be for nothing. From rebuilding the car overnight to getting the sponsorship deals brokered, Bill felt gutted as he cruised down *Conrod Straight.*

The condition of the delaminated tire was now degrading rapidly. The noise of the separated belts from inside the tire which were now slapping against the bodywork of the car was getting louder as Bill gingerly brought the car through *The Chase.*

After losing a considerable amount of time, Bill brought the car onto pit lane as he began getting ready for the driver change. Unplugging the radio connection to his helmet, the cool suit connections while also loosening the belts to the harness, Bill soon brought the car to a halt at the team's pit stall.

The car lifted slightly as the team went to work. At the same time, Bill exited the car and assisted Nick with getting situated. Helping him tighten the belts while Nick plugged in the radio and cool suit, Bill gave Nick a quick, "Good luck" before closing the door and stepping back into the pit stall.

Walking towards the garage, Bill couldn't help but notice the number of cars passing them as the car sat stationary in the pits.

The pit crew was just finishing up replacing the tires, topping off the fuel and also repairing some of the damaged bodywork done by the delaminated tire around the front left wheel by using tape designed to withstand the punishment of high speed racing.

As the car dropped back to the ground and Nick accelerated away, Bill removed his helmet and approached Richard who was sitting by a monitor which showed the current standings.

He was about to ask what the damage was regarding time lost after the entire debacle but as Bill approached the monitor, he could see for himself just how bad it was. Not only did they lose numerous positions, but due to the extended amount of time it took to get back to the pits, the leaders had passed them while the car sat in the pit stall.

They had now gone a lap down.

Bill's gutted feeling was now more evident as he slumped into the chair next to Richard. Turning to look at the Brit, Bill could tell that he was feeling the same thing. With his head in his hands, Richard peered through his fingers towards the monitor which displayed their current position. Not only were they a lap down, they had fallen to 28th position of the 31 cars in the field.

Sighing loudly, Richard sat up and slapped his hands against the tops of his legs while doing so.

Raising his brow and giving a half-hearted smile, Richard turned to Bill. "Well," he said. "At least we're not in last."

Chapter 26

As the race progressed, the team kept a close eye on events happening around the track. They took note that several other drivers were also experiencing delaminating tire issues, which left many people scratching their heads up and down pit lane. The team's head engineer, Gadget, was busy analyzing data from both Bill's previous stint as well as the information coming back to the garage from Nick who was currently out on the track.

Grabbing his clipboard, Gadget approached Richard who was sitting with Bill by a monitor which showed the live broadcast of the race.

"It's the curbs," said Gadget. "They're speeding up tire degradation. We need to tell Nick to avoid hitting them as much as possible."

Richard didn't hesitate. Once he saw Nick was on a straight as to not break his concentration while in the corners, he got on the radio.

"Nick, the word is that we need to avoid the curbs. They're hurting our tire life."

"Copy," said Nick firmly over the radio.

As the live video of the race eventually put a camera on Nick, they could immediately tell that he had adjusted his racing line to avoid the curbs.

"Let's see if that gives us one of our nine lives back," said Richard. "Good find, Gadget. Keep this information between us. We'll see if we can gain some sort of advantage before the other teams figure this out."

Giving a slight nod, Gadget turned and went back to his work station.

"That man's a bloody think tank," said Richard as he gestured towards Gadget. "Leonard Gadsby is his real name. The man eats this stuff up, digests it and then excretes diamonds. He's half the reason we're doing as well as we are."

"If you can call this *well*," replied Bill.

"Hey, we're still out there so that's good," Richard snapped back. "We're one of three wildcard entries into this race. One car is in the garage and the other is in last. Keep your chin up, Watson. It's early days and it's not over until it's over."

Bill was having a hard time believing it. Being a lap down in a road race was nearly equivalent to being dead. Outside of an absolute miracle, it was next to impossible to get your lap back. The only thing you're essentially fighting for are points, which meant nothing to Bill.

Glancing over at the leaderboard, Bill could only chuckle as he saw Derek Renshaw now in the lead with a healthy margin of about five seconds over the next car.

To Bill, so much had been riding on this race. With a number of people investing into the team, Bill felt the pressure to perform in a way he'd never felt before. Moreover, he wanted to have a strong result for Chad who was in the back of the garage with Abby and the others. With it being his last race, this would be a memory his son would carry with him for the rest of his life. Bill could only hope that he could make it a good memory.

As Bill and Richard continued to sit by the monitor watching the race, the latter sat up in his chair suddenly.

"What's wrong?" asked Bill.

Not answering him, Richard stood up and quickly moved to the entrance of the garage which faced the track.

Bill followed closely. "Richard..."

The British man silenced him by holding up his hand.

Closing his eyes, Richard tilted his head back and breathed in slowly through his nose. Bill turned around to see if any of the crew knew what the man was up to. To his surprise, every crew member in the garage was on their feet as if waiting for something. He suddenly became aware that they had all seen this before and knew it meant something of significance.

Richard suddenly snapped back to reality. Moving swiftly into the garage and towards the monitors, Richard looked on the screen to see where Nick was on the track. He was just coming out of *The Chase* and heading towards the pit lane entrance.

"Pit now, damnit!" said Richard forcefully over the radio to Nick. "BOX! BOX! BOX!"

Turning around, Richard noticed that the crew was already moving. "Get those damn tires ready!"

Bill was completely oblivious as to what was going on. "What just happened? Why are we pitting so soon? He still has several laps to go before the next scheduled stop."

"Rain, Mr. Watson," said Richard.

Bill turned to look out of the entrance of the garage.

"What the hell are you talking about? There isn't a drop of water on the ground! Why did..."

At that very moment, the floodgates opened. Rain began pouring down just as Nick had pulled into pit lane.

As Bill moved out of the way so the crew could get by, Nick brought the car to a stop just as the crew had finished getting ready. Inserting the air hose into the side which deployed the jacks that lifted the car off the ground, the crew began installing tires designed for racing in the rain while also topping off the fuel.

"Stay in the car," said Richard over the radio. "You'll be clear when you drop."

As the air hose was removed, the car dropped and Nick pulled away while avoiding wheelspin.

"Good call, Richard," said Nick over the radio.

"Eyes forward, mate, and be safe," replied Richard.

With the entire moment seemingly over just as quickly as it began, Bill could only stand there looking completely dumbfounded.

"What's slithered up your arse?" asked Richard as he noticed Bill's sudden confusion.

"How...how did you do that?" asked Bill.

"Well since you ask," replied Richard, "I was struck by lightning when I was a kid and knocked unconscious. When I came to, I had a heightened sense of predicting the weather."

"Really?"

"No, not really," said Richard with a smug grin. "I can't really explain it. I just figured out one day that the air smells a certain way right before it starts to rain. Over the years, I fine-tuned that sense into a power worthy of superhero status."

Bill chuckled at the thought of the large Brit as a superhero. "Richard Mayfield. You. Are. Weather Man."

* * *

Out on track, the other drivers were caught completely off guard as the rain suddenly began pouring all over the circuit. Even the fans who lined the stands and the various points all over the numerous campgrounds were caught completely by surprise as they now scrambled for their ponchos and umbrellas.

Now leading the race, Derek Renshaw still had a gap to the cars behind him when the rain began to fall. As the track cooled and got more and more wet with each passing second, Derek was heading through *Skyline* but doing so while carrying too much speed for his slick tires to handle in the wet conditions. He was able to make it through but not without an excessive amount sliding.

"Bring it back in one piece," said a voice over his radio.

As he approached *The Dipper,* however, he applied too much throttle for the tires to handle on the racing line. The rear of Derek's car suddenly snapped loose and he did a full 180 degree spin before coming to a hard stop on the left wall at the exit of *the Dipper.*

"Shit, shit, shit!"

Now facing the wrong way with the rear of his car up against the wall, the car was also damaged from the impact but Derek wasn't out of the woods yet.

The yellow local caution flags around him began to waive but before he could get going again, the rest of the field came stampeding down the descending corner and had nowhere to go as they noticed the now stationary car of Derek Renshaw.

Slamming on their brakes in a feeble attempt to stop their one and a half ton cars in the rain while still on slick tires, the result was pure chaos. Starting with the second placed car, which was forced to unexpectedly slow down due to Renshaw, and going all the way back to the end of the line of cars which followed, the pack snapped loose and collided with each other while heading down *The Dipper.*

As Renshaw struggled to get traction on the racing surface in an effort to avoid the coming onslaught which was barreling towards him, there was, in fact, little he could do. Running into the driver's side door of Derek's car, the second placed driver sustained heavy damage as he ultimately knocked Derek back straight. The impact was enough of a push, however, that it allowed Renshaw to continue on as the carnage unfolded behind him.

As the cars collided, body panels along with bits and pieces of debris were sent all over that section of the track. For a moment, the track was completely blocked. As the various drivers whose cars were still drivable nursed their wounded vehicles away from the chaotic mess, a lane opened up through the incident which allowed the remaining cars in the field—which had been given fair warning by their crews of the mess at *The Dipper*—were able to continue on.

A full course caution soon followed and the safety car was deployed onto the track. For many teams, however, it was too little too late. All told, there were nine cars—positions second through tenth—who received too much damage to remain in contention for a win or even a podium finish. Even with body paneling all over that section of the track, many of the cars involved were able to eventually get going again as they made the long trip back to their team's garage for repairs.

Calling back to his team, Derek made sure that they knew what was coming.

"Damage to the rear and driver's side."

It was a slow ride back to the pits as both the damage and the rain made going down *Conrod* a bit of a worrisome ride. Eventually, however, Derek made it back to his pit stall and his team began working on the damage to his car. As he glanced in his rearview mirror, he noticed that several other cars were now coming in behind him. Even the ones who weren't involved in the massive incident would be coming in and making the switch to the intermediate tires.

As his crew worked on the car in pit lane, the sound of a lone car which was still out on track and at racing speed filled the air. Derek could only wonder, "Who in the hell is still out there?"

* * *

"This is our chance! Keep going!"

Richard was ecstatic over the radio. Having pitted just as the rain began to fall, their car had made it out onto the track before the safety car was deployed. As Nick made his way around the track and eventually through the remaining carnage at the top of the Mountain, he was now hustling to get past the field of cars which had just pitted. If they could manage to get past Derek, they would be back on the lead lap.

"Remember not to pass anyone on track whilst under caution," said Richard over the radio.

Luckily, the last remaining cars who were in front of Nick were entering pit lane just as he caught up to them.

"Renshaw's still in pit lane," exclaimed Richard over the radio. "We've got this!"

As their car drove by the pit stall, everyone in the team's garage began cheering as Nick passed the leader to get back onto the lead lap. Everyone, that is, but Richard.

Standing by the television monitor as the live camera switched to their car, Richard and Bill both watched intently as the true determining factor still needed to happen.

The safety car was still out on track but moving slowly up *Mountain Straight* and with its top-mounted flashing yellow lights turned off. With the leaders still in the pits, it was waiting to pick them up before proceeding through the course.

Fearing that they would get stuck behind the safety car, which would put the leaders directly behind them on the restart of the race, Richard held his breath as Nick approached it.

Approaching the safety car, Richard and Bill watched as Nick was waved by to continue on. This now put them right where they wanted to be and officially back on the lead lap.

"YES!" shouted Richard.

The taller British man approached the smaller figure of Bill and embraced him. "We're back in this fight!"

Struggling to break free of the man's grasp, Bill could only laugh. "Alright, alright," said Bill as Richard finally put him down.

Showing his yellow teeth-filled smile, Richard put one hand on Bill's shoulder and pointed towards the sky with the other. "Bill, I don't know if you've got a friend up there or not but what just happened was nothing short of miraculous."

Turning towards the crew, Richard heaped praise on them. "Great hustle by everyone here! Let's keep this up and we may have a strong result yet."

Fistbumps and heavy handed slaps across the back were seen throughout the garage as the crew reaped the rewards for their efforts. They knew, however, that there was still a long way to go until the race was over. And on a track like Bathurst, anything can happen.

As the field of cars filtered back onto the wet track from pit lane, Nick made his way all the way around the track until he caught up with the back of the field. Under the control of the safety car which now had its flashing lights on, the field moved through the multiple turns of Bathurst in single file as the wreckage at *The Dipper* continued to be cleaned up.

While some looked at the team's current situation and saw a minimum level of hope, Nick felt rejuvenated. Although he was in the rear of the field, he was back on the lead lap. And with many of the leaders having to park their cars in the garage due to the damage they'd received in the earlier incident, the field which started with 31 cars had now been reduced to 24 with several other cars having mechanical issues earlier in the race and many others going a lap or more down. Nick felt confident that he'd be able to regain some of the lost positions.

As the field continued around the track, Richard came over the radio. "The rain will most likely continue throughout this entire stint and possibly into the next but it should be letting up a bit in a few minutes. Take care of those tires."

"Where did Renshaw end up after all of that?" asked Nick.

"He's still leading but he's got body damage," replied Richard. "Don't worry about Renshaw. Keep your head down, your eyes forward and be good to the bloody tires."

As the safety car continued its slow pace around the track, it's top-mounted lights finally turned off signifying that the race would resume at the end of the current lap.

The field straightened up and prepared for the restart. Back up front, Derek Renshaw made ready for the pace car to enter pit lane. Having already received word that Bill and Nick's car was back on the lead lap after a wizard-like pit stop just as the rain began to fall, he knew they would be on the charge. Still, he refocused on the task in front of him. All of that big talk and showmanship before the race would be for nothing if he binned his team's car into the wall on the restart.

As the pace car entered the pits, Derek wasted no time at all getting on the power as he made the final turn to start the race again.

Charging towards *Hell Corner,* Renshaw's impressive restart caused him to already have a one second gap on the next car as he completed the first turn and headed up *Mountain Straight.* Despite the rain, which was still falling, as well as the damage to his car, he was on full attack as he raced up the Mountain. Adjusting his braking point and turn-in speed, Renshaw went sideways briefly as he drifted through *Griffins Bend* towards *The Cutting.* Still getting a feel for the conditions of the track but not wanting to back off from his pace, Derek made adjustments on the driving inputs while relying on his previous experience with racing in the rain.

Derek moved slightly off the driving line as that was now the slickest part of the track. Due to the rain, the rubber laid down by all of the previous events throughout the weekend became very slippery so moving slightly off line was advantageous as rubber and water made for a slick combination. However, due to the narrow racing line at Bathurst, doing so was not always possible.

Heading through *Reid Park* and *Frog Hollow,* Derek was carrying too much speed and once again went sideways. This time, however, he scraped the right side of his car against the wall at *Sulman Park* as his car drifted too wide.

Waiting until Derek had navigated the car to the downhill section of *Conrod,* his team got on the radio.

"Let's bring the intensity level down to ten, please" said Derek's Race Engineer over the radio. "You're gonna burn the damn tires off at this rate."

Derek gave no response as he navigated through *The Chase*. With a two second gap now over the next car, Derek maintained his pace despite the feedback he'd received from his crew.

I'm the one driving the damned car. I know what I'm doing.

Further back, Nick had managed to pick up two spots on the opening lap of the restart and was now on the verge of taking another.

As the field worked its way up *Mountain Straight,* Nick moved his car to the right and completed a pass to gain another position at *Griffins Bend.* He was mindful, however, of Richard's earlier advice. Although he was eager to retake lost ground, Nick knew that a sure way to do that was to maintain a steady pace throughout the course of his stint.

As the rain continued to fall, the intensity of it slowly diminished. After about fifteen minutes, what had once been a downpour had been reduced to a slight drizzle. Still, Nick was pressing on and maintained a steady pace from lap to lap. He would catch traffic every now and again but he picked his battles and his moves carefully. Not wanting to force an issue and cause an incident, Nick waited for openings and due to the rain, he typically didn't have to wait very long.

By the time his stint was just over halfway done, Nick had succeeded in moving up a total of seven spots after starting from the rear of the field.

As the laps ticked by, Derek was still in first but his lead was slowly being reduced. After having worked himself up to a comfortable five second lead, the excessive wear on his tires was now beginning to eat away at his lap times. This was partly due to the reduced water levels on the track which can cause the intermediate tires to wear more rapidly, but also in part due to Derek's driving. Despite his crew repeatedly telling him to back off, Renshaw continued to push.

With only a few laps remaining in his stint and the rain only a slight mist now, Derek was suddenly on the verge of being overtaken. With the second place car right on his rear bumper as he navigated through *The Chase,* Derek knew that he had pushed too hard and was now paying the price for it. As such, the car behind him made a move down the inside on the final corner and Derek had no defense for it. Losing the lead, Derek tried to come out of the exchange on the rear bumper of the new leader but his tires protested.

Going slightly sideways, Derek lost even more time as the car in front of him slowly started to pull away.

Completing *Hell Corner* and heading up *Mountain Straight,* Derek's engineer came over the radio. "We're used up, mate. Box this lap and we'll get you out."

Derek didn't want to respond. He knew that his crew would be mad at him for pushing too hard and ignoring their orders. Having never won at Bathurst before, Derek was determined to make this the day. He'd wanted it so bad, in fact, that he'd let his desire to win cloud his judgement.

"Right," said Derek abruptly over the radio.

He didn't have time to dwell on how his team would perceive his response, however, due to the third place car making a move on him at *Griffins Bend* and sending him back one more spot. He knew he couldn't let this downward spiral continue. He'd fallen from first to third in less than a lap and he was now under threat from fourth.

Blocking the preferred line all the way up the Mountain, Derek knew that he'd be creating a jam behind him but he didn't care.

I'm not out here to make friends and I'm not giving up any more spots.

A cue of five cars had now formed up behind Derek as he headed down *Conrod Straight.* Driving down the middle of the track, Derek did as best as he could to hold up everyone else. But with *Conrod* being one of the widest sections of the track, there was little Derek could do as the fourth placed car stuck its nose in on the left side.

Still, Derek didn't budge. Refusing to yield, Derek was well prepared to go side-by-side through Turn 20 of *The Chase.* The other driver cautiously backed out. Given the fact that it was still slightly drizzling, he didn't want to be the one who caused an incident with the defending series champion, Derek Renshaw.

Coming up to pit entrance, Derek moved to the left side of the track and slowed to pit lane speed.

* * *

"You're currently lapping nearly two seconds a lap faster than the leader. Superb job taking care of those tires."

Nick could tell that Richard was impressed. The normally grumpy Brit would oftentimes go out of his way to show he *wasn't* impressed by too much nowadays. On this day, however, Nick could tell that his longtime Team Principal was feeling the energy which was in the air.

The rain had continued to fall even as Nick stopped for a second time to take on more fuel and tires. Due to his pace in the rain, Richard had elected to keep Nick in the car for a third stint.

"Let's hope all of that training you did with Tubbs pays off," said Richard during Nick's second stop.

Having made up two more spots in the previous few laps, Nick was now back inside the top ten but knew that he'd be pitting soon to complete his stint. Having been in the car for an extended period of time, he was getting tired. He remained focus, however, and maintained his pace.

As he headed down *Conrod Straight,* Richard came over the radio again. "Derek's just lost the lead and word is that he's going to be pitting on the next lap."

"Copy," said Nick over the radio.

Suddenly feeling energized, Nick knew that his longtime rival was most likely in trouble. The entire field had pitted around the same time, so for him to be losing the lead and pitting early, Nick was willing to bet that Derek had run his car too hard.

This wasn't the first time he'd seen Derek push too hard and use his tires up.

If I could only catch him and really put the pressure on him...

As Nick started another lap, he looked up the road and noticed a long train of cars forming as he headed up *Mountain Straight*.

"Renshaw's dropping like a brick in the ocean," said Richard over the radio. "He's down to third and holding everyone up. Maintain your form and we'll box you in a few laps."

"Copy."

Despite his fatigue, Nick was smiling under his helmet. Not just because he knew Derek was in trouble, but because he now had the leaders in his sights. Thanks to his longtime rival, Nick had succeeded at making up a large amount of ground due to Derek holding up the field.

As the race continued, the weather took an unexpected turn once again. The slight mist soon became a drizzle of rain. As Nick headed up the Mountain, he noticed that the rain was coming down a bit more heavily towards the top than it was at the bottom of the Mountain near the front stretch.

A slight weather system had formed over the track but was moving through rather quickly. This threw everyone's strategy for a spin since pit stops were approaching. All of the teams who still had cars on the track knew the weather was coming. However, reports showed that it would only last for a short while before the skies cleared.

It effectively came down to playing a game of *chicken* with the Mountain. Do you play it safe and put on more rain tires, wait for the weather to clear and then switch to slicks? Or do you take the risk, put on slick tires and avoid having to make another pit stop albeit with significant risk to the car?

Nick was just glad that he wasn't the one making those decisions.

Winding his way around the track, Richard came over the radio again.

"Derek's in the pits from third. Positions fourth through eighth were backed up quite a bit and are now just six seconds up the road."

"How much longer until I come in?" asked Nick.

"We'll pit you with the current leader," replied Richard. "Bill will jump in to give you a break and to finish his laps up. It won't be long now."

"Copy that," said Nick.

***

As Derek came in for his pit stop, he climbed out as his co-driver, Marty Osborne, stepped in. Upon exiting the vehicle, Derek noticed that the crew was equipping their Holden Commodore with slick tires as he headed back into the garage. Before he could even put his helmet down, Derek heard the sound of the tires spinning as Marty was leaving the pit box. Struggling for grip early on, Derek knew that his co-driver would have a mammoth task in front of him with navigating the car on a damp track with slick tires.

Approaching the crew, Derek said, "I can't believe you're sending him out there with slicks. We'll be lucky if he doesn't bin it into the wall."

Just about everyone in the team's garage turned to look at Derek—many with disdain in their eyes—after the low comment he had just made about his teammate.

Derek just smiled back at them as he headed towards his engineer. Turning to face the driver, Derek's engineer didn't mince his words. "What the hell were you thinking? If you didn't burn up the damn tires off, we wouldn't have had to pit so early."

Derek had no answer. He was about to have a rare moment and

apologize when a camera crew and reporter came into the garage and approached him.

"Derek, we noticed that you're in a bit earlier than the rest of the field," said the reporter. "Were you pushing a little too hard out there?"

"No, not at all," said Derek. "We're running a different strategy from the rest of the field so we'll see how it all plays out down the road."

The reporter didn't seem convinced. "Your lap times were dropping pretty heavily towards the end and you lost a few spots. Is the pressure from Lathan and Watson starting to build a bit?"

Derek tried to shrug it off.

"I don't see why I should care about those two. They've got no chance of catching us from the back of the field."

Derek's engineer cringed as he heard the words from his driver. He knew that Derek had just set himself up for an embarrassing moment on live TV.

"They're in eighth," said the reporter.

The stunned look on Derek's face was evident. If he was making any attempt to hide it, he was doing a poor job.

"Eig…eighth? Well tha…that's good. We're looking forward to the challenge."

The reporter smiled. "So are we, mate. So are we."

* * *

Despite the mist that was slowly turning into a light rain which typically helped with cooling the intermediate tires, Nick was now having a difficult time keeping the car pointed straight. Having used up what life was remaining in the tires to catch the cars in front of him, Nick noticed that his previous lap time had fallen considerably.

Back in the pits, Richard immediately took notice of it as well. "Box this lap, Nick," said the Brit over the radio. "Driver change as well."

As Nick navigated around the circuit, he noticed that the rain was slowly getting heavier once again. Every other car in the field would be sharing in similar struggles, however, as Nick carefully made his way through *The Dipper* and onto *Forrest's Elbow*, though he did as best as he could to not sacrifice speed.

Down *Conrod Straight* and through *The Chase*, Nick finally made the move to the left side of the track and entered pit lane. Engaging his pit lane speed limiter, Nick proceeded to unhook the radio, drink straw, and cool suit from their respective connections inside the car. He also loosened the straps on the harness which would allow him to exit the vehicle faster.

Nick could see the crew waiting for him at their pit box as one of the tire changers waived him in from a distance. He noticed Bill standing on the right side of the pit box ready to jump in and another set of intermediate rain tires ready to be put onto the car.

Bringing the car to a stop, the door swung open from the outside as Bill gave Nick the room he needed to safely and completely exit the car before he jumped in. Turning around to help Bill get strapped in after exiting, Nick assisted with getting the various connections which were difficult to see with a helmet on.

A quick slap on Bill's chest came from Nick.

"Good luck, mate!"

Bill gave a thumbs up as Nick closed the door to the car.

As Nick turned to walk around the back of the car towards the garage, he heard the unmistakable sound of one of the air guns used to change the tires becoming jammed. More of an impulse, Nick turned to look at what was going on. He noticed other team members springing into action to aid in getting the front right tire on the car safely. Not much time was lost, however, as the car would be stationary while it was being fueled up.

With the rain continuing to fall, Nick was momentarily fixated on the action unfolding around him—so much so that he failed to realize that he was now walking backwards towards the garage. He was both drowsy and weary from the amount of time he had just spent in the car.

He was therefore caught completely off guard when he stepped on an air hose connected to one of the air guns used for changing the tires. Losing his balance on the slippery surface, Nick was unable to regain his footing as he fell backwards and—bracing himself for the impact—landed hard on his right wrist. With his wrist unable to support the sudden weight of his body, his remaining weight collapsed onto the ground. The impact caused Nick to slam the back of his head onto the ground which, despite the fact that he was still wearing his helmet, jarred the driver's senses even more.

Several members of the pit crew rushed to Nick's aid. Lifting him up and quickly getting him off of pit lane, they carried him into the garage as the sound of Bill exiting pit lane filled the air.

Nick winced with pain as he held onto his wrist. Sitting him down, several of the crew knelt down beside him to see the extent of the damage. Some of the crew were about to assist Nick with getting his helmet off but as Richard approached, he insisted that they leave it on.

"Wait until the medical crew gets here to check him out."

Kneeling down in front of his driver, Richard asked, "How bad is it?" Nick was on the verge of tears from the amount of pain shooting through his wrist.

"I'm pretty sure it's broken, mate," said Nick. "Bloody hell. I'm so sorry, Richard. I don't know what I was thinking."

Standing back up, Richard placed his hand on Nick's shoulder. "You just sit tight until the medical staff gets here," replied Richard. "Then we need to figure out if we can still finish this bloody race."

Chapter 27

The good news was that Bill was in the car, the team still had great track position due to Nick's previous endeavors, and the call to continue running the intermediate wet weather tires proved to be the wise choice. Despite the weather looking like it would clear up as the race wore on, each passing lap proved otherwise as Bill navigated around a continuously wet Mount Panorama.

The bad news, however, came from a trackside medic after she had finished examining Nick's injury due to his earlier fall. Because of the manner in which he had landed while falling backwards, Nick had received a scaphoid fracture in his wrist and a knock to the head which, fortunately, was mostly absorbed by the sturdiness of his helmet.

If that was the bad news, the worse news was that Nick would not be able to continue the race.

Initially trying to tough it out in an effort to show everyone that he could still get back into the car, Nick even went so far as to grab one of the extra steering wheels in the garage and held it out in front of him. The feeble attempt was pointless, however, as pain shot through his wrist and forearm as soon as he gripped his right hand around the wheel.

"You're out, Nick," said Richard as he paced behind the driver. "There's nothing we can do about it."

At this point, William, Greg and Tubbs along with Abby and Chad could be seen from the back of the garage as they tried to listen to the conversation as best they could.

"So we're done then? Just like that?" asked Nick who was still on the verge of tears from the pain to both his wrist and to his ego.

"We're running the numbers now but it looks like..."

"Wait!" said a voice coming from behind Richard. Gadget appeared with his clipboard in hand and with a rare smile on his face. "The rules say that each driver has to do a minimum of 54 laps but no more than 107 total laps. You also can't have the same driver in the car for more than three and a half hours of constant driving. Nick's already met the minimum requirement by pulling a triple stint of 69 laps."

Nick chuckled. "No applause, please. Just throw money."

Gadget continued. "Bill's second stint was interrupted by the delaminated tire, so he's only completed 40 laps."

"So what you're saying," said Richard who was trying to get to the point, "is that Bill needs to stay in the car for the rest of the race."

"Precisely," replied Gadget.

"How many laps are remaining?" asked Nick.

"Fifty-one once Bill starts his next lap," said Richard.

Richard continued to pace back and forth in the garage with a perplexed look on his face. He came to a stop next to Nick and Gadget. "The original game plan was to put Bill in the car for this stint just as we did. He would then finish the stint and by doing so, complete his minimum number of laps. We would then hand the car back to Nick to finish the race.

"I don't like it but that plan's gone now. Gadget, run the numbers again just to make sure we won't cop a penalty for this. But for now, the new plan is that Bill will finish the race."

"This is unheard of," said a booming voice from the back of the garage.

Everyone turned to look at Tubbs.

"A co-driver finishing the Bathurst 1000? And an American at that?" Tubbs, realizing that everyone was now fixated on him, looked embarrassed as he held his open palms out in front of him in a child-like gesture. "Sorry. Just voicing my opinion."

"Any other comments from the peanut gallery?" asked Richard.

A few chuckles could be heard but no one else spoke.

"Right. We've still got a shot at a good result. Now let's make sure our man has everything he needs to finish this race."

The team went back to their duties to make sure, firstly, that they were in the clear with their newfound plan. Then it was crunching fuel numbers and lap times to make sure Bill wouldn't be going over the maximum allowed time of constant driving as well as the number of laps that a driver was permitted to do.

Always diligent in their reporting, the media quickly discovered the team's daring new strategy. The replay of Nick's fall was being aired repeatedly throughout the live broadcast and many in the global motorsport community were unsure if the team would be able to continue without their more experienced primary driver.

As word of the new strategy reached the various motorsport news outlets covering the event, it spread like wildfire. Within minutes, various videos and articles were being released across the globe detailing the daring plan to bring the #528 Dynamis Engineering Ford Falcon across the finish line.

The plan drew the support of many fans who were eager to see the wildcard team finish the race with a strong result after conquering so much adversity earlier in the week. Additionally, there was the idea of seeing the son of a Bathurst legend potentially crossing the finish line. On the other hand, there were some who drew up wild conspiracy theories and felt that it was all part of a staged plan just to have the American finish the race.

Race strategists attached to the various media outlets gave their opinions as well as mixed signals as to how they felt the strategy would work. The common consensus was that, although it was a daring strategy to have such an inexperienced driver finish the race, the plan in and of itself was sound.

For good or for ill, it seemed that everyone was now aware of the new plan.

Everyone, that is, except for Bill.

As all of that was going on, William approached Richard who was busy watching the television which now had Bill on the screen as he raced down *Conrod*.

"The entire world knows our plan now. When were you planning on telling the man behind the wheel? He probably doesn't even know what's happened to Nick."

Right away, Richard could tell that the man was asking not out of curiosity, but more out of concern for his son who was out there in treacherous conditions.

"When the time is right, Mr. Watson," replied Richard. "There's no need for Bill to worry about such things right now. Plus, with the rain still falling, I fear that he's got enough to worry about at the moment."

* * *

Although Bill had been hoping the weather would clear up, the track conditions had not improved. As the final forty laps of the race approached, the rain continued to fall as Bill did his best to maneuver the 1.5 ton vehicle around the infamous circuit.

After Nick's charge up the field which brought the team up to eighth, Bill had exited pit lane in 12th as several other cars elected to stay out a bit longer. However, as pit stop strategies from the other teams cycled through, Bill had not only made it back up to eighth, but he had made an additional position up to seventh while also close behind the sixth placed car.

In normal circumstances, Bill would be eager to go on the attack to try to get the next position. Now, however, he was holding back. Even as his single windshield wiper worked overtime in an effort to wipe the rain away from his view, it was proving to be just as effective as trying to light a match in the wind. The speed at which he was traveling helped push some of the rain off his windshield but the amount of water being thrown up like a rooster tail from the car in front him made visibility extremely limited. On top of that, his windshield was starting to fog up slightly on the inside.

At times, the only thing Bill could see were the tail lights of the car in front of him.

Bill was driving nervously. He wanted to be smooth and precise but found that he was being twitchy which, in turn, was unsettling the car. This was his first time racing in the rain since the accident in his TA2 car at the Circuit of the Americas all those months ago. Even so, that was only a slight mist compared to the steady rain he was now experiencing. The only advantage Bill had now was that he was on intermediate-level rain tires as opposed to the slicks he was on while racing back in Austin.

Too nervous to make a move, Bill found himself simply keeping pace with the car in front of him. Even when the sixth placed driver ran too wide on the exit of *Hell Corner,* Bill didn't move to overtake. In fact, he almost went off *with* the driver due to what's known as target fixation.

Since Bill was so focused on what the car in front of him was doing, he had just about followed the car off the track. Putting the right side tires off, Bill almost lost control as he muscled the car back onto the racing surface while losing an ample amount of time in the process. Although the car in front of him was able to get back onto the track with relative ease, Bill's brief trip off-track caused the rear of his car to swing left and right as he struggled to find grip. Because of the brief excursion, the sixth placed car was able to put a bit of distance on Bill as he left the American behind in a watery trail of cloud and mist.

The red tail lights Bill had been following for about three laps steadily began to vanish and he soon found that he no longer had a target to chase. As the laps passed by, Bill periodically checked his mirrors, but now he saw only empty track behind him. Looking up the road, Bill saw the same thing—empty track. It was almost as if he were out there all by himself.

His mind began to wander into the possibilities of what could be happening elsewhere on the track.

Was there an accident somewhere? Did I miss a yellow flag?

Bill was snapped back into reality as he made a mistake while coming out of *The Chase*. Getting on the power too hard, the rear of the car snapped out and drifted to the left. Lifting off the throttle, Bill adjusted his steering input to catch the slide. In doing so, Bill over-corrected and the rear of the car snapped back to the right. Applying a bit of power, Bill managed to straighten the car out as he headed towards the final corner.

Despite the impressive recovery, the entire incident put Bill even further on edge, and further behind.

He could feel his heartbeat pumping heavily. So heavily in fact that he could feel his heartbeat physically pulsing against his helmet as blood pumped rapidly through the arteries in his neck.

How many more laps until my stint is done?

Bill wanted to get out of the car. He was off pace, making mistakes and his heart wasn't in it.

Too much is on the line.

He had originally just wanted to finish the race but they were now in seventh. So much attention was on them now and it would be several more laps until Bill handed the car back over to Nick. Then he would be done.

Done?

The sudden thought of being *done* caused his mind to betray him. He knew that with each passing lap, he was approaching what would be the final lap he'd ever run in a race car. This final stint would determine how he would be remembered. He knew the world was watching.

More importantly, he knew his son was watching.

Feeling a sinking sensation in his stomach, Bill suddenly felt paranoid. Fear and anxiety gripped him as he felt the weight of what he was trying to accomplish land squarely on his shoulders.

What the hell am I doing in this car? This isn't how it was supposed to happen.

Bill crossed the line to start another lap. In doing so, he noticed his lap time was two and a half seconds off from his previous lap; an eternity by racing standards.

"What's going on with the car, Bill?"

Richard's voice over the radio stunned him briefly. He didn't know how to respond and honestly felt too embarrassed to say anything.

Hearing a voice of doubt rise up in his mind, it spoke to him. *Tell him you can't do this. Tell him you don't belong in this race.* Shaking the voice lose from his head, Bill pushed on but he could still hear the lingering effects of self-doubt clinging on to him.

***

The timing and scoring display didn't lie. As Richard watched Bill cross the start/finish line which updated the information on his track position and lap time, the Brit could only shake his head.

"What's he doing?" asked Nick from behind. "Why's he falling off the pace so much?"

"I don't know and he's not responding to me."

Turning to the live broadcast on the television, Richard added, "I don't think this is car related."

William, who was standing off to the side, crossed his arms in front of him as he nervously watched his son on the television. Knowing the history of Bill's previous experience of racing in the rain, he could only imagine what his son was going through.

* * *

As Bill navigated the circuit and approached the entrance to pit lane, he heard the voice again. *Park the car. Quit. You wouldn't want to crash again and embarrass yourself. How will Chad think of you?*

Bill couldn't believe what his mind was doing. He felt as if he was having a panic attack in the race car.

As he crossed the start/finish line to begin another lap, he completed the first turn and was suddenly met with the sight of headlights directly in front of him.

One of the cars which had elected to go out on slick tires hoping that the rain would subside had experienced a sudden loss of grip in *Hell Corner.* As the driver tried to apply power, the rear wheels spun and caused the car to loop around to the left side of the track.

Bill had a fraction of a moment to react.

He was suddenly back in his old TA2 car in Austin, TX at the Circuit of The Americas. He remembered the feeling of being merely a passenger as his car spun off the track in the wet conditions. He remembered the embarrassment of getting his car stuck in the sand while everyone else drove past him. He remembered the ride home...

Seeing the headlights moving in front of him, Bill adjusted his steering and just narrowly missed the spinning car. It had all happened within the span of a second.

"Shit!" shouted Bill.

He felt as if his heart was going to burst out of his chest as he heaved air in and out of his lungs. All of the sudden, he felt panic take hold as he began to look aimlessly about. With the rain still falling, his windshield fogging up and the car feeling like it was driving on ice, Bill became frantic. He had a sinking feeling that somewhere and at any moment, a random car was going to sweep out from somewhere and he'd have nowhere to go before he crashed into it.

What would Chad think?

Just then, his mind betrayed him once again as Bill's thoughts drifted to his son. Memories began to surface of Chad growing up. His birth, his early childhood, his first day of school…

Then, the image of Chad lying face down on the ground before the tombstone of his dead mother pounded its way into the forefront of his mind.

What the hell is going on?!

The voice returned. *Park the car. While you still have the chance.*

Bill felt what could only be described as impending doom. At that very moment, Bill felt that if he didn't get out of that race car, he would die. He had to make a choice. As he wound his way around the circuit again, he began contemplating ways in which he could get out of the car.

You could just crash the car. In these conditions, nobody would ever know you did it on purpose.

He would be the laughing stock of the world but it wouldn't matter. He would be finished. He knew that he would be disappointed in himself as would the team.

What will Chad think of me? I'm all he's got left. If only Lena were here...

Bill's mind suddenly stopped dead in its tracks as he thought of Lena, the woman who was the unconditional love of his life. The memories of her soothed him. Remembering the words of encouragement she would always give him when he was beating himself up too much, Bill suddenly recalled what he had read in her journal the night before the race. It was almost as if she was now sitting next to him in the car reading the words into his ear as he heard her voice as clear as day:

"To my husband, Bill. I pray God's grace and protection upon you during your race. Not just your race at the track, but your race in life. Regardless of where you finish, you'll always be my knight in shining armor, my rock, my hero, my best friend and my one true love. I know that you're wanting to win this race but know that you're already a winner in my heart. Still,

I know that you're going to go out there and give your absolute all. That's why I love you...because you don't know how to do 'just good enough'. Be the warrior and the fighter that both Chad and I know that you are and you go make us proud. God bless you, Bill Watson. Until next time..."

A sound mind returned to Bill. Just as Lena's words had always done in the past, Bill felt encouraged and rejuvenated by them. He remembered how Lena would always step in when she thought he was beating himself too much...just like he was doing now. With that brief memory, his love for his wife—a woman whom he had fallen in love with the first time he had laid eyes on her but had passed into eternity before he ever had a chance to say goodbye—had never been stronger. Like an angel descending from heaven, it was almost as if she had reached down and comforted him in what could only be described as his own living hell.

The voice of self-doubt had been banished from his mind. He felt fire returning to his heart at the thought of Lena's voice and the memory of her words. He breathed. With a clear and focused mind, Bill began putting the puzzle pieces together which were that of Mount Panorama.

Relaxing his hands on the wheel, Bill was smooth and consistent as he now drove to the limits of the tires. Experimenting with the racing line as he searched for grip on the slippery race track, Bill found ways to make up the time he had lost as he pushed on with the task at hand.

Hugging the inside line through *Griffins Bend,* Bill was able to slowly close the gap on the car which had previously escaped him after his error at *Hell Corner*. As he worked through *The Cutting,* Bill began noticing the first inklings of sunlight piercing through the clouds as the rain slowly began to subside.

Maneuvering the car over the top of the Mountain and onto *Conrod,* Bill could now see how much ground he was gaining on the car in front of him. With each passing lap, Bill saw that the next car for position was getting closer and closer.

Due to the spinning car which he had narrowly missed earlier in his stint, Bill was currently in sixth at the moment with just over thirty laps remaining.

He knew, however, that his stint would soon be coming to an end. With only a few laps worth of fuel remaining, he would soon be pitting and Nick would jump in to finish the race out. He could only hope that his previous episode wasn't too detrimental to the success of the team.

As the presence of the sunlight increased, the light glistened through the water on his windscreen which was being sprayed up by the car he was pursuing that was now just two seconds in front of him. It made visibility difficult at times but at this point, Bill had gotten used to the layout of the circuit. A line on the track was also drying out rather quickly due to the warmer temperatures from the sunlight.

As Bill completed the final corner, Richard came over the radio. "Box this next lap, Bill."

"Copy. Hopefully I put Nick in a good spot to finish the race," said Bill over the radio.

No reply.

Typical Richard.

Racing up *Mountain Straight,* the car in front of him had gotten a bad run out of *Hell Corner* and Bill was now moving to the inside. As they both headed towards *Griffins Bend,* Bill had half a car length on the inside as he braked a bit later and made the pass stick. He had successfully moved the team up to fifth position.

As Bill continued, he suddenly became aware that this would be his final lap around Mount Panorama—or any track for that matter—in a race car. He did his best to cherish the moment as he felt his eyes water up. Despite the circumstances, he had pushed through adversity and made it out the other side while also putting the team inside the top-five. It was much more than he could've hoped for.

Where there was once anger, there was now peace. Where there was once confusion, there was now resolve.

As Bill began making the mental preparations for the upcoming pit stop, he felt confident that the team's primary driver would be able to fight for an even better spot.

When Nick gets back in the car, he'll surely be able to fight for a podium spot.

* * *

"Have you told him yet?" asked William.

"No," replied Richard flatly. "I'll tell him as he makes his way down *Conrod*."

The two men watched the television in the garage which was currently showing Bill navigating through *Forrest's Elbow*. As he plunged down the long stretch of *Conrod Straight*, Richard hesitated.

"What the bloody hell are you waiting for?" asked William. Richard ignored him and continued to watch the screen. As Bill navigated through *The Chase* and approached pit entrance, the crew made ready to receive the incoming car.

Bill entered pit lane and engaged the speed limiter as Richard finally made the call. "Stay in the car, Bill."

A few seconds of silence passed before Bill responded. "What the hell are you talking about? What about Nick?"

"Watson, I need you to stay focused and stay in the car," declared Richard. "The strategy's changed. You'll be finishing the race."

Picking up on the fact that something was indeed wrong, Bill pressed the issue. "What's happened to Nick?"

"Nick's fine but he can't race," replied Richard as Bill came to a stop in the pit stall. "He took a little tumble getting out of the car. You're it, mate. You're getting a full load of fuel and slicks," said Richard. "It'll be a little wild at first but the track's drying quickly."

A moment of hesitation from Bill was soon met by complete and absolute resolve to see this through to the end.

"Copy," replied Bill. "Tell my son this one's for him."

Richard smiled. "You're clear when the car drops."

After a few more seconds of fuel, the car dropped back down to the ground. Bill rolled the car away from the pit stall and headed towards the pit lane exit to rejoin the race.

Richard, looking over at William, patted the older man on the shoulder as the two watched the screen which showed their car returning to the racetrack in fifth position.

William smiled. "Godspeed, son."

Chapter 28

Marty Osborne was not having the drive he had been hoping for. Although he had arguably the quickest car in the field with one of the most experienced teams, the weather was making things especially difficult for Derek Renshaw's co-driver. Adding to his said calamity was the fact that the team had sent him out on slick tires after seeing reports that the weather would be clearing up.

They were wrong.

Rather than having a smooth run before handing the car back to Derek to finish the race out, he instead found himself performing what could only be described as a balancing act across a metaphorical beam made of ice while juggling what felt like a nearly 650-hp chainsaw.

For only two laps, the young driver tried to finesse his way around Mount Panorama. During the process, Marty spun while attempting to get the car slowed down at the final corner. Using the escape road, Osborne swung the car back around and re-entered the racing line.

Seeing that the weather had indeed shifted course and was showing no signs of improvement for some time, the team regressed.

"Box this lap, Marty," said Osborne's crew over the radio.

He was more than happy to comply.

As he completed the lap and entered pit lane, Marty noticed that several other cars were also entering pit road, presumably the ones who'd also taken slicks. In a way, this gave Marty a small sense of satisfaction.

We're the ones everyone's basing their decisions off of. Not a bad place to be in after all.

He brought the team's Holden Commodore to a stop squarely in the pit stall. It only took a moment for the crew to change tires and top off the fuel. As the car dropped and Marty pulled away, his crew came on the radio again.

"Give us a good clean stint, Marty. Derek will be jumping in after you and we'll finish this race off strong."

"Copy," said Marty on the radio as he headed up *Mountain Straight*. "What position am I in?"

No immediate reply came over the radio. Thinking he might have a radio drama which was preventing the team from hearing him, Marty tried once again.

"Did you guys copy? What's my position?"

Once again, no immediate reply came. After several seconds, however, the team responded. "Just keep pushing, Marty."

Seeing that he was getting nowhere with this exchange, he redirected his efforts. *This must be their way of telling me to just shut up and drive.* Checking his mirrors, Marty noticed a single car behind him. Due to the conditions, it was difficult to tell who it was but he could tell by the headlights that it was a Ford.

"Damned if I'm letting a Ford past me," said Marty under his breath. The two cars continued their dance across the Mountain until they reached the front stretch to start another lap. There, Marty saw the car behind him make what appeared to be a late move while under braking for *Hell Corner*. Momentarily distracted, this caused Marty to run a bit wide at the exit of the corner.

Fearing he may have stuffed up and cost the team a position, Marty checked his mirrors again and noticed that the car behind him had made a similar mistake but had gone much further off the track. The other driver, having to now deal with additional elements on his tires, lost several seconds as Marty began to pull away.

Relieved to have a bit of a breather from the pressure of being pursued, Marty exhaled as he worked his way up the Mountain. It was difficult to get into a rhythm due to the weather, but the heightened sense of awareness Marty had for these types of conditions was helping greatly. It wasn't long before Marty had caught up to the next car.

Getting on the radio, Marty asked, "Is this car for position?"

Similar to the previous response, a voice on the radio replied, "Keep pushing, Marty."

It wasn't the answer he had been hoping for but the young driver pushed on with the task at hand.

Although he had been able to catch up to the car quickly, getting around the other driver was proving quite difficult given the conditions. Noticing the livery of the car, Marty knew that the vehicle he was pursuing belonged to one of the older drivers who had been in many battles throughout the years. He knew that the veteran driver wasn't going to make things easy for him.

As the two drivers began another lap, Marty was able to get a much better exit out of *Hell Corner* and he knew that this was his best chance at a pass. As he gained ground on the car in front of him, Marty moved to the right side of the track in order to have the inside line for the next right turn. Unfortunately, Marty showed his hand too early as the car in front also moved to the right side to block the move.

Knowing that the driver only had one move before copping a penalty for blocking, Marty moved back over to the left side of the track and was able to continue his pace until he was alongside the other car. Heading into *Griffins Bend,* Marty attempted the pass on the outside but it was a futile attempt.

Even in ideal conditions, making a pass on the outside of *Griffins* was a very difficult maneuver to pull off. In the current conditions, it was next to impossible when contending with a skilled driver such as the one Marty had in his crosshairs.

As the rear of Marty's car wobbled from the sudden loss of grip, he was able to keep it under control and continue on albeit about a second and a half further back from the driver he was pursuing. With the race approaching its closing stages, Marty was well aware of the fact that the other drivers would be racing much harder now.

Still, having fresher tires benefited the younger driver as he worked to make up the ground he had previously lost. Navigating around the treacherous circuit, Marty continued to close the gap until he was about a car length away by the time they reach *Forrest's Elbow*.

Once again, however, the car in front of Marty was making things difficult. This time, it was a bit of an odd play.

As the two headed down *Conrod,* Marty was able to close the distance as the other car moved to the right side of the track. He thought this to be a bit strange as the exit of *The Chase* was a left handed turn which gave him the inside line.

As Marty moved in, he quickly saw the reasoning behind the other driver's move.

Heading into *The Chase,* the initial right hand turn gave the inside line to the other driver. This put Marty off the racing line and onto a slippery section of the track. Unable to slow down enough to make the turn, the left side of Marty's car swung into the grass briefly before he was able to muscle it back onto the track. Still carrying momentum, he went hard on the brakes to try to get the car to stop in time for the next left hand turn. Marty had the inside line, but he was carrying way too much speed to make the pass.

Initially able to get by the other driver, Marty missed the apex of the left turn and went wide once again into the grass on the right side of the track at the exit of *The Chase.* The other driver, who was able to slow down properly, gave Marty the room he needed so they wouldn't collide and proceeded to pull a clever crossover move by moving to the left side and reclaiming the position he had momentarily lost.

Marty was starting to see red in his eyes as his frustration grew. He hated to be held up like this, and he was being made to look like a fool in the process.

As the two crossed the line to start another lap, Marty saw what appeared to be an opening and made a last second dive down the inside while heading into *Hell Corner*. The driver he was pursuing had already begun to make the left turn and noticed Marty with only centimeters to spare. Having to adjust his line mid corner, the driver lost traction in the rear of the car and spun as they exited the corner. No contact was made between the two drivers, but Marty knew he wouldn't be making any new fans after that maneuver.

Checking in his rear view mirror as he headed up *Mountain Straight* currently unopposed, Marty saw the driver who had just gone off attempt to re-enter the racing surface and nearly wipe another car out in the process.

"Six seconds and growing to the car behind," said a voice over Marty's radio. "Keep pushing."

Continuing on, Marty thought it odd that he was being told to keep pushing in these conditions despite having a growing gap to the car behind. Either way, he did as he was told and kept his foot on it.

Able to faintly see the tail lights of the cars in front of him, Marty was able to get into a solid rhythm and maintain his pace for several laps. He couldn't tell if he was actually making any ground up but he knew that he was pushing as hard as he could.

As he approached the final few laps of his stint, however, Marty was a bit shocked when he saw the headlights of a car behind him steadily getting closer and closer. Additionally, the weather was starting to clear up. So much so that he could now clearly see the car which was now right on his back bumper. Noticing the green light indicating that a co-driver was piloting the car, Marty's heart momentarily sank.

"Is that Bill Watson?" asked Marty over the radio.

"Keep pushing and keep him behind you!"

Suddenly feeling like the eyes of the world were upon him, Marty could feel an enormous amount of pressure coming from his team all the way back in the garage as well as from the car of Watson behind him.

This was why the crew were wanting me to push so hard. They knew who was behind me the entire time.

Coming into the race weekend, Marty knew that winning Bathurst was the ultimate goal. From his previous talks with Renshaw, however, he knew that beating the son of the former Bathurst legend was also a priority as it would further cement his name as one of the all-time greats in the sport.

Unfortunately, the man they were aiming to beat had just made catching up to Marty look like child's play.

"Shit, shit, shit!" said Marty aloud as he checked his mirrors heading up *Mountain Straight.*

The dive came late but it was absolute. Moving to the inside, the black Ford Falcon lunged down the right side and swept up the position from Marty.

The call on the radio came moments later.

"Box this lap, Marty," said the voice on the radio. "We're in sixth and Derek's ready for you."

"Copy," replied Marty.

Muttering to himself, he said, "Let's just hope he's ready to handle Watson."

He tried to keep a close distance on the #528 of Bill Watson, but he saw that the man had some serious pace. By the time he had arrived at the entrance to pit lane, Bill had already stretched his gap to just under two seconds and had entered the pits just in front of him.

Engaging the pit lane speed limiter, Marty disconnected the radio, cool suit and drink straw while also loosening the belts before bringing the car to a halt squarely in the team's pit stall.

The door swung open and Marty quickly climbed out and headed towards the garage. The crew member assigned to help Derek get buckled in went to work on making sure the primary driver was properly seated and had all of the connections secured. As the fuel rushed in, Marty saw the slick tires being installed and knew that, despite the rain finally stopping, the conditions would still be treacherous for slicks.

Standing by the entrance of the garage and watching the pit crew work, Marty saw that the black Ford Falcon which had just gotten by him was still taking on fuel. Undoubtedly for what would be their final stop of the race. As the black Falcon dropped and headed down pit lane to re-enter the race, Marty noticed that the green co-driver light was still on.

"Is Watson still in the car?" he asked a nearby crew member. Marty's question was quickly answered before anyone else had a chance to respond. Driving by with the sputtering of the pit lane speed limiter engaged, Bill Watson waived to Marty and gave him a thumbs up as he gingerly cruised by their car, which was still taking on fuel. Just as Watson had cleared the Holden car, the team dropped the car and Renshaw tucked in right behind his adversary. The two entered the track nose-to-tail as Marty smiled at what he knew was about to be a battle worthy of the history books.

"This is gonna be one helluva fight."

Chapter 29

Every fan in attendance at Mount Panorama was on their feet as both Bill Watson and Derek Renshaw exited the pits with twenty-one laps remaining in the race. Always taking the opportunity to stun the crowd, Renshaw wasted no time asserting himself and immediately went on the attack.

As the two cars raced up *Mountain Straight,* Renshaw fired his car up the inside to get past Watson at *Griffins Bend.* Despite being on cold tires, he made the pass stick as the two headed into *The Cutting.*

Although Bill knew he needed to be patient, he wasn't about to let Renshaw off the hook that easily. Staying just inches off his back bumper, Bill waited for the opportunity to strike. He had to be careful, however, as parts of the track had still yet to dry out.

Heading into *Forrest's Elbow,* Derek made a mistake and locked the wheels up on the downhill section due to the surface still being damp.

This was all the opening Bill needed.

As both drivers raced down *Conrod,* Bill passed the defending champion with ease due to his loss of momentum in the earlier corner. Staying nose to tail for the remainder of the lap, Bill and Derek crossed the line in front of the grandstands to start another lap. The crowd roared in excitement as if watching two ironclad warriors in a gladiatorial arena.

Racing up *Mountain Straight,* the advice which came over the radio was exactly what Bill needed to hear.

"Run your race, Bill," said Richard over the radio. "Don't run his.

Head down, eyes forward."

Not entirely sure if Richard had seen Bill on the broadcast because of the in-car camera or if he was simply using another one of his yet-to-be-named super powers, Bill knew that he was checking his mirrors too much and needed to stay focused on what was happening in front of him.

Although Bill and Derek had exited the pits in fifth and sixth respectively, the leader had received a drive through penalty for exceeding the pit lane speed limit on entry. A crushing blow this late in the race, this relegated the two drivers up to fourth and fifth.

Just behind Bill, Derek was anxious to get by his American adversary. "Keep your head cool," said the voice over Derek's radio. "There's still plenty of race to go and we don't want the leaders to get too far away. Work with him for now and get to the front."

Although the feedback wasn't exactly what he *wanted* to hear, Derek knew that it was what he *needed* to hear. Getting past Bill Watson was one thing, but winning the race was the ultimate goal. If he could accomplish the latter, he would also achieve the former.

Swallowing his pride, he backed off the attack on Watson for the time being.

In front of him, Bill was a bit surprised when Derek no longer seemed to be fighting him at the entry and exit of every turn. In fact, Bill noticed that Derek was actually settling in behind him.

Back in the garage, Richard took notice. "This could be the start of a beautiful relationship between you two," he said as he chuckled.

"Positions one, two and three are bunched up together about five seconds up the road from you. They're fighting amongst themselves so you should be catching them shortly."

With only eighteen laps to go, it was getting down to crunch time. Although the race was 161 laps, it's often argued that the *real* race doesn't start until the final twenty laps. At that point, kindness, friendship, and sometimes even team orders all go out the window as drivers are more than willing to step on the neck of the person in front of them to get by.

For the next four laps, Derek remained nearly attached to the back bumper of Bill Watson, only sticking his nose out to make sure his car didn't overheat. Although he wasn't going to force the issue just yet, he certainly wasn't going to back off just in case the American made a mistake which would allow Derek to slip by.

During that time, the leaders were having at each other as they battled for the lead of the race. All of this fighting, however, allowed the cars of Watson and Renshaw to catch them with ease.

With fourteen laps remaining, Bill and Derek had successfully caught up to the first three positions and were now less than a second behind.

Having achieved his goal of catching the leaders, Derek no longer had any need of Watson and went on the attack. With the remaining laps dwindling, Derek's goal was to get by the four cars in front of him and gap the field to take the win. With the four cars in front of him now so close to each other, it certainly wasn't an impossible feat to accomplish.

Still in fourth place, Bill could tell right away that the behavior of the car behind him had immediately changed upon catching the leaders. Were he in Derek's shoes, he would be going on full attack.

So he did.

As the pack of five cars crossed the line and made the left turn of *Hell Corner*, Bill used the draft of the car in front to pull his car right up to the back bumper. Seeing the move coming, the third placed driver moved to the right side of the track to cover. Staying left, Bill carried his momentum through *Forrests Elbow* and was able to pull alongside the third placed car heading into *The Cutting*. It was a gutsy move but the time for playing it safe was gone.

Caught off guard by the bold move, the third placed driver was forced to take a wider line through the left handed uphill turn. Losing grip in the still damp section of the track, the driver narrowly avoided the wall while also allowing both Watson and Renshaw to slip by.

Back in the garage, the crew of the *Dynamis Engineering* Ford Falcon erupted in cheers as Bill moved into a podium spot.

Sitting with Chad as well as with Tubbs and Greg in the back of the garage, Abby stood to her feet and joined the crew in cheering at the sight of the bold move Bill had pulled off. "He's moved into third!" shouted Abby.

Kneeling down by Chad, Abby noticed that the young boy was smiling. "Your daddy's one hell of a driver, Chad. I fancy you'll be one someday too."

Chad's eyes never left the viewing monitor which showed the ongoing battle with his dad and Derek Renshaw. He had seen his dad battle on the track before, but it had never been on television.

Looking to see that only thirteen laps were remaining in the race, which had been going on for several hours, excitement began to well up inside of Chad. He found himself clenching tightly to both of the armrests on his wheelchair as he watched his dad battle for position.

Finally looking away for a moment, Chad noticed that everyone in the garage was standing on their feet watching their driver on the television. He felt pride for the first time in a long time. That was his dad they were watching, praying for, and cheering for. His dad was battling some of the best drivers in the world and giving them a run for their money.

He found himself breathing heavy as his eyes fixed back onto the screen. He watched as his dad moved into second while going side-by-side with another car down *Conrod*.

He smiled as the battle raged on.

* * *

Firing past the now third placed car, Bill couldn't believe it himself. He was now in second place in the Bathurst 1000. Only a few car lengths away from the leader, Bill suddenly dared a thought—he could actually pull off the impossible.

As the lap finished and another one began, Bill made a slight mistake on the exit of *Hell Corner* and ran a bit too wide. Having to come off the power a bit to keep the car on the road, it proved to be an open door for the driver he'd just passed. With momentum on his side, the opposing driver moved alongside Bill heading into *Griffins Bend* and made the pass stick. Bill was now back in third with Renshaw right behind him again.

This time, however, Renshaw was on the charge.

Not wanting to stick around behind Watson any longer, Renshaw saw just a hint of an opening and decided to go for it.

It was a bold move by any standard. Keeping to the left and on the back bumper of Watson through *The Cutting*, Derek kept left and was able to get a run on Bill while exiting the uphill Turn 4. It was a place where overtakes are rarely attempted but Derek knew he had the car under him to pull it off.

As the track continued its uphill ascent, Derek went side-by-side with Bill, with the latter being caught off guard. Deciding not to chance an incident this far into the race or waste too much time needlessly battling, Bill backed off and gave up the position for now.

Now down to fourth after starting the lap in second, Bill had a sudden reality check at the level of competition he was facing.

Meanwhile, Derek continued his hunt for positions. Now in third, Derek had the two leaders in his sights. He was in a podium position and Watson was behind him but that wasn't good enough. There was still plenty of fight left in him and plenty of race remaining.

Tracking with the leaders down *Conrod*, Derek glanced in his mirror to see that Bill was about a car length back from him with the fifth placed car about a second and a half back from the lead pack.

As the lead group of four cars lined through *The Chase* and eventually across the start/finish line, Derek was looking for a way forward while also glancing in his mirrors. Playing both offense and defense at the same time was a difficult task, indeed.

Making their way up the Mountain, Derek was now directly on the back bumper of the second placed car and ready to pounce at the right time. Approaching *Skyline,* however, Derek made a costly mistake and went into the proceeding downhill section carrying too much speed. Seeing that there was no way he'd be able to make the turn, Derek thought better of it and elected to take the service road on the left side of the track just before *the Dipper*.

Able to get the car slowed, Derek succeeded in recovering from the incident at the expense of a position.

Seeing what looked like a care package addressed directly to him in the form of an opening, Bill Watson seized the golden opportunity and reclaimed third place from Derek Renshaw.

The crowd erupted in cheers as the action unfolded in front of them. Derek lost not only the position but a good amount of time in the process. Now over a second back from Watson and close to being under threat from the fifth placed car, Derek took a deep breath, left the incident behind him, and pressed onward.

Meanwhile, Watson wasn't about to waste this second chance he'd been given. With his adversary behind him by a growing margin, Bill pressed on towards the two leaders who were once again fighting as they approached *Conrod*.

The action was unfolding in front of Bill as the leaders went side-by-side through *Forrest's Elbow*. The crowd was eating it up, but the truth is that it was costing both cars a great deal of time. Bill took advantage of this late race battle and closed the gap. Now about a car length back, Bill watched as the leaders maintained their side-by-side battle through *The Chase*.

Approaching the left-handed Turn 21 at a high rate of speed, the inside car braked later than usual as the leader on the outside took his usual braking point. Locking up the wheels under heavy braking, the inside car couldn't slow down enough and made contact with the leader as he was attempting to complete the turn. The contact pushed the leader into the grass on the right side as the inside car struggled to regain control.

All that Bill saw, however, was a brief blast of smoke from the skidding tires followed by the road opening up in front of him. Maintaining his line and his momentum, Bill rolled past both cars and into the lead of the Bathurst 1000.

* * *

The explosion of cheers ripped up and down pit lane as the crew back in the team's garage jumped to their feet. Seeing their driver take the lead of the Great Race was more than they could've hoped for as smiles filled the faces of some with tears of joy in the eyes of others.

Even Richard, who was normally calm and collected in these types of situations, couldn't contain himself. Despite his long career in motorsports and the fact that under his leadership many drivers had won many races, he'd never so much as led a lap in a major race such as this. Hugging the closest teammate, Richard's yellow-teeth-filled smile was one of many in the garage.

And as Bill crossed the line, the timing and scoring screen updated and showed the #528 of Bill Watson as the leader of the race.

Looking beside him, Richard noticed that William was in tears. Putting his arm around the older man, Richard said, "You've got to be the proudest father in the world right now."

Wiping a tear from his eye, William looked up at the taller British man. "It's not just Bill," said William. Gesturing over towards the back of the garage, he pointed toward Chad, who was on the very edge of his seat as he watched his father lead the Bathurst 1000.

"I...I don't have the words. Seeing that boy's world light up like that just makes my heart jump. And knowing that it's my son out there making it happen…I could die a happy man right now."

Richard smiled. "Hold off on the dying part for a little bit longer. We wouldn't want to steal the spotlight away from what's going on out there."

Looking back up towards the monitor, both men saw that their team's rival, Derek Renshaw, had just moved back into third.

Richard sighed. "We've taken the lead. Now we defend it."

* * *

During the time it had taken for Bill to take the lead and the two cars he'd passed in the process to safely rejoin the race from their brief off-track excursion, Bill's lead had grown considerably. He now had a comfortable margin over the three cars behind him—including that of Derek Renshaw.

Although the incident happened in front of Renshaw, he wasn't able to fully capitalize on it as Watson had done. In fact, he'd lost time due to having to brake as the two cars re-entered the racing surface in front of him. Although he attempted to go around them both, he quickly found that there was no safe and effective way to do so.

Renshaw cursed as he watched Watson sail off into the lead with no current opposition.

The sight alone further spread the flames of fury within him. He wasn't about to let Watson take the win without a fight.

With the fifth placed car directly behind him and with second and third directly ahead, Derek knew he had a brief window of opportunity to make a quick and decisive move. With both cars ahead having gone off-road, it would take a moment for their tires to clean off. Any material stuck to a slick racing tire—especially wet grass and mud—impeded traction which ultimately slowed you down.

The opportunity came quickly and Derek moved to pounce without a second thought.

Entering the final corner, the third placed car overshot the braking zone and went wide. Quick to fill the now open gap, Derek dove down the inside and took third position before crossing the line.

Just one more car. One more car and Watson's ass is mine.

Entering *Hell Corner* as the new lap started, the second placed car had regained its momentum and was now driving defensively. The driver's team was undoubtedly filling him in on Derek's charge.

The fight went to *Mountain Straight* as Derek was about a car length back. Holding the right side of the track, the second placed car gave Derek no room to move. Even so, Derek knew the driver was a sitting duck. It was only a matter of time before an opening would come up and he would be there when it...

There!

On the exit of *The Cutting,* the second placed car got loose as the rear of the car swung out to the right. Regaining control, the driver tried to cover the position but Derek was already there.

Moving quickly, Derek filled the gap along the right side of the track but the other driver wasn't about to give up so easily. If he could somehow hold his position, he'd have the preferred line coming out of *Frog Hallow* and into *Sulman Park*.

Both cars stayed side-by-side through one of the most difficult sections of the track. Racing uphill, Derek knew he had the momentum but was off the driving line. He had to do something.

Pressure. Put the pressure on.

Squeezing the other car for every inch of space he could get, Derek did everything he could to take the position. As they entered *Frog Hallow* side-by-side, however, the car which Derek was fighting popped the inside curb on the left side of the track. The sudden force shot him out and into the side of Derek's car, causing Renshaw to have to slow quickly lest he meet the right side wall at *Sulman*

Park.

Able to recover—albeit at the price of even more left side door damage—Derek continued on. The other driver, however, wasn't so lucky.

Bouncing off of Renshaw's car, the other car lost traction and speared off to the left making hard contact with the left side wall. As the car bounced off the wall, it slid back onto the track and into incoming traffic. Miraculously, no other cars were collected as the local yellow caution flags waived. Due to the crash, however, a full course caution soon followed as the safety car was deployed.

For Bill Watson, this was the last thing he wanted to hear.

Going through *Skyline* as he saw the yellow flags waving, Richard was quick to get on the radio.

"Safety car, Bill. Full course yellow," said Richard calmly in the radio.

"Maintain your pace until you reach the back of the safety car. The road in front of you is clear."

"What the hell happened?" asked Bill who was oblivious to the incident which had unfolded behind him.

"Bathurst happened," said Richard.

Having to slow to cruising speed as he caught up to the back of the pace car, Bill's meteoric lead had now been eliminated. As the safety car led the field around the track, drivers stacked single-file behind it. Bill's heart sank a bit as his rearview mirror filled up with the car of Derek Renshaw.

"We won't be pitting, Bill. The cleanup is going smoothly and we estimate there will be five laps remaining when they resume the race."

"You've got to be kidding me," replied Bill. He grimaced at the idea of having to do a five lap duel with Derek Renshaw.

Richard chuckled on the radio. "Bathurst delivers, my friend. Bathurst delivers."

For two slow laps, Bill stayed behind the safety car as the field circled the nearly 6.2km circuit.

"The track is now clear. Get ready to go green this time by," said Richard over the radio. "This is it, Watson. Renshaw's gonna come at you with the full fury of hell behind him. Give it everything you've got. Leave nothing on the table."

"Copy," replied Bill.

Wishing he hadn't heard those last few lines, Bill could feel a fresh burst of adrenaline course through his veins as his stomach seemingly tied itself into a knot.

As the safety car exited *Forrest's Elbow*, the flashing lights on top of the vehicle turned off signaling the race was about to resume. Once the lights turned off, all of the race cars had to form up tightly. Weaving about to warm up tires once the lights on the safety car had gone off was prohibited and race officials were quick to slap you with a pit lane drive through penalty should you get caught in the act.

From the front of the field heading down *Conrod Straight*, Bill glanced in his rearview mirror to see the entire field of cars behind him. He knew they would all be gunning for him in these final five laps.

One driver in particular was keen to remove him from his current position. As the safety car accelerated away from the field and headed towards the pits, Bill now had control of the field as he maintained his speed through *The Chase*. At this point, Bill could hit the gas and resume the race anytime before the start/finish line. That was his right as the leader of the race. Many drivers would take an early jump but Bill played a different card.

Bill held the field longer than many anticipated including Renshaw behind him. He could see his adversary's car jumping as the driver inside tried to predict when Bill would go.

Completing the final turn, Bill waited for only a second, which caused Renshaw to check up behind him. That's when Bill hit the loud pedal and resumed the race.

Crossing the line with only five laps to go, the entire field of cars roared by the front grandstand as every attendant was on their feet to see the spectacle which was about to conclude in front of them.

Even as the cars screamed by, it was the booming voice of Tubbs that filled the garage.

"DRIVE, YOU SONOFABITCH!"

Chapter 30

Bill's jump on the restart of the race had paid off. With only five laps now remaining, he had succeeded in forming a one second gap to the car of Renshaw. If he could now just hold off the charge of the defending series champion, he would accomplish the impossible.

It would not be an easy task for Bill, and Derek Renshaw was keen to show him why.

As the field rounded *The Cutting* and proceeded to race up the Mountain, Bill couldn't help but check his mirrors every few seconds. He was anxious to see if his lead was holding or if Renshaw was indeed closing in inch by inch. As a result, Bill's focus was divided. He wanted to keep his eyes forward but it almost became an impulse to look up at the mirror as he could almost physically feel the pressure from the car behind him.

It was all in his mind, of course, but the nervousness of being a few laps away from winning the Bathurst 1000 coupled with having one of the most ferocious drivers in the series directly behind you was enough to make even the most seasoned of drivers a bit on edge.

As the field of cars raced across the top of the Mountain, Bill did his best to keep them at bay but he could tell that Renshaw was closing in ever so slightly. Rounding the corner at *Forrest's Elbow* and heading down *Conrod,* Bill knew his adversary would have the advantage of the slipstream.

As the field raced down *Conrod Straight,* Derek Renshaw began to close the gap.

With each passing second as he headed down *Conrod,* Bill could see Derek's car getting closer. He knew, however, that Derek wouldn't be able to make the pass this time around. At the moment, he was simply too far back. But Bill also knew that there was still plenty of time left in the race for Derek to set himself up for a pass.

Bill led the field as he crossed the line to start lap 158 of 161. Only four laps to go.

Once again Derek was on the attack. Heading up *Mountain Straight,* Bill found himself having to go slightly defensive as Renshaw closed the gap even further during the long stretch of road. Moving to the right side of the track to cover his entrance into *Griffins Bend,* Bill knew these moves were also backing up the field behind them.

Although he and Derek had a brief respite earlier in the race where they both were needing to catch the lead pack, those times were gone now. The only thing that mattered to Derek at this point was getting by Bill Watson, and he was willing to do anything it took to do just that.

Behind Bill, Derek was testing the waters. He had accomplished his goal of catching up to the back of Watson after the restart. Now, however, he was biding his time to see where the best place would be for a pass. In the process, he was trying his best to intimidate the American driver. Showing his nose in the rear view mirror or even moving completely out of his line of sight so Bill would temporarily not know where Derek was—these were tricks which Derek had picked up throughout his years of auto racing in the premier Australian category.

It was human nature to be wary of what was behind you, especially when you knew something was back there and you couldn't see it. Derek was playing to those emotions.

The field had condensed behind both Bill and Derek as each subsequent car had a gap of less than a car length between them all the way to the end of the field. If one of the drivers at the front made a mistake, it would be an unfortunate end of the race for many drivers.

Coming up on *Forrest's Elbow,* Bill could now see that Derek was right on his back bumper. Making a slight mistake going into the downhill left turn, Bill carried too much speed into the corner and locked up his wheels.

"Damnit!" he shouted to himself.

Although he avoided contact with the wall on the right side, he had to scrub speed to do so. This gave Renshaw a wide opening, which he wasted no time in seizing.

As the field raced down *Conrod,* Renshaw completed the pass and assumed the lead of the Great Race. Luckily for Bill, however, he was able to slip in behind his adversary and cover himself from being overtaken by the car in third. Using the slipstream to his advantage, Bill got through *The Chase* directly behind Renshaw and stayed on his back bumper as they crossed the line to start lap 159.

Although it was not an ideal position to be in for Bill, he knew he had a few tricks up his sleeve as well. He wasn't about to simply hand over the lead without a fight to get it back. The question, however, was would he be able to break down the defenses of Derek Renshaw in the final three laps of the Bathurst 1000.

As Bill looked for an opening, his mind thought back to Road Atlanta when he was racing his TA2 Ford Mustang while being pursued by that bright yellow Chevrolet Camaro. Now, he was in the shoes of the hunter, and he focused his mind as such.

He knew what he needed to do: stay calm, maintain his focus, and be ready when an opportunity arises. Derek was a strong driver but also a fool at times.

He always shows his hand too early, and now he'll have to drive defensively for the remainder of the race.

Bill vowed to remain patient and wait for the moment to strike. The trouble was that he was running out of time for that special moment to show up. If he waited too long, he risked giving the race away without a fight. If he moved too soon, he'd be right back in the same shoes he was in before. He didn't care about leading the race until the end. He remembered what his father used to say when he was younger:

"It only matters who's leading the race at the checkered flag."

* * *

A slight push from behind Derek caused him to glance up at his mirrors again. Watson was right on his back bumper as they headed down *Conrod Straight*. Instead of using his speed gained from the slipstream to attempt an overtake, Bill had used it to give Derek a push.

Derek wanted to smile but his nerves were too high. He knew what Watson was doing. He could tell that the American was trying to force him into a mistake. By giving him a push, Derek would be going faster down the straight which, had he not been properly paying attention, could've caused him to brake at his typical braking point which wouldn't have compensated for the additional speed. This would've caused him to overshoot the apex of the corner and ultimately surrender the lead.

If it worked, of course.

Despite the fact that a move like that could've sent Bill a penalty, Derek wasn't about to fall for such a cheap trick.

"You low bastard," said Derek to himself.

Firing through *The Chase* and down to the final corner, Watson showed his nose as if attempting a late overtake. It was expected, however, as Derek knew that the American would be continually trying to force him into making a mistake. By taking a peek in his mirrors while approaching his braking point, Derek could potentially miss it and overshoot the corner.

Again, however, Derek showed he was no fool and hit his braking point without so much as surrendering an inch to Watson.

The field crossed the line to start the penultimate lap. With only about 12.5km remaining in the 1000km race, Derek knew that Bill was quickly running out of time. The move for the lead from Watson was coming. That much was certain.

When it was coming, however, was the golden question.

As Derek completed *Hell Corner* and headed up *Mountain Straight,* he noticed that his hands were beginning to hurt due to his vice-like grip on the steering wheel. Taking a moment to compose himself, he glanced into his rearview mirror and noticed that Watson wasn't there anymore.

A brief moment of panic overtook his attempt to maintain composure.

Did he crash?

Approaching his braking point into *Griffins Bend,* Derek finally noticed that Watson had moved all the way over to the right side of the track in an attempt to cause a frantic moment for the Australian driver.

It worked.

Not knowing where Bill Watson was had caused Derek Renshaw to miss his braking mark as he looked for where his American competitor had gone. As a result, Derek was off point with his braking and ran a bit wide into *Griffins Bend.*

Behind him, Bill Watson saw the opening and committed to it. Making the apex and moving to the right side of Renshaw, Bill had almost completed the overtake but was unfortunately on the outside for the next turn. Having the ideal line, Derek was able to clear Watson and continue on their trek up the Mountain with the lead.

It was a move which showed Derek just how skilled his competitor was. Although he'd previously thought Watson was not up to the grand task of competing in Australia's great race, he'd now formed a level of respect for the American.

He glanced at his competitor in the rearview mirror.

"You're one savage sonofabitch, Watson."

* * *

Although Bill's move on Derek was ill-fated, he knew he'd gotten his point across. He could sense the change in Derek's driving style. On edge and driving defensively, this wasn't the same Derek Renshaw he'd been chasing earlier in the race. The pressure of leading the Bathurst 1000 coupled with Bill Watson directly behind him was starting to wear on Derek.

Bill just hoped that it wasn't too little too late.

As the two traversed *The Dipper* and headed towards *Forrest's Elbow,* Derek was carrying too much speed and had a slight lock up at the top of *Conrod Straight.* This gave Bill another chance to complete the overtake for the lead, but Derek was fighting for every inch of real estate.

The loss of momentum from Derek's car was felt almost immediately as he wasn't able to get the run down the long back stretch which he needed. Holding the left side of the track, Derek held the preferred line into *The Chase* as his adversary gained ground and pulled alongside. Bill had no intention of giving up easily. The crowd was on their feet and roaring as the two drivers, who were now side-by-side, traversed the dog leg into *The Chase* at full speed.

Derek once again had the preferred line on the left side of the track. However, it was a two-sided coin. As Derek was able to make the apex of the turn, Bill was able to stay along with him and prevent the Holden driver from tracking out after the turn. With the track briefly switching back to Bill's favor at the entrance of pit road, Watson had a full head of steam and a brief moment where he had taken the lead before the final left handed turn put Renshaw back into the undisputed lead.

Racing across the line, they started the final lap of the Bathurst 1000.

"Go for it, Bill! You've got this!" shouted Richard over the radio.

This was it and Bill knew it. One more lap around Mount Panorama.

One more lap...the final lap of my life.

Racing into *Hell Corner,* Bill saw Derek get a near perfect exit out of the first turn. Following suit, it was all he could do to maintain his position on the back of Derek's car. Even with the slipstream in Bill's favor, he wasn't getting the pull he needed as they raced up the Mountain.

However, Derek wasn't leaving anything up to chance. Moving to the right side of the track in an effort to block what could be a last second dive from Watson, Renshaw wasn't about to be passed on the final lap of the biggest race of his life.

As Derek moved back over to the left side of the track just as he reached his braking point to maximize his turn-in, Bill tried to juke Derek as he fired it down the inside.

Caught by surprise by the sudden appearance of a car on his right side which wasn't there mere moments before, Derek was forced to run wide to give Watson racing room. As such, the lack of grip that far off the racing line caused Derek to give up ground.

Although Bill's attempt at a pass on the previous lap at this same corner didn't work out, Bill now had a run on Derek as they raced towards *The Cutting.*

Not able to completely clear Derek's car, Bill was forced to take a wider line through the uphill left-turning section of the track as Derek had the preferred driving line on the inside. This helped the Holden driver regain some of the ground he'd lost to Bill. However, the next right turn up *Quarry Corner* switched the driving line back in favor of Bill.

Not willing to give up on the final lap, Derek refused to let go and slot behind Bill. He'd come too far to throw it all away.

The two drivers were side-by-side as they headed towards *Frog Hollow*, but it was Derek who was finally able to clear Watson while heading towards *Sulman Park*.

Now single file, the two rivals were nose-to-tail as they headed down *Skyline* and into *The Dipper*. A section of the track with a one line groove, going side-by-side was nearly impossible at race speed.

Bill knew that his chances of making a pass for the lead were quickly diminishing. With less than half a lap remaining in the race, it was all or nothing. He had to make his own opportunity if this was going to work in his favor.

Both drivers had a clean run through *Forrest's Elbow* as they progressed down *Conrod Straight* for the final time. With Bill now in the draft behind Derek, he slowly started to gain a speed advantage over his rival.

Seeing Watson coming, Derek moved to the left to hold the preferred line. Bill reacted and without lifting off the throttle, moved over to the right as the side-by-side racing reached the dogleg turn at the end of long straight.

Slamming his hands on the steering wheel hoping it would somehow siphon more power from the engine, Bill screamed at the car as he raced at full speed.

"C'mon, you sonofabitch!"

Still side-by-side, Bill ran a bit wide, missing the apex of the slight right turn. It was a strategic play, however, as this caused Derek to also run wide. Putting his left tires on the grass slightly, Derek lost a bit of momentum as he headed towards the braking zone of *The Chase.*

Watson had the advantage of being slightly ahead but Derek still had the preferred line. Getting hard on the brakes as he brought his car down to the appropriate speed, Derek made the left turn with Watson on his right side.

As the two entered the final turn, Bill moved over as far as he could to the left side of the track. Derek, not wanting to be driven into the turn on a shallow line, held his ground. The two made side to side contact as they executed the final turn.

Getting on the power too hard, Derek had a touch of wheel spin as the drag race toward the finish line commenced. Despite having to take the long way around his rival, Bill was able to get onto the power smoothly.

The crowd, everyone in the garages, and even the sports commentators were on their feet as the two drivers battled for every inch towards the finish.

Side-by-side, this final stretch seemed to hang in time as Bill watched the hood of Derek's car and vice versa to see if either driver had the edge.

With the checkered flag waving in the air, the two drivers crossed the line to complete the Bathurst 1000.

"Holy shit!" shouted Bill over the radio. "Did we get it?!"

The silence on the radio as Bill waited for a response was deafening. It was so close. Too close. So much so that the officials were having to refer to the replay footage to verify their conclusion. Timing and scoring were accurate enough to show who the winner was, but they needed to verify that with video footage.

Fans up and down Mount Panorama who had been standing for the final twenty laps or so were still on their feet. As they waited in anticipation, many had already began the post-race festivities on the sole basis that the race was indeed a fight to the very end.

After a short period of time, the decision was sent out to the teams.

Richard went to the radio. "Bill, that was one of the best drives I've ever seen in my life," said Richard. "But we just missed it, mate. Renshaw got us by a nothing margin."

The words hung in the air as Bill felt absolutely and completely gutted.

It was indeed a *nothing* margin of .012 seconds according to timing and scoring. After nearly seven hours of driving, the rainfall, the incident which took Nick out of the race and 1000 kilometers of racing to blanket the entire day, the race came down to a mere whisker of time.

"Are you sure?" asked Bill who had already started to tear up under his helmet. His voice, strained by the enormous battle he'd just fought, was barely holding together. "Are you absolutely sure, Richard?"

"Yeah, Bill. We're sure," replied Richard.

Bill could tell that Derek had already received news of his victory as he began doing burnouts for the crowd down the front stretch. As he passed him, he gave the Australian driver a thumbs up despite knowing that he probably wouldn't see it.

Bill had gained a new level of respect not only for Derek Renshaw, but for himself. He'd traversed everything the Mountain could throw at him and come out the other side just shy of winning the Great Race. However, despite it being more than he'd expected, he couldn't help but feel the strain of regret as he'd come in second place yet again.

Was there any more I could've given?

As soon as the thought entered his head, however, he quickly dismissed it. He'd given everything he had in this race, and there wouldn't be a soul on earth who could ever dispute that.

As the field of cars pulled into the service road which led to the pits, the celebrations were starting to kick off. He could see the fans jumping the fence onto the front stretch to hopefully get a spot on pit lane to watch the podium celebrations.

As Bill pulled up to where his crew was waiting for him, he could see them giving him a round of applause as he brought the car to a stop.

They immediately swamped him.

Swinging the doors open before Bill could get unbuckled, the crew dove into the car from both sides as they gave high fives, slaps on the chest, and no short amount of congratulations for what he'd been able to accomplish.

Finally able to get out of the car, Bill was again surrounded by crew members who recounted stories of what it was like watching the race from the garage. One by one, Bill thanked them each for their contribution to the team. Without their hard work of getting the car ready overnight, none of this would've been possible.

"Well done, mate!" said Nick who now had an arm sling to support his broken wrist. "You did the impossible and you stuck it to Renshaw. You earned your spot on that podium."

"Thanks Nick," said Bill as he patted Nick on the back. "I know it must've been hell for you sitting there knowing that it was supposed to be you out there in the car, but..."

"No buts, mate," interrupted Nick. "You did the team proud and made every move count. You fought to the absolute bloody end and that's what..."

Nick's words were cut off as something else had caught his attention.

Turning around to see what Nick was looking at, Bill saw none other than Derek Renshaw walking towards them.

Flanked by a swarm of cameras, Renshaw wasn't smiling as he approached. Walking past the crew and directly up to Bill, Derek stopped and stared at the American.

"I don't regret many things I've done in life," said Renshaw. "I make my decisions and stick with them. But looking back, I must say that I do regret some of the things I said about you."

A brief pause followed. "Some," he added. "Not all."

Bill and those around him couldn't help but smile at the sly comment.

"You're one helluva good driver, Watson. You raced me hard but clean. It was an awesome fight, and we gave the people what they wanted to see. More importantly, it was an honor to race with you."

In a rare moment of humanity for Renshaw, he extended his hand towards Bill.

"You're not gonna scratch your balls first like you did last time, right?" asked Bill.

Renshaw and those around him laughed as Bill met his handshake. Camera flashes were popping off all around them as the two held their handshake for a moment.

"I don't imagine there'll be a next time, will there?" asked Derek.

Bill sighed. "No. There's no next time for me."

Releasing their handshake, Derek gestured over towards Nick and his wrist in the sling.

"It looks like you'll have to get used to using your other hand for certain activities for the time being."

Nick responded by promptly giving Derek the middle finger.

Derek smiled in response.

"C'mon," said Derek. "Let's go celebrate on the podium."

As he started to head towards the podium area, Bill stayed back. "I'll meet you up there."

The crowd of cameras followed Derek as Bill's crew made their way to the podium celebrations as well. Staying back with Bill were the people who had helped him through thick and thin: Greg, Nick, Abby, Tubbs, Richard, his business partner and also the current owner of the race car, Pat Henderson, his father, and Chad.

Bill approached Pat.

"You know, I never thought all those years ago when we started this business that it'd take us to Australia," said Bill. "It's been an honor to have worked with you. I can rest easy knowing that the company is in good hands."

Pat, whose face was its typical shade of red, smiled at the remarks. "And I couldn't have done this without you, Bill. Thank you, and it was an honor to have you drive my race car."

The group chuckled as Bill stepped in front of Greg Foster.

"Greg, your hospitality is what got Chad and I here. Without you, we'd still be sitting back in Texas worrying about how we were going to make it. Thank you not just for opening your house up to us, but for looking after and taking care of Chad. You're more than just a friend of my father's. You're family to us now."

The two men embraced as Greg added, "And you're welcome to stay as long as you'd like."

Standing next to Greg was the ever-foreboding figure of Tubbs. With his massive arms crossed and brow furrowed as Watson approached, he was ready for whatever Bill had for him. Not to be taken by surprise, however, he fired the first shot.

"It was my pleasure whipping your arse in preparation for this race," said Tubbs as the group erupted in laughter. "I've gotta say that I enjoyed every minute of it."

Bill just shook his head and smiled. "Tubbs, you're one of a kind. Thanks for pushing me past my comfort levels—and not just physically. If you'd never pushed me to get in that simulator back at the bar, I'd never have met Nick and none of this would've ever come to pass."

"I…uh…" mumbled Tubbs as he searched for words.

"Don't be getting all soft on us, big fella," said Greg as he nudged the massive man in his ribs.

Bill laughed as he stepped in front of both Nick and Richard. "You guys believed in me even when I didn't want to believe in myself. Nick, thanks for your guidance during this entire endeavor. I bet you never thought inviting me out to your test at Winton would lead to this."

"I sure as hell didn't, mate," said Nick.

"I did," mumbled Richard. "I just didn't tell you."

The tall British man smiled.

"You should be proud of what you've accomplished," said Richard. "Both of you. This was a team effort and we surpassed all of our expectations. If the purpose of my life was to get both of you to this point, I can now die a happy man."

Bill smiled. "Well nobody's dying. Not yet anyways. Plus, I'm sure Nick will be keeping you busy in the near future. And you never know, you may have some future stars looking for a coach."

"Oh I think I may be officially retired at this point," said Richard as he pulled his silver flask out of his coat pocket. "We'll see how I feel after tonight's festivities. But I think Nick here would make a fine coach someday."

"Someday," reiterated Nick. "For now, I've got a bit more driving to do. Thanks to you, Bill, I may yet secure a seat for next year. Thank you. Both of you."

Bill slapped both men on their arms as he stepped in front of Abby. "You know, we didn't exactly get started off on the right foot," said Bill.

"That's fair to say," said Abby with a coy smile.

"We've certainly had our ups and downs but thank you, Abby. Thank you for sticking by my side when I just needed someone to talk to. And you've made quite the impression on Chad here, too."

Smiling, Abby said, "Well me and the little guy get along quite well. He's a good kid and you should be proud to be his father."

"I am," said Bill. "And although it was tragedy on my end which led to our meeting, it's been joy ever since. You're a wonderful woman, Abby. Thanks for your encouragement and for your compassion."

Abby, stepping forward and giving Bill a kiss on the cheek, said, "You're welcome, Bill Watson."

The other members of the group began to murmur and a few whistles from Tubbs zipped through the air. Abby's cheeks turned red as she blushed.

Stepping in front of his father, a legend in Australian motorsport, the great William Watson, Bill simply embraced him. Feeling the arms of his father wrap around him, Bill closed his eyes and soaked up the love and the memories he'd been able to share with his father. Indeed, he counted himself blessed to have been able to have a father who genuinely cared for his well-being as he grew up and even into his adulthood. Without the kindness his father had shown Greg all those years ago, long before Bill was born, he'd never have been able to make this journey possible.

As he loosened the embrace of his father, the two men held each other's gaze before Bill finally spoke. "Thank you, Dad. For everything. For always being there and for being my father when I needed a father."

William, unable to get his words out as the tears began falling down his cheeks, simply nodded his head up and down.

Finally, Bill got to the most important person of all.

Kneeling down in front of his son, Bill put his hand on the shoulder of Chad. "You've been my inspiration from the very beginning. There were so many times I wanted to give up but I always knew that you were in my corner. Your prayers, your thoughts...your love—that's what kept me going. Never forget this, Chad. Never forget what you mean to me, and never forget what happened today. Always keep fighting and never quit, even when you fall down and even when the odds are stacked against you. Fight to stand back up because you never know where you'll end up if you keep moving forward. Just know that every time you fall down, I'll be right there with you. I love you, son."

Leaning forward, Bill embraced his son as the latter wrapped his arms around his father. With his mouth next to the ear of his father, Chad—the wheelchair-enabled boy who hadn't spoken a single word ever since the death of his mother—closed his eyes and whispered...

"I love you too, Dad."

Epilogue

The skies above had changed from the clear blue of an early afternoon to a colorful display of orange and red as dusk slowly fell upon the Texas countryside. The sounds of the various birds that had once filled the air were now replaced by the sound of cicadas as well as various frogs from a nearby pond.

The old man, now sitting beside his son, wiped the tears away from his eyes as he concluded the story. He had delved deep into his past and, by doing so, had allowed memories and emotions he had once thought were long past to surface once again. Recounting the tale to his young son who sat next to him earnestly listening had in fact brought a sense of relief to the old man.

"So he lost the race? At Bathurst?" asked his son.

"By a whisker," replied the old man. "But just because you don't walk away with the winner's trophy doesn't mean you've not accomplished something great. Believe me, he did."

Reaching into his back pocket and removing his wallet, the old man pulled out a newspaper clipping, unfolded it, and handed it to his son. The clipping contained a picture of Bill Watson, his son Chad, along with Bill's father, William Watson, standing on the podium at Bathurst. Bill was performing his customary champagne drinking as he attempted to down the entire bottle while his son, seated in his wheelchair, was holding his father's racing helmet just as he had so often done. William, with his charismatic smile, stood behind Chad as he cheered Bill on.

"He was a man who never won a race in his entire life but came close several times. Some would argue how one could be proud of such a life. What did he accomplish?"

Turning towards his son, the old man continued.

"At the end of the day, it's the battles you fight in life which tell your story—and not just the ones on a race track. Some of the greatest accomplishments one could hope to achieve are the impacts they have on the lives of others. A wise man once said, 'life is measured in achievement, not in years alone.' It's our actions which define who were are. Because when it's all said and done, our actions and our words are all that we're remembered by."

The young man nodded as he let the words sink in. "What happened to him?"

"Who?" asked the old man.

"Bill Watson."

The old man let his head drop as he sighed. "Death came slowly."

The words hung in the air as the old man closed his eyes.

"About six months after Bathurst, the cancer began to take a heavy toll. Memory loss became a common occurrence and eventually he had to be relocated into a special facility where he could be properly looked after. Sure, his friends and family would stop by and see him and even an old rival came by every once in a while. But sooner than most, Bill knew that he was simply waiting for his turn to die.

"It was a great gesture then when two years after his finish at Bathurst, just before the next annual race was about to start, he was given an honorary lap around the track in a very special 1968 Ford Mustang. The same one which belonged to his father. It was his very last time on a race track, and it was his father, William Watson, who had the honor of driving his son around it.

"The very next day, Bill Watson died."

The old man tried to hold it back, but even as the words left his mouth, he began to weep at the memory as well as for the events which followed Bill's death.

Bill Watson, the man who had defied the odds and fought against the hand he had been dealt, had now faded into memory. However, it was his actions and his words which had lived on in the hearts and lives of those closest to him.

Slowly starting to regain his composure, the old man said, "That was a long time ago now. But even then, had Bill not made the choices he did, things would have been very different. In the end, he embraced his fate and charged forward anyway. He made the most of his time on this earth and because of it, his son never forgot the lengths his father went to make sure his legacy lived on long after he was gone."

The old man's son smiled. Having heard smaller versions of the grand tale growing up, the full picture of Bill Watson allowed him to put several pieces together.

Patting his father on the back, the young man said, "C'mon, Dad. We've got a plane to catch. There's still some adventuring left to do."

Smiling as his son helped him to his feet, the old man said, "You know, they would've loved you."

Just before turning to go back to the car with his son, the old man reached into his jacket and pulled out four red roses. Stepping forward, he laid one on the gravestone of William Watson. Stepping to the right, he laid another on the gravestone next to it belonging to William's wife, Charlotte. He took another set of steps to the right as he laid a rose down on the grave of Lena Watson before finally coming to a stop in front of the grave belonging to Bill Watson.

The old man stepped forward slowly as he carefully laid the red flower down on the headstone. Patting the cold stone, the old man stared at the lettering carved into the face of it as he took a step back.

Turning away, the old man walked slowly but surely as his son, with his hand on his father's elbow, assisted him when needed. The two got back to the car as the young man started the red 1968 Ford Mustang which was parked alongside the street named *Legacy Drive*. Once they were both inside, they left the cemetery and drove off towards their next adventure.

* * *

The crowds were on their feet as the events happening around them at Mount Panorama Motor Racing Circuit unfolded. From celebrity visits to performing artists to meeting their favorite drivers, the tens of thousands in attendance couldn't get enough of the atmosphere. It was an event of global proportions, and after all these years, the Bathurst 1000 was still a main staple on the global stage of motorsports.

With the cars on the grid, the drivers began to line up in formation for the singing of the Australian national anthem. Even as the drivers took to their spots, a special place up front was still vacant.

Walking through the grid, the old man noticed he had been recognized. He lowered his head, hoping the hat he was wearing would hide his face but it was too late for that. Continuing on, the crowds began to part as the old man slowly made his way to the front of the grid.

As he got closer to the front, many of the drivers instantly recognized him and extended their hands in greeting. The old man shook hands with every one of them as he made his way up front.

"Ladies and gentlemen," said a voice from the loudspeakers, "please give a resounding welcome to a two-time winner here at Mount Panorama and a third generation Bathurst competitor. Here to see the legacy continue with his son's debut race at Bathurst, please give it up for Chad Watson!"

The crowds erupted in cheers as Chad removed his hat and waived it in the air towards the crowd. Red shirts, blue shirts and all of those in between cheered for who could only be described as a hero of the Mountain.

Although he had fought in many battles both on and off the track, Chad knew his story had still yet to be told. Standing there on the same grid which he, his father and his grandfather had stood, Chad couldn't help but feel a bit nostalgic as he looked across the crowd on the grid to see his son lined up and wearing the firesuit he'd be racing in today. Giving a slight nod to his son, Chad turned back around to face the crowd, which was still cheering for him.

Taking time to observe a brief moment to himself, Chad lifted his head towards the sky and smiled.

"Thanks, Dad. For everything."

About the Author

Paul Slavonik is an American author and media production specialist who has written for such publications as Motorsport.com, RACER.com and iRacing. A former U.S. Army combat photographer and video productions specialist, Paul has a Bachelor's degree in Audio Production from Full Sail University and currently resides in Texas with his wife, Christina, and their two cats.

If you've enjoyed reading *Legacy Drive,* please consider leaving the book an honest review on Amazon. Your contribution and feedback would be greatly appreciated.

Follow Paul on social media for the latest news on *Legacy Drive* and his other writing endeavors!

You can connect with me on:

- https://www.dmgunited.net
- https://www.facebook.com/PSlavonik
- https://www.youtube.com/c/PaulSlavonik
- https://www.instagram.com/paul_slavonik
- https://www.instagram.com/dmg_united

Subscribe to my newsletter:

https://mailchi.mp/707b456a3570/legacydrive

Also by Paul Slavonik

The Guide to Road Racing on a Budget

If you're an absolute beginner who is wanting to take the plunge into the world of Motorsports but aren't sure how to go about doing it, *The Guide to Road Racing on a Budget* is for you. With valuable information which will save you from countless hours of digging through online forums, this book contains tried and true methods which set the stage for getting started including forming a budget, choosing a car, safety, track days, and ultimately getting you on the track. With the budget being the emphasis, this book aims to get budding drivers on the race track while maintaining an efficient and disciplined use of your racing funds.

Although experienced drivers probably won't get much out of this book, *The Guide to Road Racing on a Budget* is primarily for people who are just starting out and want to know how to take that initial step into the world of road racing.

CPSIA information can be obtained
at www.ICGtesting.com
Printed in the USA
LVHW091644201220
674692LV00012B/144